International

**Susan**

**Alexandra Sellers**

present

# Surrender
## TO THE
# Sheikh

*Two stories of passionate desire
and romance in the sultry heat
of the desert*

*Coming in February 2008*

# AT THE SHEIKH'S COMMAND

*by*

**Alexandra Sellers**
**Michelle Reid**
**& Carol Grace**

*featuring*

*Sleeping with the Sultan*
*The Sheikh's Chosen Wife*
*& Taming the Sheikh*

# SURRENDER TO THE Sheikh

## THE SHEIKH'S SECRET BRIDE

*by*
*Susan Mallery*

&

## SHEIKH'S TEMPTATION

*by*
*Alexandra Sellers*

M&B™ and M&B™ with the Rose Device
are trademarks of the publisher.
Harlequin Mills & Boon Limited, Eton House,
18-24 Paradise Road, Richmond, Surrey TW9 1SR

SURRENDER TO THE SHEIKH
© by Harlequin Books SA 2007

The Sheikh's Secret Bride and Sheikh's Temptation were first
published in Great Britain by Harlequin Mills & Boon Limited
in separate, single volumes.

The Sheikh's Secret Bride © Susan Mallery 2000
Sheikh's Temptation © Alexandra Sellers 2000

ISBN: 978 0 263 86578 3

024-0907

Printed and bound in Spain
by Litografia Rosés S.A., Barcelona

# THE SHEIKH'S
# SECRET BRIDE
*by*
*Susan Mallery*

**Susan Mallery** is the bestselling author of over forty books. She makes her home in the Pacific Northwest with her handsome prince of a husband and her two adorable-but-not-bright cats.

**Susan Mallery has some wonderful new novels available in November and December 2007. Look for *The Substitute Millionaire* and *The Unexpected Millionaire*, in Mills & Boon® Desire™.**

# Chapter One

"Oh, Mommy, look!"

Liana Archer glanced up from the romance novel she'd been reading and stared out the airplane window. She saw a brilliant blue sky, an unforgiving sun and nearly a dozen men on horseback riding toward the plane.

"Don't worry, Bethany," she told her daughter absently. "It's just—"

Liana's eyes opened wide as she realized what she'd just seen. Men on horseback? When the pilot had announced that the plane would be delayed a few minutes because there was a problem at the gate, Liana had assumed there was a technical difficulty or another plane in their space. She hadn't thought they were about to be assaulted by a herd of native tribesmen.

Not knowing what else to do, she clutched her nine-year-old daughter to her side. "We'll be fine," she said with a calmness she absolutely did *not* feel.

Someone else noticed the group of men. Conversation raced up and down the length of the plane. Several women began to scream. Liana's heart jumped into hyper-drive, and her breathing increased until she thought she might pass out. Why was this happening? She'd been promised that El Bahar was the safest country in the Middle East. That the king was a good and honest ruler, much beloved by his people. She'd believed the information—otherwise she never would have subjected herself or her daughter to a move that had brought them half-way around the world. So what had gone wrong?

Before she could figure out an answer, the men reached the plane. They circled around, then she heard the sound of the forward door opening and the low, gruff voices of the tribesmen as they boarded the plane.

Both Liana and Bethany shrank back in their seats. At least they were in the rear of the plane, Liana thought grimly as she looked around for the exit by the tail. Maybe she could figure out a way to open that door, and she and her fellow passengers could sneak out to safety.

"Mommy?" Bethany's voice was shaky and her face pale as she stared at her mother. "Are we going to die?"

"Of course not." Liana brushed the blond bangs off her daughter's forehead, then kissed her cheek. "I'm sure there's a logical explanation for all this and we'll—"

Several tall, dark men wearing robes and headdresses entered the main cabin. They seemed to be searching for someone.

"What do you want?" a passenger in a business suit asked, rising to his feet. "There are women and children on this plane. If you want hostages, at least let them go."

The natives ignored him. About midway down the center aisle, they paused. One of them reached for a young woman and drew her to her feet. There was an exchange of conversation that Liana couldn't hear, then the woman was led away.

Conversation exploded like gunfire. Several shrieks pierced the cabin, and Liana felt herself starting to shake. Dear God, what was happening? To think that one of the reasons she'd agreed to the job in El Bahar had been her love of sheik romance novels. But danger in the land of the sheik was much more interesting in a book. In real life, it was plain terrifying.

"Silence, please!"

A loud male voice bellowed over the din of hysterical passengers. Liana looked up and saw another of the native men standing at the front of the cabin. He was taller than the rest, and darkly handsome in a remote kind of way. He stood with his feet braced and his robe thrown back to expose the gleaming pistol at his waist. She swallowed, trying to console herself with the thought that if they were to be shot, at least it would be a quick death.

"I apologize for your fears," the man said. He glanced over his shoulder, then shook his head. "A few of the younger men were a little too involved with their assignment and took the game to heart. My instructions were for you to be informed of what was going on *before* anything began."

The man gave a low bow. When he straightened, he smiled. The smile transformed his appearance from remote to more appealing than should be legally allowed. "I am Malik Khan, Crown Prince of El Bahar. Welcome to my country. What you have just seen was not a kidnapping, nor were your lives in any danger. A young American woman employed at the palace had requested that her fiancé 'rescue' her from the plane. She thought it would be romantic to be swept away by a man on horseback."

Prince Malik motioned to the left side of the plane. "As you can observe, she is well pleased with what happened."

"Can you see?" Bethany whispered, still clinging to her mother.

Liana craned her neck as she looked across the cabin and out the far windows. She could just make out the young woman taken from the plane. She stood in the embrace of one of the tribesmen, and if their passionate kiss was anything to go by, she was plenty happy with what was going on.

"They're kissing," Liana assured her daughter. "I guess it's what the man said. Just a joke that got out of hand."

Bethany grinned, then touched her hand to her chest. "I thought my heart was going to jump right out of my rib cage."

Liana smiled at her, then kissed her soft cheek. "Me, too, kid. There they would have been, flopping around on the floor." She demonstrated with her hand, making a wiggly back and forth motion.

Bethany giggled.

"So you are recovered then, young lady? You are not afraid to enter El Bahar?"

Liana and Bethany turned as one. The tall prince stood next to their row. Bethany stared up at the man. "I would very much like to see El Bahar, but not if you're going to cut off our heads."

The prince winked at the nine-year-old. "I like your head just where it is. You will be safe here, I promise. In fact, if anyone bothers you, you tell him that you personally know the Crown Prince."

Her blue eyes widened. "You're a real prince? Like in Cinderella?"

"Exactly like that."

The man's gaze drifted over to Liana. She started to offer a polite smile and assure him that she, too, was fine, when their eyes locked.

His irises were the color of midnight. Liana felt the impact of their connection all the way down to her toes. Despite being one of the most sensible women she knew, she felt a jolt of attraction that nearly jerked her out of her seat. She found herself desperate to stand and beg this stranger to touch her and kiss her…right here on the plane if necessary. It was as if she'd been given a near lethal injection of a love drug. She couldn't speak, could barely breathe.

Fortunately, the prince merely smiled and returned to the front of the plane without saying a word.

"He's cool," Bethany said with a smile. "Wow. I've met a real live prince. He's nicer than I would have thought. And tall. Did you think he was handsome, Mommy?"

"Yes, I thought he was handsome," Liana admitted, willing her heart rate to return to normal. They both watched as the prince and his men disembarked. The door closed, and the plane began to move toward the gate. In a matter of minutes, people were disembarking. Liana collected their carry-on items and stowed away her book. As she did, she glanced at the cover of her novel and told herself that whatever ailed the heroine in this book was apparently contagious. For one brief second *she'd* found herself attracted to a tall, dark, impossible man.

Just an aberration, she told herself as she and her daughter joined the slow-moving line that would take them to their luggage. Too much traveling or the fear or maybe too much coffee had zapped some switch in her brain. That was the only explanation for her instant and overwhelming attraction to a stranger.

Forty minutes later Liana and Bethany stood waiting to go through customs. Liana had convinced herself that she'd made too much of her reaction to the El Baharian prince. Her body had still been in shock from the danger. Her instinctive fight-or-flight response to those men boarding the plane had sent a number of chemicals pouring into her system. Any thoughts she'd had about the prince had simply been the result of a fear hangover. Nothing more. Men like him didn't appeal to women like her.

"Ma'am? If you would please to come this way?"

Liana was jolted from her musings by a slight man bending over to pick up one of her suitcases.

"What are you doing?" she asked sharply. "Don't touch that."

The El Baharian customs area was a large open room with plenty of air conditioning and ceiling fans. Although the lines were long, they were moving quickly and seemed efficient. Security people moved through the crowd, and she was about to call for one when the small man bowed apologetically.

"I was sent to bring you to a shorter line," he said, pressing his hands together in front of his chest. "You have a young child and I was told that you would prefer the process to go more quickly. Just over there," the man said, motioning to a lone official at the far side of the building.

"Is that one of the customs lines?" Liana asked, wondering why no one else was going that way. She looked up and saw the overhead sign: Official Visitors and Residents.

"As much as I would like it to be otherwise," she said with a kind smile, "I'm neither an official visitor nor a resident. But thanks for the offer."

The little man pressed his thin lips together. He had dark eyes and a sparse beard. He wore an exquisitely tailored suit.

"Please, ma'am. You would be most welcome."

A uniformed security guard appeared at her elbow. "It's quite all right, ma'am. We're just trying to speed up the process."

"If you're sure," Liana said doubtfully. She allowed the two men to take possession of her luggage and lead the way over to the customs official.

"You don't *want* to be in a faster line?" Bethany asked as she dragged her carry-on bag behind her. "You *like* waiting in here?"

"Okay, okay, I was just being careful."

They came to a stop and waited while the uniformed officer began to check their passports. Liana glanced around and was surprised to see that no one else had been directed to this particular line.

"I don't understand," she said, looking at the small man, then the security guard. "Why me and not them?"

"Because I requested it."

Liana recognized the deep, resonant voice. Even before she turned to look at the gentleman who had just joined the party, she felt the hairs on the back of her neck stand straight up. She was tired, hungry and had spent the past twenty-four hours traveling halfway around the world with her nine-year-old daughter. She was not in the mood to be played with...even by her own body.

But all the temper in the world couldn't counteract the feeling of heat that swept through her, or the faint trembling in her arms and legs. She raised her gaze and stared directly into the handsome face of Malik Khan, Crown Prince of El Bahar.

The prince offered a low bow. "We have not been formally introduced. I am Prince Malik and you are…?" He reached for her passport.

"Liana Archer. This is my daughter, Bethany."

"Hi," Bethany said, beaming up at him. "Do you really live in a palace?"

"Absolutely. With my two brothers and their wives. Lots of princes and princesses. Oh, and my father, King of El Bahar."

Bethany's blue eyes widened. "And you have your own horses and gold, and lots of people bow to you all the time?"

Malik grinned. "Not as much gold as we would like and people don't bow all that much anymore. It makes it difficult for them to get their work done if they're bowing all the time."

Malik motioned to the customs official, who quickly stamped their passports, then ushered them through without so much as a glance at their luggage.

"Welcome to El Bahar," Malik said.

Liana was still speechless at seeing him again, not to mention the effect of her misplaced physical reaction to his presence. She was too exhausted to figure out what was wrong with her, so she was determined to ignore it. Yes, the prince was tall—probably six foot two or three. She was five foot eight and he towered over her. Or maybe it was his headdress that gave her the illusion of height? She studied him and decided that his clothing might emphasize his power, but it didn't add anything that wasn't already there. Nope, Prince Malik was tall, strong and intimidating. But then maybe all princes were. She didn't travel in royal circles much.

"Why did you do this?" she asked, jerking her head toward the long, slow-moving lines of people still waiting to go through customs.

Malik shrugged. "I wanted to apologize for scaring you and your daughter on the plane. I assure you, that was not our intention."

His gaze was steady and direct. She tried to ignore the way he seemed to be seeing into her soul by looking at his individual features. Perhaps if she could find fault, he wouldn't be so intimidating.

Unfortunately for her, Prince Malik was physically quite flawless. He had wide-set eyes and a straight nose. High cheekbones cut through tanned skin. His mouth was firm and a little stern, but there was the faintest hint of a smile tugging at the corners. He was the kind of man who would look good with his likeness on a stamp…or the side of a mountain.

"So, Liana Archer, why are you in my country?" he asked.

"I'm a new teacher at the American School." She shifted slightly and saw that the customs official, the little man in the well-fitting suit and the security guard were all still within earshot. None of them were overtly listening to the conversation, but Liana didn't doubt they were catching every word.

Malik frowned. "You are not."

"Excuse me?"

"You are not a teacher," he said folding his arms over his chest. "Women teachers are old and unattractive. So why are you really here, and where is your husband?"

She'd been warned that while El Bahar was more forward thinking than most Middle Eastern countries, the nation still had particular ideas rooted in the past. Obviously this was one of them.

The combination of her lingering attraction, the odd welcome they'd received on the plane and the tiredness she saw in her daughter's face made Liana speak without thinking.

"Look, Your Highness, I can't see that it's any of your business, but for what it's worth, I'm not married anymore. I can't do anything about my age, but if you'd like I'll work on popping out a few warts to make me more unattractive. Would that be sufficient?"

Behind her, she heard a collective gasp from the three men. Belatedly, she thought that sarcasm would probably not be welcomed by the Crown Prince. A vision of years in a desert prison followed by a slow and painful death filled her mind. She took a step closer to Bethany.

But instead of getting angry, the prince simply smiled. "Would the warts be on your nose?"

"Is that where you'd like them?"

"I'm not sure. I'll have to consider the matter." Then he snapped his fingers—literally—and a porter appeared with a cart.

Minutes later, Liana and Bethany were in the back of a cab speeding away from the airport. Prince Malik had let them go without doing anything more than wishing them well.

"Remind me never to try to be witty in front of royalty again," Liana murmured as she leaned her head back against the seat.

"He wasn't mad," Bethany said confidently, snuggling up to her mother. "Prince Malik liked you. I could tell."

"How nice," Liana said automatically, even though that wasn't what she felt. She was not the least bit interested in the prince's affections, thank you very much. She liked her life too much to mess it up with wishful thinking. She had plans and goals, and they did not include a dalliance with royalty—despite her body's reaction to the man.

When the cab began to circle around toward the clearly marked exit, Liana realized she hadn't told the driver where they were going.

"Do you know the American School?" she asked him. "That's where we need to go. I understand there is a main office by the housing complex?"

The dark-skinned man met her gaze in the mirror and gave her a friendly nod. "Yes, ma'am. I know the place well."

"Good. Although I have directions, if you need them."

"No. I go there many times a week. Most of the teachers there don't have cars."

Liana had been told the same thing. Many of the teachers there were, like her, expatriates on two- or three-year contracts. While the generous salary meant that purchasing a car wouldn't be a problem, most teachers didn't bother. Apparently public transportation was reliable and inexpensive, and it saved the trouble of buying at the beginning of the stay, then selling at the end.

"So what do you think of El Bahar?" she asked her daughter as the clean, air-conditioned cab moved onto the main highway.

The city was stretched out in front of them, with the Arabian Sea to the left. It was a darker blue than the sky— nearly the color of cobalt. Lush plants came right down to the edge of the highway, although in the distance she could see the barren land that was the beginning of the desert.

"I like it," Bethany announced. She sniffed. "The air smells sweet, like flowers or perfume. Do you know what it is?"

"No." Liana inhaled the scent. "A flower of some kind, I would guess. We'll look it up on the computer."

Along with a furnished two-bedroom condo, her contract had stipulated that she would be given a laptop computer, with Internet access, for use at home as well as in the classroom. All utilities, except for the phone, were included. The American School had made her a very generous offer, and Liana was pleased to be in El Bahar at last.

"Just think," she told her daughter. "You can tell all your classmates that you've already met the Crown Prince."

Bethany grinned. "You think they'll believe me?"

"If they don't, I'll be a witness."

The cab moved past a group of high-rise buildings between the highway and the sea. Liana remembered her research on the country and suspected this was the financial district. El Bahar had a stable economy that encouraged outside investors.

Up ahead the highway split and the driver took the road leading into the city. In a matter of minutes they were driving through a unique world that was equal parts modern buildings and ancient stone structures. Up ahead stood the last remnants of the wall that had once guarded the city, and beyond that a white glittering building jutted out toward the sea.

"It's the palace," Bethany said, pointing toward the large building. "I recognize it from the pictures."

"Lovely," Liana agreed. "I wonder if our condo is close to it? I remember reading that there are tours of the gardens. We'll want to do that right away."

Bethany glanced at her. "Maybe we'll see Prince Malik again."

"Sure," Liana agreed, even though she doubted the

truth of that statement. Would a Crown Prince bother with a tour group on his grounds? There was no way he would have time. No, their lone encounter with royalty was over and, for her, it had been more than enough.

The driver wove through streets that narrowed, then drove through impressive open gates. A long curved driveway circled through trees and blooming plants she couldn't identify.

Liana straightened and glanced around. Okay, so maybe the condo used by the staff of the American School had really impressive grounds. Or maybe this was part of the school itself. Or maybe a park. That was it. They were driving through a park and...

They rounded a curve in the drive. In front of them was the white building they'd admired just a few minutes before. Up close it was even more impressive, with several stories and wide balconies. A dozen or so guards stood at attention by a huge double door.

"Mommy? Where are we?" Bethany asked.

Liana didn't have an answer. Either the condo was much nicer than anything she was used to, or their driver had just brought them to the royal palace.

She looked at the man behind the wheel. "There's been a mistake."

He shook his head and grinned. "No mistake. His Highness said to bring you home, so here you are. Welcome to the royal palace of El Bahar."

Before Liana could decide what to do next, a tall man in a gray suit strode out to the cab and opened the door.

"Good," Prince Malik said. "You're here. Come, we'll get you settled."

## Chapter Two

Liana couldn't tell if they were in a really big foyer or a smallish living room. She decided it was probably the former, because this was, after all, a palace, and she doubted it had smallish anythings.

A bubble of hysteria threatened to choke her, even as she told herself it would be best for everyone if she stayed calm. Screaming like a crazy woman wouldn't do anything except upset her daughter.

Without her even being aware of leaving the cab, she and Bethany had been ushered out of the car and into this mystery room just past the main double doors. She could hear conversation behind her and had the bad feeling that their luggage had been removed from the cab and taken who knows where.

This isn't happening, she told herself firmly. Really. We're not being kidnapped, nor is this anything more than a simple misunderstanding.

"Mommy, look!"

Liana followed Bethany's gaze as her daughter stared up at an oval ceiling depicting the night sky. Glittering stars twinkled down at them, and, on what she assumed was the east side of the room, the first hint of sunrise glowed faint pink against the inky darkness. The entire picture was edged in gold paint. Or maybe real gold…she couldn't tell. The walls were the same dark color as the ceiling, but the color came from hundreds of tiny tiles. More tiles covered the floor in a pattern showing a dragon guarding a kingdom she suspected was El Bahar.

"You think the ceiling is something," Liana murmured, "look at what you're standing on."

Bethany did so, then jumped back to study the large, dangerous-looking creature.

"I stepped on his tail," her daughter whispered. "Do you think he's mad?"

"People have stepped on more than that," Prince Malik said as he walked into the room. "Welcome. I trust your cab ride was pleasant enough?"

"It was fine," Liana said, determined to ignore the way her blood seemed to sing as it flowed hotter and faster throughout her body. Yes, the prince was rugged and fabulously good-looking—and well, a prince. But she refused to let herself be distracted by him. By any of this. And how had he had time to get to the palace ahead of them, let alone time to change his clothes? Or had he been wearing that gray suit under his robes?

"You will find the palace very comfortable," Prince Malik said.

Liana wasn't sure if he was making a statement or issuing an order. Not that it mattered. "It's lovely. The palace, I mean," she said. "Impressive and not where we want to live."

Bethany came up beside her, and Liana put her arm around her slender daughter. "I am a teacher for the American School. As such, I was promised housing there. I don't know why you've brought me to the palace or what you hope to gain by it, but I insist that you allow us to go there now."

Malik waved his hand, as if brushing aside her comments. "You'll be much happier here. The rooms are larger and you may explore as you like. Transportation will be provided each morning and evening to take you to and from the school."

Liana felt as if she had a bit part in a bad movie, but she was determined not to give in to her threatening hysteria before she had all the facts. "Have we been kidnapped?"

Malik looked insulted by the question. "Of course not," he said, drawing himself up to his full and impressive height. "I am Crown Prince Malik Khan of El Bahar. I bestow on you the honor of being my guest at the royal palace."

Liana pressed her lips together, not sure how to respond to that. A soft, snuffling sound interrupted her thoughts. She turned and saw a golden retriever hovering just outside the main door. Its tail wagged frantically, but it didn't step inside the palace.

Bethany caught sight of the dog and clapped her hands together. "Mommy, can I go pet the dog?"

Liana glanced at Malik. "Is it friendly?"

"Yes. Sam belongs to my nephews, all of whom are much younger than Bethany. He's very good with children. She will be safe."

Liana nodded at her daughter. "Go ahead, but stay within sight of the open door."

Her daughter walked slowly toward the retriever, holding out her hand for the animal to sniff. Sam took a quick whiff, then licked the offered fingers, all the while wiggling with excitement at the thought of a new playmate.

Liana took the opportunity of her daughter's distraction to step closer to the prince, not because she wanted to be even more under his spell, but because she didn't want Bethany to hear what she had to say.

"We are *not* staying here," she informed Malik. "I don't know what you think you're doing, but your conduct is completely unacceptable. I am an American citizen and a guest of your country for the next two years. As such, I expect to obey El Baharian law. In return I wish to be treated with respect and courtesy, neither of which includes holding me anywhere against my will."

"You do not understand," Malik said patiently. "It is better for you to be at the palace."

He looked too intelligent not to get her point, which meant he wasn't listening. It was a trait shared by many men. Perhaps it was exacerbated by his royal status. Regardless, she had to get through to him.

Liana opened her mouth to speak, then closed it. A whisper of a memory drifted through her mind. She tried to shake it off, but it would not be denied. Then, despite the potential peril of her situation, she couldn't help laughing softly.

"Your Highness, you do *not* want to play this game with me. I've seen the movie."

He frowned. "What are you talking about?"

"The schoolteacher brought to the foreign country, the man in the royal house who refuses to let her have her own house. You are not the King of Siam and I am not Mrs. Anna. But if you have any thoughts of recreating that situation, may I take this moment to remind you that not only does the king never sleep with Mrs. Anna, he has the misfortune to die at the end."

She'd thought Prince Malik might look shocked or disapproving. Instead he startled her by leaning close. "We all die in the end, Liana," he said, his warm breath tickling her ear. "And make no mistake, I *will* have you in my bed."

"If you keep saying things like that, you're going to scare the poor woman to death."

Both Malik and Liana turned at the sound of the female voice. An attractive woman with curly light brown hair and wire-framed glasses approached. She wore a chic green dress that screamed designer, and there were the most amazing pearls around her neck. The woman shook her head at the prince.

"I can't believe you're using lines like that, Malik. Haven't you ever heard of subtlety?"

He drew himself up and glared down at the woman. Even though she wore high heels, he was a good six or seven inches taller. "I am Malik Khan, Crown Prince of El Bahar—"

She dismissed him with a wave and turned her attention to Liana. "Pay no attention to that speech. All the princes give it and we've learned to ignore them." She held out her hand. "Hi. I'm Heidi, wife of Jamal, the middle of the Khan brothers." She glanced at Malik. "You've already been tormented by my brother-in-law. What is it about these sheiks? Give them a little power and they want to run all over everyone."

Liana shook hands with the charming American and gave her a trembling smile, along with her name. She couldn't remember ever being in a more confusing situation. She felt as if she'd landed on a strange planet...and in a way she had. El Bahar was a very different place from her native California.

"I'm pleased to learn one can disagree with a Crown Prince and live to tell the tale," she said.

Heidi grinned. "Malik isn't so bad. He talks tough, and he's a fairly decent Crown Prince, but underneath all that, he's basically a nice guy."

Malik made a sound low in his throat. "You, woman, tread carefully around me."

"Or you'll have me beheaded. I've heard the threat before." Heidi leaned close to Liana and lowered her voice. "Actually, he's an excellent ruler and everyone respects him tremendously, but he can be a bit imperious on occasion."

Liana had had first-hand experience with Malik's imperiousness. "I've already seen him in action," she said. "I don't belong here. I'm a teacher with the American School."

Malik shook his head. "She is my guest."

Heidi looked from one to the other. "Interesting. What happened? You saw her at the airport and decided you liked the looks of her, so you brought her home?"

Malik looked faintly uncomfortable with the question. "I am the Crown Prince. I do not answer to you."

Heidi glanced at Liana. "Let me guess. You don't want to be here."

"Exactly."

"Well, Malik needs a willful woman in his life—even if he would never admit it. He's a bit on the stuffy side, and being challenged by a woman would help make him more human."

"I am *not* stuffy—"

"I'm not anyone's woman—"

Liana and Malik spoke at the same time.

"This is all your fault," she said, glaring at him. "Did you really bring me here because you liked the looks of me?" A voice in her head whispered it was actually a nice compliment, but she ignored the voice. She also ignored the steady thunder of her heart as she fought against her lingering attraction. "I'm not a puppy."

"I never thought you were."

Liana wanted to stamp her foot in annoyance. Nothing was going the way she wanted. She turned to Heidi. "Can you help me? I'm here to work and that's all I want to do. If I could just get to the American School everything would be fine."

Before Heidi could answer, Bethany stepped into the foyer. She walked over to her mother and leaned against her. "I'm tired, Mommy. Are we leaving soon?"

"You see," Malik said. "The child needs to rest. While you stand here arguing, you're wasting time. Heidi will show you to your rooms."

Heidi raised her eyebrows at her brother-in-law, but otherwise didn't protest. "Actually, Liana, it might be easier to give in to this tonight. You've got to be exhausted from the long trip. In the morning you can gird your loins and fight the battle anew." She touched Liana's arm. "Seriously, you are perfectly safe here. This is a royal palace and all guests are treated with the utmost respect."

Liana didn't know what to do. She had the feeling that if she gave in on this point, nothing in her life would ever be the same. The smart move would be to insist that she be taken to her condo immediately. But she *was* tired, as was Bethany. Then there was the tiny detail of spending the night in a real-life palace. That sort of thing had never happened to her before, nor was it likely to happen again.

Was she going to turn down this once-in-a-lifetime opportunity because of her pride?

"All right," she murmured. "If you're sure it won't be any trouble."

"None at all," Malik said. He offered a low bow, then disappeared down a long hallway.

"Who was that masked man?" Liana murmured.

Heidi heard her and laughed. "The princes take some getting used to. Come on. Your room is through here. Don't worry about the luggage, someone will bring it along."

"You okay with this?" Liana asked her daughter. "Do you mind spending the night in the palace?"

Big blue eyes, so much like her own, stared up at her. Bethany smiled. "Mommy, if I stay in the palace, I get to pretend I'm a princess."

"Oh, you're right. Well, that makes this very special, huh?"

Bethany nodded, then looked at Heidi. "Are you really married to a prince?"

"I sure am," Heidi said. "Which makes me a princess. We have a little boy who is also a prince."

"Wow." Bethany's big eyes got bigger. "Do you have a crown and everything?"

"You bet."

Heidi led the way down a long hall. As they followed, Liana wondered about the woman who was being so kind. She dressed like a regular person—no robes or veils—and her voice had an American accent. Liana would bet that there was an interesting story in her past. If she was going to be here longer, she might want to ask about it. But Liana and Bethany would be leaving the palace in the morning, so there wasn't going to be time to make friends.

"You're here to teach?" Heidi asked as they passed through a carved archway.

Liana glanced around them, barely able to answer for all the wonders she saw. Open doors allowed her to see into great rooms with high ceilings and western-style furniture. She caught glimpses of gardens and fountains. Every few feet they walked by a small alcove that displayed some fabulous piece of art, be it a tapestry or glassware or a statue. The floor beneath their feet was marble, and much of the wall space was tiled. No doubt parts of the palace were hundreds of years old.

"I, ah, teach math," Liana said absently as she took in the beauty of the El Baharian palace. The air was cool and faintly scented with flowers. "High-school-level algebra and geometry. Sometimes, if I have a bright group, I start them on calculus."

Heidi smiled at Bethany. "I guess with a mom who's a math teacher, you don't get to say you don't understand it, do you?"

Bethany giggled shyly and clung to her mother's hand. "No, I like math."

"Good for you." Heidi stopped in front of a single door carved with a relief of a gazelle. She pushed it open and stepped into a suite of rooms. "These will be yours," she said, motioning to the airy space.

Liana and Bethany followed her, then came to a stop in the center of the main room. In front of them were floor-to-ceiling windows that looked out over the Arabian Sea, light-colored furniture collected in two separate conversation areas, and double French doors leading out to a balcony that was almost as large as the living room. Nearly as amazing as the view was a mural on both the left and the right wall of the room. Tiny tiles had been cut and pieced together to create a herd of Arabian horses racing across the desert. The horses were depicted nearly life-size, with manes and tails flying out as fast hooves thundered across the sand.

"Oh, Mommy, look!" Bethany cried as she raced over to stand in front of the right mural. She reverently touched the tiny tiles. "Horses! Beautiful horses."

Just then two servants appeared with their luggage. Heidi pointed down a short hallway and the men disappeared. Seconds later they reappeared, without their burden of suitcases, then bowed and left as quietly as they'd come.

"You'll find the horse motif continues throughout the suite," Heidi explained. "It's one of the features of the palace. All the guest quarters have a theme. I thought with your daughter being at that horse-loving age, you two would enjoy this suite."

Liana felt stunned, as if she'd been drinking, or hadn't eaten in a couple of days. "This is a regular guest room here at the palace?" she asked. "There are more suites like this, just standing empty, waiting for company?"

Heidi nodded. Her hazel eyes filled with compassion. "I know it's a lot to take in, but you'll get used to it. There are frequent guests at the palace. Some visiting dignitaries prefer to stay at the beachfront hotels, but others like the warmth and history of the palace."

"I see why," Liana murmured. This was the most magnificent room she'd ever seen. She could only imagine what the bedrooms and bathrooms would be like.

"The balcony is a common one," Heidi went on to explain. "There aren't any other guests staying here at the moment, so you shouldn't see anyone, but don't be alarmed if someone walks by. Actually, on this level you can make a complete circuit of the palace via the balcony. I recommend the walk in the evening. It's very lovely."

"Thank you, I will."

Heidi started to leave, then paused. "I know it's terribly rude to ask, but how well do you know the prince?"

"I don't know him at all." Liana recounted the events on the plane and at the airport. "Instead of taking us to the American School, the cab brought us here. I don't understand what happened."

"Obviously you caught Malik's eye," Heidi said.

Then he can have it back, Liana thought to herself, although she didn't say it aloud. "I can't believe that," Liana said. "I'm just a teacher." Didn't sheik princes fall for movie stars and models?

"You're very attractive," Heidi said. "Tall, blonde, blue eyes."

Yes, she was those things, Liana admitted, but she was also about twenty pounds overweight and not the least bit interested in being fashionable. She preferred comfort to style. She'd been described as passably pretty, which she believed to be true. No, she was many things, but not someone to garner the attention of a prince.

"There has to be something else going on," she insisted.

"Why do you find it so hard to believe that Malik could want you? Aren't you interested?"

"Not really," Liana said honestly. "I've reached the point where I don't want another man in my life, and even if I did, I wouldn't want someone like Malik. I would never be very good in the position of wife number three or four."

Heidi smiled. "Ah, but this is El Bahar. The tradition of four wives is not allowed. Men have only one wife, and Prince Malik isn't married."

Liana told herself she wasn't the least bit tempted. Sexual attraction was one thing—marriage quite another. "If

I ever marry again, I want my husband to be interested in an equal partnership. Not likely with a Crown Prince.''

Heidi nodded. ''You're right there.'' She looked around the room. ''I'll leave you to unpack, then. If you need anything, simply pick up the phone and ask for it. Someone will be by later to take your order for dinner.'' She walked to the door and paused there. ''It was very nice to meet you both. I hope you enjoy your stay in El Bahar.''

With that, she was gone.

''She's very pretty,'' Bethany said, staring after Heidi. ''I never thought I'd meet a princess or stay in a palace. This is like an adventure in a book, isn't it, Mommy?''

''Sort of,'' Liana agreed, somewhat cautiously. ''Let's explore the rest of the suite and see what sort of arrangements the palace makes for its visitors.''

They walked down the short hallway and found two bedrooms, each with its own bath. The smaller of the two rooms was still big enough for a queen-sized bed, a desk, a dresser and a large built-in wall unit that housed a state-of-the-art television and DVD player. There was also a collection of movies in a drawer underneath. The attached bath was larger than their kitchen had been back home. The towels were thick enough to double as a mattress in a pinch and there were a collection of bath products by the oversized tub. Small versions of the mosaics in the living room continued here on the walls and floor tiles.

Liana's room was even more impressive. The king-sized bed took up barely an eighth of the floor space. The four-poster monstrosity required a step stool to reach the mattress. Crisp white linens gave the room a cool air, and fresh flowers added to the ambiance. Her bathroom was huge, with a tub large enough for a committee meeting. Instead of the horses, her bath was decorated with a floral design. In addition to the baskets of bath products, Liana found an array of makeup, brushes and body lotions…all unopened, but calling her name.

"Wow," she said as she finished her tour.

Bethany tucked a blond strand of hair behind her ear. "I like it here, Mommy. Maybe we can stay."

Liana grinned. "Wouldn't that be nice? To live like princesses?" She pulled her daughter close and hugged her. "Maybe you could insist all your classmates bow to you."

Bethany giggled. "Especially the boys."

"Of course. All the boys. And some of the girls. The ones who aren't friendly."

Still laughing, they returned to Bethany's room and started to unpack. They'd barely begun the job when there was a knock at the door.

"Stay here," Liana said as she hurried toward the front room.

Was it Malik? Had he come to talk to her? She found herself in the uncomfortable position of being both hopeful and fearful. Which was crazy. The man was handsome and high-handed, nothing more. Besides, in the morning she and her daughter would be gone, and she would never see him again.

*But first you have to get through the night,* a voice in her head whispered.

She opened the door and saw an attractive woman in her thirties standing in the hallway. She had dark hair and eyes.

"I'm Dora Khan," the woman said. "May I come in?"

"Of course." Liana stepped back to allow her to enter. "Did you say Khan? So you're…"

"The wife of Khalil, the youngest of the king's sons." Dora wore her dark hair swept up in a chignon. She had perfect skin and her dress was as stylish as Heidi's. Apparently princesses knew how to shop, Liana thought with a brief flash of wistfulness. She tried not to think about how rumpled her jeans and shirt were after nearly twenty-four hours of travel.

"I just wanted to tell you that I heard about what Malik has done," Dora said. "I know you've been dating for a while, but this is high-handed even for him—to force you to live at the palace when you want to stay at the American School. I understand you have a daughter. Obviously you're trying to protect her from the scandal this would create."

Liana blinked twice. "Excuse me? What on earth are you talking about?"

"Your relationship with Malik. I was led to believe that you've been seeing quite a lot of each other and that's the reason you came to El Bahar."

Were they all crazy, or was it her? Had crossing all those time zones affected her brain? She looked at the attractive woman standing in front of her. "I met the Crown Prince earlier this afternoon when he and several other men barged onto the plane and took away one of the women. Apparently she was engaged, and that was her idea of a romantic welcome back to El Bahar."

Dora looked confused. "You just met him today? Then what are you doing at the palace?"

"My question exactly." She recounted the events of the afternoon, starting with the customs line-up and finishing with her entrance into the suite.

"How strange," Dora said slowly. "This isn't like Malik at all." She gazed at Liana speculatively. "It's been a long time since Malik has shown any real interest in a woman. His father will be pleased."

Liana held up her hands in a gesture of protection.

"He's not interested. He can't be. He doesn't know anything about me. I'm not sure why he did all this, but please be aware that I'm leaving in the morning, just as soon as I get this mess straightened out."

"Of course." Dora continued to study her. "Well, welcome to El Bahar, Liana. I'm sure you'll enjoy your time here." She smiled. "If nothing else, it's going to be interesting. Let me know if I can do anything to help. If you really want to leave the palace, I can arrange it. Just say the word."

"I will, thank you." Liana watched her guest leave, then closed the door behind her. How odd. Who could have told the princess that she and Malik were involved? She'd only been on the palace grounds an hour or so. Had Heidi hinted at something or was it Malik himself?

The idea of the arrogant Crown Prince laying claim to a relationship that didn't exist was so ridiculous as to make her laugh. Except that the situation wasn't exactly humorous. It was more…intriguing, she thought to herself as she remembered her unexpected response to being in Malik's presence. Something about him was appealing. Not so much his money and position—both of those would be more off-putting, at least for her. She was willing to admit he was plenty handsome. There was something about his height. Or was it his dark eyes? The way they seemed to see into her soul without giving away anything of their own….

She shook her head. "Stop fantasizing about a guy you don't even know," she told herself. "You're leaving in the morning and you'll never see him again."

There was another knock on the door. Liana sighed and pulled it open. A tall, thin man with a white beard stood in front of her. He wore a suit with an odd pin on the lapel.

"Let me guess," she said before she could stop herself. "You're the king of El Bahar, and you're here to congratulate me on my pending engagement."

"No, ma'am. I'm the butler and I'm here to see what you and your daughter would like for dinner."

By the time they'd finished unpacking, had eaten the wonderful meal delivered to their suite, and Bethany had taken her bath, it was after nine. Jet lag had hit them both and Bethany barely made it between the sheets before falling fast asleep.

Liana stood at the foot of her daughter's bed and watched the sleeping girl. Her head might be spinning with confusion and exhaustion, but her heart was true and on course, as it had been from the second she'd found out she was pregnant. From that moment to this, everything she'd ever done had been with her daughter's best interests in mind.

Bethany was her entire world. She'd come to El Bahar because of her daughter, and she would gladly travel greater distances if it was the right thing for Bethany.

"I love you," she murmured, even though her child couldn't hear her. Then she walked into the hallway and shut the door.

Liana couldn't remember ever being so tired in her life, yet she didn't want to go to bed. An odd restlessness gripped her. She walked into her bedroom and thought about taking a bath. Deciding that a shower would be quicker, she first crossed to the French doors that led to the wide balcony. They unlocked easily, and she found herself moving out into the evening.

Instantly she was assaulted by the wonderful scents of the desert. The ocean, the sand and the hundreds of plants on the palace grounds combined to create a unique aroma that energized her. Even with her eyes closed she would know she was in a foreign land.

El Bahar. For years she'd heard about the country but hadn't given it any more thought than the North Pole. She'd never planned to visit. Her budget didn't allow for much in the way of world travel, and she and Bethany had contented themselves with the occasional weekend trip down to Sea World and the famous zoo in San Diego. Then she'd found out about an opportunity to teach here, and she'd seen the job as the answer to so many problems.

So here they were, in El Bahar. Living in the royal palace, if only for the night. Thinking of the palace made her think of Malik and his odd behavior. Why had he brought her here? And why had he told his sister-in-law that they'd been dating? Or had that come from Heidi? She felt as if she'd stepped into the middle of a play, but no one had told her the story or bothered to give her a script.

Who was this man, this Crown Prince who meddled in people's lives with all the impunity of a child rearranging blocks?

She crossed the width of the balcony and leaned against the broad stone railing. Floodlights illuminated the gardens below. She could make out a large fountain and several paths. Even though the afternoon had been warm, the evening air was cool and carried with it a lovely sea breeze.

Very exotic, she thought, closing her eyes to inhale the sweet scents from the garden. Magical El Bahar. Just like in her romance novels. Now all she needed was the handsome prince to appear.

"Good evening," a male voice said.

Liana spun toward the sound and found herself staring up at Malik. Be careful what you wish for, she thought, not sure if she should laugh or run for safety.

## Chapter Three

"Are you enjoying the night?" Malik asked.

"Sure," Liana told him, trying not to notice that her body had begun to melt with each step of his approach. If he moved any closer, she was going to be little more than a puddle on the tiled floor of the balcony. "It's very pretty. What are you doing out here?"

"I willed you to join me."

He spoke with such seriousness that Liana couldn't help laughing. "I thought only vampires willed women to do their bidding. Crown Princes can too?"

"Absolutely."

He stopped next to her and leaned casually against the railing. He still wore his gray suit and it still fit perfectly. The fabric seemed to emphasize the breadth of his shoulders and his white shirt gleamed in the night. His features blended together in the shadows until it was difficult to make out the firm shape of his mouth or the high cut of his cheekbones. Nonetheless, his good looks made him far too lethal for her safety.

"I'm not going to be easily persuaded," she told him honestly. "I doubt you'll get what you want from me."

"Don't be so sure. I can be very patient."

They were teasing, right? This was El Baharian flirtation? Liana wasn't so sure that Malik knew this was a game.

"Patient?" she repeated, questioning his choice of word. "Whisking me off to the palace before asking my permission is hardly the action of a patient man."

"Agreed, but it was effective. I'm interested in results, as well."

"Look, Your Highness, I'm not sure what you're expecting from me, but let's clear up a few things. I'm not interested in a fling of any kind. It's not my style."

His dark eyes regarded her steadily. He stood close enough for her to inhale the masculine scent of him—and darned if it wasn't plenty appealing.

"What *is* your style?" he asked.

"I don't have one." She bit her lower lip and figured she might as well get everything out in the open. "Look, I appreciate your attentions. They're very flattering, even though they make no sense. I mean, I'm not a fashion model, right?"

She went on without waiting for a reply. "The point is, I'm not looking for romance. I'm here to do a job."

"At the American School. I know."

"No, you don't." She turned until she was facing him. "This job is important to me. I'm a math teacher and I love what I do, but it's not the greatest paying job. I have a young daughter and we're pretty much on our own. It's up to me to provide for her future. When I heard about the school, I was intrigued because the salary is generous and the living expenses are all provided. In two years working here I can save enough to fund Bethany's college education and still have enough left over for a down payment on a small house back home. That's what's important to me—my daughter's future and our joint financial security.''

''I see.''

Malik continued to stare into her face. It was most disconcerting, she thought, especially when his attention seemed to become as tangible as a touch. It was almost as if his fingers were stroking her cheek, her nose, her mouth. Her lips actually began to tingle, as if he'd kissed her.

She swallowed against the sudden dryness in her throat. What was wrong with her? Jet lag only explained so much of her wild and strange attraction to Malik Khan.

''You have your life planned out,'' he said at last. ''Very forward-thinking of you, although it sounds lonely.''

She wrinkled her nose. ''If you're talking about love, I'm not interested. Been there, done that.''

''I understand. You're a widow who mourns the unexpected and premature passing of a much-loved husband.''

She rolled her eyes. ''Not exactly. I'm divorced and my ex gets on my nerves. I have no intention of going through that again.''

''There's a small bench just past that bend in the balcony,'' Malik said. ''Would you please join me there for a few moments before you retire for the evening?''

His old-fashioned courtesy disarmed her. What had happened to the imperious man who insisted on getting his way? Knowing that Bethany was safe asleep, she found herself moving in the direction he'd indicated.

Worse, Malik put his hand on the small of her back where the individual fingers seemed to burn against her suddenly sensitized skin. She wanted to shiver. She wanted to move closer and rub against him like a cat. She wanted to beg him to touch all of her in the most intimate way possible.

The wayward thoughts made her stumble, and she sat down barely in time to prevent herself from falling on her face. She had to get a grip, she told herself. Okay, so there was a chemical attraction between her and Malik. Or maybe it was all on her side. She couldn't tell. Either way, she had to be very careful that she didn't make a fool of herself.

"Why did you bring me here?" she blurted before she could stop herself.

"I find you attractive." Malik settled next to her on the bench. They weren't touching exactly, but he was close enough to make it hard for her to think.

"But I'm not attractive. I don't wear a bag over my head or anything, but I'm firmly in the average category."

Malik shrugged. "We'll have to agree to disagree on that. I find you unique."

Yeah, right. "Is it a blond thing? I mean, most of the women in this part of the country have dark hair."

She wore her hair to her shoulders in layers that let the natural wave give the style body.

Malik had reached forward to touch one of her curls. "It's not a blond thing," he told her. "Tell me about your ex-husband. Why are you divorced?"

"Because Chuck is thirty-one going on twelve." She sighed at the thought of Bethany's father. "He isn't a bad man, he's just too caught up in his dreams to be much of a husband or a father."

Liana allowed herself a small smile. "He was great fun in high school. He always had the fastest car around."

She glanced at Malik. "That's what he wants to do with his life—race cars. He works to raise money to buy new engines and tires and whatever else cars need to go faster than is safe. When we were first married, we had a great plan for our lives. But then I got pregnant, and we found ourselves parents before we'd finished growing up."

"Your daughter seems very smart and well-mannered."

"I love her," Liana said. "For me, Bethany was a blessing, but Chuck found being a father too confining. He would head off to the race track every chance he got." She shifted on the stone bench. "I have some blame in what went wrong. I was raising a child, working and I'd returned to college. I couldn't figure out a way to make it all work out, so my marriage suffered. Chuck came last more often than not. We're equally at fault, I think."

"How did you become a teacher? Did your parents help you?"

"Not really. My mom did some babysitting for me, but my folks are retired and not around much. They don't have any extra money. I made it happen myself. It took me a long time to get through college and then to earn my teaching certificate, but I did it."

"You sound like a strong woman."

"I'm not a quitter. And I don't believe in fairy tales."

"Nor do I."

Which brought her back to her earlier question. Why was she here? But she didn't ask it this time. She was sitting in the magic of the desert night with a handsome prince. It was a moment she wasn't ready to completely destroy. If this were Hollywood, Malik would take her in his arms and kiss her senseless. Unless it was an R-rated movie, in which case he would do a lot more.

She found herself shivering at the thought of being close to him. Chemicals, she decided in an attempt to think her way out of a situation entirely controlled by hormones, were more powerful than she'd ever given them credit for.

If only he weren't so good-looking. If only she had a little more experience with his kind of man. Although, as a single mom living in a small town seventy miles due east of Los Angeles, she hadn't had much opportunity to run into many princes. So where exactly would she have practiced?

Was he going to kiss her? Was he going to try and make love with her? The thought sent heat flooding through her body. She'd never had a one-night stand in her life, and she wasn't about to start now. In fact, she'd only ever been with Chuck, but there was something about Malik that made her want to throw caution to the wind and....

"Heidi tells me you're not married," she blurted out, then could have cheerfully cut out her tongue. Talk about a dumb thing to say.

"That's true."

"So you're the perennial bachelor, using your princely charms to seduce women?"

Unexpectedly, he rose to his feet. "Thank you for your company this evening, Liana. I've enjoyed talking with you very much."

And then he was gone. Liana stared after him, her mouth open, her eyes wide. What had she said, she wondered, completely stunned by his sudden departure. Had she insulted him with her teasing? But he did try to use his princely charms on women. Why wouldn't he?

"The rich really are different," she muttered as she stood and headed back to her bedroom. "And confusing, and the sooner we're out of here, the better."

\* \* \*

Malik paced the length of the living room in his suite. He'd left the French doors open, and the scent of the Arabian Sea just beyond the palace drifted in. He drew in a deep breath, hoping to chase away the lingering fragrance of the woman.

Liana Archer.

What the hell had he been thinking, bringing her here? He'd dragged her to the palace without her consent, as if he were some barbarian. His behavior was irresponsible. Worse, just a few minutes ago he'd wanted to rip the clothes from her body and make love to her right there on the balcony. He'd wanted to be inside her, plunging deeply until they were both so lost and mindless with passion that even time stood still.

The image in his head was so powerful, he felt himself growing aroused. The need produced an ache. Not surprising. He couldn't remember the last time he'd been with a woman. Casual relationships were an easy pleasure he did not allow himself. As the Crown Prince of El Bahar, he was held to a higher standard than everyone else. He could not risk exposing himself or the country to the potential disaster of an exposé in the tabloids—or an unexpected pregnancy.

He felt as lost and out of control as a ship in the middle of a violent storm. In truth, *he* felt violent. If he couldn't have the woman—and he couldn't—he wanted to punish, to destroy. He wanted to inflict and feel physical pain. He wanted to move, to run, to force his muscles to work past the point of exhaustion, to make his lungs gasp for breath. He wanted to feel anything but the desire that threatened to rip him apart from the inside.

*Why did you bring me here?* Liana had asked him the question and he'd been unable to answer. The truth would have terrified her. He'd brought her to the palace because he'd been unable to let her go. In that moment on the plane, when he'd first seen her, he'd felt something. A connection, a link that was so powerful, it had nearly pulled out his soul. Not once in his life had he ever been so emotionally exposed. Not even with Iman—his wife.

He paced to the windows and back, telling himself that in the morning he had to let the woman go. He had no right to keep her. He might be the Crown Prince of El Bahar, but in these modern times he would not be allowed to kidnap an American citizen, no matter how much he might want to do so.

He ached. Not just to make love, but for so much more. He saw his brothers with their wives, and he envied the emotional intimacy they shared, an intimacy he would never be allowed to experience. He longed to be just like everyone else, and that was the one thing he could not have.

So he'd brought Liana here, if only for the night, because of the unexplained desire he felt for her. Because for their brief time together he could pretend that he was like other men, that he might meet a woman, find her attractive, date her and perhaps even fall in love.

He could allow himself this fantasy for a single night, knowing it could never be. He'd learned his lesson well as a boy, and now he lived it as a man. No one breached the walls that surrounded his soul. His wife never had, although she hadn't much tried.

Iman. Just thinking about her changed his passion to anger. He welcomed the transformation. He forced himself to remember how badly it had all started and the tragedy of how it had ended. The saving grace was that he'd never loved her. He'd never loved anyone. He never would.

But not loving couldn't take away the wanting, and

reality prevented him from having that which he needed. So he continued to pace alone in his room, desperately forcing himself to ignore the ache, the need and the loneliness which had, over time, become his closest friends.

Carl Birmingham was unfailingly polite and sympathetic, but so unhelpful that Liana wished she could throw a chair through the window. At least then her frustration would have an outlet. As it was, she had to sit quietly in her seat across the desk from the American School administrator and grit her teeth to keep from screaming.

"It seems to me," he was saying in a calm voice, "everything would be so much easier if you would simply accept the Crown Prince's invitation. You said you were told this morning the Prince wished you to remain as his guest. Is that so terrible?"

Carl Birmingham, a portly man in his mid fifties, leaned toward her and smiled. "Have you considered the great honor? You are a visiting American teacher being invited to reside in one of the greatest palaces in the world. You have the opportunity of becoming a close friend of the royal family."

Liana wondered why she'd thought anyone would understand. Apparently the situation was strange only to her. Everyone else thought she should be grateful that Malik intended her to continue to live at the palace.

"I do appreciate the honor," she said, careful to keep her tone level. "However, I never asked to live at the palace. All I want for my daughter and myself is the housing we were promised in my contract. A two-bedroom condo. Just something of our own."

Mr. Birmingham straightened the papers on his desk, then glanced at her. "Of course if you feel you and your daughter are in physical danger, the situation must be rectified at once. I did not realize you felt threatened.''

Liana sighed. ''It's not that. I'm not worried about being attacked in the night, it's just...''

How could she explain the sensation of being overwhelmed by a force larger than life? Malik Khan was a man used to getting his way, and for reasons that made no sense to her, he'd plucked her from obscurity to be the focus of his considerable attention. While she was flattered, she was also very nervous. Her own attraction to the man made her vulnerable. Not to mention the fact that no one looked forward to being used then discarded.

''Ms. Archer, the American School exists because of the support of the royal family,'' Mr. Birmingham explained. ''Prince Malik sits on the board of directors. He was instrumental in changing our policy so that teachers could be chosen based on skill rather than gender or marital status. Not many years ago, a single woman would not have been invited to join the staff.''

''Why should that matter? I'm good at what I do, with or without a husband.''

''I agree. But we are both Americans. Life is different here in El Bahar. The country is very progressive, but it is still foreign, with different laws and a different culture.''

She was beginning to get a message, and she didn't like what it said. ''You think I should live in the palace.''

''Ms. Archer, I would never presume to tell you what to do. However, we are talking about the Crown Prince. He is a powerful individual, while you are simply one teacher.''

Liana leaned back in her chair and bit back a scream. Basically she was trapped. Her generous contract had a clause that allowed the school to dismiss her for almost any reason. In return, they had to provide a return ticket and three months salary. While that would keep her and Bethany from starving while she looked for a job back in California, it wouldn't do anything about funding her daughter's college education, or providing them with a down payment on a house.

"Look at it this way," Mr. Birmingham said with a smile. "Prince Malik hasn't shown much interest in a woman for years. Not since..." His voice trailed off.

"Not since what?"

He shifted on the seat. "Yes, well, not since the unfortunate incident with his wife."

"His wife? But Princess Heidi said he wasn't married."

"He's not. He was, but Princess Iman is no longer with us."

Liana thought about asking how the woman had died, then figured it wasn't her business. Nor did she care. What was important was where she was going to live.

"You want me to stay at the palace," she said flatly.

Mr. Birmingham shrugged. "You are welcome to move into your provided housing. The unit will be kept available. I cannot tell you what to do, Ms. Archer. It's your decision."

Liana nodded. "Thank you, Mr. Birmingham. I won't take up any more of your time."

With that she rose to her feet and left the room. Once she was in the hall, she swore softly under her breath. She was trapped. Well and truly trapped. If she made too much of a fuss about living at the palace, she could lose her job. Not something she wanted before she'd even had a chance to start.

Malik glanced out the window of his office and told himself he was simply checking the weather. He wasn't actually keeping watch to see if Liana had returned from her first day teaching at the American School.

He knew that she'd already spoken with the administrator about her living arrangements at the palace. Carl Birmingham had phoned earlier to relay the details of his talk with Liana and had emphasized the fact that he'd informed Ms. Archer of the great honor the Crown Prince had bestowed upon her. If this were a hundred and fifty years ago, Carl Birmingham would be one of those annoying personal assistants to the crown who spent his entire day parroting back the monarch's words and bowing as he walked.

Malik frowned. He would have had a whole lot more respect for the man if he'd challenged Malik's actions. Who was the prince to keep this woman in the palace? Malik leaned back in his chair and stared mindlessly out the window. He was playing a dangerous game, and it couldn't go on much longer. He would have to allow Liana to move into the American School's housing.

But not just yet, he told himself. Perhaps tomorrow, or maybe at the end of the week. For now he wanted her close by. Even though she was unlikely to want to speak with him or see him, he liked knowing she was within the palace walls, that if he were to command that she be brought to him, she would be forced to appear.

He was a fool, and that was something he'd always tried to avoid being. He wished he could explain why he was so interested in this woman. What combination of features, personality and fate had made him act so out of character? Perhaps Fatima had cast a spell on him.

Malik grinned at the thought of his very practical grandmother dabbling in love spells. Fatima was too down-to-earth to have patience for such things. No, he was going to have accept responsibility for his actions all on his own.

A flicker of movement caught his attention. He looked up and saw Liana's young daughter moving in the direction of a stable. He allowed himself a faint smile. No doubt she wanted to see the many horses there and perhaps find out about riding one.

Despite the meeting due to start in ten minutes and the pile of work still awaiting his attention, Malik rose to his feet and left the office. He informed his startled male assistant that he would be out for an hour or so and please to reschedule the meeting for a more convenient time. Then he hurried toward the stables on the far side of the palace.

Less than five minutes later he found young Bethany Archer gently touching the soft nose of a bay. The child had changed from her school uniform into jeans and a T-shirt. Her hair was about three shades lighter than her mother's, and she'd pulled the blond strands back into a braid. Her nose wrinkled as she gazed earnestly at the gelding, petting him with a wistfulness that betrayed her heart's desire.

"Do you ride?" he asked.

The girl jumped and spun toward him. "I was just saying hello," she said as she took a large step away from the stable door and tucked her hands behind her back. "I'd never hurt them."

He held in a smile. "I know that."

She glanced up at him. "Are you angry? I didn't exactly let my mom know I was coming to see the horses because I was afraid she'd tell me no. So I said I wanted to look around. You know, get to know the palace. Then she said to stay inside and not to wander too far or get in the way." Her mouth twisted slightly. "Grown-ups have too many rules. And they never write them down. Sometimes the rules change. My mom's real good about keeping the rules the same, but not everyone is like her. Don't you hate it when that happens?''

Blond bangs fell to her eyebrows, emphasizing the blue of her irises. He could see a lot of her mother in her. She was pretty and smart and probably the most charming child he'd ever met.

''I do hate it,'' he said solemnly, even though he wasn't sure what he was agreeing to. ''So you like horses?''

She nodded. ''Very much. They're lovely. I've always wanted to ride. Where we lived, back in California I mean, there was a lot of horse property. Old Mr. Preston used to give riding lessons, but they were expensive. I was going to think up ways to earn money this year so I could take some. He's got ten horses. A couple are old, but the rest are nice.''

He motioned to the long row of stalls. ''Would you like to meet my horses?''

She pressed her hands together in front of her thin chest. ''Sure. How many do you have?''

''There are a half dozen or so for riding. I also own some race horses, along with breeding stock. The horses are a hobby of mine.''

Her eyes had widened. ''So you have way more than Mr. Preston.''

''I would think so.'' He led the way, walking down past a few stalls, then stopped in front of an oversized pen. ''This is Alexander the Great. He's my favorite riding horse. He likes attention, so it's safe to pet him. In fact, he's a bit vain. If we ride by water, he likes to go slowly so he can stare at his reflection.''

Bethany giggled, then slowly reached up her hand to

touch the black stallion. Alexander snuffled her palm and gave a snort of disgust.

"He wants a treat." Malik pointed to a small bin set against the center of the far wall. "You'll find oats in there. You may feed him a handful, but no more. Too much will make him sick."

Bethany nodded, then ran over to collect the treat. She carefully flattened her hand to feed the horse and was rewarded when the animal consented to be petted. The girl sighed with pleasure.

"When I grow up I want to own lots of horses. I'll ride all day and learn to jump and it will feel like flying."

Her blue eyes sparkled as she spoke of her dreams. There was color in her pale cheeks and an energy that made him feel old. Had he ever had such simple hopes for his own future? Doubtful, he thought. He couldn't remember a time when he hadn't known he would someday rule El Bahar. But Bethany's life was very different. He envied her her freedom, all the while knowing that even if given a chance he wouldn't change his destiny.

"You'll need to start by learning how to ride," he said. "I would be happy to teach you."

She stared at him and pressed her lips together. Her entire body quivered with excitement. "Really? You'd teach me on one of your horses?"

"Yes. I have an old gelding who has just the right temperament. He has a white star on his forehead, which makes him very handsome, although he's not vain like Alexander here."

"Thank you," Bethany breathed reverently, then tilted her head and gave an exaggerated grimace. "Except I have to ask my mom, and I'm afraid she'll say no."

"Why would she do that?"

"I don't know. Moms can be difficult sometimes." Her

expression brightened. "But maybe because you're a prince and all, she won't mind so much." Bethany smiled. "I asked about you at school today and everyone says you're going to be king of El Bahar one day."

"That does seem to be the way things are going."

"I think it would be *very* romantic to be a princess, but my mom doesn't agree. You don't exactly fit into her plan."

Of that Malik was sure. Liana's plan included enough money for a house and her daughter's college education. From what he could tell, the single mother had tried to think of everything. He doubted a royal prince had figured into her expectations.

"I would still be happy to teach you to ride," he said. "If you would like."

"Oh, I'd like that very much. I'll ask her right away."

"Fine. If it's all right with your mother, we'll start tomorrow when you return from school."

Bethany shrieked and jumped, gave him a quick, unexpected hug, then tore out of the stable as if her shoes were on fire. Alexander snorted his displeasure, but Malik didn't agree with the horse's assessment. To his mind, Bethany was a most charming young lady who admired him. Now if only he could find a way to make her mother as much of a fan.

## Chapter Four

Liana paced around the living room, muttering under her breath. She could *not* believe this was happening to her. She felt as if she were trapped in some Victorian novel, perhaps as a governess newly arrived, only to find out that her employer had murdered his wife and was now raising the knife toward her. Ridiculous. Malik might be arrogant and annoying, but he wasn't threatening her life, even if it did feel as if she was well and truly trapped.

She couldn't get Carl Birmingham's words out of her head—he'd said Prince Malik was a member of the board of directors at the American School. Not to mention the fact that she should be *honored* to be the prince's guest.

"Honored," she grumbled as she paused in front of the French doors to the balcony. "Yeah, right. Next he'll be telling me not to worry my pretty little head about it."

Her gaze settled on the view before her. The blue Arabian Sea stretched out to the horizon. It was dark and vivid and probably the most beautiful thing she'd ever seen. Slowly, she turned in a circle, taking in the exquisite horse murals, the expensive furniture, the objets d'art. The bedrooms were just as lovely and spacious, and was she crazy to want her own place rather than accepting the hospitality of a royal prince?

She was a single mother from San Bernardino. Her dad was a retired postal worker, her mom, a homemaker. Liana's sister worked as a hairdresser. Liana herself, the only one in the family to make it through college, taught high-school math. And here she was complaining because she'd caught the attention of the Crown Prince of a wealthy and respected nation.

"Maybe I *am* insane," she said aloud. "Maybe I should just give in and stay here. It's not so horrible. After all, the food is great, and there are hot and cold running servants."

Liana sank onto the sofa and took a deep breath. As tempting as the palace might be, she couldn't stay because nothing was going to be that easy. She didn't know why Prince Malik had brought her here, but she doubted it was because he thought she would be a great ornament. Did he expect her to sleep with him? Was this all about sex?

Liana bristled at the thought. In this day and age women were not kidnapped to be placed into a harem. At least not women like her, with twenty extra pounds settling on her hips and thighs and a body with the still-visible marks of childbirth.

No, she told herself. A handsome prince like him would want perfection. And he'd have plenty of choices—what with women falling all over him everywhere he went. Liana had felt the powerful chemistry of his attraction. She, too, had been all a-twitter at the thought of being close to someone like Malik. He'd made her heart race and her blood boil and whatever other fabulous phrases filled the pages of those romances she so adored reading. At least between the covers of those books, the women always found a wonderful man and sexual fulfillment. If only life were that tidy.

But it wasn't, and, regardless of her wayward hormones, she had no intention of falling for Malik, either in or out of bed. Not that he was going to ask her, which brought her right back to where she'd started...what on earth was she doing here?

The suite door opened and Bethany sailed inside. Her bright eyes and glowing skin told of a wondrous adventure. Liana smiled and patted the cushion next to her on the sofa. "Come tell me all about it," she told her daughter.

Bethany plopped down next to her and gave an exaggerated sigh. "There are so many horses," she said, leaning against Liana. "Rooms and stables of them. They're all big and pretty and Prince Malik was there and he introduced me to his favorite. Alexander the Great is a very vain horse. He looks at himself in the water, admiring his reflection!"

She gave a giggle of delight, as if a vain horse were a wondrous thing indeed. Liana was less amused. "Prince Malik was with you?" What on earth had he been doing in the stable?

Bethany nodded. "He talked to me and everything." She straightened and looked at her mother. "He's very nice. He said that he would like to teach me to ride and I told him that I had to talk to you first and make sure it's all right, but I know it is because he said he has a very special horse that is perfect for a girl like me and I wouldn't get hurt and you really wouldn't mind, would you, because you know I've wanted to ride forever." She paused to draw in a much needed breath. "It's all I've ever wanted in the whole wide world."

Blue eyes stared beseechingly up at her. Liana grabbed hold of the anger flaring inside of her. None of this was her daughter's fault, she reminded herself. Bethany was an innocent in whatever game Prince Malik might be playing with them both. But she couldn't ignore the fury building inside her. How dare that man use her daughter to get to her? Riding lessons. Yeah, right. Every good prince gave them to absolute strangers on a regular basis. It was probably part of their training.

She forced herself to smile at her daughter and smooth her bangs from her face. "I think learning to ride is a wonderful idea, and if it doesn't work out here, I'll check into it in the city. I'm sure there's a stable close to the American School. Even with all the money we need to save, I'll bet there's enough left over for lessons."

Her daughter opened her mouth to protest, but Liana stopped her with a shake of her head. "I need to talk to the prince first, Bethany. While I'm gone, please start on your homework. After dinner, I thought we'd watch a movie. Would you like to pick it?"

Bethany's natural good nature asserted itself. "You won't forget about the riding lessons?"

"I promise I won't."

"Okay." Her daughter kissed her cheek, then stood and skipped out of the room. She paused in the doorway and glanced back at her mother. "I looked this morning and there are Disney movies on the shelves in my room, along with *The Little Princess*." She giggled. "Maybe we should watch that one."

Liana looked at her daughter. Bethany was a pretty child. She still had freckles on her pert nose, and with her slender, athletic body, in a few short years she was going to be a heartbreaker. But for now she was still a little girl. Liana would do anything to protect her, even risk an international incident...or her job.

"*The Little Princess* sounds great. Will you be all right while I'm gone? I should be back in about twenty minutes."

"I'm nine!" Bethany reminded her. "I'm not a baby."

"I know. You're practically a grandmother. Promise you'll stay in the suite."

"Promise," Bethany called in a sing-song voice as she headed off to her room.

Liana waited until she heard the door close, then she rose to her feet and went in search of Prince Malik.

The palace was huge, and, in a matter of minutes, she found herself completely lost. All the long corridors looked similar enough to confuse her. By the time she'd passed the stone nymph fountain for the third time, she knew she wasn't going to be able to find her way on her own. Of course, her journey was hampered by a lack of knowledge about her destination.

Finally Liana spotted a young servant and stopped the woman. She explained she was looking for Prince Malik. Complicated directions followed, ending with Liana being escorted to a large set of double doors.

"Here, ma'am," the young woman said with a smile. "Prince Malik. Good evening to you both."

"It won't be a good evening for him," Liana muttered as a way to gather her suddenly lacking courage. "I plan to tell him exactly what I think of him. How dare he thrust himself into our lives like this and expect..." She verbally stumbled as she realized she had no clue about his expectations, except a burning certainty that they couldn't possibly either be acceptable or match her own.

That decided, she pounded on the door.

She fully expected to be let into a suite of offices and then to have to explain her presence to a host of secretaries and assistants. Instead, Prince Malik himself opened the door. The sight of him disconcerted her, as did his state of dress.

Liana stared and swallowed and vowed that *this* time she was going to ignore the heating, melting sensation filling her body. It's not as if the man were naked, or even close to naked. He wore black slacks and a formal white shirt. He'd been in the process of slipping in cufflinks when he'd answered the door.

Dark eyes locked with hers and the intense expression there nearly caused her not to notice his still-damp hair and the clean look of his freshly shaven face. He was a handsome man—too handsome for comfort—and she had the most disconcerting urge to offer to finish fastening his cuffs for him.

"Liana," he said, faint pleasure lacing his voice. "This is a surprise. I was on my way out for the evening."

"I can tell," she told him, firmly squashing the irrational flare of jealousy that ripped through her. Going out, was he? As in, with a woman? Fine by her. She didn't care. In fact she was pleased he was going out because then he wouldn't be around to bother her. Not that he'd been a bother, but he *was* keeping her here against her will which meant the bothering bit was bound to occur sooner or later.

"I have something to discuss with you, Your Highness," she said, stepping into his suite. "While it won't take very long, I consider it most important."

"Of course you do," he said with a smile, then motioned for her to take a seat on one of the large sofas in his living room. "And please, call me Malik."

The request disconcerted her, which made no sense. She found herself slightly off balance and trying not to be intimidated by the luxury and grandeur of his living room.

He had the same view she did, although from a different angle, as his rooms were at the far end of the palace. There was no mural. Instead beautiful paintings covered the plain cream walls. She recognized a couple of the pieces from photos in books. Malik seemed to favor Impressionists, although there was a smaller collection of modern pieces in the dining area to their left.

Between the opulence, her racing heart and the heat rolling through her body like the tide, she was afraid she was going to pass out right there on the thick Oriental carpet that was probably older than the United States and worth more than a car. Then she remembered why she'd come in the first place.

Facing him and planting her hands on her hips, she said, "I don't know what rules you've lived by in the past, nor do I care. I suppose you're used to having your way and damn the consequences. Let me assure you I'm not someone to be trifled with, and I don't care if you're a prince or a king or the ruler of the universe. You will *not* use my daughter in your traitorous scheme. She is a wonderful, intelligent, active girl who deserves to be treated with respect. How dare you play with her emotions?"

Malik stared at her for several heartbeats. "Are you quite finished?"

"I haven't even gotten started. I'm not afraid of you or your power. They mean nothing to me. It's bad enough that you've brought me and Bethany here against our will. As I'm sure you know, I've spoken to Mr. Birmingham at the school and he's informed me that you're a member of the board. The inference was very clear. Either I do what you say or you have me fired. I can accept all of that, but to think you'd sink so low as to use an innocent child to get what you want. It's disgusting. How dare you try to weasel your way into her affections—bribing her by offering to teach her to ride? She might be young and inexperienced and therefore gullible, but I am not.''

''A weasel?'' Malik questioned. ''Interesting choice. I've not seen a weasel, at least not in person. Now meerkats are something different. I've seen them in Africa. On a tour.''

He spoke blandly, as if they were discussing the weather.

Liana wanted to stamp her foot in frustration. ''Are you even listening to me?''

''To every word, more's the pity.'' He took a step toward her and loomed over her. ''The problem is you're not making any sense.'' With that, he wrapped his arms around her and drew her close.

Liana was so stunned she actually stopped breathing. All the air left her lungs, but she couldn't seem to draw any back in. She went willingly because she couldn't command herself to move away. No messages were getting through to her nervous system. What was he doing and why was he doing it? She hated being this close to him, hated the way...

Suddenly, his mouth came down on hers. The action shouldn't have surprised her, yet she couldn't believe it was happening. The warm pressure of his lips moved against her in a way that left her feeling branded and impossibly aroused. His grip on her was firm and unyielding, forcing her up against him until they touched completely from shoulder to knee. Her breasts flattened against his broad chest and her hands were trapped between her hipbone and his thigh.

She told herself to protest, to object, to squirm and pull

away…but it had been a long time since a man had done this to her, and she was too weak to fight him.

Malik shifted, freeing her arms. He used one hand to brush against her back and the other to cradle her head, as if he feared she might pull away.

There was something about his lips—the heat, the firm softness, the way he took control while at the same time inviting her to come along on a sensual journey she couldn't begin to imagine. Or maybe it was his body, right next to hers, hard and unyielding to her feminine curves. Her breasts felt so good pressing against his chest. Her nipples were hard points of desire. Her hips seemed to be pulsing and thrusting of their own free will. She didn't understand her body or herself for not pushing away. In fact she found herself raising her arms until they encircled his neck. She drew herself up on her toes so that her body fit better against his.

He was kissing her with slow, sweet kisses that were almost innocent, yet incredibly seductive. The masculine scent of him surrounded her, filling her with an intoxication that she knew she would remember for the rest of her life. It was not just that she would now be able to find him in the dark—she would crawl over broken glass for the privilege of inhaling that scent one last time before she died.

Then he brushed her lower lip with his tongue. One slow, deliberate act of passion that nearly made her cry out. Without thinking she parted her lips to admit him, aware that she was crossing a line, and that once she did so, there could be no retreat. She wanted him with a desperation that left her shattered and afraid. Yet, as he entered her, she welcomed him with darting brushes of her tongue against his.

And then whatever civility still existed between them

disappeared, burned to dust by the explosion that rocked through her like lightning cutting through a tree. She shook violently as he invaded her mouth. No longer gentle or smooth, he plunged and explored like a man on an urgent mission. He discovered the secrets of her mouth, what made her surge toward him, what made her gasp. He buried his fingers into her thick hair and moved them up and down her back. He slipped lower and cupped her behind, squeezing the full curves and making her pulse against him in a way designed to make them both think of the ultimate act of love.

She found herself wanting to tear off her clothes, to expose herself to him so that he would know how much she wanted him. She thought about them making love right here, on the sofa, or perhaps on the dining-room table. She needed him the way she needed air, and knew that if she didn't have him right now, she wouldn't survive.

The sense of being out of control was so unfamiliar that it shocked her into stepping away from him. Without wanting to, she raised her fingers to her mouth and pressed them against her throbbing skin. Her body still trembled and the heat continued to pour through her, arousing her to a fevered pitch.

"I can't," she whispered, not sure if she meant she couldn't do that again, or if she couldn't bear to stop.

Malik's dark gaze was unreadable, his expression as hard as his body had been. He seemed to be caught up in his own private hell, and she wondered if she'd been the only one to feel the fire between them. What a cruel joke of fate that would be—that the first man to make her understand what all the fuss was about when it came to passion was also a man who was immune to her. Could that be possible? Had she been the only one to feel the intensity of their connection?

"I don't need your daughter's help to get your attention, Ms. Archer, and I'm disappointed you would think that of me," Malik said in a low, steady voice. "I offered to teach Bethany to ride because I enjoy her company. For no other reason." Then he turned on his heel and walked down the hallway of the suite.

Liana stared after him. Was that it? Had the bastard just been trying to prove a point? He'd certainly made an impression on her—and not one that she wanted to repeat. How dare he act so...so... She swore silently in frustration when she couldn't complete her thought.

She took a single step, then another. Gradually her breathing returned to normal. That kiss. It hadn't just exposed her to passion, it had redefined her world. It wasn't supposed to be like that, she thought in confusion. She was thirty years old. She'd been married, had a child. Nothing about what went on between a man and a woman should be new to her.

And yet it was. It was a very different world than the one she was used to.

Still reeling from all that had happened, Liana managed to make her way back to her own suite. At least Malik had more than proved his point. He *didn't* need Bethany to get Liana's attention. Another couple of kisses like that and she would spend all her time rubbing against him like a cat. It was disgusting what she'd been reduced to. Here she'd been worried that all he would be interested in was sex. Now she found herself hoping that was the case. Just over twenty-four hours in a foreign country and already she was not herself.

She turned the doorknob and entered the room. All right, so maybe she'd over-reacted. She would simply put the incident behind her. It wasn't going to be repeated; she would be on her guard to make sure of that. After all, the last thing she needed was to spend her day as some Middle Eastern Prince's sex slave. In the meantime she would tell Bethany that riding lessons with Malik were fine and—

Liana realized there was a strange older woman sitting in her living room.

"Good evening," the woman said, rising to her feet. "I hope you don't mind that I made myself at home, but at my age, it's difficult to stand for long periods of time without experiencing some discomfort."

"What? Oh, of course, it's fine," Liana said, caught off-guard for the second time in a single night. "I'm Liana Archer."

"I'm Queen Fatima, the king's mother and Malik's grandmother. Welcome to the great palace of El Bahar."

The next few minutes passed in a blur. Somehow tea and biscuits appeared. Liana found herself acting as hostess in a room where she felt very much an out-of-place guest. Fatima—like her son, she had insisted her title be dropped—was a tall elegant woman of indeterminate age. Her silvering hair had been swept up into a chignon that was reminiscent of a different era, although her clothes were contemporary, flattering and obviously haute couture. Her pale blue dress looked to be silk and the pearls around her neck were large and perfectly matched.

By contrast, Liana still wore the dress she'd put on early that morning, and a day of teaching had done nothing to improve its bargain-store appearance. She tugged on the hem and smiled brightly.

"The palace is very beautiful," she said as she held her tea in one hand and a biscuit in the other.

"I'm glad you think so," Fatima told her. "There have

been some modernizations, but all in all, it hasn't changed that much since I was brought here as a young bride." She smiled. "You must promise to come visit me in the harem. It's very lovely and peaceful there."

Liana had just taken a bite of her biscuit. Now she choked as it went down the wrong way and it was several minutes before she could speak again. "Harem?"

"Of course. I've kept all the original mosaics and much of the furniture. The gardens are as lovely, although most of the parrots are gone." Fatima sipped her tea. "Parrots were always kept around the harem so that men could not hear the voices of the women and be tempted to climb the walls."

"I see," she said, even though she didn't. Harem. "So there are women there? Women kept for the princes?" She deliberately kept her voice sounding mildly interested so that the queen would not guess her repugnance at the thought of females on demand for any group of men. She'd thought that El Bahar was a forward-looking country, but obviously she'd been—

"I'm the only resident of the harem now," Fatima said blandly. Her calm expression gave Liana the uncomfortable feeling that the queen knew exactly what she'd been thinking. "The harem as you would define it was disbanded a year or so after I was married. King Givon, my son, never kept any women there for himself and none of the princes do either. So it can be a bit lonely for an old woman like myself."

Despite her embarrassment at being caught out with such obvious questions, Liana couldn't help laughing. "I doubt anyone thinks of you as an old woman, Fatima. You are too elegant."

"Thank you, my dear. One tries one's best. Now, enough about my life. Tell me about your relationship with my grandson. I've heard several different rumors, and I'm not sure which one to believe.''

''There's nothing to tell,'' Liana said, refusing to think about the kiss they'd just shared. While it had been amazing, it didn't *mean* anything. She quickly recounted her meeting with Malik and how she'd come to be at the palace rather than the teacher residences at the American School.

''Most intriguing,'' Fatima mused. ''Not like Malik at all.'' She regarded Liana thoughtfully. ''Malik is a great many good things, but he's not what you Americans refer to as a *people person*. He's generally reserved. Heidi, his sister-in-law, can get through to him. She always has. I believe it's her irreverence for his authority, and the fact that she treats Malik like a regular person.''

''He *is* a regular person,'' Liana reminded the queen. ''He has exceptional responsibilities, but that doesn't make him any less human.''

''Really…'' Fatima took another sip of tea. ''How interesting you should think so. Most of Malik's acquaintances would not agree with you. They would say he was quite removed from the rest of us.''

Probably because they hadn't been kissed by him, Liana thought humorously. There was nothing like a passionate embrace from a handsome prince to remind a woman that he was very much a mortal man.

''So how are you adjusting to life in El Bahar?'' the queen asked.

As far as smooth transitions went, it left much to be desired, but Liana was determined to play along. She found herself liking the grandmother of the Crown Prince.

''I've never lived in a palace before,'' she admitted. ''It has its benefits, as well as its drawbacks.''

''The palace is very beautiful,'' Fatima said. ''You and

your daughter must visit me in the harem for tea. Perhaps on Saturday.''

''That would be nice.'' Liana answered politely even as she wondered if they would still be here on Saturday. Just because she'd had a moment of mind-stealing passion didn't mean that she'd changed her views on having her own place. If Malik thought he could seduce her into staying at the palace, he was going to find himself very startled when she left.

Fatima smiled at her. ''I hope you're going to be very good for my grandson. He needs that.''

''Because he misses his late wife?''

Fatima's friendly expression faded as if it had never been. Her expression hardened just as Liana had seen Malik's do. Fatima stiffened, then set her teacup on the table.

''I will not speak of that woman,'' the queen announced as she rose to her feet. ''She might have been of royal blood, but she was not worthy of the house of Khan.''

''I'm sorry,'' Liana said quickly. ''I didn't mean to say anything offensive about Malik's late wife.''

''You did not. You could not, as you are unaware of what happened.'' Fatima smiled tightly. ''Do not trouble yourself, child. While Iman will never be dead enough to suit me, she is out of our lives and we are the better for having her gone. I have trespassed on your hospitality long enough. I bid you goodnight.''

With that, Fatima departed, leaving a very bemused Liana staring after her. The rich and royal truly were different, she thought, feeling slightly bemused and very confused by all that had happened.

## Chapter Five

The girl caught on quickly, Malik thought with some pleasure. After three days, Bethany was fearless on horseback, which meant their riding lessons had been successful. He wanted her to learn the mechanics of a good seat and a combination of gentle firmness with which to guide her mount rather than have to overcome any terror at being on top of such a large animal. She was a natural, taking to the saddle with the balance of someone born to the sport.

"I want to gallop across the desert," she said with a small pout as they circled the large training ring. "This is boring."

"This is practice," he told her patiently. "You would not like falling and breaking a bone. Casts are uncomfortable and itchy."

The pout turned into a grin. "What did you break?"

"My arm. Twice."

Blue eyes gazed at him. "Mommy says that to make a mistake once is good. It means we're stretching ourselves and learning something new. But to make the same mistake again is really…" Bethany pressed her lips together and didn't finish her sentence.

Malik wondered if her reticence was good manners on her part, or a sudden realization that he was a prince and it didn't do to call him stupid. He hoped it was the former because he liked being with Bethany. The majority of her charm came from her intelligence and her artlessness. She didn't know the first thing about having a conversation with a member of the royal family. To her, he was just an adult who had agreed to grant her wish of learning to ride.

"My father told me the same thing," he said solemnly. "He also forbade me to jump my horse again."

She frowned at him. "But if you broke your arm twice, that means you didn't listen to him."

"You're right. And I paid the price."

She mulled that over. "I think I'll listen to my mom and to you. I don't want to break anything." She eyed the gate of the training corral, then sighed. "If we can't go out, can we at least go faster?"

"Of course."

She flashed him a grin of pure pleasure, then urged her horse into a trot. The patient gelding did as she requested, bouncing her along in a bone-jarring gait that made her thick, blond braid dance up and down on her back.

"Try cantering," Malik called. "It's more comfortable."

Bethany's expression changed to one of concentration. She leaned over the horse's neck and squeezed her thighs for all she was worth. Malik doubted the horse felt the pressure, but he sensed her intent and switched to the smoother stride. Bethany circled him around the ring, then executed a perfect figure 8 before slowing to a walk and moving next to Malik on his horse in the center of the ring.

"Can we go out of the ring tomorrow?" she asked.

"Yes," he said. "I think you are ready."

She beamed at him and together they turned toward the stable. The groom on duty opened the gate to let them through.

"I'm having the best time in El Bahar," Bethany confessed. "I thought I'd miss home a bunch, but I don't. I mean, I miss my friends and all, but I'm making new ones. Mommy promised I would and she was right."

"What about your father?" Malik asked before he could stop himself. "Do you miss him?"

Bethany reined in her mount. They were on the tree-lined path between the corrals and the barn. Malik stopped next to her. He reached over and touched her arm. "You don't have to answer that if you don't want to," he said. "I didn't mean to make you sad."

"I'm not sad," she told him. "I don't miss my dad very much because I don't really see him." She wrinkled her nose. "It's kinda complicated, but the main thing is he's really interested in racing cars. So all his free time and money goes into that. He would rather buy a new car engine than send child support."

She paused. "Mommy always says it doesn't mean he doesn't love me, but instead that Daddy isn't practical. He doesn't understand that buying me shoes and stuff is more important than his race cars." She shrugged. "I didn't mind that so much, but I used to cry when he would promise to come see me on Saturdays and then he'd forget. Or he'd take me to a race and leave me in the pit all day by myself. I didn't like that. It was scary and loud."

Malik stared at her young face. She seemed too small and innocent to carry such burdens. He thought of Liana's ex-husband and wished the man were a resident of El Bahar. The laws here were quite strict on these matters, and if Bethany's father had missed even two payments of his child support, he would find himself living most unpleasantly in an El Baharian prison. Or if that could not be arranged, Malik would be pleased to take it upon himself to teach the man a lesson he would not soon forget.

"What did your mother tell you about that?" he asked.

"That Daddy still loves me, but he's not really mature enough to handle the responsibilities of having a child. We decided, Mommy and me I mean, that it would be better if I didn't see Daddy for a while. Not until he was ready to be there when he said."

"I'm sorry." Malik knew the words were inadequate, but didn't know what else to say. He couldn't comprehend a man turning his back on his responsibilities.

Bethany shrugged. "It's okay, I guess. I want to believe that he still loves me, like Mommy says, but I don't know. I mean if he loved me wouldn't he want to be with me?" She looked up at Malik. "You wouldn't forget to pick up your little girl, would you?"

"If I had a daughter like you, I would move heaven and earth to be with her," Malik told her honestly.

"See, that's what I thought." She slumped a little in her saddle.

He felt badly that he'd upset her, but didn't know how to fix the situation. "You have your mother," he reminded her. "She loves you and always puts you first."

Bethany perked up a little. "You're right. That's why we're here in El Bahar. They pay a lot at the American School and there will be enough left over for college and for a house and everything." Her expression turned wistful. "I wonder if we can get a house big enough for a horse."

"It would have to be pretty big," Malik said. "And no stairs. Not if you're going to keep it inside."

She burst out laughing. "You don't keep horses in the house, silly."

"But that's what you said. A house big enough for a horse."

"I meant the backyard."

The laughter chased the sadness from her eyes and made her cheeks glow with lovely color. Malik found himself enjoying his time with Bethany. In many ways she reminded him of Heidi, his brother Jamal's wife. Heidi teased him and treated him with the irreverence of a sibling. To him, she was the sister he'd never had. While the brothers were close, they were all acutely aware of their position in the El Baharian government and their duty to their country. That caused a certain distance. But Heidi would tease him about anything and not give a damn that he would one day rule El Bahar.

Bethany was like that. Part of it was her age. Children quickly forgot that they were supposed to be impressed. But most of it was her bubbly personality.

"Race you back to the barn," Bethany said. "It's not far," she added quickly, "and I promise not to fall and break anything."

"You're on," he said, turning Alexander so that he faced the path, then giving the horse a light squeeze with his thighs.

Although he could have easily won the competition, he instead kept pace with Bethany, as much to keep her safe as to make her feel that it was a battle to the finish. As their horses ate up the grassy ground between the trees and the stable, he remembered what it had been like when he'd been Bethany's age. They were worlds apart.

At least Bethany had Liana on her side. Whatever the child's father might have done wrong, her mother more than made up for it by giving the girl a warm home and unconditional love and support. What more could a daughter ask for?

"I really don't have anything to wear," Liana said, staring at the brief note. Fatima had invited her and Bethany to dine with the royal family, and her limited wardrobe was not up to royal standards.

"You'll still be the prettiest one there," Bethany said loyally. "Besides, Prince Malik is really cool. You'll like him."

Liana glanced at her daughter stretched out on the large bed in the master bedroom. The girl couldn't put two sentences together without prefacing one of them with the phrase, "Prince Malik says." No doubt Bethany thought the prince was "cool." Liana, however, didn't have the same easy camaraderie with the Crown Prince. In fact, in the past three days, she'd barely seen him.

And now this. An invitation to have dinner with him and his family. At least she assumed Malik would be there. Liana briefly closed her eyes and prayed he would be. She didn't want to have to dine with two princes, their wives, a king and a queen mother, all without the presence of the man responsible for her being there in the first place.

"This is insane," Liana said, throwing her hands up in the air. "What are we doing here?"

"You're looking for a dress," Bethany said pointing into the closet. "Wear the blue one, Mom. It makes your eyes sparkle and you want to be pretty for Prince Malik."

"It's what I live for," Liana agreed, as she drew the blue dress out and studied it.

The garment was silk and shimmery, with a simple boat neck and long sleeves. The soft fabric skimmed over curves and bulges, which was always a good thing. With her hair pulled up in a fancy chignon and her lone pair of good pearl earrings, she just might manage to get through the evening without making a fool of herself.

Bethany rolled onto her back and studied her fingers. "Can I paint my nails?" she asked.

It was a familiar question. "Nope."

"Can I wear makeup?"

"No again, pip-squeak."

"Oh, Mommy, why not? Can't I be beautiful, too?"

Liana replaced the dress and headed for the bathroom to freshen her makeup. On the way she paused by the bed and leaned over to tickle her daughter. "You are already beautiful without all of that. If I let you become even more beautiful, you'd outshine every other woman so much that we'd turn to stone and you'd be left alone."

Bethany shrieked with laughter. "Uh-uh," she managed between giggles. "I'm not that beautiful."

"Of course you are. And smart. And funny. In fact, I'm going to have to lock you in a tall tower when you turn sixteen, just so the boys don't steal you away."

Her daughter smiled and held her arms open for a hug. "I won't leave you, Mommy. Not for a silly boy. Besides, I'm going to college, remember? And I can't do that in a tower."

"I guess not."

She pulled her daughter close, savoring the familiar feel of skinny arms holding her tight. These were the moments that she would remember when Bethany was grown and gone, she told herself. The bits of magic that made it all worthwhile. Whatever else she might do with her life, Bethany would always be the very best of her.

This dinner was her worst nightmare, Liana thought nearly two hours later. The large table in the family's private dining room had room enough for all, with Bethany sitting next to her and Malik directly across from them. The king sat at one end, and Fatima at the other, with Dora and Khalil next to Malik and Heidi and Jamal next to Bethany. The problem was everyone was being so darned *nice,* Liana thought frantically as she took another sip of her wine. Not that she wanted them to be rude or mean, but they were acting as if she were already a member of the family, or at the very least, a close personal friend. It was disconcerting.

She wanted to complain about the situation, but what was she supposed to say? "Could you please ignore me?" would be misunderstood by everyone. So she forced herself to keep smiling and was thankful that Bethany's manners had always been exceptionally good.

"I heard a rumor," the king said, glancing at Bethany, "that someone at this table beat Malik in a race back to the stables."

Bethany laughed. "That was me." She lowered her voice conspiratorially. "But I think he let me win. Prince Malik is a really good rider and his horse is fast. But I'm getting better and I'm gonna beat him on my own one day."

King Givon nodded approvingly. "If you work hard, then you certainly will. Although I have to warn you, my son is a very good horseman."

"And not one to be beaten by a girl," Malik teased.

Bethany raised her chin. "Being a girl has nothing to do with it."

Malik glanced at Liana. "That attitude would be your fault, I believe."

"Thank you for the compliment," she said blandly, trying not to notice how his dark eyes gleamed with a light that had little to do with humor and instead reminded her of the passion that had flared between them only three evenings before when he'd taken her in his arms and kissed her until she was breathless and shaken.

"I've decided we shall have a girl next," Khalil said, placing his arm around Dora's shoulders. "We have two sons and it's time for a change."

Dora turned to her husband. "What makes you think you get to choose?"

He looked insulted by the question. "I am Prince Khalil Khan of El Bahar."

"As if that explains anything." Dora leaned toward Liana. "The men in this house are insufferable. Khalil thinks he can get his way simply by announcing his title. As if the waters would indeed part simply to please him."

"They would," Jamal said cheerfully. "Happens every time *I* want them to."

Heidi, Jamal's wife, rolled her eyes. "This is all your fault, Your Majesty. You've turned reasonably intelligent men into impossibly arrogant princes."

The king smiled. "To quote our honored guest," he said nodding at Liana, "thank you for the compliment. I am the king of this great country. How else would my sons be?"

"How about warm and sensitive?" Dora asked.

King Givon dismissed her with a wave, but Liana saw the affection twinkling in his dark eyes. He obviously adored both his daughters-in-law. In fact, from what she could tell, the entire family was close.

All three brothers had similar dark hair and eyes. They

were tall men, over six feet, with broad shoulders and trim yet muscular bodies shown off to perfection by tailored suits. King Givon had a bit of gray at his temples, but he, too, was a good-looking man well into his prime. Liana knew that he had been a widower for some years and wondered why he'd never remarried.

It was quite a gene pool, she thought as she gazed around the table. And both the married princes had chosen American wives. Although she vaguely recalled that Prince Jamal had lost his first wife, who had been from a minor Middle Eastern noble family, in a tragic traffic accident.

As much as they made her nervous, she was pleased to be part of the family, if only for the evening. Being with these warm, generous people made her think of her own parents, although their small, three-bedroom home in an older part of San Bernardino was a far cry from life in the palace. She could only imagine what her sister, the hairdresser, would say about her current living arrangements. Chrissie would squeal and laugh until she fell off her five-inch platform shoes.

Malik leaned toward her. "How are you adjusting to teaching at the American School?" he asked.

The room went quiet and everyone looked at her. Liana could feel herself blushing. "It's only been a few days, but so far I'm enjoying it. My students are bright, which makes the school year more interesting, but also more of a challenge. In the advanced algebra class I'm hoping we'll have time to start learning calculus."

"You teach mathematics?" the king asked, as a servant entered with a tray of coffee and dessert.

"Yes. At the high-school level."

"Have you always wanted to be a teacher?" Queen Fatima asked.

Liana felt like an observer at a tennis match. She had to turn to the other end of the table to answer the Queen Mother. "Yes. Since I was about Bethany's age. Math was always my favorite subject. I never changed my mind."

"Mommy wants to go back to college," Bethany added helpfully, half distracted by the individual chocolate souf-flés being placed in front of everyone. She touched the thick, warm sauce with the tip of her finger and quickly licked the skin clean, then grinned. "It's yummy."

"I'm so pleased you like it," Queen Fatima said, then returned her attention to Liana. "More college?"

Liana nodded. "I would like to get my master's and maybe even my doctorate degree. In theoretical equations."

"What exactly are theoretical equations?" Malik asked, waving away his dessert and taking coffee in its place.

"You don't want to know."

He smiled. A slow smile that was a hundred percent masculine and equally seductive. Liana had the brief thought that she would be willing to give up her own dessert to see that smile again. Then she came to her senses and quickly dug her spoon into her treat.

An hour later Liana and Malik strolled through the lush gardens of the palace. Heidi and Dora had taken Bethany off to see their young children and Malik had offered to walk Liana back to her suite. Liana hadn't been sure if the events had occurred spontaneously or if they'd been planned. She also wasn't sure if she cared. After all, how many times in her life had she spent time in the company of a handsome prince? As long as she kept her head firmly on her shoulders and out of the clouds she'd be fine. Besides, real princes did *not* fall in love with schoolteachers, however much she might like the truth to be otherwise.

"What do you think of the gardens?" Malik asked as they passed a grove of orange trees. "Parts of them are centuries old."

"They're lovely," she admitted, inhaling the sweet scent of flowers she couldn't identify.

The evening air was warm and seemed to surround them in a gentle embrace. She smiled, knowing she was being fanciful. While she might tell herself to stay sensible, she couldn't help hoping that Malik would kiss her again. She wanted to know if it had really been that wonderful or if she'd imagined the excitement and desire that had raced through her. Plus, except for that one kiss, it had been years since a man had held her in his arms. She'd forgotten how nice it was to be physically close to someone.

Malik half turned toward her as they walked. "Bethany is doing very well with her riding," he said.

"So I've heard." She smiled. "She likes to relive the lesson in exquisite detail." Her smile faded. "You're being very kind to her. Thank you. I'm sorry I jumped to conclusions before. About why you were doing it, I mean."

Despite the lamplight illuminating the paths through the garden, Malik was more in shadow and she couldn't read his expression. He gave a slight nod of his head.

"I like your daughter. I'm enjoying our time together."

Liana believed him, although she was a little surprised. She wouldn't have thought that a Crown Prince would have a good time with a nine-year-old girl. But then, what did she actually know about the royal set and their entertainment requirements?

"She talked a little about her father today," Malik said.

Liana wasn't surprised. "What did she say?"

"That she didn't see him much when you were in California. That she's sure he loves her, but he's not practical enough to do things like send child support or visit regularly."

Liana stopped in the middle of the path and folded her arms over her chest. "It's bad enough that I made a mistake with my life, but I really hate that Bethany has to pay for it, too."

"You mean your ex-husband?"

"Yes. While I have a lot of regrets about the marriage, I can't regret her at all. Bethany is my life. But it's horrible that Chuck is such a jerk about seeing her. I've reached the point where I don't even care about the money, but in addition to not sending child support, he would set up weekends with her, then not show up."

Liana sighed. "That was the worst," she murmured. "Sitting with her by the window while we both waited. As it got later and later, she would try not to cry. Her effort to be brave nearly broke my heart. She didn't make excuses for him, but I could see she wanted to. Finally I had to ask him to stop contacting her at all. The disappointments were horrible for her."

She stopped talking and pressed her lips together. "Sorry. I didn't mean to dump all that on you." She wasn't sure where the confession had come from. She wanted to blame it on the wine with dinner, but she'd barely had half a glass. Maybe the rich chocolate dessert had loosened her lips.

"Not at all. I'm glad I could listen," he said. "Bethany is a special girl. It's her father's loss that he doesn't want to spend time with her."

She looked at him and smiled. "Thank you for saying that." She glanced away and said, "Chuck and I were too young. Plus we weren't really compatible, although I didn't know that at the time. Still, my marriage gave me Bethany, plus I learned a lot. I learned that I want my next marriage to be a partnership between equals. With Chuck I was always the grown-up and he was the kid. I hated that.''

''I can see why. It would be difficult to be romantic while scolding your husband about some transgression.''

''Exactly.'' She tilted her head and thought about the mystery surrounding Malik's wife's death. ''So what did you learn from your marriage?''

Even in the shadows she saw his expression harden. ''Not to marry an ugly, barren woman.''

She blinked. ''That wasn't exactly what I meant.''

''It remains the truth.'' He motioned toward the path. ''Shall we continue walking?''

''Sure.'' She fell into step beside him.

''It doesn't matter what I think about my first marriage,'' Malik said. ''The time is coming when I must take another wife.''

He spoke so matter-of-factly that Liana didn't know what to do with the information. Especially given the way he'd kissed her a few nights ago. ''Are you…um…seeing anyone special?''

''No. Nor does that matter. Like my first marriage, this match will most likely be arranged.''

That stopped her in her tracks. ''You're kidding?''

''I don't see the situation as humorous,'' he said, pausing beside her. ''I am the Crown Prince of El Bahar. There are political ramifications to any marriage I make. When the time comes, I'll do my duty.''

''I can't believe we're talking about this,'' she said honestly. ''An arranged marriage? What if you don't like her or you don't get along?''

"I have a duty to my country."

She saw that he was completely serious. He would marry a stranger for the sake of El Bahar. While she admired his dedication, she wanted no part of it. "Your life is so different from mine. I can't imagine living that way." She waved her hand in a dismissing gesture. "You can keep your title and crown and whatever else you have. I'd rather have my privacy."

"Don't be so quick to judge, my prim friend. There are compensations for the lack of privacy."

"Don't call me prim. I'm not some dried up old virgin schoolteacher."

"Agreed, but you are smug and convinced you know what is right."

She didn't know how to respond to that. She was pretty sure he was wrong. She wasn't smug. At least she didn't think so. But instead of entering into a debate, she asked, "What compensations?"

"Travel, wealth, power."

"None of those really work for me. Anything else?"

"Just this."

Before she knew what he was going to do, he bent over and took her in his arms. Despite the fact that they'd only kissed once before, she found herself slipping into his embrace as if she'd done it a thousand times. Her body pressed against his eagerly, her head tilted back and she found herself wanting to surge forward and take the kiss he offered. She knew that if his mouth didn't touch hers, she would die.

Passion exploded with that first brush of his lips. He started with a gentle exploration, but she wasn't in the mood to be seduced. Instead she wanted to be taken…and taken now.

She raised one hand to his head and tunneled her fingers

through his hair. As she did so, she pressed on his head, urging him closer. She parted her lips and when he entered, she sucked on his tongue, teasing him, arousing them both.

Suddenly his hands were everywhere. On her back, her rear, her hips, then moving up toward her breasts. Their hips pressed together. She could feel the hardness of his arousal jutting against her belly. Between her legs heat and wetness made her ache with a need she'd nearly forgotten. It seemed a lifetime since she'd wanted a man and she knew she'd never wanted one as much as she wanted this one.

If he'd pulled her up against him, she would have wrapped her legs around his hips and clung to him. If he'd started undressing her, she wouldn't have thought to protest the act, nor the intimacy that would surely follow.

Even as his tongued plunged into her mouth over and over again, she knew how it would be between them. Her breasts swelled and her nipples tightened. She gasped in anticipation as his hands moved higher and when he finally cupped the aching curves, she held in a scream of pure pleasure.

She was hot and ready. She was willing to do whatever he might ask, and damn the consequences. What was going on? This wasn't her at all. This was—

He brushed his thumbs against her nipples. The jolt of electric pleasure was so intense her legs nearly gave way. Answering heat flared in her most secret place and she was afraid if he kept touching her like that, she might actually climax right there in his arms.

The thought was so startling that she jerked herself out of his embrace and stepped back.

"Stop," she commanded, her breath coming in gasps. "I can't do this with you."

Malik's dark gaze met her own. Except for his equally heavy breathing and the ridge pressing against his fly, he looked completely calm.

"Why are you upset?" he asked. "You enjoyed my attentions."

"Yes, but it's not right." She pressed a hand to her flushed face and closed her eyes. When had the world gotten so crazy? "You're a prince. I'm just some high school math teacher. This doesn't make sense to me."

"It makes sense to me."

She opened her eyes and looked at him. "Is that what this is about? Did you bring me to the palace to sleep with me?" She felt a shudder of desire race through her and knew that she was right. She also knew that if she didn't stop them both, she was going to give in without a second thought.

"Don't bother answering," she said quickly. "I get it. This is some kind of game with you. Playing with the hired help. You're on the board of directors for the school, so I can't even protest to my boss about you, or I risk getting fired." She took another step back. "Is that how you do things here? Trap women into situations that are impossible, then take advantage of them? Can't you leave me alone?"

Malik stared at her for several seconds, then nodded. "My apologies, Ms. Archer. It seems we have both misunderstood the situation. I won't disturb you again."

He turned on his heel and walked away, leaving her alone in the shadowy darkness of the beautiful garden. Liana stared after him and knew that she'd over-reacted, speaking without thinking. Except everything she'd said was true. He *was* taking advantage of her and the situation. The fact that she'd liked his attentions only made it worse.

If only he were a complete jerk, she thought, making her way toward the palace and the sanctuary of her room. But he wasn't. He was charming to her, attentive to her daughter and she enjoyed his company...not to mention his kisses. More than enjoyed. And that was the danger. Because if Malik continued to press his suit, she would give in, and then where would she be?

## Chapter Six

An insistent knocking woke Liana well before seven the next morning. She stumbled out of bed and into her robe, then made her way to the front door of the suite.

After the events of the night before, Liana hadn't been able to fall asleep. Now she found herself with gritty eyes and a sense of exhaustion as she opened the door and peered blearily at the three servants waiting patiently in the hallway.

"Prince Malik sent us," Rihana, a young woman in her mid twenties said. She gave a quick bob of a curtsy. "Sorry to wake you so early, ma'am, but he wanted to make sure we had you packed before you left for the school."

Liana blinked several times, both to clear her vision and to give herself a second to absorb what she'd just heard. "Excuse me?"

"Prince Malik said to tell you that he apologizes for

any inconvenience. If you will allow us to enter, we will pack your belongings. They will be taken over to the housing on the property of the American School. You will be in your own apartment by the time you finish with your classes.''

Rihana spoke politely enough but Liana could see that the young woman didn't understand why anyone would want to leave the palace. At the moment, Liana sort of agreed with her. Why was Malik letting her go?

Then she remembered their conversation. And the accusations. Obviously Malik had been listening.

''Mommy? What's happening?''

Bethany was already up and dressed, but then she'd had a more restful night. Liana smoothed her daughter's long hair. ''These ladies are here to help us pack. We're moving to the housing by the American School today.''

In her plaid jumper and white shirt, a uniform the school required of all their students, her daughter looked older than her actual nine years. But at the thought of leaving the palace, tears filled her eyes.

''Mommy, I don't want to go.''

Liana didn't want to either anymore. But they didn't belong here. ''We've imposed on the royal family enough. We need to have our own place.''

''What about riding? Will I still be able to do that?''

''We'll find a place near the school and you can take lessons.''

Bethany's lower lip quivered. ''It won't be the same.''

''I know. But it will still be fun.'' She turned to the three women still waiting by the open door. ''I appreciate the offer, but we can pack ourselves.''

Rihana shook her head. ''Prince Malik insisted. He said he didn't want either of you to be late.'' Her pretty face softened with a smile. "He also said to tell the little missy that he would still like to teach her about horses."

Bethany's tears faded as quickly as they'd formed and she clapped her hands together. "Oh, can I, Mommy? Please say yes. Please?"

"Of course you can still ride here. When the prince has time for you."

What else could she say? Her quarrel was with Malik and his treatment of her, not her daughter. And she wasn't about to deprive Bethany of a wonderful experience just because she, Liana, had to get some distance from the prince.

It would all be for the best, she told herself as she opened the door wide and let the women into the suite. She and her daughter would be much happier on their own. They would have a chance to make friends with the other teachers and their families, to take part in the organized tours and really see the country.

Liana was still busy convincing herself as she hurried toward the bathroom so that she could get ready for school. As she stepped into the shower, she had the wistful thought that she'd already seen more of the El Baharian royal palace than would ever be allowed on the most expansive tour.

The building that housed the staff of the American School had been built with comfort in mind. There was a large grocery and video store across the street and a burger and pizza place on the main floor. Liana's fourth-floor condo was open and spacious. There were two bedrooms, each with its own bath. A study, gourmet eat-in kitchen, full-sized living room and a powder room for guests completed the floor plan. They had lovely views of a garden, along with the school's playing field.

While the furniture was utilitarian and wouldn't win any decorating awards, it was sturdy and looked comfortable. The condo had been decorated in shades of blue and beige, with light oak wood accents. The dining set was oak, as was the bedroom furniture. There were bright prints on the walls and a silk hanging in the small hallway.

A porter had carried up their bags and while Bethany settled herself into her room, Liana explored the kitchen. She opened cupboard doors and studied the dishes and cooking utensils available.

"There's a popcorn maker," she called to her daughter. "We could make a big batch of caramel corn after we go rent some movies."

"Okay."

But her daughter didn't sound very enthused about the plan. If anything her voice held that "I'm humoring my parent" tone. But Liana knew they were going to be fine here. The rooms were large and airy. The other teachers had been welcoming at work and she was sure they would be just as friendly here in the condo. Besides, it was only for a couple of years. When they left El Bahar, it would be with enough money to buy their own house back in San Bernardino.

"What do you think?" she asked when Bethany strolled into the living room and plopped down on the blue-and-beige plaid sofa.

Her daughter had changed into jeans and a T-shirt. She put her bare feet on the oak veneer coffee table and shrugged. "It's not the palace."

"I can't argue with that."

Liana had a brief flash of longing for the marble floors and ocean views of her suite there. The horse mosaic had been a work of art. The palace had offered dozens of treasures to be found at every turn—the fountains in the main building and outside, the gardens, the artwork, the elegant dinners, the servants.

She sank onto the slightly frayed sofa and put her arm around Bethany. "Do you think we'll be happy here?" she asked.

Blue eyes so much like her own regarded her thoughtfully. "We're together," her daughter said. "That's what matters. I know you felt funny about living at the palace, even though I didn't." Bethany shrugged. "I just miss it."

"You'll have friends here. Girls your own age."

Bethany smiled. "I'm not upset, Mommy."

"I know. I'm simply pointing out that there are some advantages to this place."

"There aren't any horses."

No princes either, although Liana told herself that was a good thing.

"What if I buy you a picture of a horse? Or one of those plastic ones? We'll put it on the coffee table."

"Mommy, that's silly."

Liana glanced around the room. "I don't think it will fit in here as a permanent resident, but if you can get it in the elevator, I guess you could have a horse over to visit. Although it has to be potty trained or you'd have to keep it on the balcony."

Bethany giggled and cuddled close. Liana hugged her.

"What do you want for dinner?" she asked. "There's exactly nothing in the refrigerator so I was thinking we'd go to the grocery store across the street, buy sensible food, then order pizza from the place downstairs. What do you think? I haven't had pizza in so long, I think I forgot what it tastes like."

Bethany smiled up at her. "That would be nice. Thank you."

"You are so very welcome."

They hugged again and as Liana released her, the doorbell rang.

"I'll get it," Bethany announced as she sprang to her feet. She raced to the small foyer and pulled open the door. "Mommy, come look."

Liana followed her daughter and saw a delivery man holding a huge spray of flowers. The arrangement was so wide, it barely fit through the door.

"I know who they're from," Bethany announced in a sing-song voice as her mother set them in the center of the kitchen table and opened the small card tucked in among roses and lilies and sprays of lavender.

Liana had a fair idea of the identity of the sender as well, and she noticed her hands shook as she opened the envelope. She read it over twice, noting the strong, no-nonsense handwriting of the Crown Prince of El Bahar.

"Prince Malik says that he hopes we're settling in nicely and that he's looking forward to resuming his rides with you tomorrow. He'll be by at four to pick you up."

"Yippee!" Bethany took the offered card and scanned it as she bounced around the room. "We're going riding. I knew he wouldn't forget. I knew it!"

Liana watched her and smiled, despite the faint sense of disappointment settling over her. She was glad that the prince meant to keep his word where her daughter was concerned. He was a very kind man. And the flowers were lovely. It was just...

She sighed. Okay, so she couldn't make up her mind. On the one hand she'd been anxious to leave the palace and get into her own place. On the other hand, she was hurt because Malik wanted to see Bethany and not her.

Be logical, she told herself. Last night she'd practically

accused him of sexual harassment. Of course he wasn't going to see her again.

But what about the kisses, a little voice in her head inquired. Hadn't they meant anything to him? Was he just going to walk away from all that fire?

Liana steered Bethany into her bedroom to finish up her homework so they could go food shopping. While she unpacked her own bags, she decided that she was being completely contrary. She couldn't have it both ways. If she was interested in the prince in *that way* then she shouldn't have made such a big fuss last night, or talked about leaving the palace. If she wanted her independence, then she had to put the memory of those magical kisses behind her.

Which meant she had to act like a grown-up.

"I really hate it when that happens," Liana said with a grin. Life was much easier when one was allowed to behave like a child. But she didn't have a choice this time. So she would be grateful for the prince's kindness to Bethany and refuse to think about him ever again.

The following Friday, a week and a day after they'd moved into the condo, Liana found herself rushing around like a teenager getting ready for her first prom. All because Malik was due over.

Her plan of not thinking about the prince hadn't worked well at all. Bethany never tired of speaking about him. Every sentence started with, "Prince Malik said…." Or, "when Prince Malik and I were riding we saw…."

Bethany's school day ended about an hour before her own. There was on-site day care for the children of the instructors, and Bethany spent her time there until her mother was finished with her work. But on the days Bethany rode with Malik, she brought her riding clothes to school and changed there. Malik picked her up from the day care and returned her to the apartment. He didn't come up to the condo often, and when he did, he spoke pleasantly but briefly, leaving Liana hungry for more conversation. She told herself it was just because he was an intelligent, articulate human being, but she knew she was lying. She missed seeing Malik and talking to him because of how he made her feel. She missed the palace, the gardens and the other members of the royal family. And if she lost any more sleep over the memory of those darned kisses, she was going to have to keep her eyelids open with toothpicks.

But today her classes had ended at noon, which meant Bethany was home and Malik was coming here before as well as after the riding lesson. In the past, when she'd invited him in, he'd made the excuse of being dirty from his ride. He couldn't do that this time.

Liana paused in front of the mirror and checked her freshly applied makeup. "You're pathetic," she told herself, wishing she'd stayed on her diet long enough to lose the extra twenty pounds she'd carried since she'd become pregnant. Here she was fussing over her appearance as if Malik was even going to notice. She'd told the man to get lost and he'd listened. Did she think she could win him back with her charms now?

"A girl can hope," she murmured to herself as she left her bedroom and went to check the living room. She'd thought about putting out a tray of snacks, but that seemed so obvious, and coffee was too datelike. Which meant she didn't have any food or drinks to offer casually.

She kept coming back to the thought that if she'd liked him so much before, why on earth had she left the palace? Liana came to a stop in the center of the living room and for the first time admitted to herself that given the chance to do it all over again, she would probably stay. Even if princes did not fall for schoolteachers. Even if she allowed herself to slip into his bed she would only end up losing her heart to him and getting hurt.

The doorbell rang. Liana nervously smoothed her palms over her thighs, wondering if a silk shirt and tailored slacks was too dressy. Should she have put on jeans? she wondered as she reached for the handle and turned it. Or left her work dress on, even though it wasn't one of her favorites and—

"Hello, Liana."

The tall-dark-and-handsome cliché didn't come close to describing Malik. His brown-black eyes mesmerized her until she was sure he could see clean through her. His broad shoulders looked strong enough to support the weight of the world and what single mother hadn't at one time or another wanted someone with whom to share the load?

He wore a plain white shirt and riding jodhpurs. She didn't even want to think about the boots, or how well they worked for her. She could feel her throat tightening as her mouth went dry. What was it about this man?

His sensual mouth turned up in a smile. "May I come in?"

"Hmm?" She realized she was leaning against the door like a mooning teenager and blushed. "Sure. Of course. Please, won't you come in, Malik?" She stepped back to let him move inside, then closed the door and motioned to the living room. "Have a seat. Bethany will be right out."

"Thank you."

He settled on the plaid sofa and she was again forced to acknowledge that while this condo was serviceable, it wasn't even close to a decent substitute for living at the palace. In truth, living there those few days had spoiled her. She'd decided the best way to handle the transition back to real life was to think of her stay at the palace as a lovely, once-in-a-lifetime, never-to-be-repeated vacation. Of course seeing Malik again brought all the longing back.

"You are enjoying yourself here?" he asked, looking surprisingly at ease as he leaned back in the sofa.

"Yes. Thank you. The privacy is very nice." She gave him a quick smile as she took a seat on the loveseat opposite. "I'm willing to admit it's not nearly as lovely as your home, but this is better for us."

He raised dark eyebrows. "Why is it better?"

Because she very much wanted to slide next to him on the cushions and have him take her in his arms and kiss her soundly. Maybe even do more than kiss. Liana shook her head. She didn't understand her reaction to this man. The instant heat and desire had never happened to her before, and she found it confusing. Although quite life-affirming. Still, she had to remember their respective positions and her goals for her and Bethany's lives.

"Malik, you were very kind to both me and my daughter, but we don't belong in your world. This is us." She glanced around the room. "Simple, serviceable, but not the least bit royal. I found living at the palace confusing."

"You should not have been confused. You were my guest."

"I never meant to be ungracious," she told him, forcing herself to meet his dark gaze. "That last night when I accused you of, well, of taking advantage of the situation. I know it wasn't that, exactly."

He looked at her with a steadiness that made it difficult to breathe. He hadn't moved and neither had she, yet she felt as if they were physically closer. It was as if she could feel his heat and hear the sound of his heartbeat.

"What was it exactly?" he asked. "Do you know why I brought you to the palace? Why I wanted you to stay?"

"I don't have a clue," she whispered and had to swallow against a suddenly dry throat.

He smiled then. The slow, masculine smile that made her bones melt and her most feminine place swell and dampen in readiness for an act of pure possession.

"One day you will understand, Liana. And then we'll talk about it."

They were playing some kind of game, and she didn't understand the rules. "Yes, well, I'm sure it will be great fun," she said, feeling incredibly lame as she spoke. Talk about inane conversation.

Maybe she was bewitched. Maybe she'd fallen under the effects of an ancient El Baharian love potion or something. She leaned back and tried to relax. She was a grown-up; she could handle the situation.

Malik studied her. "Next weekend I've been invited out to dine with one of our nomad tribes. They make their homes in the desert, but once every year or so, they find their way into El Bahar and settle relatively close to the city for a few weeks. Their way of life hasn't changed for hundreds of years and I enjoy the chance to spend a few hours living a more traditional life. I thought you might like to join me for the evening. The camp is three or four hours away, so we wouldn't get back until very late. However, Fatima has already offered to have Bethany as her guest in the harem until the next day so you would not have to worry on her account."

A thousand thoughts whirled through Liana's head. Was it a date? Was he asking her out because he wanted to spend time with her? Elation filled her. But he was a prince. Why would he date her? Not that she was ugly, but she wasn't young and thin and beautiful. Not a model or an actress or a princess. She was just a single-mom schoolteacher. So Malik couldn't be interested in her in any romantic way. So why the invitation? Was he apologizing for keeping her at the palace? Was it—

"You have the most curious expression on your face," he said. "What are you thinking?"

That she would rather die than let him know what thoughts filled her mind! Did she really care why he'd asked? Hadn't she just spent the past week wishing she had the chance to see him again? Had she really always been this contrary? "That I would love to go. Thank you for asking."

It was obvious Malik knew she'd been thinking other things, but he didn't press her. "Good." He hesitated. "As a sign of respect for the tribespeople, you'll have to dress traditionally. Fatima has the appropriate clothes at the palace. Perhaps you wouldn't mind getting ready there."

Liana had visions of a bikini with harem pants, but hoped that wasn't what Malik meant. No doubt she would have to be covered and veiled. After all she was entering a very different kind of world.

"Of course. I'll wear whatever is right for the occasion."

He rose to his feet as Bethany, in her riding clothes, ran in. "I look forward to it, then."

Liana stood as well and tried to keep her feet pressed firmly on the ground, although she was sure her bright smile gave her pleasure away. "Until Friday."

The blue silk shimmered like clear water in sunlight. Liana turned in the mirror and studied herself from different angles. The dress wrapped around her in a way that covered her completely, yet left her free to move. A sheer matching veil covered her hair. Fatima had already shown her the white velvet robe she would wear over the dress and the veil that would hide the lower part of her face from prying eyes.

"The nomads believe that if an unknown man sees one of their women, he'll be tempted to steal her away. Or at least ravish her," Fatima explained as she lined Liana's blue eyes with kohl. "It is quite a compliment."

"I'm sure the women appreciate their concern," Liana agreed. "Especially the ones who don't feel as attractive."

Fatima smiled. "All women are beautiful. Didn't you know that?"

Liana smiled. "A lovely philosophy, and one we in the west could learn from."

Fatima rubbed a red stain on Liana's mouth, then studied her handiwork. "Perfect. And in your case, it would be best to keep yourself covered, my dear. All that lovely blond hair is sure to be a temptation. Why, I would guess that Prince Malik could get two or three dozen camels for you."

"As much as that," Liana said, not sure if Fatima told the truth or not.

When the older woman stepped away, Liana looked at herself in the mirror. Her eyes seemed huge and mysterious, while her lips were dark with the stain. Between the eastern-style dress and the veil, she hardly recognized herself.

Maybe this was all a dream, she thought. After all, she stood in the middle of a harem talking about being sold for a few camels.

Fatima touched her arm and smiled. "You are loveliness itself, Liana. I hope you have a wonderful time with my grandson. Don't worry about not speaking their language. The people of the desert are most expressive, and you'll figure out what they're saying. Besides, Malik will be there. He is fluent in their tongue.''

The queen drew the white velvet robe around her shoulders and fastened it at her neck, then draped the veil over her face.

''It ties in these two places,'' she said, demonstrating how to secure the covering. ''Although you'll probably want to wait to wear it.''

Liana felt like an El Baharian princess. She was even going to meet her very own prince. What did it matter if it was only for the evening?

''Thank you for everything,'' she said, turning and impulsively giving Fatima a hug. ''You've been so kind.''

''My pleasure. And while you are off to the desert, I'm going to spend the evening with your charming daughter, who, I believe, is currently with the children in the nursery.'' Fatima glanced at her diamond and gold watch. ''Malik will be waiting for you. Enjoy, my dear. This will be a night to remember.''

## Chapter Seven

"You look lovely," Malik said as he held open the rear door of the limo waiting at the main entrance to the palace.

"Thank you," Liana murmured, hating how nervous she felt now that she and Malik were together. She wanted to tell him that he looked pretty good, too, what with his robes and traditional headdress. The rich-colored garments emphasized his dark strength and made him appear even taller than usual.

She couldn't remember a time when she'd felt more awkward—not even on her first date, back when she'd been all of sixteen and excited because Chuck Archer had asked her out to a movie.

"I'm a little surprised by our mode of transportation," she said as she slid onto the butter-soft leather seat. "I would have thought we would need a four-wheel-drive vehicle."

Malik nodded at the chauffeur hovering by the door, then moved in next to her. "Usually we would, but our friends have set up camp not that far from a paved road. Sandy will drive us out into the desert and we'll walk the last quarter-mile." He glanced at her shoes. "I told Fatima you would need sensible shoes. Did she listen and pass the information along?"

Liana held up one foot. Her sandals were flat and very comfortable. "She warned me to wear something I could walk in."

"Good." He gave her a quick smile, then looked up when the driver lowered the glass partition. "Yes, Sandy?"

"Are you ready to leave, sir?"

Malik nodded. "We're in your capable hands," he said pleasantly.

"I shall endeavor not to disappoint, sir."

The glass closed silently as the car began to move down the circular driveway.

"Sandy has been with the family for years," Malik said, motioning at the man barely visible through the smoky glass. "He's originally from England, but he moved to El Bahar when he was in his twenties. My father prefers him to all the drivers. In fact, Sandy is the one who taught my brothers and I to handle a car."

She looked at the silhouette of the fifty-something chauffeur and grinned. "Then I'm surprised he doesn't have more gray hair."

"Actually, so am I." He shrugged. "Strong genes, I suppose."

"I suspect one would need that to deal with you three princes." When Malik opened his mouth to protest her teasing, she quickly changed the subject. "Tell me what will happen tonight."

He drew his eyebrows together. "Do you really think I'm that easily distracted?"

"No, but I think you're that nice a host."

"First you try to trick me into changing the subject and now you flatter me. Obviously you need a good lesson in respecting royalty."

"Obviously," she murmured, not quite able to believe she was actually flirting with the Crown Prince of El Bahar. But up close, Malik seemed almost like any other man...aside from the incredible good looks and the fact that they were riding in the back of a limo.

"I shall think of something appropriate," Malik promised, then gave her a wink. "Now, about the welcoming ceremony. We'll be led into a large tent. Generally the women sit apart from the men, although, as you are my guest, they'll make an exception. We'll be fed, there will be a few speeches and then Bilal, their chief, will present me with a prize goat or camel."

Liana had been listening intently, right up until that moment. She burst out laughing. "A goat or a camel? Are you serious?"

"Very."

"But what will you do with it? There's hardly room for it to ride back with us."

Malik shrugged. "I'll insist on holding a competition of some kind. A race or a game of skill. The prize will be my gift. So the tribe gets to make me a present of something of value without actually losing the animal. Customs are observed and everyone is happy." He paused. "Are you thirsty? Would you like something to drink?"

Liana smiled. "That would be lovely," she told him.

Malik opened the small refrigerator on his right and pulled out a chilled bottle of champagne. He removed the foil covering and the wire netting, then expertly popped the cork without spilling a single drop.

Once he'd poured them each a glass and handed hers to her, he set the bottle back in the tiny refrigerator, then touched his glass to hers.

"To a night unlike any other."

She wanted to believe he meant their being together, but she knew better. Malik was talking about all that she would experience in the nomad encampment. "To the night," she agreed.

She took a sip of the bubbly liquid. It was smooth and faintly sweet, yet tasted as light as if it were moonbeams.

Liana chuckled, then glanced around the spacious passenger compartment. The wood trim wasn't simply a polished strip of walnut, but was instead inlaid in various pieces that created a beautiful spiraling pattern. Underneath her feet was the softest carpet she'd ever felt. She took another sip of the bubbly liquid and sighed.

"The rich really are different," she said. "If you're trying to get me to regret moving out of the palace, you're doing a good job."

Malik didn't return her smile. Instead he set his glass on the small inlaid table above the refrigerator. "Do you regret your decision?"

She noticed he asked the question without actually issuing an invitation to return. Not that she blamed him. No doubt he'd gotten over whatever minor attraction had caused him to take her there in the first place.

"*Regret* is a strong word," she said truthfully as she looked at him. "I've had a twinge or two, but most of the time I know it's the right decision. I mean there were dozens of compensations, but Bethany and I need to be grounded in the real world."

"The palace is real."

"For you, maybe. Not for us. For me it was like living in Disneyland. It's a great vacation, but on Monday morning there are still those pesky bills to pay."

He shifted on the seat, settling into the corner and angling toward her. "Do you think my life is so easy? That I don't, as you put it, pay my own bills?"

"I don't know."

She drank more of the champagne and was surprised to find she'd finished the glass. Malik poured her another, then leaned back against the leather.

"I guess I shouldn't make assumptions," she said, suddenly intrigued by his question. "Tell me what it's like to be the Crown Prince of El Bahar. Is it wonderful?"

"At times. I enjoy representing my country when I travel. I have the satisfaction of knowing I can influence hundreds of thousands of lives for the better. I work hard, but I am well compensated by my life-style."

It all sounded very nice. "What was it you once told me? Money, prestige, power?"

"All of that," he agreed.

The champagne went down so easily, she thought as she swallowed another mouthful. "But it can't be perfect every moment," she said. "What aren't you telling me?"

"Ah, you want the seamy side of life at the palace."

He was teasing, but she didn't return his smile. "I'm not saying it has to be seamy, but there are prices for everything. For example, I'll bet you didn't have a normal childhood."

He shrugged. "It was normal for me. I was taken from my mother when I was four and raised primarily by my father and his ministers."

Liana blinked. "*Taken,* as in, you didn't see her anymore?"

"Not often," he agreed blandly. "My father was concerned that I grow up to be a strong and self-sufficient man. I couldn't be coddled by women all the time, running to my mother for every little scraped knee or bruised feeling.''

Liana remembered what Bethany had said—that Malik had broken his arm twice when he'd been a boy. ''What about broken arms? Did you get coddled then?''

''I was fine.''

But he didn't meet her gaze as he spoke, and she thought she glimpsed something lost and painful in Malik's dark eyes. ''Were all your brothers raised the same way?''

''No. Jamal and Khalil stayed with our mother until she died. Then they had a nanny and tutors. For them, the responsibilities of being a prince weren't so all-encompassing. But then they weren't going to grow up to rule El Bahar.''

Liana wondered if she could really read between the lines of what he was saying or if she was assuming too much. It all sounded very sad and lonely to her. She could picture a much younger Prince Malik being told that he had to be strong and brave, that he wasn't allowed to cry or show weakness, no matter how much he hurt or how tired he might be. But was that reality or fanciful thinking on her part?

''What about now?'' she asked. ''Are you still held apart from your brothers?''

''We are close,'' Malik said, staring past her out the darkened windows. ''But their lives are different. I have the responsibility of the country's oil production. I negotiate favorable terms with our customers, maintain our alliance with our neighbors. I also have my duties here, within the boundaries of El Bahar. My father is still a young man, but he is ready to have me take over some of his functions.''

"Sounds like a lot of work.''

"Perhaps, but it is all I've known. I am the future leader of my country. The people of El Bahar look to me to be strong and always to do the right thing. For them I am the lion of the desert. Powerful, moving forward, fearless.''

"I think you do a good job,'' she said, then finished her glass of champagne.

Yes, Malik was a fine Crown Prince, but he was also a man. Who did he go to when he was tired of being the lion of the desert? Who held him when he was broken in spirit, if not in body? With whom did he trust his doubts, his hopes and his fears? For he had to have them. He was human, like everyone else.

"You must get very lonely,'' she said.

Malik looked surprised by her comment. "In a palace full of people? Not possible.''

She wasn't sure if he was denying it because he didn't want to talk about it with her, or if it was because he really didn't know how isolated he was. His entire life was designed to keep him apart from everyone else. Her heart ached for the young boy taken away from the loving support of his mother and given to the care of ministers designed to turn him into a man who wouldn't dare feel any weakness, let alone show it.

How did Malik pass the long nights when the ghosts of the past seemed to lurk around every corner and the emptiness of the future loomed on for eternity? Or was she projecting? Maybe she was assuming that Malik was enough like her to long to have someone special in his life to ease the burden and make the good times even better.

It was the champagne, she thought, even as he poured her another glass. She'd been too excited to eat much that day so the bubbles and alcohol were going to her head.

"I'm very impressed with your daughter," Malik said as he set the bottle back in the small refrigerator. "She's going to be an excellent horsewoman. She's also very bright. I enjoy her company."

"Does that surprise you?"

"Yes. I've never spent any time in the company of children."

"I suppose not." She eyed his glass and tried to figure out if he'd filled it as well as hers, or was he still on his first drink? But she wasn't sure, and it was suddenly so very unimportant.

"I'm sorry I accused you of using her to get to me," she said earnestly. The words sounded slightly off to her ears. Was her tongue thickening? What had she been talking about? Oh, yes. "What I mean is, your relationship with her is separate from the one you have with me. Not that you really have one with me. She adores you, by the way."

"I suspect I'm something of a father figure to her."

"You need to have children of your own," Liana told him. "Heirs and all that. Your brothers have children."

"I know."

He leaned toward her and took the glass from her hand. She wanted to protest its absence, but he was moving closer and she had the sudden thought that given the choice between drinking the bubbly moonbeams and kissing Malik, the kiss would win every time.

"So, have you forgiven me for bringing you to the palace?" he asked.

"Oh, sure. It was fine." Malik momentarily swam out of focus, then reappeared. Was she drunk? On less than three glasses of champagne? She considered for a moment and decided it was very possible. She'd never been much of a drinker. "I mean I'm glad we stayed friends."

He moved closer still, slipping his arms around her and lowering his head to hers. "Is that what we are? Friends?"

"Yes." Her voice was a bare whisper.

"How disappointing."

"Why? What did you want us to be?"

"I'm not sure." His mouth brushed hers. "Perhaps something more…intimate."

"That works, too," she managed before his lips claimed hers in a molten kiss that left her breathless.

It was as it had been before, she thought hazily as the magical heat began to flood her body. In a matter of seconds she found herself aroused and hungry for him. Maybe it was the champagne, or maybe it was the man himself. All she knew was that he hadn't even touched her with his tongue and her body was aching for them to make love.

The need increased when he brushed her lower lip, causing her to part for him. He entered her mouth slowly, but with a sureness that left her breathless. He explored her, returning to favorite spots that made her moan and writhe and clutch at him. His headdress prevented her from burying her fingers in his hair, so she contented herself with slipping them under his robe and exploring his strong, broad back.

Outside, the sun had set and all was darkness. Malik turned off the interior lights and plunged them into blackness. Then he placed his hands on her waist, shifting her until she straddled him, her thighs cupping his hips, her hands resting on his shoulders.

"Liana," he breathed as he kissed her cheeks, her nose,

her chin, then trailed down her neck to the folds of cloth that covered her.

He peeled away the first layer, exposing her chest down to the top of her bra. She felt a shiver of anticipation, then gave in to the gentle caress of his lips and tongue against her sensitive skin.

He licked the sweet valley between her breasts, then explored as much of her curves as were available to him. She found herself clutching his head in her hands, urging him to do more, yet half afraid he would unfasten her bra, exposing her to him. Despite the aching dampness between her thighs and the pressure in her breasts, she wasn't sure she was ready to take that next step. After all, she barely knew Malik and she'd only ever been with Chuck, and what woman in her right mind made love in the back of a car with a prince?

As if reading her mind and understanding her indecision, he returned his attention to her mouth, kissing her deeply, making her writhe until her sensitized feminine place settled directly on the hard ridge of his arousal.

And then she was lost. She reached for his hand to draw it to her breast, more than willing to make love right here, right now. She would worry about the consequences in the morning. But as her fingers closed around his, the limo drew to a stop.

Malik sighed. "Talk about lousy timing," he said, his words muffled against her throat. "With the privacy glass in place Sandy has no idea what we've been doing, so he'll be around to open the door in about five seconds."

Liana squeaked as she scrambled off him. He helped her smooth her clothes back in place, then gave her a wolfish grin. "I can't tell you when I've enjoyed a car ride more," he said.

"Yeah, right," she mumbled, suddenly feeling awkward about what they'd done. "I'm sure this sort of thing happens all the time."

The passenger door opened, but Malik ignored it. Instead, he cupped her face and forced her to look at him. "I've never done anything like this before. Not with anyone else."

His gaze was steady, and, for reasons that made no sense, she actually believed him. A smile tugged at her mouth. "Good."

The walk to the camp was shorter than Liana had expected. The night was clear, and hundreds of stars illuminated their way. Bilal, the leader of the nomad tribe, had sent scouts to guide them. She and Malik found themselves surrounded by short, powerful-looking men in traditional robes and carrying torches.

When they crested a rise, she could see the camp sprawled out below them. Dozens of tents circled three sides of a huge fresh-water spring. There were children running about, and open cooking fires. Goats and camels were kept in makeshift pens on the far side of the camp. She felt as if she'd found her way onto a movie set.

"Are they remaking *Lawrence of Arabia?*" she asked Malik.

He grinned. "This is the real world, not Hollywood."

Perhaps, but it felt very surreal to her.

As their arrival was noticed, the tribespeople gathered around them. Conversation flowed in an unfamiliar tongue. Liana found herself surrounded by women and was suddenly led away.

"You'll be fine," Malik called after her. Liana wasn't so sure.

The women took her into a large tent where their high-pitched conversation and frequent laughter made her smile as well. Using mime to communicate, they had her remove her robe, then gasped in wonder at the sight of her blond hair. She was fawned and fussed over, then found herself agreeing to having henna applied to her hands and feet. Sweet tea was passed around, and children were brought in to be named and shown off by their proud mothers.

Liana accepted all the attention with good humor and found herself thinking that there were parts of Malik's world that she liked very much. Then she wondered if the prince was being made welcome in the same way.

"What the hell is all this?" Malik demanded after Bilal had bowed and offered words of respect.

Bilal raised his hands, palm up. "Why is the lion of the desert unhappy? I have simply done as you requested."

Malik paced the length of the tent, then spun back to face the other man. "I requested a welcoming ceremony."

"At first, yes. But later I received a message from the palace asking for the change. Is it not so?"

"It is not," Malik told him.

"But Your Highness, you must," Bilal insisted. "Your most faithful people have seen it written in the stars. She is your destiny. The foreign woman might come from far away, but she has the desert in her heart." Bilal, a normally wise and conservative man, spat and muttered a curse. "She is nothing like the evil one."

"No argument there," Malik said, knowing that Bilal would have his tongue ripped out before he actually spoke Iman's name. "But I can't agree to this other thing."

Bilal shrugged. "Perhaps you don't have a choice. Perhaps this is already written. There can be delay, but not escape.'' The older man placed a strong hand on Malik's shoulder. "Come, let us continue as we have begun.''

Malik stared at the man who had been a second father to him. He didn't want to disappoint Bilal or his people, but he also knew this was wrong. He had no right to play with Liana's life this way. Who had requested the change? Was it his father? Fatima?

He shook his head and decided it didn't really matter. He had to call it all off. If he'd thought Liana was annoyed with him for keeping her at the palace against her will, he couldn't imagine her reaction to this if he let them go through with it.

"We can't do this," he said firmly.

Bilal shook his head. "We must. I told you. It's in the stars. She is the one.''

Malik started to tell him no. He had to. It was wrong to make any other decision. Except... If the truth were told, he *wanted* Liana to be the one. He wanted this. Knowing how she would react and the price he would pay later, he was still willing to risk it all. Which made him a fool and a liar. For, by not telling her the truth, he was going to make her hate him. But at least he would have had her as his own...if only for a short time.

This was the oddest dinner Liana had ever attended. She and Malik seemed to be the center of attention as dish after dish of food was brought to them. They each tasted from the same plate, then the food was taken away and another brought in its place.

She found it hard to concentrate on her surroundings. When she'd first entered the tent, she'd had an impression of a bigger space than she'd expected. Tapestries covered the walls, and there were thick rugs underfoot. She and Malik had been led to large cushions where they'd knelt together in front of a low table. Bilal, the leader of the tribe had spoken, then touched each of them on the head.

She leaned over to Malik as yet another plate was set before them. "So, *welcoming* really means *feeding* to these people?"

"We're nearly done. After the sweets are brought to us, we'll be allowed to go."

Just then a pretty young woman set a tray of dates in front of them. She motioned for Liana to take one and bite into it, then hand the other half to Malik. Liana did so.

"It's very different than I expected," Liana said as Malik chewed. "I thought it would be more of a party."

"That comes later," he said, avoiding her gaze. "But we aren't expected to stay for it."

That didn't make sense. Weren't guests supposed to be made welcome? "Because we're outsiders?"

"Something like that." Malik shifted on the cushion. "Bilal's people are gracious, and they've offered us the use of a tent for the night. Or we can have Sandy drive us back to the palace." Finally his dark gaze settled on her face. Fire leapt between them. "It's up to you."

Liana swallowed and was suddenly grateful her meal had been measured in single mouthfuls. A knot settled in her stomach and her thighs trembled. She glanced up at the people milling around, watching them, smiling encouragingly. She didn't know all that much about El Bahar and even less about their nomadic tribes, but she wasn't afraid. In fact, she'd felt very much at home with all the women earlier, even if she hadn't been able to speak their language.

But that's not what Malik was asking. He was, instead, asking her where she wanted to spend the night. At home alone...or with him. A shiver of anticipation rippled through her, but she held back and told herself to be sensible.

"Bethany—" she began.

"—is with my grandmother, probably staying up late and hearing wonderful stories about the harem. I doubt she'll worry."

Liana knew he was right. Bethany was staying with Fatima and didn't expect her mother to pick her up until close to lunchtime tomorrow. Which meant she wasn't going to know where Liana spent the night.

She looked at Malik. "What do you want to do?"

"I think you know that."

She nodded. She *did* know. He had told her everything with his passionate kisses.

It had been so very long for her, she thought, as physical longing swept through her. While it was probably a mistake for her first affair since her divorce seven years ago to be with a royal sheik, she knew if she told him no she would regret it for the rest of her life.

She offered him a shaky smile and held out her hand. "I've never spent the night in a tent. Is it fun?"

## Chapter Eight

Liana's courage lasted right up until they left the large tent and entered a smaller one on the far side of camp. Once again there were tapestries on the walls and dozens of thick rugs underfoot, but instead of cushions and low tables and people, there was only a bed. A really big bed, obviously designed for much more than sleeping.

"Oh, God, oh, God, oh, God," she murmured under her breath, coming to a stop just inside the entrance. "I don't think I can do this." She turned to Malik and stared at him. "Do you know how long it's been since I've been with a man?" She was shaking all over and her voice carried a distinct tremor with the words.

"How long?"

"Years. Not since Chuck and I split up. I've been busy. I've been distracted. I think my sexual side has been on hold or something. But I haven't minded very much. Occasionally I'd wish for a man in my life, but then I'd go out on a couple of dates and it was never very exciting, so I would give up until the next time I felt that way. Bethany keeps me busy, and I suppose I always thought I would get involved again when she was older.''

''We're only going to be in the desert for one night,'' Malik told her. ''Is that going to make her old enough?''

''You're laughing at me,'' she protested, although she wasn't really upset.

Malik took her hand and led her over to the bed. Once there he urged her to sit down, then settled next to her. He removed her veil and headcovering, then his own headdress.

''You don't have to do this,'' he said, even as he cupped her face in his hands. ''I would very much like to make love with you tonight, but I'm not going to force you or even try to persuade you. It's completely your decision. Sandy is still in camp and it would be easy for him to drive us back to the palace tonight. You could stay in one of the guest rooms or return to your own place.''

She glared at him. ''If you're going to be logical, I refuse to have this conversation with you.'' How was she supposed to explain the conflicting emotions whirling inside herself?

''It's not that I *don't* want to be with you,'' she said, hoping she sounded a little less confused than she felt. ''It's just…this is so strange. I mean, look at you.''

''Hard to do without a mirror.''

She made a face. ''The thing is, you're not just a guy I met and to whom I'm attracted. You're a prince. That puts you *way* out of my league. I feel like I'm some backwater hick who doesn't know how to play these games. What if you hate the way I make love?''

Malik stared at her. His hand dropped to his side. ''You're nervous.''

"Of course I'm nervous," she moaned. "Why wouldn't I be?"

"I haven't made love with anyone in more than two years. Despite what you think about me, I don't date models and actresses. I'm very careful about who I let into my life and into my bed. If anyone should be worried about embarrassing himself with a poor performance, it's me."

Two years? As in he didn't have a mail-order bimbo of the month flown in to entertain him? "Really?"

He touched her face again. "Of course. I want you, Liana. I have from the first moment I saw you. Everything you accused me of is true. I did take you from the airport, using my position and power to keep you against your will. I wasn't, as you put it, playing with the hired help, but I was making your life difficult. It was wrong and I apologize, because you deserve my respect. But none of that changes the fact that I wanted you then, and I still want you."

Liana couldn't breathe anymore. She'd only ever been with one other man, and while Chuck had wanted her, it had been his eighteen-year-old hormones talking. Chuck had been little more than a boy, while Malik was very much a man.

"You're one of the most powerful men in the world," she said slowly. "You could have any woman you want."

"I want you."

Wow. Talk about a great line. She didn't even care if he meant it.

"Okay, but I have to warn you. I've had a child. That means my body isn't perfect. And, well, I kind of never lost the last twenty pounds from my pregnancy, so if you're imagining someone from a magazine, this is not going to work."

"Is that a yes?"

She found herself staring at his throat and ignoring the flush on her cheeks. "Yes," she whispered.

He wrapped one arm around her and lowered her onto her back. "Good. Because I haven't been imagining being with someone from a magazine. I've been imagining being with you."

And then he kissed her.

She should have been prepared for the impact of his lips against hers—after all, they'd kissed before, and she remembered that each time she'd be left gasping and aroused. But even with the warning of her past reactions, she still found herself falling into the middle of a powerful current and being swept away by the fire that flared inside her at the first touch of his mouth.

It was heaven. It was ten kinds of magic and she never wanted him to stop. Malik brushed back and forth, as if discovering her again. It was the same, and yet it was so very different. For one thing, she was on her back on a soft romantic bed in a tent in the middle of the desert. If she had the strength or will to open her eyes, she would see the tapestries and rugs and pillows. For another thing, Malik was pressed against her in the most delicious way. His body snuggled close to hers, one of his legs resting between hers.

She brought up her arms and wrapped them around him, holding him close even as he angled his head and touched his tongue to her lower lip.

A shiver rippled through her. The flames spread until every part of her was on fire. She found herself opening to him, welcoming him, savoring the tremors and the heat and the glorious melting as her body prepared to be with him. After so many years of denying her sensual side, she found that part of her was wonderfully awake and hungry for satisfaction.

Need swelled throughout her body. She had to be with Malik the way she had to breathe to stay alive. Closer, she thought, stroking his tongue with hers, then closing her lips around him and sucking. Closer and harder and faster and just plain more of everything.

He broke their kiss with a harsh gasp of breath, then rested one hand against her cheek. Laughter lurked in his dark eyes and pulled at the corners of his damp mouth. "If you're so passionate, I won't be able to control myself." He touched a fingertip to her mouth. "That was an observation, not a criticism. I can feel the desire inside you and it creates a very physical response. But I don't want to shock you by ripping off your clothes and simply having my way with you."

She knew what he meant. The first time they made love it should be slow and tender and romantic. Lengthy, gentle touches, hours spent in discovery. She was sure that was what every other woman on the planet would want. But Malik had made her think about things she'd nearly forgotten. And the need he'd awakened could not be denied.

Even now she felt herself readying for him. Between her legs, the dampness grew. Her breasts were tight, swollen and aching with the need to be touched. Liana knew in her head that she would be completely fine if she and Malik didn't make love right now, but in her heart, she thought she might very well die.

She slipped her fingers through his thick, dark hair and drew him back to her. "I don't shock so easily," she murmured just before she plunged her tongue into his mouth.

Malik held still for all of a heartbeat as her words sunk

in, then he growled low in his throat and began to touch her.

His hands were everywhere. Her face, her shoulders, her hips, her thighs. He tugged at the folds of her blue silk dress, working it loose until he could unwrap it in the front and expose her to his gaze. Even as his tongue brushed against hers, his fingers searched for and found the tight points of her aroused nipples. He teased her, stroking and gently tugging, sending ribbons of need through her body to settle into the feminine core.

He reached behind her and unfastened her bra, then pulled it off and tossed it to the ground. Shifting slightly, he lowered his head to her breasts and kissed every inch of sensitized flesh. Liana found herself half rising off the bed as waves of sensation washed over her. She wanted...she needed.... She'd never been so desperately aroused in her life.

When his lips closed over her right nipple, she let out a moan that started in her belly. The pleasure was so intense. His fingers matched the movements on her other breast, forcing her to cup his head and hold him in place. It was too wonderful, too perfect. If he kept doing this, she would surely die.

"Don't stop," she begged.

"Never," he promised, the word lingering on her skin.

He flicked the folds of the dress open and reached down to slide his fingers under her panties. As his hand moved over her stomach she thought briefly of stretch marks and those pesky twenty pounds. But before she could figure out what to do, his fingers were in her damp curls and searching for the center of her being. And then she didn't care what she looked like because it felt too good to matter.

He explored her with the sensitivity and thoroughness

of a man on a very important assignment. First he gently slipped into the protective folds of skin and found the place that would bring them both the ultimate release. He eased inside, first one finger, then two, moving in and out, making her writhe beneath him.

"So wet," he murmured, still teasing her breast. "So hot and ready."

He moved slightly, shifting so that he could kiss her mouth again. As he did so, his fingers found the tiny spot that was the center of her being. He brushed over it, making her jump. He circled the place, moving lightly around until he settled into a rhythm that made her gasp and plead and wrap her arms around him. Her hips began to pulse; her thighs trembled. She felt both hot and cold, and it was all too much.

He stopped suddenly and pulled off her panties. Then he slipped out of his robes. Underneath he wore a simple linen shirt and slacks. Soon he was out of those as well, and when his briefs hit the floor, she saw him in all his naked glory.

He was powerful and tanned, with broad shoulders and narrow hips. A light dusting of hair bisected his flat belly, drawing her gaze to his impressive, throbbing need. When she reached out to touch him, he drew back.

"I couldn't stand it," he said simply, returning to her side and lowering his mouth to hers.

His fingers trailed down, once again finding that one spot that made her strain toward him and beg.

He worked slowly, arousing her to a fevered pitch, then backing off until she was nearly calm. Again and again, she felt herself building. She moved her hands over him, discovering the feel of his warm skin and the way his muscles bunched at her touch.

She'd forgotten what it was like to be with a man, she

thought hazily, as once again she spiraled higher and closer to the goal of her release. She'd forgotten about the warmth and the weight and sense of well-being. Except this wasn't exactly what she remembered from her past. It was altogether much better.

And then he brushed over that one place and she couldn't think anymore, because regardless of what happened in the rest of the world, her course had been set. She wrapped her arms around his neck and kissed him deeply, then shuddered as her body contracted and released in a rhythm that made her feel as if she were bathed in the most perfectly exquisite light. Pleasure rushed through her, emptying her of tension, of worry, of everything but the glory of having Malik touch her in this way.

He continued to touch lightly and evenly until she had finished her climax, then he moved over her and pressed himself against her.

He paused long enough to put on protection.

She would have thought there wasn't anything left inside her, but as he entered her so very slowly, filling her, stretching unused muscles in the most delightful way, she found herself collecting to tense and release again.

She opened her eyes and their gazes locked. He breathed her name and shuddered.

She tilted her hips to accept all of him. He felt so right. She adored the weight of him, the way her body trembled and the building pressure that promised she was far from finished.

He bent low and kissed her, then raised himself again so he could watch her face.

The swift but gentle action made her body contract in an unexpected spasm.

"Again," he demanded and she found herself doing as

he wished, until she was caught up in a cycle that made her release with each thrust.

"I can't," she gasped, knowing that her body was no longer hers to control. "I'll die of it."

Malik said nothing. Instead he continued to move, watching her. She was sure he could both see and feel her releases. She felt wanton and sensual and more feminine than at any other time in her life.

And then he was moving faster, and she felt him ready himself. She prepared for him to thrust deeply one last time. He stiffened and groaned. Her body contracted around him, pulling him in, and she held him close as he relaxed against her.

Happiness filled her. Perhaps this wasn't the smartest thing she'd ever done in her life, but she refused to have any regrets. Even if it was just for tonight, making love with Malik had been glorious.

"Not bad for two out-of-practice people," she murmured, then nibbled on his earlobe.

"You were most adequate," he told her teasingly.

She laughed. "As were you, my handsome prince. As were you."

Malik sat in the low cushioned chair across from the bed and watched Liana sleep. After making love, they'd pulled up the covers and rested together in each other's arms. But although she'd drifted off, he couldn't stop the whirling thoughts in his head.

There was no excuse for what he'd done, he told himself. When she found out the truth, which would probably happen in the morning, there would be hell to pay. If Liana hadn't appreciated his attempts to get her to live at the palace, she was hardly going to forgive his latest transgression. He should have more forcefully told Bilal no.

Malik closed his eyes. But instead of picturing the leader of the nomadic tribe, he saw Liana as she'd lain naked in his arms. He replayed the memory of how it had felt to slide into her waiting body. For that single moment, they truly had been one being.

She was so many things, he thought watching the way the faint light from a glowing lantern caught the golden blond in her hair. Beautiful, affectionate, intelligent, caring, humorous. How was he supposed to resist her? For a man who had lived alone for most of his life, the promise of her acceptance had been more than he could resist. He'd known it wasn't going to last, that it wouldn't last even now, but he'd been unable to walk away from her. For the first time in his life, he'd understood what it meant to be intimate—in more than a sexual sense.

So for this evening, and for as long as she would let him, he would pretend that it was real. That she cared about him and wanted him and that they were together. It wasn't love. It could never be love. But it was as close as he was allowed. Surely his duties and responsibilities could excuse him this one time—for these brief hours— and he could be like other men.

"What are you thinking?"

He looked up and saw that Liana had awakened. She sat up, watching him, her hair mussed and her eyes still half closed.

"I'm thinking about you," he said honestly. "About how we were together."

"Oh, are you? And how was that?"

"Amazing."

"Hmm, my thoughts exactly." She pushed back the covers and rose to her feet. Naked, she crossed the carpeted floor and stopped in front of his chair.

He remembered that she'd worried about her body—

that she'd borne a child and wasn't as slim as she would like. But when he looked at her, he saw only perfection. The full breasts of a mature woman. Rounded hips, long legs and one or two marks that proved she was a fertile, vital goddess.

"You are a fantasy," he said, leaning forward and pressing his mouth against her belly.

She cupped his head, then tilted his chin so that he stared up at her. "Somehow I think you're the winner in the fantasy department," she told him. "Very few men daydream about schoolteachers, but nearly every little girl in the world has dreamed about a prince."

"A man from a fairy tale. Not someone real."

"You're real?" she said, teasing him with mock disappointment. "And here I thought you were the manifestation of every childish daydream."

She sank to her knees and pressed her palms against his bare thighs. "Although the good news is if you're real, you won't disappear at midnight or whatever it is fantasy princes do when they leave."

"It's past midnight and I'm still here," he said.

"Good, because if you were a fantasy, I might just shock you by doing this."

He sat naked in the low chair. Liana gave him an impish smile, then leaned forward and took his rapidly swelling arousal in her mouth. The combination of movement, moist heat and her long hair brushing against his inner thighs made him swear aloud. He tensed as a wave of pleasure rushed through him. In less than a heartbeat he was as hard as he'd ever been. Pressure built quickly and purposefully and he knew he had to distract himself or he would give way in a matter of seconds.

He closed his eyes and thought of other things, but the

relentless movement of her mouth as she raised and lowered her lips against him was more than he could stand.

''What are you doing?'' he asked as he put his hands
under her arms and drew her up from her sensual task.

''Just giving in to temptation. When I woke up and saw
you sitting there all naked and thoughtful, it seemed to be
an invitation.''

Malik rose and drew her to her feet. He studied her
face. ''You are a woman of many surprises.''

''Why? Because I enjoy making love?'' She shrugged.
''I've never been opposed to it, in the right circumstances.
My experience was limited to my marriage, but while
Chuck and I were getting along, I rarely told him no. If
you're going to complain that I'm too wild, it's your own
fault. While I'll accept responsibility for long-denied desire waking up, you're the one who made it so good.''

Her words made him swell with pride—in more than
just his chest. He had a fierce need to claim this woman
again, to take them both to paradise and back. They might
have only this night, but he wanted to use every minute
to his advantage.

''I want you,'' he said, moving close and kissing her.

With their bodies still pressed together, and their
mouths joined, he moved them toward the bed. When she
tumbled onto the mattress, he followed her onto the yield-
ing surface, but he didn't kiss her again. At least not on
the lips. Instead he did to her what she'd done to him.

He licked the soft, quivering skin of her inner thigh,
then moved higher to her woman's place. There he parted
the blond curls and studied her beautiful body. He used
his tongue to find all the places that made her gasp and
call out his name, knowing that her body, unlike his own,
could be coaxed by him to experience ultimate release,

only to have it happen again and again when he was inside her.

He licked her thoroughly, plunging his tongue into her waiting depths. She was sweet and hot, and he knew he would never forget a single moment of their lovemaking—not in this life or the next. He circled that one point of need, teasing it until she trembled and pulled her knees back toward her chest.

''Malik, please,'' she pleaded, her voice soft and shaking, her breath coming in gasps.

He slipped two fingers inside her and pressed up, stroking her from the inside as he matched those movements with his tongue. She cried out. The single sound tore through him like a blade, finding sanctuary in his heart. Then all was forgotten in the convulsion of her muscles as her body contracted in waves of release. She pulsed around his fingers and he moved against the beats, drawing out the moment to make it last longer. He touched her more and more lightly until she was still, then he rose over her and plunged himself inside.

She grasped him to her and spoke his name over and over, like a talisman against the dark. As he moved in and out of her, the contractions began again, the quick, deep pulses making a mockery of his attempt to make it last longer this time. Instead he found himself speeding toward his own release, lost in the pleasure and the welcome he saw in her blue eyes.

She was, for this one brief, glorious night, his very own. And he would lose her in the morning, with the surety and speed of sand slipping through an hourglass.

Last night had been, hands down, the absolutely most amazing experience of her life, Liana thought hazily, some time the next morning. She lay on the soft bed and stared up at the tent's ceiling. She knew that she was grinning like a fool and she couldn't stop herself.

"You're not supposed to be able to do that to me," she said lazily.

Malik had already risen and dressed. The man had more energy than was human, she decided, watching him pull on his boots.

"I would say we did it to each other." He looked at her and smiled. "But if you want me to take all the credit, I don't mind."

She rolled over and onto her stomach and pressed her cheek into the pillow. "I'd been *married* and I didn't know it could be like that. Obviously Chuck and I needed to take a remedial course in sex or something. I had no idea my body was capable of doing that."

And with a virtual stranger, she thought, still bemused by all that they'd been through together.

"I've always thought those romance novelists were lying," she murmured as Malik sat next to her on the bed and rubbed her bare back. "I mean they write about all that great sex stuff and I figured it was just poetic license. But now I have to say those ladies do their research."

Malik leaned down and kissed her. "While I want to take all the credit for last night, I can't. I've never experienced anything like it before, either."

She turned to face him. The sheet didn't travel with her, and she was naked under the covers. When she realized her breasts were now bare before his gaze, she found she didn't much care. Especially when he began to gently stroke the full curves.

"So it's chemistry?" she asked.

"Or fate."

"Fate, huh?" She kind of liked the sound of that.

Liana closed her eyes, giving herself over to Malik's

sensual touch. Maybe she'd been hasty to assume they couldn't have any kind of a relationship. Maybe a short-term affair wasn't out of the question. She was going to be in El Bahar for two years, and if he wanted to be intimate with her for a few of those months, was she crazy to agree?

The trick would be to keep her heart firmly out of reach. She couldn't risk caring about him. In fact, if she were completely honest with herself, she was already a little nervous about having bonded. She didn't think she was the one-night stand type. So she would have to be careful to keep her heart firmly locked up. Still, it might be worth it. After all how often did a woman like her get to—

A young woman stuck her head into the tent. Liana dove under the covers while Malik rose. "Good morning," he said. "Have you brought coffee?"

"Yes, Your Highness," the woman said in slow, careful English. She nodded at Malik, then moved toward the low table and set down a tray.

She looked to be in her late teens or early twenties. The shapeless robe and veil over her face made it difficult to tell.

"Don't worry," Malik told Liana. "This is simply desert hospitality at its finest. It's a great honor for her to serve us coffee."

"Yeah, and she caught me in your bed. What on earth are the tribespeople going to say about that? Aren't they fairly traditional in their beliefs about sex?"

Malik didn't meet her gaze. "It's not a problem."

She opened her mouth to question him more, but the young woman claimed her attention by approaching the side of the bed. She stopped and knelt on the thick rugs, then, with a glance back at Malik as if confirming he would stay where he was, she dropped her veil and smiled.

"Good morning, Princess Liana," she said, speaking slowly, as if reciting a prepared speech in a language that was difficult for her. "Best wishes to you on the event of your marriage to the lion of the desert."

## Chapter Nine

"Married? Married?" Liana knew she'd been repeating the word over and over, but she didn't know what else to say.

"It's not what you think."

She glared at Malik from her corner in the rear of the limo. She'd been silent for the first hour or so of their trip, but she couldn't contain herself anymore. "Are we or are we not married?"

"We're married."

"Then it's exactly what I think."

This was *not* happening, she thought frantically as she stared out the window at the desert stretching to the horizon. It was a horrible dream brought on by lack of sleep, or too much sex or something, because she refused to believe it was real. She and Malik could *not* be married because there hadn't been a ceremony. She was sure she would have remembered participating in one and reciting her vows, but she didn't.

Of course she didn't remember much of anything from the last hour except getting close to hysteria and insisting they return to the palace immediately. She wanted everything settled as soon as possible, and she had a feeling that wasn't going to happen while they were out in the desert. She wanted to get back to the safety of the city. Once there, all this would make sense. She would find out there had been some kind of a mistake. That was it. A mistake. And soon everything would be put to right.

"Liana, you have to let me explain," Malik said.

She spun to face him. "Explain away. I would love to hear how you and I got married, because I sure don't remember it happening. And let me assure you, I'm not going to sit idly by while you attempt to run my life again. I don't know what this game is, but I'm not playing."

Malik reached for her hand, but she pulled her arm out of reach. "Don't touch me," she said. "I'm not doing that again, either. You might be a wizard in bed, but I won't let myself be caught in that trap a second time. I can be seduced, but I'm not stupid."

He stiffened and glared at her. "I didn't seduce you. I made it very clear that whether or not we made love was completely up to you."

She pressed her lips together. Damn the man, he was telling the truth. "All right. I'll give you that one. I did agree." She'd more than agreed, she thought grimly, remembering their second time. She'd been the initiator. And it had been amazing. "But I never said I would marry you. This whole thing is probably a joke to you, but it's serious to me. We're talking about my life. I don't appreciate being made a pawn in some twisted game."

Malik started to reach for her hand again, then stopped.

"I didn't trick you," he said, then paused. "At least, I didn't start out that way."

"How kind of you," she said sarcastically. "So it was an accident?"

"Do you want me to explain or not?"

She pressed her lips together. "Fine. I'm listening."

"I invited you to join me for a welcoming ceremony," he began. "That's what I expected to happen. But when we arrived I saw right away that Bilal had arranged a desert wedding instead."

He stopped talking. She waited, but after a couple of minutes of extended silence she knew he'd finished. "That's it? That's all you have to say. Oops, there was a mistake? Did it ever occur to you to explain it to me? To let me in on what was happening?"

"I knew you wouldn't go through with it."

"No kidding!" She was so frustrated she wanted to toss him out of the moving car. "Of course I wouldn't have gone through with it. I don't want to marry anyone. I certainly don't want to marry you! I can't believe you just blindly led me into this situation. Who do you think you are?"

Malik straightened in his seat. Even though she knew it wasn't possible, she would have sworn he grew taller and more powerful as he spoke. "I am Malik Khan, Crown Prince of El Bahar. I am the future ruler of this nation, and I have done you a great honor by taking you as my wife."

She opened her mouth, but no words came. What on earth was she supposed to say to that? "Well, la de da," she managed at last, although saying it didn't make her feel any better. Fortunately, the limo had arrived back at the palace.

She waited until Sandy slowed the vehicle, then opened

the door before he brought it to a complete stop and jumped onto the paved walkway.

"I want to see the king," she demanded as she made her way past the armed guards at attention.

Malik was already behind her. He grabbed her arm and spun her around to face him. "What do you think you're doing?"

"Getting this mess straightened out. There's been a mistake. Obviously you and I aren't really married. I don't know what you think you're doing but it's not going to work."

"Married?"

"Mommy?"

Two voices spoke at the same time. Liana groaned, then jerked her arm free and saw that Fatima and her daughter had come out to greet them. Bethany's eyes were huge and her mouth quivered as if she wasn't sure if she should smile or not.

"Mommy, did you really marry Prince Malik?"

"No, I did not," Liana said, glaring at him, daring him to contradict her. "There was a little mix-up at the desert camp, but I'm going to see the king and we'll get it all straightened out."

"Malik?" Fatima asked inquiringly.

"There was a change of plans," her grandson said dryly. "It wasn't a welcoming ceremony after all. You wouldn't happen to know anything about that, would you?"

Liana planted her hands on her hips. "Don't try and pass your actions off on others. You're the one responsible." She looked at the queen. "Excuse me, Fatima, but where is the king? I must speak with him right away."

"I'll take you to him," Malik said stiffly.

"I'll see him alone, thank you very much." Liana

started toward the palace. "You've already done quite enough."

But it wasn't to be. Even as she started down one of the many hallways, Malik caught up with her and took her hand. No matter how she pulled, he wouldn't release her. And to make the situation even more humiliating, she'd turned the wrong way, so they had to backtrack to get to the king's offices.

"You're leaving as soon as we get there," she told Malik under her breath. "I will not have this conversation while you're in the room."

"Then you won't be having it, because I'm not leaving."

"We'll see about that," Liana announced, even as she thought to herself that it was unlikely she was going to get her way in this matter. After all, she hadn't gotten her way in very many other matters where Malik was concerned—except for the issue of living on her own in the housing by the American School. And a lot of good that had done her, she thought grimly. Malik had let her go, only to trick her into marriage.

They rounded the corner and found themselves facing a large set of double doors. The royal seal filled the center of each door and two armed guards stood at attention. For a second Liana wondered if they would be allowed to enter, but then a male secretary came running up and opened the right-hand door for them, bowing and announcing Malik at the same time.

King Givon sat behind an impressively large desk. There were bookcases and a large sitting area by a window that looked over a stunning garden complete with a life-sized statue of an Arabian horse.

The king rose as they entered. "What an unexpected surprise," he said, smiling at them both. "Miss Archer. I have missed having you here at the palace. I'm pleased you took the time to come and speak with me today.''

His polite greeting left Liana feeling momentarily off balance. She jerked her hand free of Malik's and nodded at the king. ''Your Majesty, I have a small problem and I need your help.''

Givon raised his eyebrows then glanced at his son. ''Are you that problem, Malik?''

''Sir,'' Liana interrupted, ''I would most appreciate it if we could have this conversation without the prince being present.''

''I see.'' The king motioned for her to take a seat on one of the low sofas by the window. ''And, Malik, do you wish to stay?''

''Yes, Father.''

Liana forced herself to settle on one of the soft cushions when all she really wanted to do was bounce to her feet and pace the length of the impressive room. The rugs underfoot looked as ancient as El Bahar itself, yet, despite their age, they were rich with color. Each design appeared to be more perfect than the one before, yet she knew that every rug had a tiny flaw worked deliberately into the weave.

King Givon sat next to Liana and took one of her hands in his. ''I'm sorry, my child. I would dearly love to grant your request of an audience without the presence of my son, but as he wishes to be here, I cannot deny him. I hope you'll understand.''

She didn't at all, but she doubted it would help to say that. Instead she nodded and stared at her hands. Her hands. Her breath caught as she took in the patterns of henna staining her skin. Her eyes closed as she remembered reading something about henna being applied to the hands and feet of a bride. Why hadn't she remembered this yesterday?

"I can't believe it," she murmured, then looked at the king. "Something horrible has happened. I understand that Malik is your son and the Crown Prince, but I hope you will put your personal feelings aside and hear me out."

"Of course." The king nodded gravely.

Malik moved to the window where he stood with his back to them. She had no idea what he was thinking, and she didn't care. "Yesterday I accompanied Prince Malik out into the desert." She briefly recounted her expectation that she was to participate in a welcoming ceremony, and how she'd found out this morning that she and Malik had somehow been married.

"It can't be true," she said urgently. "I never agreed to any of it. Someone has made a mistake. I won't be married to him. I can't be. No one asked me if I wanted to marry him."

The king patted the hand he held. "The ancient ways are different here than in the West," he began. "A traditional desert wedding doesn't require the permission of the bride, only that of her family."

"But I don't have any family here."

Wise dark eyes so much like Malik's stared into her face. "Without family to care for you—" he began, but Liana cut him off.

She pulled her hand free and rose to her feet. "I don't need anyone to take care of me or my daughter. I do a fine job all on my own." She pressed her fingertips together.

"That is true," the king agreed. "However, the old ways don't make allowances for a woman who can support herself. Instead, a woman without family will be married off to the first man willing to provide for her. Under those circumstances, her husband is held to a higher standard because the woman is without protection.'' Givon smiled. ''In our own way, we try to see that all are taken care of.''

Liana swallowed her frustration. Screaming at the king was only going to make him angry and what she really needed was the monarch on her side. Even so it was difficult to keep the sarcasm out of her voice. ''So you're saying that because I have no family, any man in El Bahar can marry me against my will?''

''Something like that. But, as I mentioned, these are the old ways. Things are different now.''

Relief flooded her. She sank back onto the sofa and for the first time that morning, smiled. ''So we're not married?''

King Givon glanced at his son, who still stood with his back to them. ''Modern practices have taken the place of desert marriages for most people, however the desert arrangements can still be valid under certain circumstances.''

Liana swallowed. A knot formed in her stomach and she had a bad feeling about what the king was going to say. ''What circumstances?''

''If you went through the desert ceremony last night and that was all, then the marriage can be annulled immediately. However, if the marriage was consummated, then I'm afraid it's completely binding. At that point the couple is truly married for a month. After that time, they may consider a divorce, but not before.''

Liana couldn't breathe. She couldn't think, she couldn't move. She could only stare at the king sitting next to her and press her lips together to keep from crying out in frustration.

"That can't be it," she whispered. "Anything but that."

Givon's bushy dark eyebrows raised slightly. "I see."

Just two words, but there was a wealth of meaning behind them. Color and heat flooded her face. Liana sprang to her feet and mumbled an apology, then ran from the room. She pushed past the startled guards and ran until the king's private office was far behind her, and she was again in a familiar part of the palace.

She stopped by a small fountain in an alcove. The splash of water sounded like tiny bells, but she barely heard the soft melody because of the harsh sobs clawing at her throat.

It couldn't be true, she thought frantically. Someone was lying. In this day and age a man couldn't really marry a woman without her permission, could he? Not even a Crown Prince. And even if it were so, why would Malik do it? And with her? Was he tricking her? Did he want to punish her for leaving the palace? But that didn't make sense, she thought as she dashed away her tears. Of course, nothing made sense anymore.

She leaned against the cool wall and continued to sniff and smooth away her tears, all the while trying not to notice the henna staining her hands. What was she supposed to do now?

Liana slowly focused on her surroundings. She'd stopped in a little-used corner of one of the side corridors by the harem. She straightened and drew in a deep breath. She had more than herself to consider—there was also Bethany. This affected her as well. If it was true.

Liana knew only one other person she could ask about the marriage, so she walked around the corner and headed for the gold doors that marked the entrance to the harem.

Inside, she found both of Malik's sisters-in-law as well

as Fatima waiting for her. Bethany bounced to her feet and raced over to her mother.

"Fatima says that you're really married to Prince Malik, which means you're a princess," her daughter said, beaming up at her. "Can I be a princess, too? Please, Mommy?"

Liana looked at the elegant queen. "So it's true?"

Fatima rose to her feet and crossed the marble floor. When she was in front of Liana, she rested her hands on Liana's shoulders, then leaned forward and kissed her on both cheeks. "Well, my daughter," Fatima said. "I'm afraid you have married the Crown Prince." A smile tugged at the corners of her mouth. "Of course, now that you have him, I can't help thinking he will be the one to change, not you. You're an excellent partner for my grandson."

The queen was actually smiling at her, Liana thought in amazement. Both Dora and Heidi were nodding with approval. As for being partners, that wasn't going to happen. Not if she could do anything about it.

"We're not really married," she said flatly, stepping back from Fatima.

"But the king called and said you are," Bethany announced. "Just now. And Fatima was happy, and now Princess Dora and Princess Heidi are my aunts and Fatima is my grandma and I have a big family." She clapped her hands together. "I've always wanted a big family, but till now it was mostly Mommy and me." She looked at her mother. "What are you going to tell Grandma and Grandpa?"

"Oh, Lord," Liana murmured. What *was* she going to tell her parents? Nothing for now, she thought. Nothing until everything was straightened out. If she and Malik were really married, then her parents would have plenty of time to deal with the fact that their daughter had married a prince. If she could get the situation fixed, they might never have to know.

Liana pressed her fingers to her temple. "I don't feel too good."

"Perhaps you should sit down," Fatima said, leading her over to the sofa.

Dora gave her a sympathetic smile. "I'll order tea."

Liana looked at her. "I don't think tea is going to help this situation." She shook her head. "This isn't really happening, is it?

Bethany plopped down next to her. "It's okay, Mommy. You'll see. You'll like being married to Prince Malik. He's really nice. When we go out riding, he always listens to me and talks to me. Not like some grown-ups. And now we can live here in the palace where there are horses and the babies. I'll still go to school, of course, and I'll study really hard and not be a moment's trouble. Really. So you'll like being here and will want to stay married to Prince Malik forever."

Her own daughter had already bought the idea, Liana realized. She'd thought Bethany might be upset, but of course she wasn't. For the nine-year-old, having Malik as a father was something out of a fairy tale. After all, he was a handsome prince who had taught her to ride a horse and now appeared willing to make all her dreams come true.

"I think I'm going to faint," Liana said as all the blood rushed from her head and the room swayed.

"Deep breaths," Fatima instructed. "You're in shock, but you'll get used to the idea." She smiled. "You're now married to a prince. That can't be a bad thing."

Liana wanted to disagree in the strongest terms possible. Of course it was a bad thing. She'd been tricked into marriage by a man she hardly knew. Nothing about her life had prepared her for this, and she didn't want to be here. If she'd known what was going to happen when she came to El Bahar, she never would have left California.

She looked at the other women in the room. They stared back with varying degrees of concern, but no one was shocked. They weren't appalled and bemoaning her fate. Was she the only one still based in reality?

Heidi leaned forward and smiled at her. "I know this must seem strange, but it's not as bad as you think. After all, you get to be married to a prince. Imagine how wonderful it would be if you fell in love with him."

Liana opened her mouth to speak, then closed it. There was no polite way to respond to that comment and she didn't want to alienate herself from everyone at the palace. In love with Malik? Not her, not ever. If she were left alone with the man for more than three minutes, she would skin him alive…or worse. In love. That was ridiculous. Just because he was sort of attractive and fairly decent to her daughter. And the sex had been spectacular, she added grudgingly. More than spectacular. It had been intense enough to change the earth's rotation. But that was lust, not love, and, as for the rest of it, she would never allow herself to care for someone who thought he could get whatever he wanted just by pushing other people around.

Besides, she had a life of her own. Which reminded her. "I have to get back to my condo," she told Fatima.

"Of course. You'll want your things."

Liana didn't want to think about the reality of having to move back into the palace. So she didn't. "Actually, I was more concerned about my lesson plan. I need to go over it for Monday."

Fatima patted her hand. "That's not necessary, my dear. You're the wife of the Crown Prince. You won't be teaching anymore. In fact, you never have to worry about working again for the rest of your life."

## Chapter Ten

Not having to work again might be someone else's fantasy, Liana thought grimly, but it wasn't hers. She enjoyed taking care of herself. Being with Chuck had taught her not to depend on anyone else, and she didn't intend ever to forget that lesson.

So she sat quietly through her tea with Fatima and the two princesses, and, when she could, she escaped back to the guest suite where she and Bethany had first stayed. There she made the first of her two phone calls. She was not about to accept her current situation without a fight.

However, thirty minutes later she was forced to concede defeat. The administrator of her school had congratulated her on her unexpected nuptials and had gone on to inform her that not only had her classes already been reassigned to other teachers, but that her account had been credited for her full two years of salary. Liana grimaced. There wasn't a doubt in her mind as to where *that* money had come from, and if Malik thought he could buy her off, he was going to be surprised.

Her second call had been to the American consulate. While the man at the office had been sympathetic and understanding, he hadn't been the least bit helpful. El Baharian desert marriages were legally binding. If she and the prince had consummated the union, then she was married for the next thirty days. After that time, she could pursue a divorce. Oh, and he had also suggested it would be very nice if she didn't make an international incident about the issue. Relations with this very rich Middle Eastern country were most cordial and the United States government intended to keep them that way.

Liana got the message. This was her problem and no one was going to help her out of it.

No matter how many times she replayed the situation in her mind, it didn't make sense. Why her? Men like Malik didn't fall for women like her. She knew he wasn't in love with her. And while the sex *had* been amazing, that had occurred *after* the so-called marriage ceremony. He was a prince. She was a schoolteacher. They did *not* belong together, so why had he done it? She glared at the phone, picked up the receiver, then slammed it down again. This couldn't be happening, she thought frantically. She wouldn't let it. When had she lost control of her life? Was El Bahar really so very different? Had she truly been trapped into marriage without her consent?

"Mommy, why are you mad?"

Liana hadn't heard her daughter enter the room, but now she glanced up and saw her standing by the entrance to the suite. Familiar blue eyes stared at her in confusion.

Liana held open her arms and her daughter ran over to her. They hugged each other, then Liana settled the child on the sofa next to her and brushed her bangs out of her face.

"I'm not angry so much as frustrated," Liana admitted.

"But Fatima says that now we get to live in the palace and I can ride horses every day."

Liana pressed her lips together. When the situation was described like that and viewed from a nine-year-old's perspective, what was there not to like? Bethany could live in a real castle, have a prince for a father and a bevy of aunts and uncles ready to spoil her at every turn.

If only life were that simple for adults, Liana thought sadly. "Prince Malik and I are married," she admitted, although she hated giving in on that point. "But it's not a permanent marriage. It's like summer school. You know, shorter than a regular semester. Well this marriage is going to be shorter than most. Just a month. And when the month is over, you and I are going back to America."

Bethany's eyes filled with tears. "But I want to stay here forever. I want Prince Malik to be my daddy. He likes me and talks to me, and he's never too busy or forgets to come get me. Please, Mommy. Can't we please stay? I'll be really good and Prince Malik will buy you flowers every day and you'll never have to worry about having enough money to buy me school clothes and I'll go to bed right on time every night, I promise."

Her daughter's pain cut through Liana like a knife. She knew that Chuck had let his daughter down, but until she heard Bethany glory in a man who picked her up when he said he would and took a few minutes to give her attention, she hadn't realized how deep the wound went in her little girl. Tears flowed down Bethany's cheeks and caused Liana's eyes to burn as well.

How was she supposed to explain that what Malik had done was wrong? That no man, prince or not, could trap a woman against her will? But Bethany wouldn't see marriage to Malik as a trap. For her it was a dream come true.

"I'm sorry," Liana murmured, holding her daughter close. "I wish I could explain it better. We're going to have to stay for a month, but that's all. I want you to enjoy your time here, but don't forget it's just for a short time and then we must go home."

Bethany pressed against her shoulder and sobbed as if her heart were breaking. Which it probably was, Liana thought grimly. Sometimes being a parent was the hardest job in the world.

"I'm going to pray every night that we get to stay," Bethany said, her voice still thick with tears. "I'm going to ask God to change your mind and make you want to stay here." She raised her head and sniffed. "Or maybe you could fall in love with Prince Malik and then you'll never want to leave."

And pigs could fly, Liana thought. In love with Malik? Yeah, right. In what lifetime? The man had bullied her from the moment she'd set foot in his country. He'd brought her to the palace against her will, he'd tricked her into marriage and now who knows what more he expected?

Liana swallowed against the sudden tightness in her throat. Bethany stared up at her with such hope that she couldn't help wishing there was a way to give her daughter everything she wanted. Malik had been good to her daughter, she admitted grudgingly. He'd been consistent and patient. From what Liana could tell he actually liked spending time with her.

He was also incredible in bed, not that his skills there excused anything or made the slightest bit of difference to her. All right, so he was good-looking and intelligent.

And maybe their talk on the way to the desert had given her some insight into the stress of his life. After all, where did a Crown Prince go at the end of the day? How did he relax and to whom did he talk? From what she'd been able to tell, Malik was very much alone. So she *was* the tiniest bit honored that he felt he could trust her enough to share some of his life with her. But that didn't excuse one thing he'd done and there was no way in this lifetime that she was ever going to do something so incredibly stupid as to fall in love with the man.

Later that afternoon, Malik returned to his father's office. They'd both had urgent business to take care of, but the conversation about Malik's marriage to Liana Archer couldn't be put off forever.

Malik knew the questions his father would have. Questions any sane person might ask. Why had he done it? Malik had asked himself the same question, but he wasn't sure he was willing to share the answer with anyone. He could barely acknowledge it himself. Except for that one moment when he'd realized that Bilal had prepared for a wedding, not a welcoming, Malik had felt as if he could finally touch all he'd ever wanted. His decision had been impulsive. He might have to pay for it for the rest of his life, but he couldn't regret it.

He walked into his father's private office and found the older man waiting there, along with Fatima. He greeted them both, then stood in front of the sofa and braced his feet. An American expression came to mind—the best defense was a good offense. He glared at his father.

"You contacted Bilal and changed the ceremony," Malik said.

King Givon shrugged. "I might have suggested something of the sort, but I never thought you'd go through with it."

"Of course you did. Otherwise why bother?"

Fatima leaned forward. Elegant as always, the Queen Mother looked much younger than her nearly eighty years. "Malik, it's been so long since you've showed any interest in a woman. We thought we would plant the seed in your mind that she might be someone worth pursuing." She waved a slender hand. "If you'd married her and not bedded her, or if you'd at least told her the truth, the marriage could have been annulled."

Malik drew his eyebrows together. "You meddled in my life and now you're concerned because you got what you wanted?"

Fatima sighed. "It seems we might have misjudged the situation. Liana is not one to take kindly to being tricked into marriage."

"I can't blame her for that," he said blandly.

"But you're the one who tricked her," Givon said forcefully. "Why did you do it?"

Malik shrugged. "I was surprised when I realized what Bilal was doing. I thought about taking Liana and leaving, or even telling her the truth and letting her decide." He paused. "But she would have said no. There was also the matter of offending Bilal and his people. So I married her without her knowledge because I wanted her for my wife."

"But she's not going to simply allow this to happen," Fatima said. "She's furious, and I'm not sure I blame her. Our ways are not her ways." She stared at her grandson. "Why this one? Why do you want this woman?"

He didn't know how to answer that. "She intrigues me."

"Heidi intrigued you," the queen pointed out. "She

saw past the title and duties to the man inside. Why is Liana different?''

Malik considered her statement. He'd known Heidi for years. As a teenager, she'd been a frequent visitor to the palace. Somehow his position had never impressed her. Even now she took great pleasure in teasing him unmercifully.

Malik smiled at the memory. "Heidi was always for Jamal," he said. "Even when we were younger, I knew they belonged together. And even if they hadn't, she and I would not have been right together. My feelings for her are purely brotherly. Nothing more.''

"You care for her very much," Fatima reminded him.

"I know." With Heidi he could feel almost human. It was an immeasurable gift.

"So, you have a month in which to win your new bride," his grandmother said. "A month in which to make her fall in love with you and a month for you to learn to love her back.''

Malik nodded, agreeing with all but the last. He would do his best to win Liana—to make her fall in love with him. But he would never love her, or anyone. He could not. Love was a weakness he could not allow himself. That was a lesson he'd learned at a young age and one that had never left him.

Knowing he couldn't put it off any longer, Malik went in search of Liana. They had to talk about all that had happened. By now she knew that she was no longer employed by the American School. She might have even called the American consulate. He wasn't sure what they would have told her. Perhaps the truth—that in El Bahar, a desert marriage was still valid, and that for the next month she was his wife.

*Wife.* He turned the word over in his mind. He'd been married before. But Iman had taken that simple word—*wife*—and had made it into something evil. She had defiled their marriage bed and had humiliated him a thousand times over. Worse, she had weakened him in front of his countrymen. There could be no greater sin.

But Liana was not Iman, he reminded himself. He had seen the truth of Liana's character reflected in the artless conversation of her charming daughter. A child repeats what it hears and learns, and Bethany spoke of a warm, loving woman with a generous heart. She confessed to times of loneliness and poverty, but only casually. Liana had given her child all she had. She could not be more different from Iman.

He paused outside the guest-room door. After knocking once, he entered and found her alone, standing by the French doors overlooking the Arabian Sea.

Sometime since he'd seen her last she'd changed her clothes, exchanging her traditional blue gown for jeans and a T-shirt. Her long blond hair hung loose about her shoulders and he couldn't help remembering how it had felt brushing against his thighs the previous night when she'd knelt in front of him and taken him in her—

"What do you want?" she asked, continuing to stare out at the view. She hadn't turned to face him, nor was there any anger in her voice. She sounded tired and resigned.

"Where's Bethany?"

"She ran to tell the horses the good news. That she was going to be living in the palace and could see them every day. I've informed her that we're only here until the month is up, but she's hoping for a miracle."

Liana slowly turned to face him. She wasn't wearing any makeup and her skin was pale. Except for the henna staining her hands, she looked like a typical American woman ready for a casual Saturday of housework and errands.

"I've been standing here trying to make sense of it all," she said, raising her gaze to his face. "The truth is I can't. Why did you do this, Malik? Why did you trick me into marriage?"

"I didn't know the ceremony had been changed until we arrived in the camp. Once I realized what they were doing, I went along with them."

"Why?"

"I needed a wife."

She stared at him. "As simple as that? No explanations or excuses?"

"Do you want to hear any?"

"Not really."

"I thought as much. So why bother? I've told you the truth."

"You needed a wife?" She shook her head in disbelief. "Okay, say I buy that. Why me? There must be hundreds, no, thousands of women more suited to the task. I don't know the first thing about your world. I don't have family connections or the training. My idea of high fashion is buying a cotton blouse that's *not* on sale. I don't know how to make political small talk with visiting dignitaries, and I'm sure not beautiful enough to grace a magazine cover."

Malik studied her critically. Technically, she might not have the classic features of a beauty, but when he looked at her, he saw pure loveliness. The face of the woman with whom he could almost be himself. Someone worth bothering about.

"No man could be dissatisfied with your appearance," he said.

"There's a compliment." She shoved her hands into her back pockets. "I don't know what to say to you, or even what to think. My entire life is out of control."

"Your life is very much in control."

"Oh, yeah, and you're the one doing the controlling. I hate that. Who gives you the right?"

"Ancient tradition allows—"

"Screw ancient traditions," she said, interrupting him. She pulled her hands free of her pockets and approached him. "Who gave you the right to mess with *my* life and why on earth did you pick me?" She stopped a couple of feet in front of him and rubbed her temples. "Is that what the sex was all about? Did you do it just to keep me?"

How was he supposed to answer that? If they hadn't made love, she would be free to leave him now. But that hadn't been the reason he'd wanted to be with her. He weighed his options, then decided to speak the truth.

"If we hadn't made love last night, I knew I would die." Perhaps not on the outside, but certainly in his soul where the last vestiges of his humanity clung by a thread. Being with Liana had given him new life…if only for a short time.

She glared at him. "Great line. Did you think it up yourself?"

"It's the truth."

"Sure. And I'm the queen of…" Her voice trailed off. "Never mind. I might just be queen of something, after all." She turned toward the window, then spun back to face him. "I don't want this," she told him. "I can't believe I came half-way around the world only to end up with someone exactly like my ex-husband."

Malik stiffened. "Do not compare me with him. We are nothing alike."

"Aren't you? Chuck made all kinds of decisions without consulting me. He took our savings, which we had in theory agreed was for a down payment on a house, and bought a new race car and an engine and tires. He never asked, he just did what he wanted. Frankly, I can't see that you're any different.''

''I have taken nothing from you,'' Malik reminded her. ''You have only gained from knowing me.''

''If we're talking about the money you had placed in my account, you can forget it. I'll be giving that all back. While it's a generous payment for one night of sex, I refuse to be your whore for any price.''

He grabbed her upper arms. ''Is that what you think? That I paid you to service me?''

Her eyes glistened with unshed tears. ''What else could it be?''

''Perhaps it was my way of making sure your dreams were not affected by all that has happened. It is not my intention to have you go when the month is up, but if I can't stop you I don't want you to leave El Bahar without what you came for. The divorce would have provided you with a generous settlement, but I thought you might be stubborn about that. I thought you would at least take what you expected to have earned from teaching. If you return to your country with that money, then both you and Bethany will be taken care of. You will have your house, and she will have her money for college.''

He shook her slightly, but didn't give in to the rage boiling inside of him. ''How dare you imply I treated you as anything but a precious part of my life? I didn't take you last night without regard for your feelings. I asked you. I had you choose what you wanted. If you had refused me, I would have walked away. I have honored you by marrying you and yet you accuse me of treating you in such a despicable way." He thrust her from him. "You know nothing of me."

"You're right," she said, her breathing coming in hard pants. "I don't know you and I don't want to. I had my whole life planned. Everything was fine. I do a damn good job taking care of my daughter and myself, and we don't need you." A single tear slipped down one cheek. "But we're stuck with you now. So tell me what's going to happen? What about Bethany and how this is going to affect her? She's going to be destroyed."

"Why? I care for her."

"Isn't that nice. Well, guess what? She cares about you, too, and living here is only going to make that worse. She's going to start to have expectations."

"I will be a good father to her."

"Will you visit her when we're back in California? Do you plan to fly in every other weekend? Don't you realize that a month is plenty of time for her to get her heart broken?"

"I don't want it to be just for a month. I want you both to stay."

"Oh, that's so nice," she said sarcastically. "But this may be one of those times when you don't get what you want."

He refused to think about that. Liana was here and she was going to stay. Somehow he would convince her.

"You and Bethany will move into my suite today," he said. "Someone has already been sent to pick up your things. I will give you a few days to settle in, and then I'll be joining you in our bed."

She bristled. "I don't think so, Prince Malik. I might be stuck in El Bahar, but I'm not staying in the palace."

"You are my wife. Your place is at my side. Besides,

you don't have a choice. The housing at the American School is no longer available to you.''

She blinked. "Because I don't work there anymore," she said slowly, as if it was all just sinking in. "Let me guess the rest of it. No one will rent a room to me if you tell them not to."

"You are my wife," he repeated stubbornly. "Your place is here."

"I'll go to the American consulate," she said. "They'll have to help."

He wasn't sure if she didn't see that she had no choice or if she was determined to fight him to the end, regardless of her lack of options. He suspected the latter. Liana could be most stubborn. While that trait made things difficult now, he knew it would be a great help later in their life together. She would fight for what she believed, and when they had sons together her strength would help them to rule El Bahar with wisdom and courage.

Liana continued to stare defiantly. He touched her shoulder. "They will not help you."

Her whole body stiffened, then she seemed to collapse upon herself. She walked over to the sofa and sank onto a cushion. "It's not fair," she whispered.

"Perhaps not, but we must live with the situation as it exists. We are married. Nothing can change that. Would it be so difficult to make the best of things?"

She raised her head. Fire glowed in her eyes. "You haven't won, Malik. I might be here for the next thirty days, but when the time is up, Bethany and I are leaving."

"No. You will fall in love with me and you will stay."

Her lips curved into a smile, but there was no humor in her expression. "Want to bet?"

Now it was his turn to smile. She couldn't know that he was betting his very life on her staying. She was his last hope. Only with Liana did he have a chance of surviving, of being a man rather than a machine. She had the key to his heart and if she walked away from him, it would stay locked forever.

But he didn't tell her any of that. For one thing, she would never believe him. For another, he couldn't imagine allowing himself ever to be that vulnerable to another person. He'd been raised to be autonomous. He was Crown Prince Malik and he needed no one.

"You will love me," he repeated. "And you will stay."

"You will rue the day you tricked me into marriage," she retorted.

He met her angry gaze and knew that only one of them was going to be right. But which one?

## Chapter Eleven

"Mommy is really mad at you," Bethany confided the following day as their horses picked their way across the open desert.

Malik glanced at the child riding next to him. "I'm not surprised. She was angry last night when we spoke." While Liana had conceded that it was necessary to stay in the palace, she'd not given in easily, nor had she moved into his suite. Instead, she and her daughter were back in their original guest quarters.

He tried not to think about the humiliation of being rejected by his wife less than twenty-four hours after their wedding. He knew there was talk in the palace, and soon it would drift out to the city. Still, he would survive this; nothing Liana could do would ever compare to Iman's transgressions.

"You're gonna have to do something," Bethany informed him. "Otherwise she's gonna stay mad forever."

Malik stiffened in the saddle. "I'm Prince Malik Khan. I do not compromise."

The nine-year-old looked at him. She wore her blond hair pulled back in a braid under her riding hat. The combination of light-colored hair and the black cap made her eyes appear even more blue than usual.

"If compromising means you've made a mistake, and you have to admit it, I think that's what Mommy wants." Bethany flashed him a smile. "She says she wants a lot of other things, too, but I don't think she really means them. Especially not the part about cutting off your head and leaving it on a stick in the center of town."

"How very visual," he said dryly.

"Mommy has a great imagination. She can make really boring stuff interesting. That's why she's such a good teacher. Oh!" His riding companion brightened. "She's mad about losing her job, too, and she's even more mad about her getting all her money, even though she didn't finish teaching." Her voice lowered confidentially. "You're kinda in trouble, Prince Malik. I didn't know grown-ups could be in trouble like kids, but they sure can."

He didn't know how to respond. He understood that Liana was annoyed with him for tricking her, but she'd overreacted to the situation. After all, he was a prince, and he'd married her. It wasn't as if he'd taken advantage of her then cast her aside. He had willingly given her his name, then set her up as his country's future queen.

Yet in return she insulted him by refusing to move into his quarters. Didn't she understand that he wanted her there? Not only so they could be lovers again, but because he wanted to think about her living where he lived. He wanted her fitting into his life, using his belongings, appreciating the art, enjoying the views, just being a part of his world. Was that so wrong? Couldn't she see that he had not wanted anyone else to do that? Did she know what it cost him to open up enough just for this?

He stared at the horizon where the sun was barely visible in the cool, clear dawn. Sometimes his life felt as empty and cold as the desert in winter. Liana could be his sun—offering both warmth and light. Yet she turned her back on him and rejected him. Then he reminded himself that he should expect little else from her. The price of his position was isolation.

"I don't understand why Mommy is so upset," Bethany said a few minutes later when they'd turned the horses and were heading back to the stables. "I think she likes you, but she doesn't want to say that. And she's so mad now that she keeps talking about you being just like my dad." Bethany glanced at him, her expression confused.

"You're not like Daddy at all," she said confidently. "You never forget our plans to go riding, and you're never too busy to talk to me. You're always nice, and we have fun. I told her that, too, but she said I'm too young to understand."

Malik didn't understand either, but he wasn't about to share that with Bethany.

"I'm sure we'll come to some agreement," he said.

"I hope so, because I don't want to leave El Bahar. I want to live in the palace and be a real princess."

"I'll have to see what I can do about that."

Bethany grinned. "Then everyone in school will have to bow to me, and I won't have to do what the teachers say."

"Unfortunately, little one, it's not that simple. Sometimes being royal means doing a lot of things you don't want to do, even when all your friends are going out to play. There are many responsibilities."

Bethany sighed. "I guess it couldn't be as wonderful as I think." She glanced at him. "Is that why you married Mommy? To have her help with your responsibilities?"

"Some," he admitted. "Some of the reason is that I didn't want her to go away."

"But she says we're going away anyway, and in a month, not in two years like we were at first." She frowned. "You're gonna have to do something, Prince Malik. Because if Mommy doesn't stop being mad at you, she's not going to stay here at the palace."

"I know." The problem was he didn't know what to do to change Liana's mind. "Do you have any suggestions?"

She rolled her eyes. "I'm only nine. I don't know about grown-up stuff like that. Except in those books she reads, the men are always getting the ladies to fall in love. And then they get married and live happily ever after. I think you forgot the in-love part. You should have done that first. Then she wouldn't want to leave."

They were by the stables. Malik slid off his mount, then helped Bethany down. "I suspect you're right. I did do things backwards."

"So make Mommy fall in love with you. It can't be too hard. Those women in her romance novels are always falling in love. You could read one, then do what they do." She beamed. "If you get it right, we won't have to leave."

Malik was not the kind of man to take advice from a book, but he couldn't quite explain that to a nine-year-old.

"I'll think about it," he said at last.

Bethany hugged him, her small arms going around his waist. "I'll try to talk to Mommy more," she said. "So we never have to leave."

Malik removed her hat and then smoothed her sleek blond hair. "I don't want either of you to leave," he said.

What he didn't dare tell her was that she was part of the reason he'd married her mother. Not only was Bethany proof that Liana would be a good mother for his sons, but he'd actually grown to care for the child. She was intelligent and spoke her mind with a frankness he found refreshing.

Sometimes when he was with her, he allowed himself to forget all the responsibilities waiting for him when he returned to his world. In Bethany he saw how life would have been had he not been the Crown Prince.

So different, he thought, remembering all the afternoons he'd spent watching from the window as his brothers left the schoolroom to go riding or out to the *souk* with their tutor. But his days lasted long after the hours of study. When he had finished with his tutor, he reported to his father. In the afternoons, the king and his ministers trained him in matters of government. After dinner, there had been more lessons, or state events he was expected to attend. While his brothers had been free to return to their mother's side to be cuddled and read to or sung to sleep, Malik had lived alone. He'd been deemed a man at the age of four and had been expected to act like one at all times.

Malik didn't want that for his children, but he knew no other way. So he needed Liana to be the loving force in their lives. She would fight for them, protect them, even from him. She would make sure they knew what it was to love and be loved. With her as their mother, he wouldn't have to worry that they would grow up with a black soul and an empty heart.

Liana felt she and Malik were still at a draw. He'd forced her to stay in the palace, but she'd insisted on living in guest quarters rather than moving into his rooms. She wasn't teaching, but she also wasn't a part of his life. Unfortunately, the victories weren't very helpful, and after two days of pacing the length of her suite, she was ready to go crazy.

There was nothing to do with her day. She was used to always being on the run. Between teaching and Bethany and her house, she'd had a list of things to do that stretched into next month. Every day had been busy from the time she woke up until she fell exhausted into bed. But now there was nothing. Bethany was in school all day. The suite didn't require cleaning—there were servants who got insulted if she so much as made her own bed. Someone else did the cooking. She had no friends and no one to talk to. Worse, she sensed that her marriage to Malik—not to mention their unusual living arrangements—was the subject of much gossip and speculation.

A part of her felt guilty that people might think badly of Malik because of her actions. But then she reminded herself what he'd done to her, and she got mad all over again, and that made her swear she wasn't going to give in.

Her life had become very complicated, she thought to herself as she stared out at the beautiful view. She still didn't understand why Malik had married her. Nothing about her screamed ''great catch.''

She didn't think he was madly in love with her. She thought he might like her and she was reasonably confident that he'd enjoyed making love as much as she had…at least she hoped so. But that was all temporary when compared with the act of getting married. Which brought her back to her original question of what on earth he'd been doing.

"I need some answers," she said aloud and turned her back on the view. That was the problem. She had too many questions and not enough information. Therefore she had to go to the source and find out what exactly was going on.

That decided, Liana stalked out of her suite and made her way into the working wing of the palace. She remembered some of the way from when Malik had taken her to see the king.

After a wrong turn and detailed directions from an assistant, she found herself standing in front of an imposing desk, staring down at an official-looking man with short blond hair and wire-rimmed glasses. He was pale and slight, but with an air of importance that made her tug at the hem of her short-sleeved cotton sweater.

The man continued typing on his computer for what seemed like hours. Finally he looked up at her and raised his eyebrows. "Yes?"

"I'd like to see Prince Malik," she said, trying not to sound as intimidated and out of place as she felt.

The man smiled, but the gesture wasn't the least bit friendly. "I'm sure you would, but that's not possible. At the moment he's meeting with the king. Later he has a meeting with Prince Jamal. There is a parliamentary session this afternoon and a formal state dinner tonight. I just don't see where I can squeeze you in." He clicked three keys on the computer. "The prince might have something at the end of the month. Would that be convenient?"

Instead of answering, Liana looked around the room. She'd given the open space a quick perusal when she'd first entered, but now she noted the original oil paintings, the coat of arms on the far wall, the richness of the carpet and the odious little man barring her from her husband.

The truth hit her like a bolt of lightning. She'd really

married a prince. A future ruler of a real country. Not just a wealthy man or a successful man, but an honest-to-God prince. What on earth had she been thinking?

"Well, do you want the appointment or not?"

Liana blinked at the man and shook her head. "No. Thanks."

She backed out of the room and quickly made her way down the marble hallways. There were fountains and statues and priceless rugs.

She hurried back toward the more familiar section of the palace. When she rounded a corner, she saw the golden doors that marked the entrance to the harem. Gold, she thought, feeling dazed. These were solid gold doors that had been carved or hammered or whatever it was people did to gold to make it decorative. She traced the intricate pattern, then pushed her way inside. She wasn't sure what she wanted here, she only knew that at least in these rooms the men weren't allowed.

Liana shut the heavy door behind her and leaned against it. In front of her, Dora and Heidi sat on two sofas, talking.

Dora looked up and saw her first. She smiled. "You look terrified. Whatever has happened, we can help. Please join us." She motioned to the tea set on the low table between them. "We sent Rihana to your suite with an invitation, but you weren't there."

Liana crossed the marble floor and sat down next to Heidi. She gave them both a wobbly smile. "I was at the other end of the palace. I wanted to see Malik, but his secretary told me I needed an appointment."

Heidi wrinkled her nose. "Don't get me started on Malik's secretary. I don't like Zachary very much. He's too self-important for me. But I suppose he's efficient. At least that's what Jamal says."

Dora shrugged. "I agree with you about him not being my favorite." She looked at Liana. "Next time, tell him who you are. I suspect he didn't know. Otherwise he would have let you right in."

Liana wasn't sure if that was the case, but she nodded because it was expected. Rihana entered then, carrying a tray of more tea and sandwiches. As the afternoon snack was served, Liana tried not to think about the fact that she was having English tea with two princesses in the harem of the palace in El Bahar. She felt as if she'd followed Alice down to Wonderland, only she had to contend with more royalty than just the Red Queen.

Dora passed her a cup of tea. "What on earth are you thinking? You have the most peculiar expression."

"That I'm a nobody from a small town no one has heard of and I'm sitting here with two princesses and I'm married to a prince. How on earth did this happen?"

Dora brushed her comment off with a wave. "Don't get caught up in the whole royalty thing. I was an executive secretary until I was thirty. Then I met Khalil. Now, Heidi here actually attended Swiss finishing school, which is pretty close to princess school if you ask me."

"I didn't," Heidi said teasingly. She tucked a strand of long, light brown hair behind her ear and sighed. "Don't let it get you down, Liana. I know that getting used to being in the palace and married to Malik is going to take some time, but it's not so very horrible. You do have us to help, and you can take things as slowly as you need to."

Liana studied both women. They were attractive and well-dressed in clothes that probably cost more than she paid in rent in a month. She wanted to believe that they had something in common, but it couldn't be true.

"I don't even know how I got here," she admitted.

"One minute I was teaching math at the American School and the next I was married to a prince."

Dora sighed. "I don't know all the details about what happened, but I think I know enough to understand how you feel. For what it's worth, Khalil married me under false pretenses. It took a long time for us to come to terms with our marriage. Eventually I managed to tame him...or he managed to make me more wild, I'm not sure which." Her mouth curved up at the corners. "Either way, we're very happy."

"She's right," Heidi said, leaning forward and touching Liana's arm. "The Khan men aren't easy but they're worth the trouble."

"You're both talking as if I'm going to stay."

"How do you know you're not?" Dora asked.

Liana was so stunned by the question, she had to stumble for an answer. "I don't know him. He doesn't know me. I'm still clueless as to why he wanted to marry me in the first place. We have nothing in common. I don't know how to be a princess. I'm the first person in my family to graduate from college. What on earth are we going to talk about? How will I keep from completely humiliating myself and Malik? Why would the people of El Bahar accept me?"

"All good points," Heidi said calmly. "Sounds like you've been doing a lot of thinking."

Dora nodded. "But you left out the most important question, Liana. What do *you* want from this marriage? Are you so very sure you want to leave Malik before you've found out what it's like to be with him? I won't disagree that he had no right to trick you into marriage or that you both have to take the time to get to know each other. But this is a wonderful opportunity. You need to be sure you're not interested in this life before you turn your back on what you have. Once you walk away, there's no returning.''

''She's right,'' Heidi said. ''You're stuck here for a month, right? Why not take the time to get to know Malik and learn about El Bahar? You don't have to make up your mind today.''

They were both so calm and rational, Liana thought, slightly stunned by all they were saying. She was still reeling from the reality of her situation, so the thought of stepping back and taking some time to think things through hadn't occurred to her. But according to all she'd learned, she wasn't leaving for a month. Should she take that time and assess her situation?

''What have you got to lose?'' Heidi asked. ''If you find this isn't what you want, you were planning to leave anyway.''

''You make it sound so simple.''

''Maybe it is.''

Maybe...but it wasn't. First of all, she had Bethany to think of. The more time her daughter spent with Malik, the more the girl became attached to him. Then there were her own feelings to consider. For reasons she wasn't willing to explore, she was a little cautious about getting to know Malik any better than she did. As if something deep inside warned her this man could be dangerous to her heart. The last thing she needed was to fall in love with him.

But the alternative was to spend the next few weeks hiding out in her room. Running away from a problem had never been her style. She wouldn't have gotten through college and been able to raise Bethany on her own if she'd allowed fear to get in her way.

Maybe it wouldn't be such a bad thing to get to know the man to find out if they had anything in common...anything other than an ability to spontaneously combust when they got too close.

"Right now we're barely speaking," she confessed. "I wouldn't know how to start getting to know him."

Dora and Heidi looked at each other. "There's a state dinner tonight," Dora said. "Were you planning to attend it?"

Liana shook her head. "The first I heard about it was earlier when Malik's secretary recited his schedule for the day. It included the dinner."

Heidi smiled. "Gee, as the new wife of the Crown Prince, I think you should attend."

"Obviously Malik doesn't," Liana said, suddenly hurt by the realization. "He didn't say a word."

"Did he have a chance to?" Dora asked bluntly.

Liana swallowed. "I guess not." She looked at her new sisters-in-law. "Do you think I should go? I mean, would I be allowed?"

"Of course you're welcome. But as to whether you should or not, that's your decision."

Liana pressed her lips together. If she wanted to get to know her husband, she was going to have to start to understand his world. In her mind, attending a formal state dinner was about as appealing as a foot surgery and a root canal on the same day. But it would give her an idea about what she was up against.

"I'd like to go, but I don't think I have anything to wear."

Dora smiled "That is the least of your problems. Between us, Heidi and I have dozens of gowns, many of which have never been worn. In fact—" Dora tapped her forefinger against her lower lip "—you're a couple of inches taller than either Heidi or myself, but I do have a gown that is a little long. I haven't bothered to have it taken up, mostly because I didn't think the style would flatter me.'' She patted her hips. ''Those of us shaped like a pear have to worry about certain dresses emphasizing the wrong thing. But you're more balanced.''

Liana was about to point out that she was also twenty pounds overweight, but she figured there wasn't any point. Either Dora's dress would fit or it wouldn't.

''If that doesn't work, I'll bet we can find something else,'' Heidi said encouragingly. ''Then we'll do your makeup and pin up your hair and you'll really feel like a princess.''

Liana doubted that was possible, but she decided not to point out the obvious—that she was a nobody and would remain a nobody. Maybe she could fake being a princess for a night.

Dora rose to her feet and led the way out of the harem. ''How do you feel about tiaras?'' she asked, her expression serious.

Liana blinked. ''I've never thought about them one way or the other.''

''Then you'd better start thinking about them because you'll be wearing one tonight.''

An honest-to-goodness tiara, Liana thought three hours later as she stared at herself in the mirror. Actually she was staring at a woman who looked a lot like herself but was really someone else. She'd never known she could look this good!

Maybe it was the dress or the makeup or the diamonds glittering in her hair. Maybe it was a magic night, and she was caught up in the glow. Whatever the reason, she felt as if she actually looked like a princess.

The gown Dora had loaned her was midnight-blue velvet. The sweetheart neckline dipped low enough to show a hint of cleavage. The fabric smoothed over her body, emphasizing the good curves and hiding the bulges. Small capped sleeves left her arms bare, while the flowing fabric covered the rest of her to the floor.

After Liana was dressed, Heidi had seen to her hair, pulling it up and away from her face. Pins secured the elegant chignon in place. Her bangs had been curled and sprayed and behind them glittered a real diamond tiara. The gems sparkled, and that light added a glow to her eyes. Or maybe it was Fatima's makeup. Liana had never been one to bother with cosmetics, but the king's mother knew secrets that made eyes widen and skin seem porcelain perfect.

Liana's gaze drifted over her reflection, taking in the color staining her cheeks and her mouth, the way her hairstyle made her neck appear long and slender. For the first time in her life she felt truly beautiful. Even if all the finery disappeared at midnight, she didn't care. At least she'd had the experience of looking like a princess.

A knock at her door startled her. She walked slowly toward the entrance, her unfamiliar high heels slowing her down. But instead of finding Bethany or one of the servants waiting in the hall, she saw Malik standing there.

He wore a black tuxedo and white shirt. The combination of perfect tailoring and his impressive body nearly took her breath away. He was beautiful enough to star in all her daydreams for several lifetimes. Dark eyes regarded her thoughtfully.

"You look lovely," he said.

She had to force herself to inhale before she could speak. "Ah, thanks."

"I heard that you wished to attend the dinner tonight. We honor our neighbors to the east. Bahania is a country much like our own—a nation with a monarchy and a desire to maintain a hold on the past while moving toward the future. My grandmother is from that land.''

She nodded. Fatima had already told her a little about what to expect at the dinner. "Do you mind if I come along? You didn't mention it to me, and if I'm intruding...." Her voice trailed off.

Malik's expression hardened. "I didn't tell you because you made it clear you weren't interested in acting as my wife in any capacity. If that has changed, you are welcome to be at my side."

He'd answered the question without telling her what he was thinking. But that didn't surprise her. She'd hardly been open and friendly since finding out about their marriage. Not that he had any right to expect anything different from her. After all, he'd been completely wrong to trick her into marriage. Still, she was realistic enough to know that if she was really going to take the time to get to know the man, she had to stop being mad at him all of the time.

Before she could figure out what to say next, Malik thrust a wooden box into her hands. It was about the size of a loaf of bread.

"These are for you," he said gruffly. "They are yours alone. They did not belong to Iman. What was hers was sold. I gave the proceeds to the poor."

Liana had no idea what he was talking about until she opened the lid of the box and found herself staring at a collection of jewels. Diamonds, sapphires, rubies, emeralds and pearls lay tangled together. The display was so opulent, she had a fleeting thought that they couldn't possibly be real. Yet she knew they were.

"I don't know what to say," she murmured in complete truthfulness. What *did* one say when presented with such a gift? Malik reached into the box and drew out a stunning sapphire and diamond necklace that he fastened around her neck. When he was done, she saw the matching ear-rings and put them on. Then she glanced at her reflection.

"I'm a stranger," she said, looking at the sophisticated woman staring back at her.

"You are most worthy," Malik informed her.

She met his gaze in the mirror and had the oddest feel-ing that he meant she was worthy for much more than attending the evening's dinner. But how could he be sure? He barely knew her. She could be many horrible things he'd yet to discover.

Still, he held out his arm and she slipped her hand into the crook of his elbow. At least she had the next few weeks to find out the answer to that question…and many others. The most important of which was—would she stay?

*Chapter Twelve*

Liana managed to keep breathing right up until they walked through the open double doors of the ballroom, but when she saw the milling people and heard a loud voice announcing "Crown Prince Malik and Princess Liana," she felt she would pass out from a combination of anticipation and fear. To make matters worse, every person in the room turned to look at them.

For the second time that day reality crashed into her with all the subtlety of a herd of wild Arabian horses. If she stayed married to this man, one day she would be queen.

"I suggest you start breathing," Malik murmured into her ear. "If you smile and nod, they'll start talking with each other again, but I promise, if you pass out, you'll be the center of attention all evening."

She sucked in a breath. "I don't want that."

Malik smiled at her—one of those slow, male smiles

that was as sweet, rich and tempting as freshly made Christmas fudge. "Try to relax, Liana. You're charming and very beautiful. No one but me is going to know how close you are to throwing up from nerves."

She nearly stumbled on the smooth floor. She didn't know which shocked her more. That he'd figured out how close she was to losing control, or his comment that she was beautiful and charming. Was that how Malik saw her?

She didn't get a chance to mull over his words because she found herself swept into a river of introductions. The royal family formed a reception line with her tucked neatly between Malik and his brother Jamal. A uniformed officer introduced the guests to each of them. Liana shook hands with ministers, a visiting European head of state, the King of Bahania, all four of his handsome sons, along with his spirited-looking daughter. She was verbally admired, congratulated on her marriage and generally made to feel as if her marriage to Malik was nothing out of the ordinary.

Her mind whirled, her mouth hurt from smiling and she found out that her lovely dyed-to-match shoes had not been designed for over an hour of standing. Just when she was sure she wouldn't survive another moment, everyone was invited to move into the dining room. King Givon and the King of Bahania escorted Fatima into the great hall. Malik and Liana went next, walking alongside the Crown Prince of Bahania.

If the ballroom had been awash with glittering lights and jewelry, the dining room was a fairyland of opulence. Thick brocade tablecloths fell to the floor. There were candles everywhere, the flickering light reflecting in the crystal and fine china. Exotic blossoms in different shades of red formed elegant centerpieces. In the far corner, a small orchestra provided background music and several

dozen uniformed servers moved silently to assist guests
to their seats.

Overhead, thousands of tiny white lights twinkled like
stars against a darkly tiled ceiling. As in most rooms of
the palace, the floors were marble. Liana found herself led
to a table set up on a dais, where she was seated between
Malik and the King of Bahania. They were to dine in full
view of all their guests. She swallowed hard.

Malik leaned close. "What are you thinking?"

"That I really don't want to spill my water or drop
food off my fork in front of all these people."

He reached under the tablecloth and found her hand.
After squeezing her fingers gently, he released her, seem-
ingly oblivious to the fire that flared between them with
the light touch. "You'll get used to it. Besides, once the
meal is served, most people are more concerned with their
own dinner and the conversation at their table than what
is happening up here."

She shifted so that her lips nearly touched his ear. "Am
I supposed to make small talk with a king?"

"You've had conversations with my father."

She wanted to point out that that was different, but she
wasn't sure Malik would understand. After all, he'd
grown up in this world and it was all he knew.

"Don't worry," he said. "You'll be fine."

His steady gaze spoke of his faith in her abilities. Although she knew that she could very easily mess up, she
found herself wanting to prove him right—for his own
sake as well as hers. Oddly enough she liked that he believed in her and assumed she would do well.

She glanced around the room and smiled when she
caught someone staring. A flash of movement caught her
attention and she turned to see a young man speaking with
a girl a few years younger. The teenagers stood awk-

wardly, as if they would run from each other at any moment.

The King of Bahania noticed her interest. "My youngest," he said proudly. "He's just discovering the charms of the gentler sex."

"He's very handsome," Liana said and realized she wasn't the only one noticing the innocent flirtation. Several other guests were observing the young prince's activity with the girl.

How horrible to grow up in such a limelight, she thought, wondering what it must have been like for Malik. Had he ever had a moment's peace or privacy? For the first time she considered that his emotional reserve came from self-protection. How else could he have learned to shield himself while being constantly the center of so much attention?

She remembered her determination to get to know the man who was now her husband so that she could decide her future logically rather than emotionally. Yet her heart went out to the small boy who had been expected to act like a man. Who had hugged him when he was afraid? Who had held him close and whispered that he was special and loved? And if no one had been around to offer that kind of support, did he still carry that emptiness inside himself?

She looked at her handsome husband, taking in his confident air and closed expression. He held so much inside. What would happen if he felt safe enough to share his heart? How would he respond? Perhaps she should take the time to find out.

They danced in the light of a thousand candles. Malik held his wife in his arms and spun her across the floor, only to gather her close and fight the need to kiss her. He was vaguely aware of the other couples, of the music and the voice of reason in his head reminding him he had a responsibility to dance with other women and make polite conversation with the visiting royalty from Bahania. What he wanted instead was to take Liana to bed.

He desired her. Worse, he needed her. He needed to lose himself in her lushness, to allow himself to find refuge in her answering passion. Desperation added a sharp edge to his desire, making him long to ignore protocol and duty and simply disappear with her. Instead he held her against him as the song ended and told himself that one more dance with her wasn't so great a sin.

"You're looking fierce about something," she said, gazing at him, her eyes bright and her smile welcoming. "Compared to you I'm a pretty horrible dancer, but I was hoping you wouldn't notice."

"You're doing very well."

"I'm counting frantically in my head," she confessed. "I guess you took lessons. Probably from the Russian ballet when they were in town."

"Something like that," he admitted, beginning to move to the soft, romantic music. "When this dance is over we'll have to change partners."

The humor fled her face and her eyes flashed with panic. "Oh, great. I've never stepped on the toes of a visiting monarch. At least I'll have something to write home about."

Malik shook his head. "He'll be charmed, as I am. You didn't have any trouble speaking with him at dinner."

"That's because we were talking about Bethany. I mentioned how much she adored all the horses in your stable and we were off and running, so to speak."

"The king is a great cat lover. Ask him about his fa

vorites. That should be enough to get you through a dance.''

Malik took in Liana's pretty features and the way her tiara caught the light. Tonight she looked every inch the princess, and while she was quite beautiful, he found he preferred Liana dressed as a regular woman. Or in nothing at all.

He closed his mind against that image, because he didn't want to have to deal with the natural result. His blood already flowed so hotly that it would take no more than a light touch for him to become aroused.

''Is there some sort of briefing for these kinds of functions?'' she asked, oblivious to his thoughts. ''If I have to attend another one of these, I'd like to be a little more prepared.''

''Yes. The staff gathers complete files on all the guests. Had I known you were interested in attending, I would have made sure you were prepared.''

''Next time,'' she said, swaying in time with him.

''Next time,'' he agreed, even as he wondered if there would be a next time. After all, days moved by quickly. If she kept true to her word and stayed only a month….

But he wouldn't think about that. He didn't want to believe she was leaving him. He had just over three weeks to convince her to stay with him for always. Three more weeks, as his grandmother and Bethany had pointed out, to make her fall in love with him. An easy enough plan…if only he knew how.

''I had a very nice time,'' Liana said awkwardly as they approached the door to her quarters.

When Malik had offered to walk her back to her room, she'd had high hopes for more than idle chit chat. After all, his smoldering gaze had followed her all evening while she'd danced with dozens of visiting dignitaries. She'd found herself stumbling over polite conversation as she imagined herself making love with Malik. But since leaving the ballroom, he hadn't touched her once; maybe she'd simply imagined his interest.

Which made life more confusing, she thought as they paused in the hallway. Hadn't he been the one promising to share her bed after she'd had a chance to get settled? Well, she was about as settled as she was going to get, so what was he waiting for?

"I'm glad you enjoyed yourself," Malik said formally.

Wasn't he going to do anything? Didn't he want her anymore?

A more mature, braver woman would have asked. But she felt neither. Instead she sidestepped the issue. "Would you like to come in for a drink?" she asked. "Bethany is spending the night in the nursery with Dora's two, so we wouldn't have to worry about waking her up."

She felt like a brazen hussy. After all, she didn't doubt he could read the desire in her eyes. Her skin was hot and her face felt flushed. She'd been partially aroused since their first dance. Being so close to him and unable to touch him had been torture, but Malik had been politeness itself. Maybe he'd forgotten how it had been between them. Should she remind him or just let it go?

"A drink would be nice," he said, as she opened the door and stepped inside.

Ah, a neutral response, she thought as she made her way to the fully stocked wet bar in a corner of the living room. He wasn't giving anything away.

"Have a seat," she told him, then reached for a bottle of cognac and waved it in the air. "Is this all right?"

"Perfect."

He sat on the striped sofa, not at one end, but not exactly in the middle either. Which meant she had to decide how close to sit to him when she gave him his glass. She poured a splash into each snifter and sighed. Getting to know a man had always been complex. The intricacies of new relationships were one of the reasons she generally avoided them. Being with Chuck had been easy. They'd been young and had thought they were in love. Passion had allowed them to gloss over the rough spots. While she and Malik had shared plenty of heat, it wasn't enough to allow them to mesh their lives with ease. Perhaps if he'd been just a regular man that might have been possible, but he wasn't.

As she walked over to the sofa, she paused to open the French door leading to the balcony. Scented night air drifted into the room.

"I think it's getting cooler," she said as she handed him his glass. She settled herself on the same sofa, about as far from the right corner as he was from the left.

"I agree. Winters are mild in El Bahar, but the summers can be difficult until one adjusts."

So they were going for scintillating and witty conversation, she thought humorously. Perhaps next they could do a fashion recap on who wore what to the party.

"We have our own version of the changing seasons," he continued, after taking a sip of his cognac. "There are different festivals in the winter. The English garden is at its best in the spring when all the plants are blooming. When the wind is right, their scents travel as far as the main roads around the palace grounds."

She started to say she couldn't wait to experience it all but then she remembered she probably wouldn't still be in El Bahar in the spring. It was mid-October. If she only stayed for her required month, she and Bethany would be home for Thanksgiving. Oddly enough, the thought made her sad.

"What do you think of my country?" he asked.

She shrugged. "I haven't seen enough to form an opinion. The palace and the grounds are lovely, of course."

He reached up and loosened his formal black tie. The dangling ends contrasted with the snowy white of his shirt and looked amazingly sexy.

"I would be happy to put a driver at your disposal," he said. "You could go wherever you like."

Her mouth twisted. It's not as if she didn't have the time to see all of El Bahar. Her days were pretty empty. "While I appreciate the gesture, Malik, I don't think that's going to be enough." She set her drink on the low table in front of them and folded her hands together in her lap.

She gazed at him. "I've always been a busy person, and I'm more comfortable going and doing all the time. Right now I spend my days wandering around these rooms. Bethany is in school, and everyone else is busy."

"What do you want to do?"

She didn't have an answer to that. As much as she would like to return to teaching, she knew it was out of the question. "I don't know," she admitted. "Dora is busy with her political work, forwarding the rights of women, and Heidi spends all her free time working on ancient texts."

"You said that you always wanted to continue your education. Obtain your post-graduate degrees. El Bahar has several prestigious universities. Two of them are right here in the city."

"Yes, there's that," she said quietly. Except she wasn't going to be around long enough to take one class, let alone get a doctorate.

"You are thinking there isn't much you can do toward that in a month," he said, his voice faintly accusing.

She felt herself flush and had to bite back a defensive retort. She had no reason to feel guilty, she reminded herself, even if she didn't believe it.

He leaned toward her, his expression intense. Darkness filled his eyes until the pupils and irises were the same color and impossible to tell apart. "Is it so horrible here?" he asked. "Is that why you don't want to stay?"

"No. Of course not. It's just…" How could she explain the distance between them if he refused to acknowledge its existence? "I'm not sure I can fit in. I wasn't raised to be a royal princess. While I'll agree there are wonderful advantages, it can be a difficult life. I saw a bit of that tonight. Everyone was staring, and I was terrified I would put a foot wrong."

"You were fine. Everyone adored you."

"This time. But what happens when I say the wrong thing or accidentally insult a visiting dignitary? I don't want to be responsible for starting an international incident." She rubbed her temple. "I can't figure out if you really don't understand or if you just don't want to. Didn't Iman have any doubts?"

He stiffened. "I will not discuss her with you."

"Of course not. Everything always goes your way, or it doesn't go. Isn't that right? You wanted to marry me and we're married. You want me to stay and you expect that to happen as well. You don't want to discuss Iman or how she died, or what was so horrible about your relationship, so we don't." She glared at him. "You can't have it both ways. Either I'm your wife or I'm not. If you want me to take this seriously, you have to do the same. Circumstances do not bend to your will, however much you might wish them to."

Malik put his glass on the table and stared at her. She half expected him to leave, but instead he rose to his feet and crossed to the French doors. Once there, he stared out into the darkness.

Tension radiated from him. Tension and something that might have been pain. For a moment she thought about going to him and wrapping her arms around him. Not because her body ached for his touch, but because he looked so alone standing there, as if once again the burden was his to bear, and no one was going to share the load.

But before she could decide if that was a sensible idea, he spoke, and his words immobilized her.

"Iman isn't dead."

Her lips parted. She tried to speak, failed, then tried again. "But everyone said…" She paused and recalled what had been said to her. They hadn't actually said she was dead. "They implied she was dead."

"A subtle difference, but there all the same. She has left El Bahar and will never return. That is what matters. While it would have been better for all of us if she had died, she did not."

"I don't even know what to say to that," she admitted. "You're sorry your ex-wife didn't die." A thought occurred to her and she gasped. "You *are* divorced, aren't you?"

He glanced at her over his shoulder. "I assure you, my marriage to you was completely legal. Iman and I have been divorced for years."

"Oh. Good." Although if they hadn't divorced, her problem would have been solved. Odd how she felt relieved to hear otherwise. She pressed her lips together. "Why are you so angry with her?"

He shrugged and returned his attention to the darkness beyond the balcony. "Anger doesn't describe how I feel."

He paused. "Ours was an arranged marriage, as most are for those in my position. It was a disaster from the start. We had nothing in common. Despite that, I attempted to get to know her. I thought we could at least be friends. And perhaps with friendship would come caring."

He hadn't said love. Liana had the brief thought that he hadn't experienced very much of that in his life, so he was unlikely to expect it in an arranged marriage.

"But that didn't happen?"

"No. Iman was beautiful, but her heart was cold and ugly. She had been forced into our marriage against her will and she made no attempt to conceal her hatred both of me and the situation. When we finally consummated our union, I discovered that she'd already been with another man."

A virgin bride might be an old-fashioned concept back home, but Liana suspected it was expected for the bride of a soon-to-be ruling monarch. "You couldn't forgive that?" she asked.

He turned to face her. "I couldn't forgive her lover following her here and continuing to claim her favors. I couldn't forgive her for making a fool of me and, by association, my country. I couldn't forgive the fact that many of the servants knew of her infidelities but were afraid to tell me the truth, and that rumors abounded in the *souk* where the street sellers told stories about the new princess. And I couldn't forgive her stupidity and carelessness in allowing me and my father to walk in on her while she entertained her lover in our marriage bed."

All the blood seemed to leave Liana's head. She felt dizzy and confused. Malik's stark words painted a clear picture of a faithless wife making a fool of her husband.

"The name *Iman* means faithful, but in her case it was a lie," he continued. "When I realized the extent of her transgressions, I banished her and divorced her. Everything she had ever touched was destroyed and her name was no longer spoken here. She betrayed us all, for what is done to the Crown Prince is done to each citizen. I care not about what she did to me, but it is unforgivable that she so defiled the glory of El Bahar.''

Lines of tension stiffened his body, but his face was expressionless. Except for the clipped harshness of his words, he might have been discussing a current movie.

But Liana knew him well enough now to sense what the truth cost him. While she didn't understand what it must have been like for him to have his wife's infidelities spoken of throughout the country, she felt his pain now as clearly as if it was her own. Her heart ached for the proud man standing in front of her. He wanted only what was good and right for his country. He'd sacrificed himself in ways no one could ever truly appreciate. He *was* El Bahar, and he would give his all for the betterment of his people. His last thought, his last breath, would be for them.

His words echoed in her brain. ''What is done to the Crown Prince is done to each citizen.'' Which meant Malik's humiliation was also theirs. Would he be humiliated if she left him? Would her legacy be as brief and painful as Iman's?

She didn't want to think about that. She didn't want to know that she had the power to hurt him. But she couldn't escape the reality of what telling her about his past had cost him. Malik was a proud man and he'd laid open his shame at her request.

''Thank you for telling me,'' she said at last. ''I appreciate knowing the truth and I promise to honor your confidence.''

He dismissed her with a flick of his wrist. ''Even the

street cleaners know the truth. There is no confidence to keep."

She told herself he felt embarrassed by his past and that was why he treated her so casually.

"You asked me once what I learned from my first marriage," he said. "I'm grateful I never loved her."

His pain was so clear to her, she could have traced the still bleeding soul wounds. She saw the child who had been thrust into a frighteningly adult world and left to survive without comfort or affection. She saw a young man coming to terms with his sexuality in full view of an interested nation. She saw a husband who, despite his claims to the contrary, must have secretly hoped for someone to finally love him and share the burden of his office only to find himself rejected and then humiliated by his new wife. She saw a determined leader—a lion of the desert—alone. Untouched by kindness or love.

Without considering the consequences of her actions, she rose to her feet and crossed to stand in front of him. She wrapped her arms around him and rose on tiptoe to kiss him.

He grabbed her upper arms and thrust her away from him. "I don't want your pity," he growled, his eyebrows drawn together, his mouth a straight line.

Despite his obvious irritation, she smiled. "Malik, you inspire many emotions in me—mostly anger and frustration. I promise, I've never once felt pity."

"Then why do you come to me now, after I've told you about the whore who was my wife?"

She slid her hands under his jacket and again pressed a kiss to his forbidding mouth. "Because you're finally more man than prince. While the prince is scary and annoying, the man is very appealing. I would like to kiss him before he changes back."

His expression softened and he placed his hands on her waist. "I'm not annoying. I'm considered charming and an enjoyable companion."

"Yeah, right." She gazed into his eyes and watched the first flickering flame ignite. "So, do you want to talk all night or could I interest you in something a little more physical?"

Dark eyebrows raised slightly. "Are you propositioning me?"

"Absolutely."

## Chapter Thirteen

Malik knew that making love with Liana again would be a mistake. While he kept Liana at a distance, he knew that he was safe. But if he allowed himself to touch her again, to be with her, to claim her, then he knew that he would be forced to expose himself in ways he never had before. And once he'd allowed the light of Liana inside himself, he could never again be content to survive in emotional darkness.

So, even as her mouth pressed against his and he felt himself growing aroused and ready, he resisted. If he held some part of himself back from her, he thought he might be able to contain his growing need. If he could channel the energy and make it all about sex, they would both survive.

Yet, even as he attempted to hold himself apart, to keep his mind clear and his touch impersonal, he felt the fire growing. It burned through his reserve, melting the edges of his being until they blurred and connected with the wonder that was Liana.

He cupped her face, then moved his hands to her hair. He unpinned her tiara, then freed the long strands from her elegant hairstyle.

"You were magnificent tonight," he murmured as he kissed her soft cheeks, then her mouth. She tasted sweet and hot. Her lips welcomed him with nipping kisses, her tongue stroked against his, making it impossible for him to maintain his distance.

"I was terrified," she whispered between kisses. "All those people staring and waiting for me to say or do something wrong."

"No." He raked his fingers through her long hair and kneaded her scalp. "They were watching because they were envious. All the women admired you and all the men wanted you. Tonight when they make love with their wives, they'll imagine you in their beds."

She drew back and looked at him—her blue eyes were bright with a combination of passion and laughter. "I don't think so. I'm willing to admit that I clean up pretty good, and the dress was amazing, but I was just—"

He claimed her mouth to silence her. He plunged his tongue inside her, relearning the secrets of her mouth, her taste, her heat. He pulled her closer and she trembled in his embrace.

"You were everything," he breathed. "Perfect and lovely. You are my wife."

He felt her shiver. "Malik, do you have any idea what you do to me?"

He knew because he felt the same uncontrolled passion growing inside himself. As much as he wanted to jerk up her dress and sink himself into her right now, he wanted to make it last between them forever. He wanted to touch

nd taste every inch of her body. He wanted to lick her
ll over, then have her do the same to him. He wanted to
lip his tongue into her waiting heat and have her take him
n her mouth, then he wanted to be on top of her, plunging
1ome, claiming her, marking her. He wanted to spill his
.eed in her again and again until her body had forgotten
vhat it was like to be with any man but him. He wanted
o brand her with his kisses and his touch until she existed
mly for him—as he would exist only for her.

He kissed her mouth, then moved lower—trailing a
damp path down her throat and onto her chest. The sweet
aste of her skin made him hungry for all of her. With
ingers that weren't as steady as they should have been,
te lowered the zipper of her dress and pushed the velvet
)ff her shoulders and down to her waist.

She wore a lacy bra that teased by hiding her tight
1ipples. He saw the puckered flesh pushing up against the
abric. Supporting her weight, he urged her back, until her
)reasts thrust up toward him. He leaned over her and took
)ne nipple between his teeth. He gently moved back and
'orth, making her skin harden and her breath come in
hort gasps.

"Malik," she sighed, holding on to his shoulders.
'You're making me crazy."

"Good."

He brought her back to a standing position. Her face
vas flushed, her eyes glazed. He knelt at her feet and
ugged off her dress, then had a little breathing trouble of
his own when he realized she wore a garter belt and stock-
ngs. He swallowed hard and ignored the pressure be-
ween his legs. A voice in his head screamed for him to
:ake her now, to free himself and plunge into her, carrying
:hem both to paradise. Instead he forced himself to gently

tug off her panties, leaving her in stockings and a bra. Then he drew her to the sofa and had her sit.

Kneeling before her, he kissed her deeply. She hugged him, making it easy for him to unfasten her bra. When the garment fell away, he studied her rounded breasts and the pattern of veins under pale skin.

"So lovely," he murmured as he began to explore the curves.

He cupped her fullness, then stroked the exquisitely soft undersides. With his tongue, he flicked against her nipples, touching quickly and lightly, making her gasp. He tasted the sweet valley between the curves and licked all of her.

She squirmed and spoke his name and buried her fingers in his hair. Her hips moved, shifting closer until her heat pressed against his need and she began to rub up and down, driving them both to the edge. When he couldn't stand it anymore, he dipped lower, kissing her ribs, her belly and the hot skin of her thighs. Only when he felt her shudder did he part the protective folds of her feminine place and love her there.

She was already so hot and wet that he knew she wouldn't last long. He found the one tiny spot that made her cry out. With his lips and tongue, he circled and stroked, his steady rhythm matching the tightening of her leg muscles. He used one of his hands to dip inside her, pushing up so he touched that most sacred place from above and below. With his other hand, he reached up to cup her breast.

Heat radiated from her as if she suffered from an intense fever. Perhaps she did. She was a wildly sexual creature—untamed and magnificent in bed. When she drew her knees back to urge him on, he moved more quickly and thrust his finger deeper. Her breath caught, then stilled.

and he knew that it was her time. He focused all his considerable attention on the messages of her body, willing her to experience the ultimate release in the most perfect way possible.

She cried out and convulsed into spasms. Her strong internal muscles, her legs, her stomach all flexed and released with thousands of pulses. He continued to touch her, lighter and lighter, drawing out every second until she was spent and still.

He looked up and saw that a flush covered her from her breasts to her hairline. Her gaze met his, and he saw the tears in her eyes. For a second, fear gripped him, but then he knew. Her release had been so complete that she'd lost control in more ways than one.

"No one has ever made me feel like that before," she whispered. "Not ever."

He had known he had to be strong—to stay away from her or he would be lost. Yet it was too late. With Liana, most especially in her arms, he was just a man like so many others. Human—imperfect—alive. When he was with her he could succumb to the allure of her body and forget himself. He knew the truth. He'd seen the darkness that awaited him, but for these few moments he could pretend.

He wanted to tell her that if she left him, there would be nothing for him but dust and blackness. Yet he would not speak the words because she would never understand. So instead of responding, he simply moved closer. And when her hands reached for his trousers and unfastened them, he allowed her to pull him free.

Her fingers were small yet sure. She stroked him to a state of readiness that made him grit his teeth.

"I want you," she breathed as she kissed him.

Wrapping his arms around her, he pulled her to the

edge of the sofa. Her legs parted, and she welcomed him as he slipped home.

"Be with me," she whispered. "In me. Let me make you feel all the things I felt when you touched me."

They danced as lovers have danced for thousands of years. He let himself fill her, savoring her damp heat and the sensation of finally being home.

When he began to move, she wrapped her legs around his waist, holding him close. She was tight and the friction made it impossible for him to hold back. He moved faster and faster, losing himself in the passion. She clung and her breathing increased in speed.

"I can't believe it," she gasped, straining to get closer. "It's happening again. Malik, please. Don't stop. Do it harder. Take me."

The words were wrenched from her, guttural, as if they'd escaped against her will. She aroused him to a feverous pitch, yet he held back, restraining his own release until he felt the first rush of her body's rippling as release overtook her. Then he cried out into the night and poured himself into her.

The sensation ripped through him like a sword, tearing him into pieces, destroying his thin veneer of civilization, making him savage and greedy. He pressed in hard and deep, claiming her, joining with her until he truly couldn't tell where he ended and she began.

Consciousness faded. There was only the moment and the feelings and the woman who offered him a haven. He held on to her, needing her close, breathing in her scent, her sounds, her heat, knowing that when they finally separated he would feel as if he'd lost a piece of himself.

*Stay,* he thought frantically even as she leaned back against the sofa and smiled at him. *Stay with me because I will not survive without you.*

But he didn't say the words. He barely acknowledged that he thought them. For reasons he didn't understand, he was the one. He would do anything to keep her. Somehow he must find the secrets necessary to bind her to him forever.

Fatima was right. He had to make Liana fall in love with him.

Liana got out of bed in time to see her daughter off to school, then tumbled back onto her mattress where she slept until after nine. When she awoke for the second time, it was to a room full of bright sunshine and a sense of well-being unlike anything she'd ever experienced before.

It wasn't just that she and Malik had made love the night before…and again in the quiet hours that preceded dawn before he'd left her room to return to his own quarters. She was willing to admit that some of her happiness came from her body's physical contentment, but there was something else going on. When she'd been in Malik's arms, she'd felt a true connection. As if all the talk about being joined as one person finally made sense. While he held her and they made love, it was as if she could see into his very soul.

"Ridiculous," she told herself as she stepped out of the shower and began drying. "Two really don't become one—despite the words in the marriage ceremony." Yet she couldn't shake the idea that there was more between them than just chemistry.

She wrapped the towel around herself and stared at her reflection. Was it real or was it wishful thinking on her part? Had she found a way to touch her husband that had nothing to do with physical contact and everything to do with hearts? Last night had been a revelation on many different levels. She'd learned that she wasn't anywher near prepared to be the wife of a ruling monarch and tha she didn't think she would enjoy many aspects of the life But she'd also seen that Malik's world was even mor empty than she'd imagined, and that he was desperatel alone. The fact that he'd reached out to her—marryin her and drawing her into his world—made her feel so and squishy inside. As if he was willing to trust her an only her.

Did she want that, she asked herself, as she began ap plying her makeup. Did she want to be the one perso Malik went to, the keeper of his confidences? That kin of relationship implied an intimacy that was foreign t her. Malik was nothing like Chuck, yet that was hardly bad thing. With her ex-husband, she'd never felt like partner in marriage. With Malik, she wouldn't be a fu partner either. There was so much that he would contr by virtue of his title and position. Yet if he truly let he into his heart and soul then they would be partners on much more important level.

"More questions," she murmured as she smoothed o eye shadow, then reached for her tube of mascara. Ques tions of a different kind, but no more answerable than th question of why he'd picked her.

Maybe it was because he felt it, too, she thought sud denly. Maybe he'd sensed their connection from the be ginning, long before she'd realized it was there. Was tha possible?

The concept of being so intensely close to another hu man being both intrigued and frightened her. If nothin else, she was going to have to be even more sure that sh was making the right decision at the end of the month Although, now that she knew the truth about Iman, leav ing Malik was not going to be so easy. She didn't war humiliate him in front of his people. Nor did she want to make a mistake with either of their lives. But she couldn't stay if it was wrong for her and Bethany to be here.

"Talk about a tangle," she said as she walked to her closet and began looking at her clothes. She didn't have any real plans for the day so it probably didn't matter what she wore. Maybe she should—

A knock at the door of her suite interrupted her thoughts. Still wearing a robe and nothing else, she crossed the living room and opened the door to admit Fatima followed by half a dozen servants. Every one of them had an armful of clothes.

"Good morning," the elegant queen said, kissing her on the cheek. "I've decided that it's time for you to start dressing like the princess you are. But I could not face a day of shopping so I had the store come to you."

As Liana watched, more servants came in carrying boxes and bags. There were dresses and ballgowns and dozens of shoes and purses.

"Put them wherever you can," Fatima said. "Then leave us." She smiled at Liana. "Rihana will bring us lunch later, so take your time trying on everything. Only pick what you truly love. You can always go shopping in Paris and London later in the year."

"Okay," Liana said, stunned by the opulent display.

By the time the servants left, there were clothes everywhere. On sofas and chairs, in boxes stacked in the center of the room and on all the tables. She bent over to finger the skirt of a purple dress, feeling the smooth, cool silk, and wondering how much it all cost. Not that she was going to ask. For one thing, she doubted Fatima would tell her. For another, it didn't matter. The royal family had a degree of wealth that was beyond imagining.

"Are you overwhelmed?" Fatima asked as she pushed aside a lovely beaded black gown to make room for herself on the sofa. "I've been waiting for you to realize you need new things, but last night, when I saw how lovely you looked in your ballgown I decided to take matters into my own hands. Do you mind?"

Liana looked at the beautifully dressed woman, wearing perfectly matched pearls and a green suit that probably cost more than Liana had made in a month...or two. She knew that Fatima was only being kind. Considering how her grandson had married his new wife and the potential for scandal, the queen was taking it all very well. Liana was grateful for the offer of help and friendship.

She smiled. "Yes, I'm overwhelmed, but I'm not the least bit offended. I wouldn't have known where to start with clothes." She looked around the room. "Although I have to admit I would have begun with a little less stock to go through."

Fatima waved her hand. "It will be fun to try on everything. Go put on some undergarments, including pantyhose. While you're doing that, I'll sort. It's better to try on all of one kind of thing at a time. Day dresses and suits, cocktail dresses, then ballgowns." She raised her dark eyebrows slightly as she smiled a slightly wicked smile. "I might have even brought along a few daring nightgowns...if you're interested."

Liana felt herself blush. She had a feeling that everyone in the palace knew where Malik had spent the night. "We'll, um, do those last."

"Of course."

Four hours later Liana was exhausted but happy. She'd gone through all the clothes and most of the shoes. She now had a wardrobe fit for a princess, although according to Fatima, she needed dozens more things.

"We might not be as well known as the British royal family," Fatima said as she sipped her tea, "but we do still find ourselves photographed for tabloids and magazines. Never forget you have a duty to be as lovely and well-groomed as possible. As Malik's wife, you need to present yourself in such a way as to make the people of El Bahar proud. Young girls will pin pictures of you on their walls and women will copy what you wear."

Liana shook her head and leaned back into the chair. Dozens of open shoeboxes were scattered around her on the floor. She hadn't known there were so many styles in existence, let alone ever thought she would have them all in her living room. And the purses. She'd been the kind of woman who had a dark bag for winter and a lighter bag for summer. Now she had more than she could count.

"I can't imagine anyone hanging a picture of me anywhere," she admitted. "This is all so strange and more than a little frightening."

"You were fine last night," Fatima reminded her. "You held your own with the King of Bahania."

"Beginner's luck," Liana insisted. "We mostly talked about Bethany and her love of Arabian horses."

"Not luck." Fatima stared at her intently. Despite helping Liana get in and out of nearly a hundred different outfits, Fatima looked as fresh and relaxed as she had when she'd arrived that morning. "Some people can spend a lifetime traveling in royal circles and still never get it right."

Liana wondered if she was talking about Iman. If she'd known the queen better, she might have asked. Instead, she shifted the conversation to a safer topic. "Malik does well. I suppose it's because he was born to the job."

"Perhaps," Fatima agreed. "If nothing else, he's had plenty of practice." She sipped her tea and eyed Liana.

"Did he tell you how he was taken away from his mother when he was only four?"

"I'd heard." Her heart still ached for the lonely little boy he must have been. "His father raised him after that."

Fatima nodded. "I never agreed, but my son refused to listen. After all, he'd been taken from me when he'd been that age. I had fought with my husband about the practice, but the old ways can be difficult to change." Her gaze turned speculative. "I suspect you wouldn't allow such a thing."

Liana was shocked. "Allow my child to be taken away from me when he was four, simply because he was one day going to be king? No. I wouldn't let anyone do it."

"Malik is very stubborn. What if he fought you?"

Liana set her jaw. "I mean no disrespect, Queen Fatima, but I find the practice inhuman and wrong. Malik might be the Crown Prince, but he doesn't frighten me. I would not submit to that kind of tradition."

The older woman sighed with pleasure. "I'm glad. I admire your strength and determination. It took me many years to learn to assert myself, and, by the time I did, it was too late for Givon. And his mother wasn't very strong at all, so she never fought her husband. So Malik was taken away and expected to be a man from the time he was four.

"I still remember when he fell and broke his arm for the first time. He cried from the pain. His father was gone, but one of the ministers found him and humiliated him for his girlish tears." Her mouth twisted in remembered anger. "Those were his exact words. *Girlish tears.* He scolded Malik for the weakness and locked him in his room for the rest of the day. It was only the next morning that he finally took the child to a doctor to get the bone set."

She set her cup on the table. "Fortunately Givon agreed the man had gone too far, and he was relieved of his position. Still, it wasn't enough. No one comforted Malik. I tried to go with him to the doctor, but I was not allowed. That night I sat in the hallway outside his room and wished I could hold him close." She pressed her lips together.

"I can't imagine what that was like," Liana said grimly, knowing that she would have torn through the door if someone had tried to keep her from Bethany.

"That is why you are so right for Malik. When you have a son, you will be there to remind Malik of his past and to help him find a new way...a different way...to raise a Crown Prince."

Liana didn't know what to say. She hadn't made up her mind yet as to what she was going to do. While last night had given her reason to think that she and Malik might have a chance of making a marriage between them work, she wasn't sure she wanted to be a part of the royal family.

Fatima rose to her feet. "Enough about the past. We have a glorious future to celebrate. Now that you've chosen your clothes, I'll have the others sent back." She smiled. "Rihana can move your new things for you."

Liana frowned. "Move them? I don't need her help for that. I can carry them into the bedroom myself."

"Don't be silly. You don't need to carry your things across the palace. Without help, it would take too many trips."

At first Liana didn't understand what the other woman was saying. Then her meaning sank in. Fatima thought she was moving into Malik's rooms rather than staying here.

"Fatima, I appreciate all your help and your confidences today,'' she began gently. ''I hope you'll understand when I tell you nothing has changed. Malik married me against my will and I'm not sure how I feel about that. I don't know what's going to happen between us and until I do, I think it's important for Bethany and myself to stay in these rooms.''

Fatima stiffened. ''You can still say that? After what I told you?''

Liana felt small and ungrateful. She'd never meant to make the queen angry with her. ''Everything is so complicated,'' she began. ''I have a lot to think about.''

''I see.'' Dark eyes met her own. ''I thought you had realized that Malik was worth fighting for. Obviously I was wrong. Forgive me for taking up your time and boring you with stories from his past.''

Tears sprang to Liana's eyes. ''Fatima, please don't be like this. I don't want to be estranged from you.''

''It seems we have no choice. I love my grandson. I thought you were on your way to loving him as well. I thought you would be the one to see past the distance he always keeps to the man underneath. But I was wrong about you.''

''What do you expect from me? When I first got here Malik practically kidnapped me to keep me at the palace, and then he tricked me into marriage.''

Fatima's mouth was a thin disapproving line. ''Yes, I can see how his determination to have you in his life would be distressing. You prefer men who can walk away from their family without a second thought.''

The low blow landed squarely on her pride. She didn't know how Fatima had found out about Chuck—probably from Bethany—but it didn't matter.

''You're not being fair,'' Liana said. ''I know that Malik is a much better man than Chuck. I just have to be sure.''

"I might not have been able to protect him when he was a child," Fatima told her coldly. "I know now that I should have fought my son on that point. Nor was I able to protect him from the horror of his first marriage. But you can be sure I will not let anyone else destroy him."

"I would never do that."

Fatima glared at her. "What do you think leaving him will do?"

*Chapter Fourteen*

Much as she tried, Liana couldn't get Fatima's words out of her head. She felt that the queen was blaming her for wanting to be sure that her marriage to Malik was the right thing for both of them. But the older woman either wouldn't or couldn't see her side of things.

Their unfriendly parting made Liana restless, and she paced in the luxurious suite until she felt as if she knew every square foot of marble flooring by heart. Time passed slowly. She kept glancing at the clock, but even the approaching late afternoon wasn't going to make any difference. Bethany was staying at school until dinner so she could work on a special project with two new friends and their teacher, so she was all alone, with only her memories and her conscience for company.

Was Fatima right? Would her leaving hurt Malik? Did he care about her? How on earth was she supposed to be able to figure that out? The man wasn't overly forthcoming with his feelings. And what did *she* think of him? While he could be charming and a pleasant companion, he was also dictatorial and demanding. She paused by the French doors and touched the cool glass. On the other hand, he was a sweetheart with her daughter and an incredible lover. The tiny glimpses she'd had into the workings of his mind told her he was both intelligent and incredibly isolated. He'd held himself apart for so long, she wondered if that would ever change. Was he capable of an emotionally intimate relationship, and did she want to stay if he wasn't?

Once again she had more questions than answers. Last night had been wonderful. Not just the sex, but before. She'd actually had a good time at the state dinner, even though she'd been terrified. She and Malik had worked well together—they had the potential to be a good team. She sensed that he desperately needed someone on his side—someone he could depend on and trust.

She stared at the beautiful ocean in the distance. Maybe she was going about this all wrong, she thought suddenly. Maybe instead of figuring out what she wanted, which was impossible because she didn't have enough information, she should figure out what Malik wanted. Did he want emotional depth in his relationship? Was he looking for a surrogate daughter and easy sex, but little else? Her decision depended somewhat on his expectations.

"There's only one way to find out," she told herself and quickly left the room.

This time the journey to his office was relatively simple. She remembered where to turn and soon found herself once again facing the imperious Zachary, who gazed at her with faint disapproval.

"You didn't make an appointment yesterday," he said

by way of greeting. "And the prince is just as busy today. I'm afraid you can't see him."

She leaned forward, bracing her hands on the desk and bringing her face to within inches of the secretary's. "I am Princess Liana, wife of the Crown Prince, and if I want to see my husband, I will. You may either announce me or get out of my way. Those are your choices."

Zachary flushed. "I'm sure there's no reason to be rude."

"Then don't be."

She straightened and headed for the closed door on her left. If Malik wasn't in there, she would keep opening doors until she found him. She might not be sure what was going to happen with her marriage, but while she was here she was not going to let anyone push her around.

"You can't go in there," Zachary said as he hurried to get in front of her. They reached the door at the same time. The secretary threw himself against the wood and glared at Liana.

They were about the same height and Liana was fully prepared to take the man on. She was confused and tired and feeling more than a little lost in her current situation. Her husband was an enigma, her grandmother-in-law no longer approved of her, and she had to worry that any decisions she made about her personal life were going to have international ramifications.

"Get out of my way," she ordered.

Just then the door swung open. Malik stood in the opening looking tall and handsome and annoyed. Liana swallowed, half-afraid he was going to take Zachary's side. Instead he turned his attention to her and smiled.

"Have you come to see me?" he asked, sounding pleased.

She nodded. "I don't have an appointment, so that seems to be a problem."

"No problem." He took her hand and drew her past the secretary. "This is Princess Liana. She is always welcome and you will interrupt me whenever she asks you to. I don't care who I'm with. Do you understand?"

Zachary's flush deepened. He nodded, then gave them both a slight bow.

Malik ushered her into his office, which was nearly as nice as the king's had been. She had a brief impression of a huge desk and bookcases before he led her to a corner grouping of low sofas. She settled on one of the cushions and Malik sat next to her.

"He's an annoying little man," she said, motioning to the now-closed door.

Malik squeezed her hand. "I agree. However, if there was a way to organize the sands of the desert, Zachary would find it. He's most efficient, so I put up with his pretensions. However, I will not have him insulting you."

The tone of possessiveness made her knees go weak. Just being this close to Malik, taking in the freshly shaven jaw and the way his suit emphasized his strength, made her want to throw herself at him and beg him to take her. Around him she felt wildly alive. And safe. As if he would always take care of things. Which was insane. She could take care of herself, thank you very much. Still, the feeling lingered, and she found herself wanting to move closer to him.

"Thank you for last night," he said.

She smiled even as she felt a faint heat on her cheeks. "Yes, well, it was amazing. Thank you."

"We do well together. Not just in bed," he added. "I thought we were well matched at the dinner."

His comments mirrored her own thoughts. She stared

at him, at his dark hair and the strong line of his mouth. Centuries of wisdom seemed to glow in his eyes. He had a history, both recent and ancient, that she couldn't possibly understand. Their lives had nothing in common. Yet she felt as if she understood him. She wanted him and liked him. She cared about him. Which meant it wouldn't be very difficult for her to fall in love with him.

She pulled her hand free of his gentle hold and laced her fingers together on her lap. "What do you want from me?" she asked. "Is our relationship about sex? Are you looking for a friend and a companion? What do you expect from me? What is my role in all of this? I can't make any decisions until I understand your goals."

Malik was silent for a long time. Liana studied his face, trying to figure out what he was thinking. But she didn't have a clue. Finally, he leaned close and touched her cheek.

"You have slender ankles."

She blinked. "What did you say?"

He picked up her hand again and held it. "I can wrap my fingers around your wrist with room to spare. You are a delicate flower of a woman, yet so very strong inside." Then he kissed her palm.

"Malik, what are you talking about?"

He stared intently into her eyes. "Your ankles. They are delicate. I imagine them, seeing them, touching them."

Something was very wrong, she thought through a haze of confusion. "I'm trying to have a serious conversation about our relationship and you want to talk about my bones?"

Warm fingers stroked her knuckles. "All of you is wonderful."

If she didn't know better, she would think he was

drunk...or deranged. Was this an El Baharian thing? Maybe they were having a culture clash, and he thought this was how to woo a woman. "I don't want to talk about body parts right now. What about us?"

"Your skin is the color of cream."

She jerked her hand free. "You're not making any sense."

"I want you to know how much I cherish you."

"Cherish is all fine and good, but what do you want from me?"

His adoring expression changed into something unreadable. He released her hand and straightened. While he didn't turn cold, he definitely withdrew from her. At first she felt hurt. As if all his compliments had been some weird game. But then she knew with a clarity she couldn't explain that Malik wasn't playing—he was protecting. Her question had terrified him and he didn't want her to know.

The truth appeared without warning. It burst into her mind like flowers blooming in spring—all bright and beautiful and tempting. Was she right? Could she truly believe?

"You want me to stay," she breathed. "You want me to fall in love with you."

He rose to his feet. "Of course," he said curtly. "What did you think? Now if you'll excuse me, I have a meeting in five minutes."

Still stunned by Malik's revelation, Liana didn't know what to make of an invitation to dine with the family that night. She was more than a little nervous about seeing Fatima again and wondered if she was going to be lectured by the king and Malik's brothers. But instead she and Bethany were made welcome in the private dining room and spent a pleasant evening enjoying their host's company. Afterward, Malik walked them both to their suite.

"I'm going to bed now," Bethany said as soon as they entered the living room. "I'm really, really tired, and I'm sure I'll be asleep in five minutes."

She gave them each a hug and a good-night kiss, then skipped down the hall and into her room. When the door shut, Liana sighed.

"My daughter is many things, but she's not subtle."

Malik stared after her. "She is a wonderful child. You're very lucky to have her."

"I know, but thank you for noticing." She shifted uncomfortably, not sure if she should invite him to sit down or simply throw herself into his arms. "I appreciate that you've taken so much time with her."

He turned his steady, dark gaze on her. "I do it because I want to. For no other reason."

She smiled. "That's what makes it so meaningful. Bethany thinks the world of you." She pressed her lips together, then decided this wasn't the time to explain to Malik that her daughter thought of him as a surrogate father. It was too late to prevent Bethany from being hurt if they left El Bahar. Better for her to enjoy her time here. And who knows. Things might work out between Malik and herself. Speaking of which...

She cleared her throat. "What were your plans for the rest of the evening?"

He stepped close and cupped her face. "You are a light in the evening sky."

"Huh?"

"All other beauty pales before your radiance."

"Malik, you're being weird again. It makes me nervous."

He kissed her mouth. "I want you to know how I appreciate your womanly charms."

She felt herself melting against him. "You have some impressive male charms, as well." She wrapped her arms around his waist. "I don't think Bethany will be asleep in five minutes, but it's not going to take her too long to settle down. Would you like a drink while we wait?"

He brushed his lips against hers again…slowly, seductively. His tongue moved against hers and made her gasp. She was already on fire. Heat filled her and she felt her panties growing damp as her body readied for his invasion. The thought of having to wait even five minutes was physically painful.

"I will dream of your slender ankles, your pale skin and the sweet scent of your essence," he said, stepping back.

"Would you please speak in English?"

Malik shrugged regretfully. "Sorry, Liana. I'm not staying here tonight. You are my wife and when we next make love, it will be in my room, in my bed and with your daughter sleeping down the hall."

Irritation joined the passion. It made for an interesting combination. "You're blackmailing me."

"I told you I wanted you to move into my suite. It's where you belong."

Her gaze narrowed. "You expect me to give in on everything. What do I get in return?"

He didn't answer. Instead he turned and left.

She stood staring after him, then grabbed a pillow from the sofa and tossed it at the closed door. The childish gesture didn't make her feel any better, nor did it make the situation any more clear. Malik's sudden flowery compliments were very strange. And she hated his insistence that she move into his rooms. What was that all about?

She paced the room, something she'd been doing a lot of these days, and knew she wouldn't be falling asleep any time soon. She was too aroused, too ready for her lover' touch. Damn the man. She could only hope he was a uncomfortable as she.

"Do it," a little voice in her head whispered. "Woul it be so terrible to go live with him?"

But that was too much like giving in. She was alway the one who bent in this relationship. Just once she wante him to be the one to give in.

"You're making Mommy really crazy," Bethany con fided later the next week as she and Malik walked bac from the stables.

Malik wasn't sure if she offered good or bad new "How do I make her crazy?"

The nine-year-old removed her riding hat and smoothe her blond braids. She smiled up at him. "She says we ea with you every night and all you do is talk about im impersonal stuff." She stumbled over the word, then con tinued. "And when you're alone you keep talking abou her slender ankles and her porcelain skin. She says she beginning to feel like the doll of the month on a cable shopping channel."

Her small nose wrinkled. "Do you really like her an kles?"

"I'm sure they're very nice," he said. "But they're no my favorite part."

"Then why do you talk about them all the time?"

They walked into the main garden outside the rear of the palace. Malik led them to one of the many ston benches along the path and sat down. Bethany settled ne to him.

Their daily rides had darkened her skin to the color of

oney and added a dozen or so freckles to her cheeks.
he still had an expression of wide-eyed innocence that
nade him want to hold her close and protect her from
verything bad. He couldn't imagine what his life had
een like before this amazing child had burst into his
world and changed it all around.

"I took your advice," he admitted, faintly embarrassed
y the fact. "After I married your mother, you suggested
nat I find a way to make her less angry with me. You
nentioned those romance novels she's always reading, so
picked up a few." He shook his head. "The men in
nose are always talking about the women's slender an-
les."

"That's pretty dumb," Bethany said.

"I agree. But I thought it was worth a try."

"Try something else," the child offered. "The ankle
ning isn't working. Besides, she's also worried about the
act that you two have nothing in common and that you're
xactly the wrong kind of man for her." She glanced
round as if to make sure they were alone, then lowered
er voice to a confidential whisper. "I think she's kinda
cared about being a royal princess. She was telling me
nat it's fun to read about and dream about, but living that
fe is very different. She doesn't want to mess up and
mbarrass you or the country."

"She could never do that. Your mother is very poised
n every situation."

Liana putting a foot wrong was the least of his worries.
Ie was more concerned that she wouldn't give their mar-
iage a chance. Time was slipping through his fingers, and
e didn't know if he was any closer to making her fall in
ove with him than he'd been when she'd first arrived. All
is compliments didn't seem to be helping. Not making
ove with her was slowly killing him, but he was deter-

mined to bring her into his bed. His gut told him that i
he could get her into his quarters he would be that muc
closer to keeping her in his life.

But not being with her meant that he couldn't sleep
He had trouble concentrating while he worked, which ha
never happened to him before. He needed Liana not t
leave. Somehow he had to convince her to stay past th
one-month deadline. But how? What words could he use
All his life he'd been taught to be strong and in contro
but no one had taken the time to show him how to get
woman to do what he wanted.

"Malik, now that you and Mommy are married, are yo
my new dad?"

Bethany asked the question without looking at him. Sh
turned her riding hat over and over in her hands as if
were the most interesting thing she'd ever seen.

When she was riding alongside him, her braids blowin
behind her and her seat so comfortable and relaxed on he
mount, he forgot that she was just a little girl. But now
with her sitting next to him and obviously afraid of hi
answer, she seemed small and defenseless.

He put a hand on her shoulder. "Your father back i
America will always be your real father. Nothing ca
change that and no one will take his place. If you're ask
ing if we're now a part of each other's lives, the answe
is yes."

She raised her head, and he saw tears filling her blu
eyes. Eyes so like her mother's. "But what happens if w
leave? Mommy swears we're still going at the end of th
month and if that happens, you'll forget all about me."

A single tear spilled onto her cheek. It was as if she'
cut him with a knife. The pain sliced through him, makin
his muscles stiffen.

Slowly, he brushed away that tear and the one that fo

owed. He looked at her sweet face and knew that while Bethany might be the biological child of another man, she would always be the daughter of his heart. Because if Liana left him, he would not marry again. He couldn't enter into an empty union of convenience now...not even for his beloved El Bahar.

"Did you know that your name has a meaning in Arabic?" he asked.

She sniffed, then shook her head. "What is it?"

"In that language, Bethany means *daughter of the Lord*. In time I will rule El Bahar, which makes me lord of this country. So in some ways, that makes you my daughter, too." He pulled her close and hugged her. "Don't worry, child. I will never forget you."

Bethany clung to him. "I don't want to go, Malik," she breathed. "Don't make us go."

"You are welcome as long as you would like."

She raised her head and looked at him. "I love you."

Her words completed the job her tears had begun. The knife cut clear through to his soul and all his life's blood began to seep away.

He didn't say anything, he simply held her close. As much as he wanted her to care about him, he didn't want her hurt when she left. And she would be hurt. He should have seen that before, but he hadn't. As for loving her back...he shook off the thought. Love was not a part of his life. Long ago he'd vowed never to love anyone. Nothing had happened to change his mind. He wouldn't love Bethany and he would never love Liana. Still, he promised himself that he would find a way to make them stay.

"If I kill a prince, will they cut off my head?" Liana demanded as she paced her sister-in-law's living room.

Dora laughed. "I suspect they might. If they got the

chance. However, Malik is much loved by his people, and you'd probably be killed by a vicious mob instead.''

''Gee, thanks.'' Liana stopped in front of the chair opposite the sofa and rested her hands on top of the back.

''I've been living with an El Baharian prince for some time now,'' Dora said. ''They are difficult men. Passionate and incredibly loyal, which helps, but never easy. They have the normal annoyances inherent in all men, plus the idiosyncrasies that go along with being a member of a royal family. It's not a life for the faint of heart.''

Dora sat on a pale yellow sofa that brought out the gold in her brown hair. She was as elegant and regal as Fatima, and just as well dressed. Liana had heard the stories of her marriage to Khalil and it was hard to reconcile the princess in front of her with the image of an abandoned executive secretary standing alone and jobless in an airport.

''But I think it's worth it,'' she added. ''Khalil is the most wonderful man I've ever known. I would change the tide for him if he asked. As he would for me.''

Liana nodded. She'd seen the love between husband and wife with both Dora and Khalil, and Heidi and Jamal. Sometimes when she and Malik dined with the other two couples, she felt a sharp stab of envy for their happiness. She wanted that, too. A caring relationship with a man who loved her as much as she loved him.

''I don't know what he's feeling,'' Liana confessed. ''I can't figure out why he wants me to stay.''

''Does it matter?'' Dora asked. ''Isn't it enough that he does? He chose *you,* Liana. Out of all the women in the world, he picked you.''

''I know and because I can't figure out why, it's driving me crazy.''

''I do empathize with your position, but I'm also selfish. I think you're wonderful for Malik and I don't want you to leave.'' Dora spread out her hands, palm up. ''What do you want?'' she asked. ''What isn't Malik doing right?''

''I don't know.'' Malik was doing a lot of things right. If she ignored the fact that he'd tricked her into marriage, he was being a real sweetie. He was charming and attentive whenever they spent time together. If he seemed a little obsessed with her ankles, it wasn't such a big flaw. He still wanted her to move into his rooms and wouldn't sleep with her until she did—which she hated but understood.

As for what she wanted…she remained clueless and completely confused.

''I'm going to go talk with him,'' Liana said and glanced at her watch. It was nearly two in the afternoon. He was probably still in his office.

''I can't wait to hear the outcome of this conversation,'' Dora called after her. ''I want the details later.''

Liana was still smiling when she marched into the foyer of Malik's office. Zachary took one look at her face, then buzzed his boss and announced her.

Rather than waiting to be let in, Liana walked into Malik's office and closed the door behind her. Her husband raised his eyebrows.

''An unexpected treat,'' he said.

''Yeah, yeah, lay off the ankles this time, okay?''

''As you wish.''

He was so polite all the time, she thought grudgingly. And handsome and attentive and emotionally distant and complicated and good in bed.

''I thought you wanted this marriage to work,'' she said.

''I do.''

"But you won't sleep with me."

"Not until you share my bed."

"And I can't just come in for a few hours and then leave?"

He didn't bother answering that one.

She sighed. "Fine. Bethany and I will move our things in this afternoon." Her gaze narrowed. "But don't think for a second that I'm going to beg you to make love with me."

A slow, male smile tugged at the corners of his mouth. "I promise you won't have to beg."

## Chapter Fifteen

Liana decided to make the move on her own. She didn't
want to get one of the servants to help and have the news
spread all over the palace. Not that it was going to be a
secret for very long. There were too many clothes for her
to transfer everything in a single trip, but it was easier to
carry over armfuls of clothes than to pack them all up and
then unpack.

As she draped dresses over her arms, she found herself
both excited and disappointed. Somehow she'd hoped for
more than a teasing acceptance from Malik. After all, her
giving in was a big deal. She'd promised herself that he
was going to be the one to bend this time, and he hadn't.
What did that say about her strength of character? Or did
it mean she was realistic?

She hated that she spent so much of her time second-
guessing herself. Before meeting Malik, she'd always
known the right thing to do, and now everything was up-

side down. But a part of her was thrilled at the thought of being with Malik again. As much as she might want to tell herself she needed to live with him to give their marriage a fair chance, she couldn't deny the anticipation that raced through her at the thought of being able to see him and touch him whenever she wanted.

She paused at the entrance to his private rooms and realized belatedly she didn't have a key. Not all the doors were kept locked inside the palace, but his suite might be. However, she tried the knob and found it turned easily. After shifting the clothes to a more comfortable position, she pushed open the door and stepped inside.

She hadn't thought much about what his suite would look like. From what she could tell, they were all variations on a theme. Living quarters faced the ocean and were large and spacious. She'd expected sofas and chairs, a small dining area and artwork reflecting his taste. She found all that in the room, but the elegant furnishings weren't what caught her attention.

Instead she looked around in amazement at the roses decorating every surface. White and pink and peach and deep red. Yellow and plum and shimmery silver. They stood in bowls and vases; their petals littered the floor and their fragrance invaded her senses.

Malik stood in the center of the room, his expression as unreadable as usual. But she sensed his tension, his need for her to be pleased.

There was a chair by the door and she set down her clothes. "It's been less than a half hour since I told you I was moving in," she said, then waved at the roses. "How is this possible?"

"I work quickly."

"You couldn't have had the flowers here all this time."

"No. They've been in a large refrigerator. They've

been replaced two or three times while I waited for you to make up your mind.''

It was a silly, expensive, romantic gesture and she didn't know if she should thank him, burst into tears or tell him not to waste that kind of money on her. Instead she walked over the petal-littered floor until she stood less than a foot in front of him.

"Will I ever understand you?'' she asked.

"Given time.''

"Do you understand me?''

He smiled. "You are a woman. You and your kind will always be a mystery to mere mortal men.''

He reached into his jacket pocket and drew out a small jeweler's box. Her breath caught as he opened the velvet top to show her a brilliant marquise-cut diamond set on a diamond and sapphire band.

"I never gave you a wedding band,'' he said by way of explanation, then slid the ring on to her finger.

"It's beautiful.'' Liana didn't know what else to say. Was she supposed to thank him? A wedding ring. Somehow that made their marriage feel all the more real.

"Be with me,'' he said, gathering her close and kissing her. He pressed his mouth to her lips, then her cheeks, her forehead and finally returned to her mouth.

She felt him shaking in her embrace, as if her being here really mattered to him. All her doubts fell away, as did her questions as to whether she should have given in or not. Need filled her. Not just passion and the desire to be with this man, but a longing to understand him and heal him. To be his haven. She wanted to empty herself into him, to fill him up and take away all his pain.

It was as if her feelings were so large and overwhelming that she couldn't keep them to herself. She kissed him back, opening her mouth and welcoming him, touching him, teasing him, beginning the dance that would bind them together in unforgettable passion.

She reached for his shirt buttons. He shrugged out of his jacket, then stilled her hands.

"Not here," he said. "In my bed. I need you there."

She looked at him. His face was all harsh angles and planes. A muscle twitched by his mouth, and she saw the tremors in his fingers. He was already hard and his arousal pressed against the front of his trousers.

Her power over him humbled her. She wanted to promise that she would never take advantage of her ability to transform him from proud prince to mortal lover. But her throat was too tight for her to speak.

"I need you," she breathed as he led her toward the hallway.

"And I, you."

Without warning he picked her up and carried her into the bedroom. He placed her on the bed and began to remove her clothing. She found herself fumbling first with his buttons, then her own. He pulled her shirt from her slacks and she did the same. She had one shoe on and had lost the other somewhere.

They were kissing and undressing and trying to touch at the same time. She pulled off her blouse and unfastened her bra. He slipped down the lacy cups and began to suckle her breasts. She fumbled with his fly, then drew him out and wrapped both her hands around his silky hard length.

Finally they were naked, and he was pressing himself into her. She was wet and ready. It had been too long— perhaps all of a week, but it felt like a lifetime.

"More," she gasped as he entered her. She drew back her knees.

Malik reached between them. Even as he plunged in

leeper, he rubbed her small center, bringing her immediate pleasure. She screamed out his name and he swallowed the sound with a kiss.

Over and over he drove into her, taking her back to the point of release, making her writhe and beg and gasp. As he neared his own completion, he opened his eyes and stared into her face. She could see to his soul.

Both of their bodies tensed. "My wife," he breathed as the first waves of pleasure swept over him.

"Husband," she managed, then lost herself to one final shuddering release.

Then they were caught up in each other, joining in a timeless union of man and woman. Carried forward on surrender and promise.

After they'd both regained their ability to breathe and had settled under the covers, Liana snuggled close to Malik and rested her head on his shoulder.

"I should have moved in long ago," she teased. "If you'd been clear about what I could expect I might not have fought you so hard."

"I doubt that. You can be very stubborn."

She laughed. "As if I'm alone in that. You were determined to have your way in this."

He looked at her. "I had no choice."

There was always a choice, but she wasn't about to debate that with him. Not now, with her body still pleasantly relaxed and her muscles all liquid and rubbery from the lovemaking.

"Who are you, Malik Khan?" she asked idly as she rubbed her hand over his chest. "You say that in time I'll begin to understand you, but I'm not so sure. Sometimes I feel as if I know everything you're thinking, but other times you're a complete stranger."

"How well do we know anyone?" he asked.

He was being elusive again. She turned so that she lay on her belly, and rested her chin on his chest. He picked up a strand of her hair and rubbed it between his fingers.

"You have lovely hair."

She smiled. "Aren't you going to comment on my ankles?"

"I've decided to let that go."

"Thank you. It was starting to scare me. I was afraid you had a secret foot fetish or something."

"Nothing like that."

She looked at his face. In time, if she stayed, she would get to know every inch of him. She would trace his scars and bumps and curves and muscles until they were as familiar as her own. Together they would create a history that would give them strength through the difficult times. If she stayed.

And if she left? What would happen then?

Liana found she didn't want to think about that. It was too frightening and sad.

"I'm still not sure I know how to be a princess," she said.

"You will learn. Just as I will learn to be a good father to Bethany."

"Doesn't being a father frighten you?"

"Sometimes. I have no experience."

"I get scared, too," she admitted. "When that happens, I just hang on and love her. It's amazing what a full heart can accomplish in a relationship." She pressed her lips together, then decided she might as well take the chance.

"What happens if I fall in love with you?" she asked.

"Then you will stay in El Bahar and be happy as my wife."

She poked him. "Wrong answer, Malik. You're sup-

osed to say that you'll love me back. *Then* I can stay in
El Bahar and be happy as your wife.''

She thought he might tease, as a way to distract her
from talking more about the *l*-word, or change the subject.
Instead he grew serious.

''I am your husband, Liana. I will be faithful to you
and take care of you and any children we may have together. But you must understand I am first and foremost
the Crown Prince of El Bahar. My very best is for my
people. As such I cannot allow myself to be weakened by
emotions such as love. I live for the greater good.''

She stared at him. ''I can't figure out if this is a bad
joke, or if you actually believe what you're saying.''

''I mean what I say. I will be all things to you, but I
will not love you.''

His words slapped against her, and she found herself
scrambling into a sitting position. After pulling up the
sheet to cover her nakedness, she stared at him. ''You
really mean that?''

''Yes.''

Something inside her cried out in pain. She didn't want
it to be like this. She didn't want him to reject her before
they'd even had a chance to make things work.

''And yet you expect me to stay here and love you?''

He looked uncomfortable and would not meet her gaze.
''Loving is not required. A successful marriage is based
on many things, including mutual respect and an honest
desire for the other's happiness. I believe we can build on
that.''

She couldn't take it all in. Did he really think he could
hold himself apart from his feelings so completely? ''You
might be a Crown Prince, Malik, but you're also a man.
You can't command your heart not to love.''

''I have so far, and without much effort.''

She didn't doubt that. His life hadn't exactly made him the poster child for happiness.

"You mentioned an honest desire for the other's happiness. What if the only way I can be happy is for you to love me?"

He rose from the bed. "You are speaking about events that may not occur. I don't wish to discuss all the unlikely possibilities at this time."

She still hurt, and if she let herself think about all he'd said, she knew she would start to cry. "Every time I start to believe we can make this work, you tell me something that makes it impossible."

He stiffened. He stood naked in front of her, and she was able to see all his muscles tense at her words. He moved close and touched her bare shoulder.

"You don't understand," he told her. "I can give you everything. You say you don't want money, position or power, but that's because you haven't experienced them. Your life will be the envy of millions all over the world. You will want for nothing. Bethany will have every opportunity. We can have children of our own. Children who we will help grow to be great leaders. We can begin a dynasty that lasts for a thousand years." His gaze narrowed. "Will you throw all that away because of a few words?"

"They're not just words. They imply a commitment."

"I have committed myself to you. I take you as my future queen. I lay El Bahar at your feet. How can you ask for more?"

When he put it like that, she felt selfish and greedy. Once again he'd completely confused her.

"What about children?" she asked. "I would never agree to raise them the way you were. I wouldn't let you take our oldest son from me when he is four and force him to be a man. A child remains a child until he is ready to be man. No one should interfere with that.''

He sank onto the bed and pulled her close. He was warm and strong and she could feel the steady sound of his heart. ''That is why you must stay,'' he told her. ''Because I don't want that for my children either. I need you, Liana. Stay with me.''

How was she supposed to refuse him when he was like this? She wrapped her arms around him and held him close. But in the back of her mind she heard the faint ticking of the clock. Her month continued to speed by, and she was no closer to knowing what to do than she'd been the first day she'd found out she was married.

''You seem to have settled in well,'' Fatima said a few days later when she joined Liana for lunch.

They sat on the balcony at a small ebony table that had been a gift from a Chinese emperor nearly five hundred years ago. Liana traced the pattern of the flatware and tried to smile. Her mouth curved up on demand, but she had a feeling that she didn't look all that happy.

The older woman leaned forward. ''Are you still angry with me?'' she asked bluntly. ''I was a bit harsh with you before, and I'm sorry for that. I reacted out of disappointment. I thought that you were going to be so good for Malik, and then when I found out you were still thinking of leaving, I was surprised and hurt.''

Liana looked at Fatima. ''Don't be so quick to assume that everything has changed.''

''I don't understand. You're here, living in his rooms. When you two appear in public or with the family, you seem very happy.''

Liana shrugged. ''We are. In a way. I mean...'' She took a sip of her iced tea and sighed. ''In a way everything is going very well between Malik and myself. He's attentive, kind and wonderful with Bethany. He's begun talking about some of his responsibilities with me. He's brilliant about politics, and I'm learning a lot.''

"Givon says that Malik appreciates your opinions," Fatima told her. "He respects you."

"As I respect him." She paused before going on. She and Malik were also making love every night, and that part of their life together was marvelous. Not that she was going to share the details with his grandmother. "I could very easily fall in love with him."

"Then what is the problem?"

Liana drew in a deep breath. "Malik has told me that he will never love me. He believes that the best part of him must be saved for El Bahar, and he won't let himself get tangled up in any serious emotions. So he will care for me and be faithful, but he won't allow himself to love me. I'm assuming he intends that to also encompass our children, should we have any. So how can I stay with a man who vows never to give me the one thing I want?"

Fatima regarded her with dark, wise eyes. "Is love so very important?"

"Isn't it? Chuck and I had infatuation, childish affection and lust. When that wore off, we weren't left with very much."

"All the more reason to be sensible the second time around."

"Sensible," Liana repeated softly. "It's not exactly what every young girl dreams of for her marriage."

"But you are not a young girl. You are a mature woman who has experienced some of life." Fatima touched her glass, but didn't pick it up. "Did it ever occur to you that Malik is deceiving himself? That he speaks

the words because he wants them to be true, not because
they are?''

Liana blinked. ''I hadn't thought of that.''

''Perhaps you should. How much has he told you of
Iman?''

''I know that she's not dead, and that she was unfaithful
to him.'' She shivered. ''I can't imagine how that must
have humiliated him. Malik is a proud man.''

''I believe it was one of the darkest moments of his
life. Not only because everyone knew what had happened
and how his wife had tricked him right here in the palace,
but because in his mind, he'd let down his people. He
couldn't see that her betrayal made him so much more
human in their eyes. He was no longer a young god, but
a real man who could make a mistake. He'd always been
adored, but afterward he became truly loved.''

Liana considered Fatima's words. ''I don't think Malik
sees it that way.''

''He doesn't. He sees only his mistake and he has
vowed it will never happen again.'' Fatima tilted her head.
''Why did he choose you as his wife?''

''I haven't got a clue. It's a question I ask myself all
the time.''

''Perhaps you should ask Malik instead. Perhaps you
should think about Iman and of how he would make sure
he never repeated that kind of mistake again. We are all
products of our past. Malik's history has had an influence
on him.''

Liana thought she understood what the other woman
was saying. ''But it's different with Malik. He never loved
Iman.''

''How do you know?''

''He told me.''

''What else would he say?''

That had not occurred to Liana. If Malik had loved his wife, or if he'd been allowing himself to soften towards her and then she'd betrayed him, he would have been destroyed inside. He would have questioned his judgment and would have vowed to never be caught that way again.

He'd lived so much of his life emotionally alone. Oh, there were plenty of people around him, but no one special to hold him and look out for him. No one who didn't demand but instead gave.

"Perhaps he needs to be shown that he's found a safe place again," Fatima said softly. "I believe it is in both you and your daughter to heal his bruised heart and allow him to open himself again. If he were to *be* loved, he might allow himself *to* love. Look at his actions, not his words. Then think about what you see there. Don't be hasty, Liana. Be very sure on this. Isn't he worth that at least?"

Once again the queen had given Liana plenty to think about. Later that afternoon she stood on one of the high balconies on the north end of the palace and looked out over the vast land that blended into the desert.

The sea was to the south of the palace and the city stretched out on both the east and west sides of the royal grounds. But behind the carefully cultivated gardens was only wilderness. Liana didn't know how much land the Khan family owned, but she knew their property stretched for miles.

From where she stood she had a clear view of the riding trails and the stable. Two specks appeared in the distance. In time they would show themselves to be her daughter and Malik, out for their afternoon ride.

Despite his busy schedule, he always made time for Bethany. Sometimes they rode in the morning and some-

mes after she returned from school, but at least six days
ut of seven found them together on horseback.

She'd been wrong about him, Liana thought to herself.
he'd accused him of using her daughter to get to her,
ut that hadn't been his plan at all. For reasons that didn't
nake sense, his devotion to her child seemed easy and
natural. Why did he do it? Liana loved her daughter with
ll her heart and believed her to be bright and charming,
ut she was still only nine. Hardly a sophisticated companion for someone like Malik. Yet he sought Bethany
ut, and seemed to find pleasure in the relationship for its
own sake.

Fatima's words—that she and Bethany had the power
o heal Malik's heart—came to her. Was that true? And
f it was, how on earth was she going to walk away from
him? No woman in the world could resist such a chal-
enge. To heal a man such as Malik would be the most
extraordinary work of her life.

She glanced around at the seldom-used balcony garden.
She'd found it last week and had begun to rearrange the
potted plants and trees until they created a secluded private sanctuary just as she'd done on the rooftop garden.
Her latent interest in gardening and decorating had begun
o assert itself, and she'd found herself wondering if there
was a detailed inventory of the treasures in the palace. If
not, it was a job she would enjoy. She'd seen the storerooms and knew that there were hundreds of wonders
here. Different antiques needed to be rotated in and out
of the public rooms so that all could enjoy them. And
what about preservation and restoration? Had anyone seen
o that?

She knew what was happening to her. She was slowly
making a life for herself here at the palace. It was a dan-

gerous thing to do, because she still didn't know how to handle her future. Was she staying?

She turned back to the view and saw that Bethany and Malik were already at the stables. Malik dismounted, then helped Bethany down. Her daughter surprised her by throwing her arms around the prince. Malik surprised her even more by hugging her daughter back. There was something comfortable and familiar about their actions, as if they'd been performed dozens of times before. Actions not words, she thought, as Fatima had instructed her.

Her chest tightened as hope filled her. Was Fatima right? Could she and Bethany heal Malik to the point where he would admit he loved them?

She sighed. Who was this man who had tricked her into marriage? For a long time she'd assumed he was so arrogant that he'd just assumed he would get his way. But perhaps it was something else entirely. Was it possible that he'd acted to hide a fear of losing something he wanted or needed?

Liana sensed she was on the verge of discovering a very important truth. She thought about Malik's childhood and how desperately alone he'd been. She thought about Imar and her betrayal. Both had taught Malik not to depend on anyone but himself. He couldn't risk making a mistake about relationships, so he no longer invested in them.

But didn't he still have the same needs as other men?

Her fingers laced together in front of her waist and she drew in a deep breath. He was afraid of being rejected again. Of being offered something he needed to survive then having it taken away. She would have to show him that she really was a safe haven for him, and that he never had to worry about being alone again.

## Chapter Sixteen

"Why did you choose me?" she asked later that night when they were alone in bed. They'd just finished making love, and she lay in Malik's arms, safe and content.

"You are my wife. It would be inappropriate for me to make love with anyone else."

She smiled and touched his lower lip. "That's not what I mean and you know it. Why did you marry me? You could have picked someone entirely different. Someone more appropriate."

He settled back on the pillow and tucked his hand under his head. "You were the one I wanted," he said. "At first there was just an attraction I hadn't felt before, and I responded to that. Later, as I got to know you and your daughter, I realized you had all the characteristics necessary to make both a good queen and a good mother."

He looked at her. "Bethany is a wonderful child. You

love her deeply and would do anything to protect her. wanted that for my children.''

She nodded. His words made sense. After all, look wha had happened to him.

''Also,'' he continued, ''you weren't impressed with the fact that I was a prince. I couldn't imagine spending the rest of my life with someone in awe of me.''

''Instead you find yourself with someone who will always tell you exactly what she's thinking.''

''I don't mind. If I don't agree with you, I simply won' listen.''

She wanted to laugh, but she knew he was telling the truth. She thought about what he'd said about why he'd picked her. Was her being a good mother to Bethany also about her capacity to love? Had he chosen a woman with a big heart so that he could find a place for himself there?

She wanted to ask, but knew he wouldn't answer. A least not honestly. Malik kept his emotions firmly in check. However, she wasn't like that. Her feelings spilled over, even when she didn't want them to. Right now, she knew that while Malik might be arrogant and annoying at times, he'd somehow found that place he'd been looking for in her heart.

She'd figured out the truth that afternoon when she'd watched him with her daughter. Now she reached up and kissed his mouth. ''I can't imagine a world without you, Malik. I love you, and if you want me to stay with you, I will.''

She waited expectantly for his excited reaction. A smile hovered at the corners of her mouth.

But instead of whooping or gathering her close and beginning to make love with her, he simply nodded.

''I'm pleased,'' he told her. ''You've made the right decision. Except for telling my immediate family, there shouldn't be any changes in our lives. We will have to talk about when we're going to start our family. I would like to begin that process as soon as possible.''

He continued talking about children and a belated honeymoon and a ceremony to give her a title in her own right. Liana listened, but none of the words made sense. Instead she felt icy claws sliding all over her, and she couldn't help shivering in response.

Had she been wrong about Malik? While she hadn't expected a heartfelt declaration in return, she'd thought he would at least seem happy.

"Don't you care?" she blurted out. "Doesn't any of this matter to you?"

He frowned. "Of course. I told you I'm pleased."

"Gee. If you're pleased about this, imagine how excited you'll be when the dry cleaning returns on time."

He sat up in bed and looked at her. "Why are you upset? I want you to stay and you're staying. We have details to discuss. If you would prefer we can talk about them later."

"I don't care when we talk about them," she said, her voice thick with disappointment and anger. "I want you to be happy that I told you I love you. I want you to say you're thrilled and pleased, and that you were afraid I would leave and you would be alone. I want to know this matters, that I'm not some interchangeable part in your life."

"We have been over this before," he said patiently. "You are my wife. I am your husband. I have great respect for you, and I have honored you by taking you as my future queen."

She scrambled to her knees and glared at him. "Not good enough. I have given in on every point, Malik. I'll live on your land and be your wife. I'll learn the customs and raise our children to be good and wise rulers. But you and I don't have an arrangement, we have a marriage. It's not about duty and position, it's about loving each other. You've won every single battle, but you're not winning this one. I matter to you. I know it and you know it, and by God, you're going to tell me.''

His expression tightened and turned unreadable. "I will not love you.''

"You're afraid to admit it. Maybe just to me, or maybe to yourself as well. I understand that you had a lot of horrible things happen to you. I'll even give you time to heal and to learn to trust me more. But you will have to bend on this one eventually.''

"Never.''

This time she was the one to stand up and look down at him. She crossed her arms over her bare chest. "It's very simple. If you love me back, I'll change the world for you. If you don't, you'll lose me forever. I won't go away, but I'll die a little inside until the very heart of me is gone.''

"Women put too much stock in emotions,'' he told her curtly. "I'll be a good husband. Measure me by my actions, not my words.''

Fatima had said almost the same thing, and for a while Liana had believed it would be enough. But now she knew it wasn't.

Malik's foul mood lasted more than a week. He didn't understand women or their constant need for reassurance.

"Why won't she give in?'' he asked Bethany as they walked to the stable.

But the nine-year-old refused to take his side. "Mommy says she needs to know that she can trust you to always be there for us.''

"Of course I'll be here. Where else would I go?"

Bethany stopped in front of the stable door and looked up at him. Shadows darkened the skin under her big, blue eyes. She suddenly looked small and impossibly fragile.

"Malik, you gotta tell her you love her," she insisted. Her rosebud-shaped mouth pressed into a thin line. "Mommies and daddies always say they love each other. That's how they have babies together. If you don't love Mommy, she can't have a baby brother or sister for me. Don't you want that?"

"Of course. But loving her or not isn't relevant to that issue."

Bethany shook her head mutinously. "You gotta love people, Malik." She paused, then frowned. Her face paled. "I love you. Don't you love me back?"

She'd stabbed him with a large sword, and there was nothing he could do to get out of the way. "Bethany," he said, dropping to one knee and pulling her close. "You are very special to me. You know that. I enjoy our time together, and I'm very glad to have you in my life."

For the first time since he'd met her, Bethany pushed him away. Tears spilled from her eyes and her mouth quivered. "You *don't*," she accused, her voice cracking with pain. "I thought you loved me. I thought you were different from my daddy, but you're just like him. You don't love me either."

Before he could stop her, she turned and ran away. He heard her sobs and started to go after her, but then he stopped. What was he going to say?

He stood in the center of the path for several minutes, then stormed into the palace and headed for the harem. Once there, he pounded on the golden doors until his grandmother opened them.

"It's just a word," he growled. "They're all insane,

expecting me to talk of flowers and love. I'm a prince. I don't have time for this. You must speak to them and explain the situation.''

Fatima regarded him thoughtfully. "I assume you're speaking of Liana and Bethany?"

"Yes. Liana agreed to stay, then in the next breath demanded that I tell her I love her or I will lose her or some such nonsense. It's been nearly a week, and no matter how I insist, she won't let it go. You have to fix this.''

"Actually, I don't.'' She stepped into the hallway and closed the harem door behind her. "You see, Malik, for a long time I agreed with you. I counseled Liana to see your side and to give in. But now I'm not so sure.'' She traced her pearl necklace with her thumb and forefinger. "I assume she has confessed her feelings.''

He thought about that night more than a week ago when she'd told him she loved him and that she would stay. All his fears had drained away as if they'd never been. He'd been relieved and happy and he'd wanted to lay the world at her feet. The emotions had threatened to overwhelm him. Rather than letting her see that, he'd kept his feelings to himself and had talked of their future. It was safer that way.

"She had indicated she cared for me and was willing to stay.''

Two perfect eyebrows raised slightly. "Cared? Was that her exact word?''

"No,'' he said between gritted teeth. "She said she loved me.''

"Ah. But you don't love her. I can see that might be a problem.''

Love? What did he know of the emotion? He knew that he needed Liana more than was safe or even sane. Without her, he was nothing—an empty shell living in an absolute void. Without her, he would go through the motions of living, but there would be no joy. Just endless gnawing pain and the promise of more of the same until death released him.

"I have honored her by making her my wife. That is enough."

Fatima shook her head. "Your father and his ministers might have turned you into a leader, but as far as knowing how to make a woman happy, you're a complete fool. Give in, grandson. The date palm that bends before the wind lives to bear fruit another season. The date palm kept straight with pride, breaks and dies alone."

"I will never give in on this."

Her eyes filled with sadness. "Then I am sorry for you, Malik. Because you can't be a great king until you learn compassion, and you can't experience compassion without first knowing how to love. She is everything you've ever wanted. She brings you the offer of peace and a wonderful little girl who thinks you are the sun and moon in one. Yet you would lose them because of your pride or your fear or maybe both." She turned away. "I can't fix this for you. I can only tell you to admit what you already feel in your heart. If you don't, you'll regret it for the rest of your life."

The worst of it was that Liana continued to share his bed, Malik thought several days later as he stepped from his morning shower and grabbed a towel. Every night he expected her to order him to go away, even though she was in his room, and every night she held open her arms. It was too easy to lose himself inside her, and he had the feeling that when they made love he gave away a part of himself. In time, all that he was would have been given over to her, and then he would be empty inside. Yet he wasn't so sure that being empty would be any worse than the darkness before her arrival.

He found himself thinking about her throughout the day. Not just sexually. Instead he found himself remembering conversations, smiling over shared humor, thinking about what he wanted to tell her that evening. Her intelligence allowed her to grasp things quickly and he found himself interested in her opinions.

She said nothing about loving him or expecting him to love her back, but her watchful gaze told him she had neither forgotten nor given in. The issue still loomed between them—a large, living creature whose hot breath burned against his neck.

Fatima was just as bad, only she didn't keep her thoughts to herself. His grandmother expressed her opinion at every opportunity, telling him that he was a fool, and he would lose Liana if he didn't mend his ways.

To make matters worse, Bethany no longer rode with him. Although he'd tried to explain the situation to her, all she could say was that he didn't love her. When tears filled her eyes, he knew that if he still had a working heart, it would be breaking for her.

He hung the towel back on the rack and walked toward his dressing area. Liana was already up and sitting on the edge of the bed. She'd pulled on a nightgown after they'd made love the previous night. The low-cut silk garment exposed creamy cleavage that made him think about filling his hands with her breasts and kissing them until she moaned and writhed, so close that it only took the lightest touch to send her over the edge.

Her hair was mussed, her face pale, but he still thought she was lovely. Just looking at her now as she poured herself a glass of water from the carafe on the nightstand made him want her again. He could feel himself hardening. No matter what, he always wanted her.

He was about to say something by way of an invitation when she pulled a small plastic container from her nightstand drawer and popped out a tiny pill. He frowned. Was she feeling ill? Was there a problem he didn't know about or had she—

Truth slammed into him. She was taking birth control pills.

Without bothering to dress, he stalked into the bedroom. "I thought we were going to discuss starting a family."

She swallowed her pill then looked at him. No humor or desire lurked in her eyes. Instead she looked incredibly sad. "Be realistic, Malik. There aren't going to be any children."

Her words were enough of a blow to send him nearly to his knees. Only by supreme force of will did he remain standing. "We talked about them," he said, his voice low and strained. "You agreed."

"I agreed to a lot of things I shouldn't have." Tears filled her eyes, but she didn't give in to them. Instead she raised her chin and blinked them away. "I was wrong to say I would stay with you, because I can't. Bethany and I are leaving."

He couldn't speak, he couldn't breathe. The darkness approached like a judgment from God, and he could only endure the chilling emptiness and know that it would last forever.

She set her glass back on the nightstand. "I was too young when Chuck and I married. Actually we both were. We grew up and learned hard lessons. One of the most important for me was that I have to feel as if I'm an equal partner in my marriage. I was never that with Chuck. He didn't want a partner—he wanted to do things his way and have sex available. He wasn't interested in responsibilities or any future past next weekend's big race."

"I'm nothing like that," Malik told her, although he knew it wasn't going to do any good. She was leaving and he didn't know how to make her stay.

"You're right," she admitted. "You're not Chuck. Instead you're a prince and one day you'll be a king. Because of that, you and I will never be on an equal footing as far as making decisions on how we should live our lives. But that makes it even more important that there is give and take in our personal relationship. It can't be one sided."

Frantic need filled him. He had to find a way to make her understand. "Do you want to return to teaching? I'll let you do that. Or you can go to college or work in the palace. You're not trapped here."

She brushed away a single tear. "You still don't get it Malik, I don't need you to *let* me do anything. Not return to teaching or even give me a child. I already have that. What I need is for you to care about me and my daughter. I need you to love us."

She stood up and faced him. "I would have risked it for myself," she said. "I meant what I told you before. I do love you and I would be willing to stay. But I can't now. I'm not the only one who lost her heart to you. Bethany did as well. As a grown woman I can take a chance on you changing your mind and admitting your feelings. As a mother, I can't let you continue to hurt my daughter. You've destroyed her, Malik. She thinks you're just like Chuck. That you made her promises that you're not going to keep. It's ironic. I came halfway around the world to find a man so like my ex-husband."

"I am *not* him," he growled, insulted by her comments. "I've kept every promise I made to your daughter."

"But you won't tell her you love her, and that was an implied promise. I hoped you would be able to remember what it was like when you were young and project those feelings on to her. Like the time you broke your arm and one of the ministers thought you were being a crybaby. You were sent to your room and not taken to the doctor until the next morning."

The memory threatened, but he pushed it away. "I would never do that to her."

"I know, but she needs more than responsible parenting. She needs to be loved. The way things are now, I could hire a nanny to do what you're doing with her."

He took a step toward her. "How dare you insult me in this way?"

She didn't back down. "How dare you hurt my child? I would have forgiven you everything. I would have waited. But the day you made her cry was the day I knew we had to leave."

The bottomless abyss threatened, but he ignored the cold fear tickling the base of his spine. He turned his back on her. "Go if you must. I don't give a damn."

"I know," she whispered. "That's the point."

Malik stood at the top of the palace and watched the black limo pull away. The rooftop garden retreat had changed from the last time he'd seen it. Probably because of Liana. He'd heard that she'd taken to spending part of her afternoons up here.

As the dark car disappeared around a curve in the driveway, he tried to find some part of her presence still lingering near him, but she was truly gone, and there was no way for him to bring her back.

He should have told them good-bye, he thought. He should have said something to Bethany. But he couldn't face the pain in her small face, or the disappointment in her mother's expression.

The irony was that a single phone call would prevent both of them from leaving the country. But to what end? Liana had made it clear that she didn't want to be here any longer, and he couldn't blame her. A heavy yet familiar weight settled on his shoulders. Once again he'd let his people down. News of his wife's departure would spread quickly, and everyone would know he'd failed again.

He should never have married her, he told himself angrily. She knew nothing of the pressures of royal life. He should have allowed his father to arrange a suitable match with someone appropriate.

But despite all that happened, he could not regret his time with Liana. Given the chance, all that he would have changed was the fact that he had hurt Bethany.

He closed his eyes and wondered how it had all gone so wrong. She was a young child—he knew what it felt like to be abandoned and alone. Telling himself she had her mother wasn't an excuse, so he didn't allow himself to take comfort in the fact. He had thought he was a good ruler, a decent man of strong character. Ironic that it had taken a nine-year-old girl to show him that he was really nothing more than a selfish bastard.

"There you are, my son."

Malik turned and saw that his father had joined him. The king walked over to the edge of the garden and stared at the view of the palace grounds.

"Liana is gone," the older man said unnecessarily. "The women are up in arms. Fatima is raging and I suspect Dora and Heidi of plotting. Already Jamal and Khalil are concerned they will have no peace from their wives until this matter is settled."

Malik shrugged. "They will get over it in time."

"Perhaps. But their accusations weren't all directed at you. Some of the sharpest barbs were thrown directly at me."

Malik glanced at his father in surprise. The king was nearing sixty, but still stood tall and strong. Gray blended into the dark hair at his temples. His mind had never been quicker, his health was excellent and he could easily rule for another twenty years.

But that had never been his plan. He'd often talked about giving Malik time to get his personal life settled and grow comfortable with his responsibilities. Then Givon would step down while Malik was still relatively young. It had been that way in El Bahar for a thousand years.

"Why are they angry with you?"

The king shrugged. He touched the iron balcony railing. "Do you remember your mother much?"

The odd question surprised Malik, but he searched his mind for an answer. "She died when I was eight so I should, but I never saw her much after I turned four, so no. Not really."

"She was a wonderful woman. Beautiful, intelligent, caring." The king sighed. "Her greatest flaw, perhaps her only flaw, was that she adored me to the exclusion of all else. She denied me nothing. Not even my oldest son when I came to take you away."

He looked at Malik. "I believe we have many wonderful customs in our country, but the practice of taking the Crown Prince away from his mother and siblings is wrong. I hated it when it happened to me, yet I did it to you. I'm sorry I didn't change the old ways, but it's not too late for your son.''

Malik grimaced. ''I doubt I will have one.''

''Because Liana is gone?''

''Yes.''

Givon studied him. ''You could marry again. I can arrange it.''

''It doesn't matter,'' Malik said, staring into the distance. Was she at the airport yet? In a matter of hours she would be gone and he would never see her again.

''Would it matter if I told you that I am proud of you and I believe history will find you one of the greatest leaders of our country? That I've often wondered how I was so fortunate to be blessed with such an heir. I don't worry about the people or the country. You will always do the right thing. But I do worry about your heart, my son. I have always loved you and I never told you before.''

Malik didn't dare look at his father. He felt odd inside. His chest tightened, and yet he felt as if some heavy burden had lifted. He swallowed. ''I, ah, thank you, Father.''

A strong hand settled on his shoulder. ''I loved your mother, as well. Loving her made me strong, just as loving Liana will make you strong. Love is what holds us together in times of trouble. It heals us and gives us the courage to try to be better. I would have walked through the fires of hell for her if she'd but asked, and I have never regretted loving her.''

Malik finally faced the king. ''Is that why you never remarried?''

Givon nodded. ''My ministers pressured me for a time, but I already had you and your brothers. I didn't need more heirs. I have had companions over the years, but I could not imagine taking another woman for my wife. My heart had been given away, and I didn't have it to give to someone else. I suspect you would experience the same problem if you tried to marry again.''

His father's words flew around him, stinging and buzzing until they finally started to make sense.

''I didn't have a choice about losing the woman I loved,'' his father said. ''You do. Bend on this matter, Malik. Bend and speak the truth. Then you will know a strength and peace of mind you can't begin to imagine.''

''I don't want to go,'' Bethany said, tears running down her cheeks. ''I want to stay in El Bahar.''

It was all Liana could do to keep from crying as well. They were already seated in their plane and about to push back from the gate.

She hugged her child close and wished she had words of comfort to offer. What she'd told Malik was true. If it had just been her, she would have taken the chance of making him fall in love with her. But she couldn't play with her daughter's feelings. Ever since Bethany had figured out that Malik didn't love her, she'd been like a broken doll. She refused to go riding, barely ate and wasn't sleeping. Liana knew it would take time for her to recover, but the process would go a whole lot smoother when they'd left El Bahar.

''Mommy, don't make us leave,'' her daughter begged.

''It will be okay,'' Liana promised, understanding Bethany's conflicting emotions. Liana felt them as well. On the one hand she knew in her head that leaving was the best thing for all of them. But in her heart, she thought he was going to die.

She didn't know how she was supposed to survive without Malik in her life. He'd become her husband, her lover and the keeper of her heart. For Bethany, he was

the only father she'd ever known. And what about Mali
himself? Liana hated to think about all that he would hav
to go through as news of her departure spread throughou
the kingdom.

But she didn't have a choice. He'd hurt Bethany an
she couldn't allow that to happen again.

The plane moved slowly backward as they were pushe
away from the gate. Liana continued to hold her daughte
close and murmur soft promises of better times ahead. He
own eyes filled with tears as she wondered how long i
would take to stop loving Malik. What other man coul
measure up to the glory that was her handsome prince?

She had a bad feeling that she would love him foreve
She would grow old with only her memories for company
She thought of the condoms they'd used and birth contr
pills she now swallowed faithfully and had the fleetin
regret that she wouldn't have his child.

Bethany looked up at her. "Maybe he would hav
learned to love us back," she said. "Can't we give hir
another chance?"

"I wish we could," Liana said. "But some peopl
don't change. He hurt you, sweetie, and I didn't want hir
to go on hurting you."

"I'm better," her daughter said through her tears
"Please, Mommy. Just one more chance?"

Liana was tempted to jump up and demand that the
let her and Bethany off the plane. But she resisted th
impulse. "It will be easier when we get home. You'
see."

The lie tasted bitter. Being home wouldn't help. Noth
ing would help for a long time. But eventually time woul
start the healing process and they would—

"Mommy, look!"

Bethany pointed out the window. Liana stared, the

blinked. In the distance a group of men on horseback rode toward the plane. Dust billowed up around them until they reached the paved runways. The plane lurched to a stop.

"Ah, ladies and gentlemen, this is your captain speaking. There's been a slight change in plans."

He continued talking, but Liana wasn't listening. She recognized the man on the lead horse. Despite the robes and headdress, she knew his face, his body, even his heart. Gladness filled her. More tears spilled over, but these were of promise and joy.

"He's not letting us go!" Bethany screamed in delight. She unfastened her seatbelt. "Hurry, Mommy. Let's meet him at the door. Oh, I knew he wouldn't let us go."

Liana gave a slight smile to the stunned passengers sitting around them. She and her daughter slid into the aisle and started toward the front door. As it opened, a stunned flight attendant tried to stop them.

"You'll have to return to your seats," she said in a stern voice.

"Don't mess with her," Bethany said. "She's gonna be the queen."

Liana didn't say anything. She simply maneuvered herself and her daughter past the woman. But before they reached the door, a tall handsome man entered the plane. His dark gaze found her at once, and his hard expression softened.

Her heart rose in her chest, and her body began to shake. Her love for him filled her.

"I couldn't let you go," he said, then looked at Bethany.

To Liana's surprise and great relief, he crouched down to child level and held open his arms. Bethany cried out his name and barreled into him. She wrapped her thin arms around his neck and clung as if she'd never let go.

"I'm sorry," Malik said quietly. "I was very wrong t⌐ hurt you, and I promise to do my best to keep it fron happening again. Of course I love you. You are the daugh⌐ ter of my heart. You will always be my sweet Bethany."

"Are you my daddy now?" she asked.

Malik looked at Liana as if waiting. She nodded.

"Yes," he told the little girl. "If that is what yo⌐ want."

"I love you, Daddy."

Malik's eyes closed briefly as he held her tighter. "⌐ love you too, daughter."

Then he rose to his feet. Still holding Bethany's hand he reached for the microphone.

"Ladies and gentlemen. I'm sorry for the delay in you⌐ departure. You'll be on your way shortly." He paused then set the microphone back in place and turned to Liana "You left me because you thought I did not love you⌐ daughter."

"You're right."

"You said you were willing to take a chance on me i⌐ you didn't have to worry about her."

"I still believe that."

"So you will now stay?"

"If that is your wish."

He smiled. "Liar. You want more. You want it all."

Her joy grew. "Of course."

"Very well. I am Malik Khan, Crown Prince of El Ba⌐ har. This is my land and these are my people. You ar⌐ Liana Khan, wife of the Crown Prince. Your place is a⌐ my side. Stay." He held out his free hand to her. "Sta⌐ because you are the possessor of my heart. Stay becaus⌐ I need you. Stay because I love you now and will for al⌐ time."

As her daughter had before her, Liana threw herself ⌐

im. He caught her against him and held her close. "I love you," she whispered as spontaneous applause broke out among the passengers. "And I will stay with you forever. On your land, with your people."

"My wife," he said gently and kissed her.

For Malik, the sense of homecoming was complete. The last crystal of ice surrounding his heart melted, and he knew that he'd found the one thing he'd been searching for all his life. As he acknowledged his love for Liana and Bethany, he felt the peace and strength flowing through him.

Years from now, Bethany Khan would tell her grandchild about that day on the airplane when a future king had become her father and how his great love for her mother had been the start of a visionary dynasty that would rule for a thousand years. But that is a different story altogether.

\* \* \* \* \*

# SHEIKH'S
# TEMPTATION
*by*
*Alexandra Sellers*

**Alexandra Sellers** is the author of over twenty-five novels. Born and raised in Canada, Alexandra first came to London as a drama student. Now she lives near Hampstead Heath with her husband, Nick. They share housekeeping with Monsieur, who jumped through the window one day and announced, as cats do, that he was moving in. What she would miss most on a desert island is shared laughter. Readers can write to Alexandra at PO Box 9449, London NW3 2WH.

# One

Winter was taking a last swipe at the mountains. A strong wind had started to blow soon after lunch, and within an hour the beautiful spring weather had developed claws. Now, wearing the anorak and jeans that had been perfectly comfortable this morning, Lana Holding was shivering, and probably it would get worse.

Static screeched in her ear again. "Nothing," she reported briefly, turning down the volume on the CB mike and tossing it through the truck window onto the passenger seat. She leaned against the truck and looked down at where Arash was tightening the wheelnuts, his left leg bent, his right leg extended awkwardly away from his body.

She could have helped with the job, but when, in his usual autocratic way, he had told her not to bother, she hadn't forced the issue. She was determined to en-

joy this trip through the breathtaking Koh-i Shir mountains in spite of his presence and the jinx that seemed
to be dogging them. Getting into a heated argument
with Arash over changing a wheel wasn't her idea of
a good time.

She sighed with ill-suppressed anxiety. "They must
still be miles behind us."

Arash pulled the wrench off the last nut and straightened. "They probably have not left Seebi-Kuchek."

Seebi-Kuchek was the village where they had spent
the night. Their little convoy had consisted of two
trucks when they set off from the palace yesterday, one
carrying Arash and Lana, the other two of Arash's
staff, who had come along as bodyguards or advance
men or something. Or for all she knew, their role might
be just to make sure she and Arash wouldn't have to
be alone.

If so, that was fine with her. Lana didn't want to be
alone with Arash, either—she didn't want to be with
him *at all*—but she had been impatient to get into the
mountains. This morning, when the other truck had
developed minor engine trouble, it was she who had
suggested setting off without them.

"They can catch up with us at lunch time," she had
urged. "The weather is so beautiful. I want to get up
into the mountains while the sky is clear, and what if
it doesn't last?"

She regretted it now, even more so because her in-
stincts had been right. Clouds were building around the
magnificent peak of Mount Shir, and soon this road
would be just any old desolate stretch of road with no
mountain views to entrance the eye.

Arash had agreed without a word, though she knew
he hadn't liked it. They had dawdled at their lunch

break, waiting for the others to catch up, but it didn't happen, and so they had gone on again. An hour later one front wheel had hit a pothole hard. Replacing the broken wheel, which had unbelievably stubborn bolts, had cost them too much time. She knew they would have to hurry if they were going to reach the village they were aiming for on the other side of the pass today.

She eyed him now. "Should we go back?"

"Your choice," Arash said, moving to set his tools into the back of the truck. He slammed the double doors. "We can go forward or back. The distance is about the same, and each way it is unlikely we will get down out of the pass before nightfall."

She eyed him in alarm. "What does that mean?"

"It means spending the night in the mountains."

Lana closed her eyes and heaved a sigh. "Why is this trip so *jinxed?*"

"I know no better than you," Arash said, in a calm voice which had the effect of irrationally irritating her.

"I know you don't know, Arash," she told him levelly. "Haven't you ever heard a rhetorical question before?"

His response was to eye her steadily for a moment and then say, as if she hadn't spoken, "Which shall it be, Lana? Forward or back?"

She could hear the suppressed impatience that was almost always in his voice when he spoke to her, and of course this stupid situation was no easier for him than for her. However much she disliked Arash Durrani ibn Zahir al Khosravi, cousin and Cup Companion to Prince Kavian, she knew he returned the compliment with at least equal force.

She couldn't imagine how he had been talked into

being her escort to Central Barakat, any more than she could understand—now—why she had accepted the situation.

She had wanted, unofficially, to be the first to travel through these fabulous, awe-inspiring mountains on the newly-built Emerald Highway which her father's money had made possible. And when Alinor—her best friend from university, now Princess of Parvan—had said that Kavian had a particular reason for wanting Arash to be her escort, had hinted that she would in this way be providing cover for a secret diplomatic mission, Lana just hadn't known how to tell her friend that the thought of making the journey in Arash's company would leach all the joy out of the adventure for her…

So now here she was, stuck in practically the most desolate mountains on the face of the earth with Arash al Khosravi, a man who got on her nerves at the best of times.

Who was still waiting for her to decide. "You're here, too," she told him. "What do you want to do?"

"Let us go on," Arash said.

Arash shifted gears for another climb on the tortuous road that, with a small chunk of Jonathan Holding's vast wealth, was being built through the mountain ranges of Shir and Noor to link Parvan with the Barakat Emirates.

He thought back to that moment when Kavi had asked him to accompany Lana Holding on her misguided pilgrimage on the still-unfinished road. Arash had never before pleaded with his prince for any favour, but he had been horrified by the request.

He had resisted in the strongest terms.

*Kavi, I ask you not to ask this of me. I cannot be the one to take her through the mountains. Surely any of the others…*

"As the most trusted of my Companions, Arash, you are the only one I can ask this favour," Kavi had replied uncomfortably, and Arash had realized there was more to this request than he himself had been told. "We owe her everything. How can I entrust her safety to any other?"

He gazed at his prince for a long moment as certainty crept over him. "Who has requested this, Kavi?"

"I myself make the request," Kavi said, but with a tone in his voice that belied the words. Arash opened his mouth to say that it would be worse than useless for him to make this trip, and then subsided into silence.

It was true. Kavi and the country owed Lana Holding everything. Kavi had two reasons now to bless the luck that had put him and Arash at university at the same time as Alinor, now his wife, and her friend Lana. Lana, who had turned out to be the daughter of the American billionaire Jonathan Holding, had fallen in love with Parvan, and had persuaded her father to aid the tiny kingdom in the aftermath of its savage and destructive war against the Kaljuk invaders. So this was a small sacrifice for Kavi to ask of his closest and most trusted Companion.

Between Kavi and Arash there could be no such thing as a command. Arash had not sworn to obey the Durrani, for such an oath could not be asked from one of his ancient line. But he had sworn his loyalty, and such a wish, expressed in such a way, was more powerful than a command.

*On my head and eyes, Lord,* he had said then, bowing formally in the most ancient of exchanges.

But he wished Kavi had laid any other mission on him.

The way Arash was pushing the truck, Lana wondered if he had changed his mind after all, and intended to get down out of the pass before they had to stop for the night.

*"Mash'Allah,"* she reminded herself, in the way that she had learned during her time in Parvan. *Whatever God wills.* In terrain like this it was easy to remember the maxim that, whatever man proposes, it is God who disposes.

He heard the murmur and glanced over.

"Pardon?"

"I was just thinking that we might still make it down out of the pass to where we originally planned to stop if you keep it up like this."

Arash shook his head. He wished it were true. "It will be dangerous to drive after sunset."

He meant that they could not afford to risk hitting another pothole in the darkness.

Lana glanced nervously at the sky. She had been trying for the past hour to tell herself that the thick heavy clouds were moving east and the area of clear sky was no smaller than before. But they were not moving east, and the amount of blue was definitely shrinking.

He followed her gaze, but said nothing.

They rounded a curve, and he braked sharply. A spread of stones and rocks and snow had come down off the side of the mountain to spew across the road. He bumped slowly over it.

At night, without benefit of a moon, they would almost certainly have hit it before he saw it. Suddenly Lana accepted that they really would have to spend the night up here.

"What if there's a storm?" She tried to sound matter-of-fact, but she couldn't hide the note of dismay in her voice.

Arash flicked her a glance.

"Is there any protection up here?" she pursued.

He shrugged. "It is as you see."

She knew in a storm they should find cover. But here, in the remotest region of Parvan, landmine warnings were still posted prominently on both sides of the road. The snow-covered, uninhabited mountains, almost as much as the valleys, had been liberally strewn with butterfly mines by the Kaljuks in the last days of the war, before their retreat.

Anything might be a landmine in disguise—a comb, a toy, a leaf....

There were teams all over the country working hard on mine clearance: Lana knew all about it, since it was her own favourite project in Parvan.

She also knew that, except for the routes that were the nomads' regular pathways between their summer and winter grounds, including this one where the road had been built, these bleak, difficult mountains were scheduled to be the last area cleared.

It made sense to clear the valleys, the towns, the farmlands and nomad trade routes first. But it meant that even if they saw a cave or overhang, she and Arash could not just climb up to take shelter. They were safe from mines only for a few yards either side of the road, and all that had been mostly levelled to make way for the road.

A gust of wind roared down the mountainside, shaking the truck as it bumped along, spattering sand and gravel against the windshield, making her shiver.

Storm and mountain—you couldn't beat them for making a human being feel frail and insignificant.

"We can't pitch the tent if there's going to be a storm. We'll have to sit it out in the truck," she observed in a level voice.

There was silence. He did not deny it.

Lana felt the first real thrill of alarm. Sitting in a truck overnight while a storm raged with only Arash and a survival candle for company! It defied imagination. The man could barely bring himself to be civil to her at the easiest of times.

She eyed the clouds again.

"Is there going to be a lot of snow?"

It was a stupid question, which she knew as soon as she asked it. When the weather was unseasonable in the first place, who could guess? But it was just ordinary human nature to ask, Lana figured. It didn't really mark her as ignorant, but by the glance Arash threw her, you'd think she was a specimen of a species that lacked basic reasoning capabilities.

Arash shrugged. "Two inches? Two feet?"

*"Two feet?"*

"It is impossible to guess."

His voice was rough and flat, not sharing anything with her, and she had to breathe deeply to calm her irritation. She had only been making conversation to ease her nerves, and besides, he must know the ropes a lot better than she did. She'd never been up here before, but his family estates were in the Koh-i Shir mountains somewhere, so why shouldn't she ask an expert?

But what was the point in defending herself?

They always did rub each other the wrong way. It was one of those inexplicable, unfounded antipathies. Each would have been happy never to see the other again, she thought, if only one of them would leave town.

But Parvan was Arash's home, and he wasn't going to emigrate. And, apart from this short break which Alinor had insisted on, Lana wasn't going anywhere, at least until after Alinor's baby was born. And then— well, she wasn't ready yet to name a day when she would leave Parvan.

She had never met such brave, strong, true people as the citizens of Kavi's little country of mountain and desert, and here—helping, with her father's money, to put the war-torn country back together—she felt that she had found her reason for being.

"What is this, Lana, adopt-a-country?" her father had demanded in amused exasperation at yet another request for a contribution. In one of his weak moments she had convinced him to match, dollar for dollar, all the funds she raised elsewhere. "Don't I already support most of the villages and roads and wells and schools? And that mountain highway—what are you calling it, the Emerald Road?—is sucking up cash like a vacuum cleaner! What else can there be?"

"Dad, face it—if you don't spend your money on something like Parvan, what'll you spend it on? Trying to buy power, that's what. And then you won't be a great guy anymore, you'll be a monster, and everyone will hate you," she had explained ruthlessly. "And I don't want everyone in the world hating my dad."

"I'm not trying to buy power at the moment, Lana,"
he had told her. "I'm trying to endow a museum."

The new museum was *his* baby, and it needed lots
of funds, too. But he almost always came through for
her. And sometimes their interests coincided, for many
wealthy Parvani families were forced into selling their
ancient treasures to finance the rebuilding of their lives.

At least Lana could always make sure the Holding
Museum paid well.

Kavi and Alinor and all the people whose lives she
touched—whose villages and homes and farms were
rebuilt, much sooner than could otherwise have been
possible, with her father's generous donations and the
money she raised with her fund-raising events—of
course were grateful.

Only Arash stood outside the circle of her admirers.
As a sheikh and tribal leader with a valley full of farms
and villages to care for, he had not interfered when his
people had received their share of the generosity. But
as the man whose own estates and family home had
suffered, he would accept nothing from her.

And although she was certain that his painful limp
could be helped with surgery, he had virtually pre-
tended not to hear her offer to finance a trip for surgery
abroad.

She had never understood his reasons, and she no
longer bothered to try.

She turned her head to run a look over his strong,
uncompromising profile as he drove, his own attention
firmly on the road. He was wearing a leather jacket
and denim jeans and boots, but he looked no less a
sheikh than when he was in full traditional dress.

"Will this thing drive if there's that much snow?"
she couldn't help asking.

"There are too many unknowns to predict anything with certainty," he said.

"So we might end up waiting for a helicopter rescue?" Her heart sank. *And how long would that take?* she wanted to ask, but she suppressed the desire. His answer would only be another irritating refusal to guess, and she was already gritting her teeth.

"I knew I should fly," she muttered.

Arash lifted a disbelieving eyebrow. "And why didn't you?"

"Well, you know the answer to that better than I do, Arash!"

"I know only that Kavi asked me to see you safely to Central Barakat and that you insisted on coming by road."

She threw him a look. "I do know, Arash, that I'm providing cover for some secret mission to Prince Omar."

Arash frowned at the road. "I am entrusted with no mission other than delivering you safely to my cousin Omar and Princess Jana in Central Barakat."

Of course he wouldn't tell her if he was. "So why was it so important that you and no one else accompany me?" she demanded sceptically.

There was a short silence.

"But this was your own choice," he said in slight surprise.

Lana's mouth gaped. "*My* choice? What, to have you along? Why would it be *my* choice?"

"Naturally I found your motive inexplicable."

Lana turned to look at him, her eyes narrowed. "Did you really think that I had asked Kavi to force you to come with me? Kavi couldn't have told you such a thing!"

He threw her a glance, shrugging. "It was one possible explanation for something inexplicable."

"Thanks for the vote of confidence!" she snapped. "What did you think my motive was, Arash, just as a matter of interest?"

The truck slowed as his eyes briefly but electrifyingly met hers.

"I thought your motive would be revealed in time. I didn't trouble, therefore, to wonder."

"Don't hand me that!" she commanded irritably. "If you thought I engineered this, you must have had some ideas about why! What was my reason, Arash?"

She stared at him, her mind whirling, fury already bubbling up inside, and she thought how dangerous it would be to be stranded alone with Arash, of all men. She knew there was a well of resentment in her towards him.... There wasn't another of Kavi's Cup Companions she didn't like, whom she wouldn't rather have been with now.

"What reason could I possibly have for wanting to be alone with you up here in God's country?"

He made no reply. After a minute, she opened her mouth on a slow, outraged breath.

"I don't believe it!" Suddenly she could hardly get the words out for the rage that assailed her. When she spoke, her voice shook.

"What did you think, Arash? Did you think I maybe wanted to get you alone to make you an offer?"

She saw a muscle leap in his jaw and was sure she had hit home.

"What kind of an offer, exactly, were you envisaging? Just a brief affair, or was I going to go so far as to propose a mutually convenient marriage of wealth with an ancient title? Was that it?"

"It was not that I believed it. It was merely one possible explanation that crossed my mind."

"You really have to be seen to be believed!"

He slowed the truck with a quick jab at the brakes and turned to her, a blaze of fury on his face.

"You deny that such a possibility has occurred to you?"

She stared at him, the words tumbling from her lips. "*Yes,* I deny that such a possibility has occurred to me! What gives you the right to speak to me like this?"

His eyes were dark with feeling, and a shiver ran all over her. What on earth could be coming now?

He lifted a hand from the steering wheel and his finger pointed at the end of her nose. His eyes flashed violet, and the fury in his voice now astonished her.

"What gives me the right? *You* give me the right, Lana. You with your quiet suggestion that I am for sale at public tender!"

# Two

It had been Lana's idea to offer a fabulous fund-raising dinner on a jet, flying guests who had paid a substantial sum for the honour overnight from London to Parvan, where they would greet the sun as it rose over magnificent Mount Shir. Then they would land at the capital to meet the Regent Prince and his wife at a palace champagne breakfast.

On board the luxuriously appointed jet, donated for the occasion by the princes of the Barakat Emirates, subscribers were also privileged to meet some of the Cup Companions....

Lana had quickly learned that Kavi's handsome Cup Companions had a drawing power second only to Prince Kavian himself, and she included them in nearly every fund-raising event. The long-suffering Companions joked that they were no better than performing bears at such times, but uncomplainingly took their turn.

It was just chance that Arash was one of the performing bears whose turn it was to appear for that particular fund-raiser—an event scheduled to last for nearly a day, and for most of which they were, of course, all captive on the aircraft.

Sheikh Arash Durrani ibn Zahir al Khosravi never failed to please women who fantasized about the Cup Companions. His charm was rough and unstudied; he never came across as practised or polished, but he had a natural charisma that had an effect in spite—or maybe because—of a sometimes impatient tongue.

Arash was tall, dark and arrogantly, powerfully good-looking, with a firmly held mouth behind a neat curling beard. His flashing dark eyes sometimes seemed black and sometimes glowed deep violet, a colour so unusual that people couldn't help remarking on it.

The fact that he had been wounded in the war with Kaljukistan and walked with a limp only added to his romantic glamour.

When in addition he was wearing the Companions' traditional state dress of flowing white oriental trousers snugly cuffed around the ankle, beaded thong sandals on strong bare feet, and a rich wine-dark silk tunic surmounted by his jewelled chain of office and his war medals—well, Lana knew it was a strong female heart that could resist.

Lana's own heart had been immunized early, so she was in no danger, but she had seen women trip over their own feet when they were still twenty paces away.

It nearly always amused her, the effect one smile from a Cup Companion could have on the donations, but it was not amusing when the Companion in question was Arash.

Probably because she didn't like him.

She also hated having to pretend enthusiasm for him with these adoring women. Arash, whose eyes sometimes seemed to hide a deep sorrow even when he smiled, was a rich source of inspiration for dreamers. She wanted to say, *Don't go anywhere near him, he's dangerous to know*...but of course she never did.

Anyone would have been guaranteed to ask how she knew. But she had never talked about it to anyone. Not even Alinor guessed that Arash and she had a past that had affected her so deeply that she still could hardly look at a man....

"I suppose he suffered an awful lot in the war," Lucinda Burke Taylor had said with clinical soulfulness an hour or so into the flight, and Lana knew that Lucinda had sought her out for a purpose.

It was going to be a bumpy night.

Usually Lana had no difficulty enthusing about the Companions to smitten women, and the donations went up when she did. But this woman had already married two high-profile, low-income men, and a Chinese poet-in-exile was already next in her sights. It was as obvious as the day was long that she thought of these transactions in terms of purchase. His culture and brains for her money. And she believed it an equal transaction.

If she was going to start aiming at Arash...but it wasn't Lana's business. Arash would have to look after himself.

"I've heard he's the Grand Sheikh of his tribe now. It sounds so fascinating!"

"If you consider losing your father and older brother in the same war fascinating."

"Oh, of course, I didn't mean—I just meant, the whole business of being sheikh of a tribe, in this day and age! It's just so—!"

After a struggle Lana mastered herself. "He's very close to the prince, too. One of his closest and most trusted advisors," she confided.

His back turned to them, Arash was talking to someone Lana had earmarked for him. She provided each Companion with his own list of three or four of the wealthiest and most charitable people at any event. They all disliked the task, but each could be counted on to speak to everyone on his list. And usually a good proportion of Arash's targets made donations afterwards.

"And he's not married, right?"

The gunsight eyes followed as Arash and the guest unconsciously moved closer to them. Lana gritted her teeth.

"Not married, and hasn't got a bean," she heard herself say flatly.

The woman's eyes brightened at this information.

"Really?" She turned to fix her gaze on Lana, who had to consciously refrain from ducking. "Do you mean he's—" Her voice dropped to a confidential murmur. "Is he looking for a moneyed wife?"

It would be husband number three for her, and incidentally would mean sinking the fortunes of the dissident poet, but why not? Arash's estates were in ruins, and just because he wasn't accepting any from Lana didn't mean they didn't need an injection of cash.

It wasn't up to her to guess whether he would consider an offer or not.

"Might be worth putting your bid in," Lana said, glad that the other woman was apparently deaf to irony.

Arash's gaze met hers briefly across the space that divided them. He had heard some of the discussion. But instead of sending him an apologetic look, as she would have with any of the others, Lana merely raised her eyebrows in a shrug and shepherded Lucinda in his direction.

"Your Excellency…" she began, giving full weight to his title because of the impact it had on most Westerners. But the way Arash eyed her she knew he suspected her of irony.

Well, to hell with him. He knew nothing about her. If he had known her at all, he would have understood that he could take her father's money without obligation.

"…may I present Lucinda Burke Taylor?"

Maybe Lucinda would have better luck. Maybe Arash would be more comfortable with a cash sale. Maybe that had been her mistake. She hadn't asked for anything in return.

Lana frowned. *Mistake?* The only mistake she had made with Arash was a long time ago, and she was far from making another.

"I was *joking!*" she said now.

"You were not joking. She came to me as one who comes to assess a horse. She wanted to count my teeth!"

"I know she did! Don't you know irony when you hear it?"

He glanced at her. "And Miss Burke Taylor—did she know irony when she heard it?"

"I can't help it if she was too stupid to get my point. You've dealt with enough stupid, greedy women. You couldn't have had any trouble with her—she wasn't up to your weight at all!"

"Thank you." He bowed ironically over the wheel.

"But Lucinda's not the point now, is she? Where do you get the jump from Lucinda to me?"

"You?"

She breathed deep, trying to quell the irrational fury that consumed her. "Even if you thought I was serious, you have no grounds for suggesting I would want to put in a bid myself. No grounds at all!"

To her surprise, he braked and pulled over to the side of the road. He slammed the gearshift into Park and turned to her.

"What are you talking about? Why do you make so much fuss about a simple mistake?"

"I'm talking about you saying I engineered this trip so I could make a pass at you!"

He stared at her. "Are you crazy, Lana? I have just told you—"

She overrode him. "It's been a long time since I threw myself at you, Arash, and if it is not already obvious, let me make it one hundred percent clear—I am not likely to do it again!"

"You did not throw yourself at me," he said. "You offered yourself to me from compassion, the way a woman does when a man is going to war and may never come back."

"Is that what you thought?" she asked bitterly.

"Is it not the truth?"

She blinked slowly, her eyes clouding. Was it? Was

that what had motivated her? She could hardly remember now, but she supposed she must have had some reason for such crass stupidity.

"Maybe," she said. It would explain something, anyway—the thing that had always mystified her. Why had she thrown herself at him when now it was so obvious they were incompatible and didn't like each other? Just out-of-control hormones?

She sighed. "It doesn't matter now, does it?"

"No, it doesn't matter now."

"And just to set your mind at rest, Arash, in case you really are afraid it might happen again, it is just possible I might be reduced to buying a husband for myself—"

"I did not—"

"But never, in a thousand million years, would I ever consider making *you* an offer, Arash. So if you were thinking that was the reasoning behind my offer to help you rebuild your palace or your valley or anything like that, you can relax."

"I have—"

"I didn't want you to come on this trip, I was blackmailed into it, and I would have flown when I discovered you were going to be my escort, only Alinor as good as begged me not to. I have no desire ever to be alone with you, for any reason whatsoever!"

"I understood this before," he said, not without humour. "You have been at such pains to make it clear that you regretted that night, Lana, that even a stone statue would have the message by now. So I know that you do not believe what you are indignantly pretending to believe, and that you know very well that what was in my mind was no more than that Lucinda Burke Taylor had asked you to open certain negotiations for her."

Heat rushed up under her skin, and she was filled with angry shame. Oh God! What a fool she was! Of course he would never imagine…what the hell had possessed her to accuse him of thinking such a thing? It was the last thing he would think. They couldn't stand each other! She must be going crazy. Mountain air did that to some people.

"I am sure that Lucinda Burke Taylor handles her own negotiations. She must be quite polished by now," Lana muttered, bending her head to conceal her embarrassment from him.

Arash laughed, and from the corner of her eye she watched the smooth movement of his throat and smiled herself. However angry she got with him, it rarely lasted. They did have that.

There was a moment of silence while she abruptly took in the fact that they were not moving.

"Why are we stopped here? Why aren't you driving?"

He leaned forward, resting his arms over the steering wheel, and gazed out at the weather.

"We have a choice to make," he observed.

A huge gust of wind hit the side of the truck, seeming to suck the warmth out of the little cabin, and she shivered. Looking out the window, she could see lots of rock, but nothing that offered real protection.

"What choice? Is there someplace nearby where we can get under cover?"

He lifted a hand and pointed out the window beside her. "That way," he said. "It's a long trek."

She turned and stared at the rocky landscape. "What—cross-country? But what about landmines?"

"There's another mule train route here, leading to a

valley. It has been cleared by your teams. It's a long way down the road to the next such track. It may be best to make for the valley. I think it is going to be a severe storm, Lana. High winds and heavy snow. It will not be safe to remain in the truck. There may be avalanche.''

They both automatically glanced out at the snow-covered slopes, as far up as they could see. The clouds were low, dark and increasingly ominous.

"Do you mean it's going to be a blizzard? But Arash, what if it starts while we're walking?"

"That is only more reason to hurry."

"But we might wander off the route! We could get blown to bits."

"I know the landmarks. Whatever else happens, we will not stray from the path," he said briefly, without emphasis. They were both silent as they considered the other fate that might befall them, caught without shelter on a mountain at night during a storm.

"We have a mountain survival kit in the truck." He seemed to come to a decision. He lifted his hand to the key to shut off the engine. "We must hurry." He opened his door and got out.

Another gust of wind smacked at them. Arash staggered under the blast.

"Arash..." she began, but he was already at the back of the truck, opening the doors and rooting around amongst their supplies.

"Dress warmly," he ordered. "Put on everything you can. More than you think you need."

Well, it might be preferable to stagger through the mountains than sit in the truck with Arash waiting for the storm to hit. But she hated listening to him give orders as if he were an army sergeant and she a recruit.

"Thank you for that advice," she muttered, to the dashboard.

She stepped out of the truck and instantly began to shiver in the icy air. He was right—her jacket and jeans would get her nowhere. She would freeze to death if the temperature dropped much further.

Her short red curls were lifted and blown flat against her head; even her eyelashes were caught by the wind.

Her jacket billowing, she staggered to the back of the truck, where Arash dragged out the bag she pointed to and dropped it at her feet. Lana bent down and started pulling clothes out of it. She hadn't packed for cold weather; she was heading to the desert, after all. She had few suitable things. But layers were the warmest way to dress anyway.

She quickly grabbed out sweatshirts and jerseys, a pair of sweatpants, socks. Then came a couple of pairs of leggings. She gazed at them in surprise, suddenly remembering having packed them, paused for a moment, then tucked them back into the case.

"Put them on," Arash commanded her.

She glanced up. She had thought he was fully engaged, but apparently he had time to watch her.

"Put them on," he repeated in a voice that brooked no argument. Another wind slammed into them, smashing one of the doors of the truck closed, rocking the vehicle violently. It was icy cold, with fingers that reached inside the cotton shirt she was wearing to count her ribs. She shivered.

"Are you crazy? I'd have to take off my jeans first! I'd freeze just putting them on!"

"You will quickly get warm again when we start to walk," he said.

She really didn't want to strip off in the middle of the road—in front of Arash—if she could help it.

"I'm sure I'll be all right with—"

"The temperature is still dropping. We have a long walk on exposed mountain."

She still hesitated, and his voice got flatter and more urgent.

"Lana, we are using valuable time. Do as I say! Take off your jeans!"

The explosion over, his words hung in the air. Their eyes met.

A muscle pulsed in his jaw. She wished they could laugh. It should have amused them. But somehow, instead, she felt heat burn up in her cheeks. Lana turned away and pulled her jacket off, reaching for a jersey.

As she pulled on all her sweaters, Arash pulled on a thick tracksuit over his jeans and shirt, then a heavy sweater and down vest, and then his leather jacket. All right for him, he didn't have to strip off his jeans, Lana thought bitterly, pulling down the zipper and shivering as she slipped the denim down over her hips.

Underneath she was wearing only a tiny pair of briefs in paper-thin yellow Lycra, and she saw Arash glance involuntarily at her bare hips and thighs before he firmly continued with his own business.

It was just male instinct, she told herself, trying to ignore her reaction to his glance. Trying not to remember the last time he had looked at her body.

Her jeans around her knees, she held down her boot heel with the other toe and tried to prise her foot free, but her feet must have swollen during the long drive— the boot was stuck.

"Damn!" she swore, wrestling with the boot for a moment before starting to hike her jeans back up.

"What is it?" Arash turned. He had dressed quickly and was packing the supplies. He held a coil of rope in his hand. "Lana, believe me, it is best if you put on everything you can."

"I'm *trying* to. I can't get my boots off!" she exploded. Now she couldn't get her jeans back up over her hips.

Without another word Arash sank down at her feet and quickly loosened the laces.

"Lift your foot," he commanded impatiently, and when she mutely obeyed he wrapped one hand around her ankle and worked the boot off with the other.

She shivered violently. It really was freezing. Hastily she stepped with her free foot on the gravelly road to let Arash draw off the other boot. She shoved her jeans down again, and he took over to pull them down over her knees and shins and off one foot and then the other.

Then she stood half naked in front of him, nothing on her lower body except the yellow bikini briefs. Lana swallowed convulsively, looking down at his dark, thickly waving hair as he lifted his head and frowned questioningly up into her eyes.

For a moment they were both silent, remembering.

"Ohhh, it's *cold!*" she cried, pretending that she had been assailed by no memory of another life, another world.

Arash got to his feet and turned to business, and Lana shook out the first pair of leggings, lifted a foot and quickly began to work them on.

When she had put on the leggings and jeans and her sweatpants she began to warm up again. She quickly pulled on her boots and jacket, tied a big silk scarf around her head and face, pulled up her hood and made

the drawstrings tight. She slipped a small toiletries bag
with the bare essentials into her pocket.

Meanwhile Arash had stuffed two backpacks full,
and was tying a rope around his waist. When that was
done he took the other end and began to tie it around
her.

"What on earth are you doing?" she demanded.

He threw her a look and went on tying the rope.

"Answer me, Arash!"

His hands stilled for one moment of what looked
like irritation and he looked into her eyes at close quarters. In this grey light his eyes were the colour of
crushed dark violets. She could almost smell their perfume.

"I am tying a rope around your waist," he said levelly.

"I can see that!"

He shrugged. "You asked the question."

"You know what I meant!"

"The reason for what I am doing is as obvious as
the action itself. What do you want me to say? If you
get blinded by the storm, do you relish the prospect of
wandering off the path away from me and getting
lost—or worse? Do not waste time on argument, Lana!
Every second counts! You must submit to me in this!
If you challenge me every step of the way, we are
doomed."

*You must submit to me in this.*

Lana swallowed. Of course he was right. He was the
expert here. "Sorry," she muttered, and then turned
and slipped into the straps of the backpack he held up
for her. A moment later he had shouldered another one
himself, larger, heavier.

"Ready?" he asked.

Together they stepped into the storm. Survival depended on mutual cooperation now. She wondered if they could achieve it.

She had gone to London to study at university, wanting adventure, wanting travel, wanting to get away from the restrictions that her father's sudden wealth imposed on her life.

Lana had been born and raised in an ordinary, comfortably-off family environment, with a father she hardly saw and a mother who was proportionately devoted to maintaining home and family. She rarely spent time with her father because his field was computers, and when Lana was about five he had taken the plunge of starting his own company.

Within ten years Jonathan Holding was almost a billionaire, and Lana's life had changed completely. She had of course enjoyed the freedoms that such wealth offered, but she had equally disliked the restrictions that it imposed.

The worst effect was in her dating life. She had only been sixteen when she had had to fight off a date rape from a guy who, when a well-placed kick had finally calmed his ardour, had drunkenly apologized and confessed that he had wanted to be able to claim he had deflowered Jonathan Holding's daughter.

He was a student at a nearby private school for boys. That night she had learned that there was a competition among the guys: the goal was to get the ''virgin's panties' of the daughter of someone famous to hang on your gym locker door. Lana Holding's panties would be almost as much of a feather in a guy's cap as those of the daughter of a high-profile movie star, who was her fellow student.

That experience had made her very, very wary. Afterwards she listened to her friends when they talked about sex, about how they had meant to resist but had been overcome by their own passion, or by a guy's, or by his arguments or bad temper, or merely by their own impatience to know what it was all about....

Not Lana. The experience gave her breathing time, and a good reason for resisting during those first cloudy, hormone- hazy days of growing up. And when the cloud had cleared a little, she had realized that she wanted a lot more from a guy than just his determination to get her underpants from her. And a lot more from herself than just her hormones crying out for relief.

She had decided to go abroad to university, where with a little luck she could be just an ordinary person again. She had taken her mother's name to become plain Lana Brooks, though at her father's insistence she had agreed to live in a building with extremely high security.

Lana had been lonely in the huge and luxurious apartment, until she had invited her best friend, Alinor, to share the place with her.

Alinor had already caught the eye of the mysterious graduate student Kavian Durran, who rumour said was an important member of the Parvan royal family. He was accompanied everywhere he went by the two Parvani friends who had come to England with him. Rumour said *they* were actually bodyguards.

One of them called himself Arash Khosravi.

# Three

___

Lana bit hungrily into a piece of *naan*. "Where are we?" she asked, chewing.

Buffeted by howling winds, they had been struggling across rocky ground for well over an hour, and if there was a path, she certainly hadn't seen any markings.

Every step terrified her. The thought of what would happen if he put his foot on a mine made her sick with fear. She had gritted her teeth till her jaw ached. *Not him,* she had silently pleaded. *After all that he's suffered, don't let him…* She didn't like him, but she was a long way from wanting to watch a landmine blow his foot off.

But he had brought them safely to their first rest stop. "Five minutes," he had said, eyeing the sky. The snow had started to fall almost as he spoke, and a layer of powder was already settling on the ground, being blown into little ridges under rocks and against stones.

Arash had set a hard pace, and his knee must be bothering him. She knew he had been hoping to reach their destination before the first sign of snow, and he did not hide his anxiety to get going again.

"In that direction," he replied now, pointing in a direction she guessed was south, "not far from the Barakat border. Maybe twenty miles."

"And in the direction we're heading?"

There was warm soup left over from lunch, in the thermos flask. It had been filled this morning by a woman in Seebi-Kuchek, the village where they had spent the night, and although of course Lana had thanked her, she was a lot more grateful for it than she had imagined being.

They had only the flask lid as cup. Arash lifted the cup to his lips once for every time she did, but he could barely have warmed his lips for the amount he drank.

"We are heading towards a river valley. There we will find shelter."

She didn't bother to ask how much longer they had to go. They would either make it before the storm broke or they wouldn't. She nodded, finishing the last bite of her bread, and dusted the crumbs from her knees. Arash held up the cup of soup to her.

"Finish this off."

She was hungry. A long time ago, in a past of plenty which she could now hardly recognize, she might have drunk the soup without a thought. Lana had always been an exhuberant eater. She had never worried about her weight, or whether people—other women, mostly—had thought her fat. She loved food and she indulged herself.

But she never took food for granted now. Too often she had seen poor villagers produce their last morsel of food for their visitors…the generosity of the people here was the deepest she had ever met.

So she stood, looking down to where Arash sat on a rock, his right leg extended. He too was much thinner now, though every gesture still carried the promise of power. "Thanks, Arash, I've had plenty."

She saw his pupils expand, all at once, like a cat's. Then his eyes fell to the cup between his hands. After a moment, he lifted it to his mouth and drank deeply.

He held it out to her again. "The last mouthful is for you."

He had drunk less than half, but she could not argue the point further. She took the cup with a nod and gratefully drained it, while Arash with quick efficiency cleaned up the remains of their meagre meal.

He stood, drawing his right foot under him in the awkward way she was used to, and Lana unconsciously tightened her lips and shook her head. She *knew* something could be done, if not to restore full function to the knee, at least to relieve the constant pain she was sure he suffered. She had asked a couple of surgeons about his case, and the prognosis was pretty clear. Why wouldn't he let her father finance the operation?

They shouldered their backpacks in silence. "Ready?" Arash asked briefly, and at her nod stepped into the wind and started off. Lana followed as the rope that joined them lost its slack.

Her hands were cold. She had only two thin pairs of gloves, and other than drawing her hands up inside her sleeves there wasn't much she could do to warm them. Pockets were out of the question most of the way—she needed her arms free for balance.

The wind was horrible; she had never experienced such cold, strong winds in her life. Thank God now, except for gusts, it mostly came from behind. Whenever it blew into her face and her nose, terrifyingly, it seemed to suck the breath from her lungs.

They had been heading downhill for some time. More than once she was blown against Arash's back. On each occasion he stopped, firm as a rock, till she got her balance, then with a brief word set off again.

"I suppose that's a knack you get when you're raised in the mountains," she called once, but if he answered her, the wind snatched away his words.

It was funny—she didn't like him, but she trusted him. There was no one she would rather have been in this trouble with, no one she would have trusted more to get her through this.

She searched for her reasons. Because he was not a man who lied to himself. Arash never disguised his perception of reality in order to bolster his ego.

How rare that was among men.

She knew there was no one Kavi trusted more. "Arash is my right hand," she had heard him say to Alinor once. "If I only think about a thing, it is done, as if my own hand had done it."

He was as fine a warrior as any of his famous ancestors: the Parvanis were a nation of storytellers and she had heard plenty of stories about Arash's war exploits, from everyone but him.

She had nothing but respect for him as a man. She had never seen him perform an ungenerous act.

Except one.

It was a pity they couldn't like each other. But chemistry was like that, sometimes. Something primitive operating in spite of all rational process.

And she, of course, had other reasons.

They came to ground that sloped sharply upwards, and here, the vegetation having got a little thicker, the path was visible. Arash turned up a defile, and the wind simultaneously changed direction and blasted fiercely at them. The snow it carried was cold and hard, stinging her face with sudden ferocity.

Losing her balance, Lana stumbled and cried out, but though the wind seemed to steal the cry right from her throat, Arash turned and stepped quickly down to her, his hand outstretched.

She grasped it and recovered her balance, her heart beating so hard and fast that she was lightheaded for a moment. She clasped her other hand to her chest and blew out a relieved breath.

"Thanks!"

Her pack was heavy enough to have made a fall nasty. She might have broken a bone. His grip was firm, and he held her for an extra second to be sure she was safe. Her heart was still going like a drumroll.

"All right?" Arash asked. "It will be easier very soon now."

She nodded, and he let her hand go, turned and went on.

For a moment she stood frowning down at her hand. Just with that brief touch his hand had warmed her freezing fingers.

After a long struggle, half-blinded by the snow, they crested the ridge, and the world was transformed. Lana, breathing heavily from exertion, gasped at her first glimpse of what lay below.

Behind was the familiar white and grey of rock and mountain and snow, but at their feet the ground opened, as if a giant knife had cut a gash in the fabric of the earth and the two sides had been pulled apart to reveal the earth's deepest beauty in a vast, rich valley.

"But it's magic!" she exclaimed breathlessly. "Oh, Arash, how beautiful! It's like—it's like Shangri-La!"

It was green with spring growth and the early buds on numerous trees. There were neatly planted orchards in a dozen directions, as well as the wild growth of natural forests.

There were villages, and farms with the neat, centuries-old terracing she had come to expect in Parvan. There were sheep and goats freckling the fields, and their bells jangled on the wild wind as shepherds hastily drove them home.

As everywhere in Parvan, there was evidence of the Kaljuks' destructive bombs. Terraced fields were smashed, a roofless house gaped helplessly at the coming storm, sad skeletons of a burnt orchard clawed emptily at the sky.

But there were also signs everywhere that the inhabitants were rebuilding their lives. A half-finished new roof, the fresh bricks of a rebuilt muezzin tower, freshly plowed land.

Far to their right, a river cut through a rocky gorge and thundered in a massive, breathtaking waterfall down to the valley floor so far below. There it continued its journey as a river again, glistening between rich hilly banks all along the valley till it was lost to view.

At their feet the path they had been following suddenly became visible as a trail leading along the steeply sloping side of the valley down towards the river. It branched out in many directions, and she realized that this path was the inhabitants' link to the caravan route and the outer world.

A blast of wind drove more stinging snow into her face as she paused to catch her breath, and Arash said, "We must hurry to get to cover. There is still some way to go."

"Has the valley been cleared of mines?" she asked.

He nodded. "This valley was mostly spared the mines in any case, being so close to the Barakat border. The Kaljuks were afraid of bringing the Barakat Emirates into the war against them. If a pilot had made a mistake, if the mines or the bombs fell across the border…"

"I thought Central Barakat came in on Prince Kavi's side."

"Prince Omar is Kavi's cousin and mine. He fought the war unofficially. His brothers, too, sent money and arms. But to engage the Barakat Emirates officially—the Kaljuks were at great pains to give them no excuse to formally declare war."

"So this valley was luckier than some."

He twisted his head in a nod. "As you say."

"What is its name?" she asked, but Arash shook his head.

"Save your questions, Lana."

He did not take the main path, leading to the left and sharply down, but a less-defined, though still visible, route to the right, in the direction of the waterfall. High on the green slope, it seemed more of a goat track than a human pathway.

Suddenly the storm broke in earnest. The muddy goatprints began filling with snow. The pattern of the wind was visible in the snowflakes' whirling dance. Her eyes traced whorls, and spirals, and long sweeping blasts, and leaping chaos, all within the space of a few seconds.

The thought entered her mind—*the secret of life is in those patterns, if only I could understand them.* Then she blinked in surprise. She must be lightheaded from exertion and lack of calories. Or rapture of the heights.

One of Kavi's bodyguards was a walking, talking sex bomb, as far as Lana was concerned. Arash Khosravi was powerfully built, and in their many discussions about the mysterious trio of Parvanis attending the university, Lana and Alinor convinced themselves that he really was a bodyguard.

He was also ruggedly good-looking, his eyes were a deep, unbelievably sexy violet, and he exuded masculine sexual confidence.

When he looked at her, Lana never felt that assessment in his gaze that she had learned to hate from men, never felt that question hovering in the air between them: *Could I?*

Arash's sexual assessment was very different. When he looked at her, she seemed to hear a voice inside her head, saying, *You have never wept with pleasure. I will make you do so.* Or *You have never been given all that you need. I will teach you how much more you need than you believe now.*

She was sure he didn't guess how far she was from the experience of real sexual pleasure.

When Kavian and Alinor started to date, Lana and Arash of course were often thrown together. Up close she had found him breathtaking. Mysterious, elemental. He was so different from the men she knew.

Even the way he carried himself was different. He walked as though the air were his own, and with every step his body seemed to restate a deep connection with the earth, as though his movements were part of the earth's breath.

For a while she had been convinced the deep, almost primitive attraction she felt was mutual. She had told herself that Arash was choosing his moment. She imagined that he was deliberately building the intensity between them, increasing their anticipation.

She wished she had the courage to tell him her anticipation didn't need any help. She had never felt such powerful sensual excitement in a man's presence. Looking forward to the day Arash would make his move, she would burn and freeze and melt and shiver all at the same time.

Maybe, if she had not been so totally inexperienced, she might have been more confident that he would welcome some move from her. But he made her so nervous. What if she was imagining it all? What if her hormones had just made her sexually crazy?

The day drew nearer and nearer when he would go home....

Each day her heart ached a little more. Each day she thought, *This will be the day*. Each day she trembled when he was near.

And then the impossible arrived. Kavi and Alinor were leaving for Parvan the next day, and Arash was going with them. And with a deep sense of shock, Lana had realized that he was never going to make his move. And she might never see him again.

That night, at a farewell party at Kavi's place, a little drunk—a little drunk and a lot desperate—Lana had stared across the room at Arash Khosravi where he leaned against a wall watching the proceedings, and knew that this was her last chance and that she could not let him go without a word....

She heard the introductory strains of a slow sexy song and, swaying across the room to where he stood, had slipped her body into his surprised hold, and her arms around his neck.

"Dance with me, Arash," she breathed softly, smiling. "You're going home tomorrow. Dance with me tonight."

They struggled along the path that Arash chose. The evening closed in, and below them, all along the valley, lights came on in villages and isolated farms. And still they walked, the path dropping very gently as it proceeded around the valley's slope, leading closer and closer to the waterfall. Its comforting rumble grew steadily louder, even against the blast and thunder of the wind and the thickening fall of snow.

She realized, after a while, that he had some specific goal in mind, and knew exactly how to get there. Several times before the snow got deep enough to cover all trace of the track, she noticed other tracks branching off, leading perhaps to this or that distant flickering light or cluster of lights marking a farmhouse or a village. But he always chose his path without hesitation.

Ahead of them there seemed to be nothing but shadow and the sound of the falls. Yet he moved surefootedly, not pausing to take his bearings.

Then at last, just before evening darkened into night, when she thought her fingers and her nose must be black with frostbite, he stopped. The snow whirled, and Lana gasped as a white-grey wall loomed up in front of her.

A door creaked, and Arash led her through into a

courtyard. There was less protection here than she would have imagined from the height of the wall, but the reason became evident when another gust swept aside the falling snow to reveal massive damage a little further along.

*"Ya Sulayman! Ya Suhail!"* Arash called, but his voice was eaten up in the roar of the storm.

There was no light anywhere.

"Is there a house?" Lana asked, peering around her. The wall was fairly typical, a kind she had seen before. It probably surrounded a large house and garden and perhaps an orchard. Generally such a place was the home of the sheikh or tribal leader, or the village chief. In her travels, finding the best projects to undertake—digging a new well here, rebuilding the mosque school there—she had often been offered the hospitality of such homes.

So it was likely that Arash had brought her to the house of the local sheikh. But it was strange that there were no lights. The house of a village chief should be full of people and lights, and, in weather like this, the courtyard and even some of the rooms might be crowded with animals. She wondered if it was even still standing.

"Yes, there is a house," Arash responded, after shouting again and receiving no reply. "What is left of it."

He moved forward, and she had to follow. Then, as they got closer, the snow briefly cleared, and she caught a broad vista of a once palatial, but badly damaged house. It had obviously been the home of an important sheikh. Probably the tribal leader of the whole valley, with a pedigree going back centuries.

Even half shrouded by the storm and cloaked in

night, the ruin made her shake her head in sorrow. It must have been a beautiful place, built on several terraced levels up the hillside.

As they walked she saw the intricately patterned paving stones under her feet, broken now, and a dry channel said that a spring had once made its way through the garden. There were the remains of delicate archways and, just visible on the far side of the flat roof, an intact dome.

Although there were some signs of industry—a neat pile of new bricks, some boarded-up windows—no extensive repair seemed to have begun.

Arash led her towards a doorway and pushed open the door, and she followed him inside, out of the wind's icy blast.

He shoved the door shut against the wind. They stood for a moment in total darkness. Catching her breath, she felt him fumble with something.

"Didn't we bring a flashlight?" she asked, and found that she was speaking in a whisper.

"One moment," Arash said, in a normal voice, and just then a match flared and she saw his hand reach for the glass chimney of an oil lamp on a small shelf just above her eye level at the doorway.

He lit the wick and replaced the chimney, then poked the small metal match back into the little box and restored it to its place behind the lamp. Dimly she wondered how he had known where the flintbox was in the darkness.

They stood looking around a large shadowed room. There were windows in one wall, a rug covered a doorway leading off the wall opposite the door they had come in by, a tiny arch opened in another. The room was intact, untouched by any bomb damage, and Lana was warmer just by virtue of being out of the wind.

She gratefully stripped off her gloves and began to rub her freezing fingers as she looked around.

There were rugs spread thickly on the paving stones, a large pile of cushions, a low square table, a carved sideboard, and a big bronze charcoal brazier in one corner.

These were evidence of wealth and an important family fallen on hard times, like the house itself. Country people, and even many city people in Parvan, sat and ate their meals from a simple cloth spread on the floor.

In the corner was a folded stack of quilts on a traditional *korsi*, so they slept as well as ate here, at least in cold weather. It seemed the actual living space had shrunk to this one room.

She blew on her hands and held them to her cold nose while Arash called again and got no answer.

"I guess there's nobody home," she said.

"No," said Arash.

"Do you know the master of the house?"

"I am the master of the house," he said, bowing his head in the traditional greeting of his people. "Welcome to the ancestral home of the al Khosravi."

# Four

The lamplight revealed some kindling wood stacked in a corner and charcoal in a metal scuttle. Arash dragged the bronze brazier over to the arched doorway in the opposite wall, lifted the rug that hung there and hooked it open. Then he began to lay a fire in the brazier.

The room was cold but not chill, and Lana wondered who was living here now, and when they would return.

There was a second oil lamp on the low table and she wordlessly knelt to light it before starting to unload food from their backpacks to create the meal they were both hungry for. Too late, she wondered if she ought to have asked permission.

It was a strange and disorienting experience to have been brought to his home so unexpectedly. Since she had come to Parvan, Arash had made it very clear he did not intend to renew any friendship with her. Refusing money was only part of it.

After an initial period of hurt confusion, she had learned to respect his boundaries—if respect was the word. She carefully avoided anything that might be construed as pushiness.

So although she had funded projects in this valley, she had never visited it. She had made a paper decision, or sent one of her team. She hadn't even known exactly where the valley was situated. She realized that she must have avoided even seeing the name on a map.

The Valley of Aram.

No, not avoided. Why should she care where Arash's home was? There were lots of valleys she hadn't been to, lots whose names she wouldn't recognize. It was only chance that this valley was among them.

Perhaps she was picking up some mood from him. Maybe it bothered him having to bring her here. She was sure only the strongest necessity could have forced him to do it. Looking back to that moment in the truck, she imagined he had made the decision with some reluctance.

And that might have nothing to do with her. Maybe that was just because it hurt him to see his home. Once so beautiful, now a ruin.

Yet it still had something…. Lana paused for a moment in her labours and looked around, like an animal sniffing the air.

"What is it?" Arash's voice invaded her thoughts.

"I don't know," she said slowly. "It's just…this place."

He was quiet for a moment. "Yes?" he prompted, when she didn't speak.

"I don't know, it's just got…it seems ridiculous to

say it, when it's been bombed, but it has such a peaceful feeling. The air seems different here. Or something,'' she said, laughing a little because that kind of imagining was really unlike her.

But Arash did not laugh. He nodded. ''It has always been so. That is perhaps where the valley got its name.''

She remembered suddenly, and smiled. It meant two things, he had told her once: in Parvani it meant the Valley of Tranquility; in Arabic, the Valley of White Antelopes.

''Have you been here very much since…have you been here recently?'' she asked, on the thought.

''Twice in the past few months, for brief visits.''

In a little rush of words she asked, ''Do you mind my being here?''

He looked at her thoughtfully. ''Mind? Why?''

Sorry that her voice had given expression to her thoughts, she shrugged.

He let the silence go on just long enough to underline it. Then he said, ''I do not mind bringing you to my home, Lana.''

In the handsome carved ebony sideboard that looked as though it had been imported from India in some previous century, Lana found dishes, cutlery, sugar, salt and pepper, everything neatly stacked and clearly in recent use. There was a woman's hand evident everywhere, from the high polish on the sideboard and the bronze charcoal brazier to the clean patterned cloth covering the low table.

''Who lives here now?'' she asked.

''Two of my father's servants.''

When the fire was going, she saw his wisdom, for most of the smoke from the brazier was drawn out through the doorway. Arash stood up, picked up his flashlight and a tin pail that stood on a small stool near the door. He disappeared out the doorway.

A warm, glowing comfort seemed to settle on the room, emanating from the two circles of lamplight and from the broad flickering fire in the brazier which sent odd moving shapes around the walls through the carved patterns in its lid.

Lana breathed deeply, absorbing the deep comfort for a moment, before getting up and moving to the stack of cushions she saw. She began to spread the cushions on two sides of the table.

When he returned with the pail full of water, Arash's hair was thick with snow.

"What's it doing out there?" Lana asked.

There was a wooden dipper on the stool and he set down the pail and put the dipper into it.

"Snowing very heavily, and a strong wind. There is a toilet. Shall I show it to you now?"

With a nod she followed him out through the curtained doorway into an adjoining room which, though she could see little detail in the flashlight's glow, seemed to be stacked with furniture. A hole in one corner of the roof let in a very cold draft and snow was drifting across the tiled floor.

Diagonally across the room there was an opening, and once through this they entered a passage. A couple of doors along, Arash stopped and opened a door.

Inside, the first thing she saw was a bucket, and her heart sank. Then, to her relief, the light brushed over a typical Parvani toilet—the white square of enamel on the floor, with a hole in the centre and two foot-shaped patches either side of it, that she had already grown accustomed to using.

Above was a cistern with a chain, but Arash said, "The water supply is damaged. There is a pail of water for sluicing."

Then he handed her the flashlight and left her.

It wasn't easy to use a typical Parvani toilet when you were wearing briefs, two pairs of leggings, a pair of jeans and sweatpants, but the icy air added impetus to her efforts. Lana was soon back in the warmth.

The fire had died down and stopped smoking, and the brazier had been moved over to within reach of the table. The carpet over the doorway was down, to keep the heat in. Arash's jacket was hanging up and his boots were by the door. He was filling a kettle as she entered, and he set it to boil on the brazier.

She moved over to the coat hooks and slipped out of her own jacket and scarf and boots. She stretched gratefully.

"Oh, that's better!"

A huge sack of rice was leaning against the sideboard. Arash took a cooking pot from a shelf high on one wall and began measuring rice and water into it, then sprinkled some salt in before kneeling to place it beside the kettle.

A charcoal brazier was really a miracle of engineering, as Lana had come to appreciate during her time visiting the countryside of Parvan. It would cook their food and provide heat, and because they were burning charcoal there would be little smoke.

This one was also beautiful to look at. The elaborate, handcrafted design that decorated it and sent haunting shadow patterns onto the walls probably meant it had descended in a wealthy family for generations. When a sheikh had commissioned such a thing from the best craftsman in an age of excellence, succeeding generations were not hasty in replacing it.

Rousing herself from her reverie, Lana moved over to sink down on the cushions by the table. Seeing him against the background of his own home, she felt her curiosity in him stirred. She didn't usually let herself think much about Arash, though she felt no such inhibition with the other Cup Companions.

"Were you born here?" she asked, when he had adjusted the pots on the brazier and relaxed back on the cushions that were kitty-corner to where she was sitting. As always, he sat with his right leg stretched out.

"Yes," he said.

"In this house?" she pressed.

He picked up two of the pieces of *naan* which she had placed on the table and reached over to balance them carefully on the handles of the brazier to warm.

"Where else?" His dark eyes moved to hers. "This is my home and the home of my family for many generations past. My ancestors were born here and *insh'Allah* my own son will be born here."

A little ripple of irritation scraped down her spine at his words.

"And where will your daughter be born?" she asked dryly, and knew only when she spoke that was not what she had wanted to say.

He gazed levelly at her. "I spoke of my son because I was speaking of his inheritance—as occupier of this house and as sheikh of the tribe of Aram. If God wills, I shall have many sons and daughters. But it is my eldest son who must inherit."

"What if you don't have a son?"

She didn't really know what prompted her to try to provoke him. Maybe just what she had feared if she was too much alone with him—a bubbling up of some nameless, long-held resentment.

When Lana had come to Parvan in the aftermath of the war and, deeply moved by what she saw, had poured her father's money like balm on the bruised and hungry land, of course she had been glad to meet Arash again. Of course she had been glad he had survived the war.

But when she tried to say so, he had looked at her gravely, as if he scarcely remembered who she was but was determined not to let her capitalize on their previous acquaintance.

Well, as if it mattered. Arash was alone in holding her at arm's length. There wasn't a Parvani citizen in the length and breadth of the land who wasn't half prepared to turn Lana Holding into a saint, among them Arash's own people.

"La-na!" they would cry, when she climbed out of a truck or helicopter or down off the back of a horse or mule, recognizing her by her curling red hair and creamy skin even if they had never seen her before, because her fame spread from valley to valley faster than her transport. "Lana!"

She soon learned that in Arabic her name meant, "he softened". For many, the "he" in question was "God," as in "God softened his anger towards us and sent us balm for our wounds." For everyone it meant that the horror of destruction was relieved by her generosity.

And the Parvanis were a people who understood generosity.

"Lana's team" would enter a village or a valley or

a field, and work for a time, and then the evil "butterfly" mines lurking in houses, in wells, in fields, in schools, mines that might otherwise have taken a foot or a hand or an eye were gone, and the people could return to the land, their homes and schools and lives.

A chief would write a letter about an irrigation system which had been deliberately destroyed by the Kaljuks, and Lana would come with her experts and find a way, and the money, to restore it. She had imported planeloads of seed and distributed it in time for the spring planting, a crucial step to recovery for the farmers, for whom the war had broken the cycle of planting and harvest. Schools and mosques everywhere were being rebuilt.

She tried never to impose, nor simply to give charity, but to find ways to help people help themselves within their own priorities. She discussed and negotiated, so that the people themselves decided what was best for them. Villages got teams of mules, perhaps, or flocks of sheep and goats, to be shared among all.

Her donations helped the many women whom the war had made widows to start herb farms, or simple factories for the manufacture and export of carpets, textiles, ceramics or other handicrafts, that they had previously produced only for their own use. In the prettiest and most historically interesting areas, they opened small tourist guest houses.

All this meant that women could earn the money to feed their families rather than be dependent on continuing handouts. And her connections abroad often guaranteed these products a market.

Parvan was beginning to thrive again, and everyone said it couldn't have been done without Lana.

Arash resolutely stood apart. His refusal to accept

any money from her various funds had always been incomprehensible to her, but of course it had never really affected her. It was his loss, not hers.

Now she was here, and could see the ruin of this once-proud house with her own eyes. And the thought that he would not compromise with his dislike of her even for the sake of restoring this beautiful estate was sharply painful.

And so, very human, she said, "What if you have no sons?"

His face closed, his jaw clenched, and he turned away from her to see to the warming bread. He carefully turned over each piece.

"If I have no son, then there will be no one to inherit the land and title," he said. "No one to carry out the sheikh's duties among the people."

His voice scarcely disguised a deep pain. She had never heard that note in his voice before. She realized that in this he was deeply, painfully vulnerable.

Lana closed her eyes, biting her lip. Her desire to hurt him had been unconscious, a basic human reaction to being hurt herself. Too late she remembered his father and elder brother, both lost in the fighting. For Arash and the people of Parvan, most of the old certainties had been wiped away.

This was not the time or place to challenge the law of primogeniture.

"I'm sorry, Arash, I didn't mean…"

"But that is a long way in the future," he continued, as if she hadn't spoken. "There is much work here to occupy me before I can think of taking comfort in a wife and family."

She glanced around them at the pitiful remains of his heritage.

"What—restoring this house, you mean?" she asked.

"This house, and the lands, and the flocks, and the valley, and the people's livelihood," he agreed.

"Are you saying you won't get married till all this—" she waved a hand, "—is rebuilt?"

"A man does not marry until he has something to offer a wife."

The charcoal brazier was hot now, shedding a very welcome warmth and a comforting red glow around the table. A pot was starting to simmer.

"Don't you think that a woman who loved you would want to share in the rebuilding with you?"

Arash gazed at her, but his dark eyes were without expression.

"A man does not marry unless he has something to offer a wife," he repeated woodenly.

Lana blinked at him.

"Are you serious?"

"Why not?"

She shrugged; it wasn't her business at all. "Well, where I come from, if a woman loves a man she doesn't wait around till he's paid the mortgage."

His eyes bored into her, his face shadowed in the flickering lamplight. She had the feeling that some of his inner control had slipped, and that she was seeing a part of him that he had been keeping hidden.

"You, of course, will not have to wait for a man to do so. You are in a position to pay the mortgage yourself."

Angry heat burned her cheeks. "What's your point? That any man will only love me for my father's money?"

"I am not such a fool," he told her flatly. There was

an expression in his eyes that she couldn't fathom. She stared as if locked by the beam, and licked her lips. Did that mean he himself found her attractive? But in that case, why…

"Well, what is your point, then?" she demanded, ruthlessly breaking into her own train of thought.

She looked away to fiddle with the intricately chased salt pot in the warm circle of lamplight, carefully aligning it out of the shadow of the matching silver sugar *qadron* so that the light glinted from its highly polished surface, as though that were an important task.

"Your father's wealth insulates you from the ordinary necessity of men and women, Lana."

"I don't think so." Ashamed of her weakness, she lifted her head and gazed deliberately into his face.

He raised his eyebrows, and she explained, "The ordinary necessity between men and women is love, and a commitment to the future. Whether two people are in this valley contemplating a bombed out ruin, or in Los Angeles trying to buy a place with a second bedroom for the baby, or in a mansion trying to book a slot at the best school, it's always going to be easier when the work is shared, isn't it?"

"This may be true where two people choose their own future. For me it is different."

"Why?"

He had spoken as though what he said was the final word on the subject. He looked irritated at being pushed.

"You think love should conquer all, Lana?" he asked dryly.

"I think I wouldn't want the man I loved to think the way you're thinking, and not many women would."

"In a situation like this—" he lifted a hand to indicate the house "—that will require many years of labour before it is habitable again, should a man ask a woman to marry him, knowing that he will be at hard physical work every day, from sunup to sundown, rebuilding all that his ancestors have built over centuries and has been destroyed?

"Should he offer a woman he loves a husband she would see only when he was racked with fatigue and frustration, too tired even to talk with her, too poor to offer her beautiful things to decorate her beauty before her youth was over? What would you think of a man who asked such sacrifice of your own youth?"

She rubbed the tip of her nose pensively. "I guess I would expect to work beside him, Arash. We could always talk while we were repairing the dry-stone walls or feeding the livestock, couldn't we?"

"I cannot ask a woman to help me in a task that is mine alone," he said, as if that argument were obvious.

"But didn't you just tell me that your son will inherit?" Not waiting for his reply, she went on, "Excuse me for pointing out the obvious, but that son will be your wife's child, too. Why shouldn't she help build an inheritance for her child?"

She waved her hand to indicate the place around them. There was a tension between them now, and she realized vaguely that it was not new.

He did not reply. "Are we talking about a real woman here?" Lana asked. "I mean, there is someone who is waiting for you to do all this work?"

He shook his head. "Once I thought to marry the woman of my choice. But the war ended that for me."

She snapped, "Well, more fool you, then."

His eyes flashed with outraged masculine fire.

"Do not call me a fool, Lana," he returned, very evenly.

"I'm sorry. But are you telling me that you have been restrained from marrying the woman you want because your life is not the same as it was before the war?"

There was another long pause as he gazed at her. Then, and she was sure he spoke against his will, he said, "Yes."

She shook her head. "And she's willing to put up with this?"

"She knows nothing of it."

Lana felt her jaw dropping. She tried to speak, stopped, tried again. "You didn't even tell her? What if she marries someone else before you're ready to declare yourself?"

"It will be best for her."

"Are you in love with her, Arash, or is this a dynastic marriage we're talking about here?"

"I am in love with her," Arash said simply, but his voice held the reflection of a deeply suppressed passion, so harsh and raw that she almost felt sorry for the woman who was the object of it. It would be like standing in a blast furnace if he ever let go.

# Five

The pot of simmering water suddenly broke into a rolling boil and, as if grateful for the interruption, Arash turned and found tea and mint in the sideboard. He tossed some into the pot, then removed it from the heat.

"I hope Suhail and Sulayman won't mind when they come home and find that we've used their supplies," Lana said, grateful too for the chance to change the subject.

Arash got to his feet and moved through the shadowed room over to the window. He wiped the glass and peered out.

Then he turned. "They will not mind." He smiled. "Have you lived in my country so long without learning this?"

Lana shook her head. "No one could be in Parvan for ten minutes without learning a whole new definition of generosity," she assured him. "Are they your father's servants you spoke of?"

"Yes. They live alone here now, as simple caretakers. I am sure they will be back soon," he said, but she wasn't sure whether it was her or himself whom he was comforting with the thought.

Lana blinked. "They won't come home tonight, will they?"

There was a curious pause, as if this was the first time the thought had struck him. "It is only a little after seven o'clock," he murmured, and his dark eyes seemed unwillingly drawn to hers. She could not read the expression in them.

Lana shivered all over her body without knowing why. Arash turned back to the window, but the shape of his back told her that whatever he saw was on his own mental screen.

"Arash, what is it? What's the matter?"

Was it possible he was worried that they were out there somewhere in the storm? It seemed so unlikely. The storm had certainly not come down without warning. But he abruptly moved towards the door, picked up his jacket and pulled it on.

"What are you doing? Where are you going?" she cried.

"To find Suhail and Sulayman," he said, as if the answer were obvious. "They are not young. The weather will make it difficult for them."

"Arash, there's a village, there are farms, aren't there? You don't really think they're out there lost in this now? They had plenty of warning there was going to be a blizzard. Don't you think they're just staying put for the night?"

"Perhaps," he agreed, nodding. "Someone will know where. I'll find them."

He opened the door, and a blast of snow came in on a devil's wind. It scurried all around her, making her shiver. The flame in both lamps flickered; shadows danced wildly on the walls. Smoke puffed from the brazier.

"In this?" she cried, utterly mystified. "You'll freeze to death yourself!"

"It is not so bad yet. If they do not come home tonight, however..."

Lana jumped up. The lamp flames were almost blown out and it seemed as if light as well as comforting warmth was being sucked from the room. Now the shadows were not intimate, but sinister. She was floundering, out of her depth.

"Arash, you *can't* go out in this!"

She reached for him in her urgency, grabbing the stuff of his jacket in both hands, as if to hold him back forcibly. She almost laughed at the futility of it. He was so big, a mountain warrior. She couldn't have held him for a second against his will.

But at her touch, as if it had such power, he stopped.

Lana gazed into his eyes, her mind racing with conjecture.

"Please," she breathed. "If you go out in this, we might both die. What will I do if you don't come back?"

He lifted his hands to hers. She resisted only briefly as he made her let him go and drew her hands away from his chest.

"You are safe here," he said. Then he shook his head and, stepping through the doorway, banged it shut behind him. The lamp by the door went black, and for a second she thought it had gone out entirely. But the flame returned as if from nowhere to renew its struggle against the dark.

Lana shivered as the cold air encircled her. What on earth did he fear? Not that Suhail and Sulayman would have set off for home in this, she was sure. They could have stopped at any home in the valley and asked for shelter. If one thing was certain, it was that the two servants were safe somewhere.

She thought of the way he had looked at her, as if wrestling with something he could not explain, and she wondered if the storm, the shadows, even perhaps their conversation had triggered some memory in him.

Did he suffer from some war trauma? Lana's mother's brother had been in Vietnam. Lana had learned a lot about war trauma over the years of her growing up.

She also knew there had been a hard winter of fighting in the mountains and that Arash had been in several of the battles.

"Oh, God, please no!" she cried aloud, and made a dive for her own jacket and boots. In a fever of impatience she got into them and tore open the door.

"Arash!" she cried. The wind battered at the door to push her back into the room. Snow blasted, hard and stinging, into her face. This time the lamp gave up and went out. Swearing, Lana forced her way out into the darkness, dragged the door shut and then stood in the blinding, white-swirled black, trying to get her eyes accustomed, trying to find her bearings.

She groped her way across the paving stones with her arms fully outstretched ahead of her, buffeted by wind, groping for the wall. She touched it before she saw it, and kept one hand on it as she moved. After a few minutes, she felt the outer door under her hands and struggled to open it.

With a roar of rage, the wind tore it from her fingers, almost from its hinges, and bashed it back against the wall. Lana was sucked out into the cold and merciless heart of the maelstrom.

"Arash!" she screamed helplessly, while the wind smashed her to her knees as if she had been hit with a club. God in heaven, where was he? In a storm like this you could die five feet from your own front door! She had heard stories of such things happening, of bodies found huddled against some tiny protection only yards from warmth and life.

Kneeling where she had fallen, trying to see, to listen through the howl for Arash's voice, Lana felt the first icy drop of terror dribble down her spine. Where was the house? She could see nothing but the whirling of the snowflakes. Before, she had seen the secret of life in their wild dance, but now she knew it for the dance of death.

Still on her knees, she turned this way and that, her face lashed raw with stinging snow. Nothing. No one. Her confused senses scarcely told her which way the land sloped under her.

Desperately she shuffled forward on her knees. Was she going uphill or down?

She stopped and reached with her arms, feeling all around her for the wall. She must be no more than a few feet away from it, but if she went the wrong way for only a yard, she might never find it.

"Arash! Arash!" she screamed, and the wind sucked the very breath from her throat and threw the words away. "Arash!"

A hysterical giggle arose in her throat—was she offering rescue, or seeking it? What the hell good was she going to be to Arash even if she did find him? All she could do in her ignorance would be die with him.

But even though she was helpless in the face of such weather, she could not have left him out here alone. If he was in the grip of some traumatic war memory, he might be blind and deaf to the true reality of his situation. God alone knew what he might be seeing in his mind.

She might at least wake him from that.

"Arash!" she cried again. If she could find him and bring him to himself—Arash was a mountain man. He would bring them home safe again.

She began to pray, moving through the snow on her knees and sometimes on all fours—it was futile to try to stand—trying to shield her eyes from the burning, driving snow as she peered helplessly around her into the storm. Her hands were already freezing cold, and she could feel the cold seeping through at her knees.

"Arash!"

*I am not going to let him die like this! What will the tribe do without him? What will Kavi do if he loses his best friend so uselessly? And Alinor, she loves him, too! How will they survive if Arash dies?*

"Arash! Arash!"

*So many people love him and count on him, and it would kill them if he died, and I am not going to let it happen! They love him, you can't let him die, everybody loves him, I...I...*

"Aaarash! Where are you? *Aaaraaaash!*"

Out of the storm, without warning, something leapt on her. Something huge. She screamed crazily and was knocked flat into a bed of snow.

For a split second she lay passive, waiting for the first slash of tooth or claw that would end the storm and life and all for her. *Is this death, then?* she asked, with a crystal acceptance.

Then, suddenly, life erupted in her with violent denial.

"I have to find him!" she shrieked, lashing out wildly and feeling the blow connect. The animal—it must be some kind of mountain cat—reeled up in surprise.

"Lana!" it cried. *"Lana!"*

Arash.

"Arash? Oh, God! Arash!"

He tried to lift himself off her, but twice the wind blew him flat. Down at ground level, the shrieking howl was muted.

"What the hell are you doing?" Arash shouted in her ear, subsiding where he lay for a moment, stretched out, half on her body, half buried in snow.

The shape of each of them was balm to the other, the reminder of human existence in a bleak and terrifying landscape, and each unconsciously clung to the certainty that was the other.

"I was looking for you! Good thing you found me!"

She began to laugh as sweet relief flooded her. They were safe now. Arash would find the way back to warmth and life and love....

Funny how warm snow could seem when you were being buried in it. Down here on the ground, with the snow already drifting against them and Arash's breath hot on her cheek, Lana could suddenly understand those strange Northern stories about people who lay down to sleep in the blizzard. She would like nothing better than to wrap him to her like a blanket and...

He shouted again, but this time the wind howled and shrieked and she could not hear. Arash struggled up on one knee. In a wind like this the inflexibility of his leg hampered his attempts to stand, but he dragged Lana to a sitting position.

"Get up!" he ordered, and she smiled.

"Easier said than done, mister!"

They struggled to their feet at last, and then he took her hand and to Lana's amazement she took only half a dozen steps and then stepped through the courtyard doorway. Astonishing how close safety was. She had felt as if she was alone in the Arctic wastes.

They fought to get the door closed and bolted against a wind that was determined not to let them, and then made their way to the inner door and the room where warmth and light triumphed over death and darkness. This door, too, they closed and bolted.

Arash turned, and his hands of their own accord gripped her upper arms. Lana felt his heat burn through all the layers of her clothes towards her heart.

She could not find words for any of the thousand thoughts that tumbled around her mind. Something more than death had beckoned to her out in the storm, something even more dangerous.

And the threat of death had passed, but that other threat was still present. It was in the purple depths of Arash's eyes, in the hungry need she felt to fling herself against his stalwart body and assure herself he was real.

This was the deeper danger—that the brush of death's greedy fingers had torn away a veil. Behind that veil lurked a truth that she must not let herself see....

His hands tightened on her arms, and her breasts

rose and fell in a trembling breath. Time gently slowed for her, to allow her to perceive every flicker of his eyelash, every movement of the muscle in his jaw, the pulse at his throat that gave the bass beat to the music of her life. The flexing of his lips as they parted and firmly closed again.

She remembered another time when he had held her like this, when her life had trembled in the balance as it did now. *I have nothing to offer you,* he had said then.

And it was true.

She closed her eyes and turned away her head, and felt how his hands tightened in a brief convulsion and then slowly let her go.

They turned to the mundane task of kicking off their boots and hung their jackets again. Then they moved over to the low table, where the lamp still bravely burned and the brazier glowed attractively red.

The *naan* was burning.

The ordinary world slid into place with a small shock. Arash bent and snatched the two pieces of *naan* up and dropped them in the centre of the table. The smell of charred bread struck her nostrils with curious sharpness, as if her senses had responded to the threat of extinction with increased appreciation of the world.

As if they were grateful for the distraction from some other need.

Lana was suddenly starving.

She flung herself down on the cushions, reached for a piece of *naan* and, though it was burning hot, tore off a piece. She dipped it in the little dish of hummus she had set out.

*"BismAllah,"* she murmured, and popped it into her mouth. The bread sizzled on her tongue and she panted

quickly to cool it and flapped her hand in front of her mouth.

"Oh, that's delicious!" she exclaimed, when she had chewed and swallowed. "I am so hungry! Aren't you starving?"

Arash, standing above her in the gloom, breathed once, deeply. "Yes," he said. "I am starving."

To her relief he sat down and reached for some *naan.*

She had put out some of the food they had brought, and after a mouthful or two of hummus Arash picked up a dish of cold casseroled lamb and tomatoes and turned to stir it into the cooking rice.

He began rooting through the sideboard and pulled out spices he found there—cumin, she thought, and coriander—and sprinkled a tiny amount of each into the mix.

Lana's stomach growled as delicious scents rose in the steam, and she unconsciously picked up her fork and watched hungrily as he served the mixture onto their plates. The physical and mental strain she had been through had turned her ravenous hunger into sheer starvation.

Then, in the silence that real hunger imposes on eaters, they ate.

"Do you really think Suhail and Sulayman might be caught out in the storm?" she murmured tentatively, when they had eaten all the rice and lamb, and Arash was pouring tea into the two delicate, traditional tea glasses that sat in chased silver holders.

Arash's thick dark eyebrows went down in a dark, surprised frown. "No," he said.

She pressed her lips together, wondering if he

wanted her to make an opportunity to talk about whatever it was.

"But you were determined to rescue them."

He eyed her with dark intensity. "Not to rescue them. To bring them home."

"But why?"

There was a glimmer of deepest violet.

"You know what it was that drove me. Why do you wish to talk about it?"

She didn't understand why he thought she knew. Did he imagine Alinor had told her something?

"Well, if I do, it's only a very general guess. I thought that you might want to get it off your chest—"

"What could be more stupid and dangerous than to get such a thing off my chest now?" he said crushingly.

She wrapped her arms around her own shoulders. "Why, would it…" She licked her lips. "I mean, I really don't understand, Arash, so if you think I've been told something, I haven't."

"Told?" he said disbelievingly. "What need have you to be told? You know it."

She was mystified and uncomfortable, and mutely shook her head.

He gazed at her unblinkingly. "What is it, then, that you imagine the case to be?"

She half shrugged. "My uncle was in a war. He—afterwards, he used to have memories that he couldn't control. He'd just hear something and flash onto some horrible thing."

Looking at his clear eyes now she knew she had been wrong. There was no shadow there of the kind she remembered in her uncle's eyes.

"I belong to a warrior race, Lana. We fought as we

have always fought for our homeland. We fought to defend our people, our homes. I have wounds, like all my countrymen. But such memories as these that you speak of are for the Kaljuks, to remind them forever of the price of an unjust war.''

She nodded, mesmerized by his eyes and voice.

''But you are not such a fool, Lana.''

''It didn't fit with what I know of you. But—what else could it have been?'' she murmured defensively.

He shook his head and was silent, bending to drink his mint tea.

''Why won't you tell me what it was?''

She heard the little clink of the glass hitting its saucer.

''Why do you press it? What is it you want?'' His voice was soft with exasperation. ''We are alone here! You know what can happen!''

She stared at him in sudden, angry disbelief as a hint of the truth dawned on her.

''What?'' she cried. ''What exactly are you saying?'' It seemed to her that fury overwhelmed her in a rush of blind heat.

He was silent, his mouth tight with impatience as he watched her make for the cliff's edge against all his warnings.

''I don't believe it! You're saying you went out into that…that maelstrom, you risked your life—in order to provide us with a *chaperone?*''

# Six

"**I** don't *believe* it!" Her blood was pumping with indignation so fierce she felt faint.

"What do you not believe?" he said in a controlled, level voice. He gazed steadily at her.

"What exactly are you suggesting?" she countered.

"In Parvan an unmarried man and woman do not stay alone together, Lana. You know this. Especially at night."

What a ridiculous, archaic sentiment! After all the stress of the day, this was just too much! She sat up straight, glaring at him.

"Why, exactly? Not because you might seduce me—you don't like me nearly enough for that! So, what then? Afraid I might try to seduce you?"

"Is it impossible?"

She gasped and drew back as if he had slapped her.

"Well, you're right, of course! It wouldn't be the

first time, would it?'' she replied bitterly. ''But we all learn our lessons, Arash. I've been immunized against your fatal charms now. I'm not likely to throw myself into your arms a second time.''

''I do not suggest that you will deliberately throw yourself at me!'' he said irritably.

''It sure sounded like it!''

''Only because you are ready to be angry with me.''

''No, I don't think so! I think I drew a perfectly reasonab—''

''Whatever you believed, and whether you had reason to do so, Lana, it is not what I meant! Why do you inflame our feelings in this way? Do you not see how dangerous high emotions are at such a time?''

''However high my emotions get, Arash, they are very unlikely to shift from anger to undying love!'' she said furiously.

He was silent, gazing at her, until she became uncomfortable.

''You are more intelligent than this. I will not argue with you,'' he said, struggling for calm. ''I am my father's heir, the spiritual and temporal leader of the tribe of Aram. My father's people would be deeply distressed to learn that I had brought to this valley and this house, and spent the night alone with, a woman who was not my wife. Let this reason be enough for you.''

''There's a blizzard, for heaven's sake!''

''That such things as blizzards can strike unexpectedly is the very reason why we should not have been travelling alone together in the beginning.''

''So what's your real point here, Arash? That we might forget who we are, or that your father's people will imagine that we did?''

"My point is no longer important. We are alone and we can do nothing about it. Except to guard against..."

"Yes, you've done it now!" She interrupted him without apology. "You probably saved our lives by bringing us here, Arash! What a pity we didn't just stay in the truck. We might have frozen to death by now, or be dead in an avalanche!"

"Why do you wish to anger me, Lana, by saying these unintelligent things? Ask yourself why! Do you not see what is already at work?"

She felt a buzz of awareness at his words, as if something in her was trying to speak, but another part of her refused to hear.

She said levelly, "I think your arrogance has to be seen to be believed. The people in this valley aren't so backward they—"

"My father's people do not receive television signals, but they know the difference between men and women. You have been raised to think you are above the human condition because of sophistication. Is it really so?"

"Are you trying to tell me that I'm going to be seized with uncontrollable desire for you, Arash, just because we're alone together? If so, you couldn't be more..."

His hand snapped across the corner of the table that separated them and closed on her wrist where her arm rested in the circle of lamplight. His strong, sensitive hand was dark and rough with outdoor work, and he cupped her wrist and showed her her own delicate bone structure, the skin that was pale and creamy after the long Parvan winter, as if it were evidence of something.

She stared at their joined flesh, frowning, puzzling over some truth in the image, as if it were a mathematical equation. Then, in the continued silence, she looked up.

His face was softly shadowed, the deep violet of his eyes reflecting the lamp's tiny fire. She gazed wordlessly into the double flames, and as if they gave off real heat her blood warmed and her heartbeat grew wild.

"I am a man," he said flatly. "You are a woman. Let this explanation serve."

And suddenly, in the rich, intimate shadows and the isolation forced on them by the storm—for something in her registered the snow-filled hurricane that surrounded the house, and was deeply and strongly aware that it was impossible that their solitude could be disturbed—suddenly, the primitive incantation took on powerful meaning, and leapt between them.

It was as if by naming a tiger he had produced one.

He was a man. She was a woman. It was a powerful, dangerous mixture, as volatile and as predictable as the chemical formula for dynamite.

She thought dimly, *Dynamite doesn't refuse to explode because people get hurt. If you hold a match to a fuse, it will blow up.*

Lana licked her lips nervously, staring at him, taking in Arash's being without a filter for the first time in a very long time.

He was fiercely attractive, powerful, a man of magnetic charisma. The passionate anger in his eyes and the set of his mouth contributed to the essence of pure masculinity that emanated from him, a perfume that could drown her senses, flood her reason.

She swallowed.

"And what does that mean?" she whispered.

He did not answer, only looked at her with a burning sensual possessiveness that was fanning a fire deep inside her, a volcano at her centre she hadn't even known was there. Slowly, as if in explanation, he lifted her wrist off the table, while his other hand came up to her throat.

With painful, erotic deliberation, he pushed her down against the cushions spread so conveniently behind her and leaned down over her. The flame of his eyes invaded her thighs and her abdomen, spread through all her limbs, with a focus of melting fire.

Her body and blood churned. Arash was deeply, powerfully, sensually attractive to her, a fact that she had somehow been able to wipe from her memory.

"Why did you push me to this proof?" he asked. "You knew from the beginning the risks."

"No," she protested weakly.

His fingers stroked her throat, her chin, with little sparks of excitement, and his mouth was only a few inches above hers. Shivers of yearning rippled through her, demanding fulfillment.

Only once before in her life had she felt such a wild flood of excitement, of desire, of the most primitive passion.

"I do not believe you have forgotten," he said. "Then, too, you knew how I struggled."

She could not speak.

He still held her wrist captive, pressed into the cushion beside her head. She lay in shadow. Only the tips of her red curls, tumbled around her head to reveal the broad, curving white forehead and ears like newly opened flowers, caught the lamplight and glinted as if with their own fire. Her eyes searched his face disturbingly.

"What shall we do, Lana? Shall we give in to this sweet madness that can have no future, and then forget again? Do you take your chances now?"

At his words her heart twisted with a pain she thought she had forgotten. She *had* forgotten. She had convinced herself it was all meaningless, and now, suddenly…

Lana closed her eyes to shut out his face, and turned her head away.

"Not this time," she said flatly. "Let me up."

"I—" Arash began, then closed his eyes, and as if he were fighting his way through glue, he lifted his head, lifted his hand from her throat, let go her wrist, like a slow-motion film. A cold draft brushed her.

He struggled clumsily to his feet and moved over to the water pail. He dipped in the dipper and took a long drink from it, his back to her.

Then he picked up the almost empty coal scuttle and his flashlight and, lifting the carpet curtain, went out.

Silent and unthinking, Lana lay where he had left her. She mechanically registered the presence of a large tin bowl that the careful housewife had set under the low table. She blinked, slowly taking it in. Then she sat up, drawing the dishpan from its place, and put it on the table. There was a thick bar of soap and a dishcloth inside. She began stacking the dishes together.

A pot of water was simmering on the brazier. She poured the contents into the washbowl, and added water from the pail. She picked up a knife and the bar of soap. It was a thick, creamy grey oblong, one side gouged out in a shiny curve. As she had seen women do all over the villages of Parvan, Lana scraped the knife along the curve, letting the flakes of soap fall into the tepid water.

She swirled her hand in the water to create a few suds. Her mind was empty. She seemed to have no past, no future, no self. She was just a woman preparing to wash the dishes. She watched her hand move through the water, sudsing the soap into a froth, as if it were someone else's hand.

"Dance?" he repeated. His hands gripped her waist, hard, and in the shadowy room his eyes had been black with a danger that thrilled her, and she knew she had not been wrong. Arash Khosravi was powerless to resist her, and the dance he had in mind now did not need music.

They danced. Slow, sinuous, second by second less aware of their surroundings, their perceptual world the limited-limitless expanse of each other. His body pressed hers, melted into hers, so that she marvelled at this new phenomenon that she was both herself and part of this other being that was both two and one....

Did he struggle with himself during that dance? She never knew. To her it was all inevitable, and when darkness enveloped her she opened her eyes without surprise to find that they had left the room, had danced down a hallway to shadow....

Kavi's apartment was on the second floor of the Parvan Embassy, a massive suite of rooms which his bodyguards shared with him. In the shadows in the deserted hall, Arash's hands enclosed her in a grasp that would have been painful if it hadn't been so thrilling, and his mouth came down and took rough, hungry possession of hers. His arms wrapped her tightly and the next thing she knew, he simply lifted her off her feet, pressing her flat against himself, and, still kissing her, was walking through another huge room, into another darkened hall....

His strength astonished her. At the door to a room he paused, and, their mouths still pressed hungrily together, she lifted her legs up to cling around his waist, dragging the skirt of her dress up around her naked thighs to free them. He opened the door and entered another suite of rooms.

Inside it was dark. Every second was measured, as if time had a weight and meaning she had never understood before. He closed the door and leaned back against it, and she let her legs slide down to the floor again, let her body flatten against his, as they still kissed.

No kiss had ever made her so passionately drunk, so hungry, so sure. The pressure of his hardened body against her made her tear her mouth away to gasp in oxygen.

He kissed her throat in the darkness. She felt his hair, his ear, his cheek under her trembling hand, and that was all she needed to know, that she was in Arash's arms. She had never been so hungry, so wild for a man's mouth, his hands....

"Lana," he said, his voice urgent and low, and she felt him grasp her arms and, a drowning man, lift his head for air. "I can offer you nothing. I have nothing to offer you."

"What?" she murmured, smiling, her mouth of its own accord planting a row of little kisses along the perfect line of his cheek, delighting in the roughness of his shadow beard, the firm line of bone.

His arms wrapped her again. He lifted his chin away from her mouth, grasping for control.

"There is no future with me, Lana. I go tomorrow, to fight a war. I will not come back. Say no now, Lana, if you hope for more than this. Say no."

She didn't believe him. His arms were tight around her with possession, and her heart told her that his need, like her own, was more than sexual.

She dropped back her head and looked at him from smiling, slanted eyes. "I'll take my chances," she whispered.

Lana had washed the few dishes and was drying them by the time Arash came back through the curtained doorway with a bucketful of charcoal, his head and shoulders covered with snow.

"How's the weather?" she asked, not to let silence fall between them after what had happened.

"The snow is very, very heavy. The wind is less fierce," he said, as if he agreed that silence was dangerous.

"I can still hear it roaring, though."

"That sound is the waterfall. You will get used to it."

She paused, taking that in. She would get used to it?

"Aren't we going to leave tomorrow?"

He looked at her without speaking, the expression in his mouth and eyes saying it for him, then immediately turned to the business at hand. There was a blackened area on the floor on one side of the room, and, using two big pads designed for the purpose, he began to drag the brazier towards it.

Lana bit her lip and for a few moments went on drying the dishes and putting them away in the cabinet.

Arash lifted the lid of the brazier and began to lay lumps of charcoal on the bright embers.

"How long, then?" she couldn't stop herself asking. She was shivering with nerves.

They exchanged another look. Of course he knew no better than she. She was just babbling.

"What will we do for food?" she asked, but it was not that fear which caused her to shiver.

"In the morning we will take stock. Tonight, we should assume that lamp oil at least should be conserved." He put the lid back on. "We must put the lamp out and sleep now."

He moved over to the corner where the large stool-shaped frame of the *korsi* was stored and lifted it to set it protectively over the brazier, while Lana obediently moved the cushions onto the rugs that encircled the patch of blackened tiles around the brazier.

Then, in a ritual that was hundreds of years old at least, together they began to spread the quilts over the two piles of cushions on opposite sides of the *korsi,* making a traditional Parvan winter bed.

There was one huge circular quilt, more than twelve feet across, all browned at the centre, and they spread that one last, over everything, *korsi,* cushions and all.

She had seen entire families sleep like this, their bodies radiating out from the brazier like spokes from the hub of a wheel. The *korsi* kept the quilt away from the brazier, so that it didn't catch fire, while the heat was kept under the quilt. With your feet at the centre, and only your head sticking out of the quilt, you slept in toasty comfort, warmed by the brazier's long-burning heat.

It had its drawbacks: if you gave in to the temptation to keep the room snug and close, you might die of carbon monoxide poisoning. But Arash hooked the rug over the doorway open, to keep a fresh draft flowing during the night, and she braved the cold again to visit the toilet.

When she returned, everything was ready in the room.

They took off only their sweatsuits before stretching out under the quilts. Silence fell without her noticing, and when she did, Lana couldn't seem to find the words to break it.

She lay down, shifting her body to force the cushions into a comfortable mould around her. As Arash blew out the fragile little lamp flame, the darkness fell over her like another quilt. She heard him settle back against the cushions, knew his feet were just on the other side of the brazier from hers.

"Good night," she murmured.

"Good night, Lana."

Then she wished she hadn't spoken, because the little exchange in the darkness seemed to underline their intimate isolation, and she wished suddenly that they could be lying closer together—side by side, for the warmth and comfort that another human body brings in times of hardship.

But she had taken her chances once, and lost.

He had led her into a darkened room and flicked on a small lamp. There was a small sofa cluster, bookshelves, and in an alcove, a bed.

Although it was decorated in the high Middle Eastern fashion, with beautifully patterned rugs and draped material swathing the walls, the room was completely impersonal. There wasn't one book, one item of per-

sonal belongings, and the stack of luggage by the door
said it all.

He gazed at her for a moment of silence as she took
it in, as if waiting for her to change her mind. In the
morning, his look warned her, there would be no trace
of him in this room....

She blinded and deafened herself to the warning, to
the real meaning, and smiled at him with heavy-lidded,
longing eyes.

"Make love to me, Arash," she pleaded softly.

He caught her wrist hard, and drew her towards the
bed. The little alcove was decorated like a sultan's tent,
with festoons of patterned cloth draped from the ceiling
to cover all the walls...and he looked just like the sultan of a dream, barefoot in leather thong sandals, flowing white trousers and full-sleeved shirt, an intricately
embroidered, jewelled, sleeveless waistcoat.

He drew her dress off over her head, just as she had
dreamed he would when, earlier tonight, she had put
on the silk underwear.... In deep green, softest, finest
silk, she wore hareem pants that banded under the
knee, a little bolero top that exposed her skin from
breasts to hips. "Hareem pyjamas," the salesclerk had
called the outfit, in the exclusive, crazily expensive lin-
gerie shop where she had found them.

She looked like a Hollywood version of a concubine—voluptuous, curvaceous, her breasts spilling out
of the confines of the top, her hips and thighs full and
female. Her skin was rich cream, her red hair spilling
over her shoulders and back to glow in the lamplight,
her eyes gazing at him with deep sexual hunger and
expectation....

Sitting on the edge of the bed, he drew her between
his open thighs, and rested a kiss on her plump,

smoothly curving stomach. His hands of their own accord stroked her naked back, her curving, silk-covered rump, her strong thighs…her arms, her breasts, her shoulders.

He drew her head down, reached up to meet her lips with his, with powerfully disturbing hunger tearing at him, fighting against his self-control.

He found himself kneeling on the floor in front of her, kissing her flesh above the edge of the silk trousers, slowly drawing the fabric away to let his mouth trail closer and closer…he reached up and unbuttoned the front closing of the little jacket, so that above him her full breasts burst free, and he felt the heavy weight against his palms, the tantalizing beading of the nipples that told him his touch was pleasure to her.…

Shadow and lamplight mingled and blended, silence and her cries or his murmurs were the same, male and female too were one as he drew her down onto the bed and stretched out beside her, above her, and at last, inside.…

He had never expected to weep at the moment of oneness, never hoped to see the full human expanse of tragedy and joy in one act, nor to feel that deep connection that said from this moment on he would understand the universe only through her.

He had never been swept with such deep, wild, honeyed pleasure, never cried a name as though it was the answer to every question he could ask the universe, now and forever.

She awoke in the depths of the night, not remembering the dream that awakened her. She had been weeping in the dream. Her head was swirling with distant nameless memories which she did not want to recall.

Slowly, resistlessly, they surfaced—she had been dreaming of the night she had asked Arash to dance. Until tonight, she hadn't thought of that night for ages. She had put it all out of her mind.

The memory was sharp, strong, immediate, as if something in the darkness made her vulnerable, carried her straight back to that time. As if she had awakened inside that night again, as the person she had been then. Letting her feel again the passion, the yearning she had had, the need to touch him, to feel his arms around her, to believe that it meant something to him.

He had not guessed she was a virgin. He was big; her gasp of mingled pain and pleasure had been disguised by their mutual wild, drunken passion...and she was not experienced enough to know that he would have said something if he had known, or that she should tell him.

Only later did she understand the deep bond that had been forged between them, a bond she should have made him conscious of....

She had fallen asleep while the birds sang their early chorus, feeling that they sang the song of her heart, with a sure sense of rightness binding her to Arash, whose firm, muscled chest was under her head, whose arm enclosed her, whose hand gripped her in a wordless message of belonging....

She had awoken to solitude and silence. She sat up with a smile, looked around the room...and saw only her own clothing laid neatly over a chair. Her little handbag, which she had last seen on a sofa in the room where the party was held, was there, too.

The pile of luggage was gone, Arash's clothes were

gone. There wasn't a sign or sound to tell her another living being was in the world.

She flew up off the bed, dashed on her clothes, and ran out of the room and into the flat. A small group of cleaners was at work in the place...Prince Kavian and the others had left for the airport an hour ago.

She returned to his empty bedroom to search for a note, a message...nothing. She asked the cleaning staff...they had seen nothing, no paper, no message had been left.

So it was there, in the massively ornate main room of the Crown Prince's apartment in the Parvan Embassy, surrounded by sympathetic but uncomprehending strangers, that Lana had finally understood her own feelings.

Slowly, with absent steps, she had left the place, had wandered into the street, had hailed a black cab...had returned home.

There was a message on the answer phone, from Alinor. "Where did you get to? I'm sorry we never got a chance to say goodbye...."

No message from Arash, of course. And now, as well as understanding herself, she understood him.

"I have nothing to offer you, Lana..."

Love, he meant. He did not love her.

She had been in love with him. Crazily, wildly, deeply and passionately in love. With a love that, when she had finally accepted that she meant nothing to him, had nearly torn her heart in two.

Now it all came back...things she had forgotten, had forced out of her mind and memories in order to survive....

He had believed that an invasion of his country by its neighbour was inevitable—she had known that he was convinced that he was going home to fight a war. Prince Kavian had still been hopeful that it could be avoided, but Lana had watched Arash when his prince spoke of diplomatic solutions, had seen the bleakness in his eyes.

Once she had asked him what the result of war would be. She had forgotten that, too. But now she remembered as if she had asked him the question tonight.

She remembered the utter hopelessness in his expression, as if he already saw the loss of everything in life that held meaning for him.

"It means our total destruction, Lana," he had said. "We are a tiny nation and our oil reserves are not easy to access—the mountains make it difficult. Kaljukistan has much oil, and markets that the West wishes to exploit. It has also the arsenal left behind by its former Soviet masters. Who will help us in this war? Who will take our side?

"We have a way of life that is centuries old. It will be wiped out. All our wealth for generations will be mortgaged to buy the weapons we will need…we will have nothing. In the end we will have our sovereignty. Nothing besides."

Fearfully, she had asked, "But they won't win?"

"They will never win unless they kill every Parvani breathing. As long as one of us has breath Parvan will fight."

If he had given her the smallest opening, she would have said, "Let me come and fight beside you," that was how besotted she had been. She had ached for him, she had yearned to go and help to fight his war. But he had given her no opening….

She had thought of him constantly after he left,

sometimes not knowing for months at a stretch whether he lived or died. The Parvani-Kaljuki war was not a popular cause with Western journalists. She had learned then that no news was not good news. No news made you helpless, anxious, terrified that the blow might fall at any moment.

One day at university a fellow student had breathlessly told her, "Did you hear that one of Prince Kavian's friends got killed a couple of days ago? One of the blokes who was here with him?"

Her heart—her heart had clenched so spasmodically it seemed to stop the flow of life within her. She remembered the pain now with a renewal of that terrible, aching breathlessness, the ugly fear...it had showed her how wide was the gulf between hopelessness and real acceptance.

It was a dark, evil twenty-four hours before she could find out whether it was Arash or Jamshid who had died, because whichever one of them lived, whoever had died, the news was horrible, and yet she couldn't stop herself from wishing that it would not be *him*....

It was not him. It was Jamshid. Lana had grieved deeply for the handsome, laughing man, so young, so senselessly dead—so deeply that she had believed that if she did hear the news of Arash's death, she would not survive it.

If she had felt any hope that he would welcome it, Lana would have gone to Parvan then, would have found him, wherever he was, and told him...

But the war had closed the borders. With money, she probably could have gotten around that. But she did not believe he would welcome her or her love. He had told her she meant nothing to him, and he had left without one word, just to underline that message.

Jamshid had left behind a wife planning to join him as soon as the war was over. She had given birth to his child a few months after the news of his death.

''What a pity she's been saddled with the child,'' people said, but Lana had never said that. Never thought it. She had envied the other girl with a feverish pain, because she had her young son as a memento.

If Arash died Lana herself would have nothing. She had never heard one word of love from him. She would have nothing except the memory of those few dark hours of purely physical passion which had meant exactly nothing.

As if her dreams tonight had stripped the armour from her heart, the old raw, tearing pain lashed through her with a heightened urgency. Lana gasped for air, pressing her hands to her mouth, trying to make no sound.

What a fool she had been, to imagine that she had sealed her heart with common sense, had learned that love was a dream. Love was reality, harsh and cruel, where you had nowhere to hide, and you never woke up.

Now, when it was too late, it was all spread out for her, like a tapestry. The truth of who she was, what she felt, what she had done.

She had come all this way, begged money from her father, from friends, from strangers, worked harder than she had ever worked in her life. She had gone hungry when his people went hungry, she had wept when they suffered, she had stretched her powers and abilities to the limit to try to restore to them their lives....

Because a man who did not even like her had said one night, with heartbreak in his voice, *We will have nothing*.

# Seven

The room was cold but bright when she awoke. There were thick designs of frost on the windows and she could see her breath on the air. Her nose was cold. Lana lay under the heavy layers of quilt without stirring, enjoying the warmth for a few more minutes.

Snowflakes were still falling heavily beyond the windows, a thick soft fall of flakes that seemed to mute the waterfall's roar. She lay drowsily, not thinking of anything.

In the next room she heard banging and lifted her head to peer around the mound of the *korsi,* disturbing the quilts and letting cold air into her cosy nest.

Arash was already up. Taking a deep breath to prepare herself, Lana eased back the quilts and got up.

''Ahh!'' she cried involuntarily as the cold air enveloped her body. The place was freezing! She went through the curtained archway in her stockinged feet and made a mad dash across ice-cold tiles to the toilet. On the way back, she saw that the banging noise came from the high corner where the roof was damaged. Arash was outside on the roof, hammering some plastic sheeting over the hole.

Back inside the main room, she carefully folded the quilts and stacked them and the *korsi* back in their corner again, then bent to the task of resuscitating the fire. There were still plenty of embers in the brazier, and a careful laying of new charcoal would get it going again.

Just like her love. It had burned down to embers, so that she had hardly known they were there. And now she had put new fuel on the embers, and it would burn her again....

What a fool she had been to come on this trip with Arash. Why hadn't she listened to that little niggle of fear, that voice that had warned her that that way lay danger? She should have abandoned the idea of the drive through the mountains, if he had to be her escort. She should have gone by air.

She forced herself to put him out of her mind and began the search for breakfast provisions. By the time Arash came down off the roof and through the door, rubbing his cold hands, there was tea and toasted *naan* with butter and apricot preserves almost ready, but she had not succeeded in controlling her thoughts....

"Great!" he said, kicking off his boots and hanging up his jacket. "Nice and warm in here!"

Compared to outdoors, perhaps. But the brazier really wasn't up to heating the whole room comfortably in a prolonged cold spell. In weather like this, a Parvani family might spend the whole day huddling under the quilt around the hot brazier.

Arash sank down on the cushions she had placed by the table. As if reading her thoughts, he nodded his head towards the other room and said, "There are a couple of empty oil heaters out there. We can have a look after breakfast to see if there's any fuel for them."

"Where did you find that sheet of plastic for the roof?"

"It was already there. The wind had dislodged it," he answered, as she pulled the hot *naan* off the brazier with her bare fingers and dropped it quickly onto the plate she had left ready, crying, "Ah, ah, ah!"

She shook her hand to disperse the heat before repeating the entire action with the second *naan*.

Arash laughed.

"There's a pot holder," he pointed out.

Lana gazed at his smiling face, his laughing eyes, and wondered how she could ever have convinced herself that she had no feelings for this man.

Now her love seemed to her to have always been there, following her close as a shadow, moving out of her vision when she turned her head, perhaps, but always there.

She had been hoping that with the clear light of day those night thoughts would disappear, like most worries that plague sleepless humans in the early hours, but all she had to do was look into his face to know that no longer could she hide behind indifference.

She had caught her own shadow.

"Arash—" she began, then choked herself off. She bit her lip in frightened astonishment. What had she been going to say? "I've just remembered I love you"? Just like that, as if it might be something he wanted to hear?

She had had no practice in guarding her tongue. She

had worked more deeply, convincing herself that she had no feelings. Now that that fence had fallen, there were no barriers between feeling and voice.

"Yes?"

"Do you want tea?"

"Thank you."

She poured, and they ate the simple breakfast in silence. Her mind was too full of thoughts to notice.

"How long will we be here, Arash?" she asked.

"If we find snowshoes, perhaps tomorrow we can leave." He spoke as if he hoped so. "We will not know for sure until the snow stops."

"Is there any chance we'll find food stores?" Lana asked.

"I am sure there will be something. In any case, there will be a gun and ammunition," Arash murmured thoughtfully.

"You mean you'll go hunting for our food?"

"If necessary. I want to make a tour of the house. We can check the stores afterwards. Do you wish to come with me?"

She wanted to see his home, as if some part of her whispered that she would know him better if she knew the place where he had spent his childhood and youth. She nodded, and a few minutes later they were on their feet, pulling on boots and jackets and gloves.

He led her through the curtained doorway and across the adjoining room in the way she already knew, and along the corridor past the toilet.

At the far end of this corridor was a short flight of stairs, leading at the top through another archway and into a massive room lined with beautifully painted tiles.

There were only a few pieces of time- and war-damaged furniture in the otherwise empty room, but nothing could hide the fact that this had once been a luxurious place, and Lana belatedly realized that they had taken up residence last night in the staff quarters.

Then they passed through a succession of rooms, while Arash seemed to take mental stock. Some were damaged, some merely uninhabited, but all showed the effects of neglect. There were squares everywhere on the walls showing where pictures or other treasures had once hung, and Lana shook her head.

"Did your paintings…?" she started to ask once, and he glanced over at her.

"They were sold to buy arms," he said shortly, and she remembered that tortured night back in London when he had foreseen this tragedy.

She thought suddenly, *If I had comforted him then, instead of just listening, if I had held him and told him I loved him…did I miss my chance then?*

"I'm sorry," she muttered. "This must all have been so beautiful."

He did not answer, merely opened another door and continued on.

Apart from the missing works of art, some of the rooms were largely intact, and as they passed through several of these, she couldn't help saying, "It would be so much better if these rooms were lived in, Arash. This furniture won't take much more neglect."

He nodded. "Yes, I will come home soon."

*When you reach my cousin Omar, Arash, I ask that you stay with him for a little, to rest before returning to the Valley of Aram and undertaking the task that awaits you there….*

Arash frowned with the memory. What could Kavi's motive be for wishing him to do this? If he believed

Lana, if she had not requested his escort—what reason could there be for such a demand?

His eyes rested on Lana from time to time as she moved through the home of his ancestors, smiling with pleasure at the sight of a decorated archway, an intricate inlay design on a bedstead or table, floor tiles that his great-great-grandmother's favourite designer had made...why had he been thrust into such proximity with her? Was this incidental to some other purpose that would be revealed only in time?

It was almost inconceivable that Kavian would have feared to give him the details of any mission before he left, and yet...

*Make love to me, Arash.*

He squeezed his eyes shut against the memories that assaulted him suddenly. Lamplight on creamy flesh, clear dark eyes smiling at him with such open yearning, the heavy weight of her breasts in his hands, the sweet cries of passion and surprise.

He had carried these memories with him across all the battlefields of his bleeding country...and each night dreamed them, as if his soul refreshed itself with a visit to a mountain spring after the daily heartbreak of the wanton destruction of his countrymen's lives.

Arash took a deep breath, his jaw clenched. He would need an iron control to get through the coming days. And last night had made it clear that after such a long period of stress his control was not made of iron.

He opened a door. "This is my mother's dressing room. Some of her clothes may still be here."

He disappeared through the door and she followed him into a corridor lined with drawers and cupboards.

Natural light came through windows high at the far end. He was opening some of the cupboard doors.

"I am not sure what my mother took when she went. Perhaps there is something that you can use."

Lana slowly approached one of the cupboards he had opened. It contained a long rack with clothes covered in white silk bags. The rich scent of spices and musk hovered over everything.

There were several cupboards along the walls, but except for this one, most were empty, or nearly empty. At the end, a wider space filled with mirrors contained a dressing table.

"Where is your mother?" Lana asked after a moment.

"When peace came, she went to live with my sister. She did not like being here alone, where she had been so happy with my father."

"You've been torn by conflicting duties," Lana commented softly.

His eyes met hers as if unwillingly, and he quickly turned away again before she could read the expression in them.

"Choose whatever you find useful," he said.

"Thank you," Lana said softly. She reached into the full cupboard at random and unzipped one of the silk bags. The silk parted to reveal an extremely fine gauze, purple and spangled with diamanté. With a smile she zipped it back up.

*If you dressed in something like that, maybe he wouldn't be able to resist you,* an inner voice tempted her.

*Yes, or maybe I'd just catch my death of cold,* she responded firmly.

"Here is something warm, I think." Arash meanwhile had reached into another closet and pulled out a garment bag. He hung it on a nearby hook and with a sweep he slid down the zipper and flipped out the contents.

It was not something warm. It was a soft, shimmering negligee in glowing turquoise. It seemed to have been made with a thousand overlapping feathers in deliberate imitation of a bird's breast, with fluffy feathers also trimming the cuffs and neckline. The front opening parted over a thin gown in silk satin, still faintly wrinkled around the hips from its last wearing.

Perfume wafted from the bag, carrying an erotic potency that said that a woman had worn this outfit....to entice a man.

Lana blinked and shook her head, loosening her neck muscles, to try to clear her thoughts.

"I've never seen anything like that!" she said brightly, to shift her mood. "That's really magic!"

"Yes," he said. "My mother liked to wear beautiful things for my father. He said she was the only woman in the world who could make a man blind to all other women."

They regarded each other in silence, without knowing that time passed.

"Was it an arranged marriage?" Lana asked at last, because surely they were lucky to be so in love if so.

"He saw her one day on horseback, down at the river. My father—his name was Zahir—was a very fine rider, the best among the young men in this valley. My mother and her companions passed him on the road. Her horse bolted suddenly. Zahir and his men gave chase. My father's mount was very swift. He caught up with her and dragged her off her horse and onto his own."

Lana smiled. "Did they fall in love at first sight?"

"She was beautiful, and his blood was up, and with his arms already around her Zahir could not resist. He kissed her."

Hearing the word *kiss* on his lips, she licked her own. "And what happened then?"

"She blushed, because of course such things are not done even today in this valley. She said, 'Is this how an al Khosravi chooses a concubine?'

"My father was furious at the insult. He said, 'It is how he chooses his wife!' He returned her to her friends, learned from his own men who she was, and the next day travelled to her father's house to ask for her in marriage."

"Is all that really true?" she asked, entranced.

Arash smiled. His voice had softened almost seductively as he told the story. "It is the story my father told. My mother sometimes added the information that her horse had only bolted under her instructions."

Lana laughed. Arash started to say something, then stopped abruptly, blinked and stared at her as if she were someone who had shaken him out of sleep, or another reality. He swallowed and turned to the task of repacking the garment.

"I thought it was perhaps a coat," he explained in a low voice, and replaced the garment bag in the closet. "You will come later and make your choice of whatever you need. My mother would wish it."

"A bath!" Lana cried, as her glance fell through an open doorway. "Oh, bliss!" Then she paused, recollecting. "Oh, but I guess it's not working?"

"Neither water nor electricity has been restored," he said.

He stood at the open doorway as she was tempted into his mother's private *hammam* in the semidarkness, touching the beautiful marble and the ornately carved fittings with awed admiration.

He remembered childhood moments here, the room filled with steam, his mother in the tub, laughing at her attendants, or wrapped in a white towel, choosing from the host of scented oils she was offered...how he had loved the perfumes, the hot steamy air, the scent of women.

''What beautiful bottles!'' Lana exclaimed.

Some of his mother's soaps and bath oils, dusty with disuse, were still sprinkled around the room, sad testimony to the life of the house that the bombs had destroyed. Lana's eyes were enchanted by the magical glass shapes and the rich turquoise and purple and gold and green oils within.

She picked up one at random, opening it and being transported to another world. These were the scents of a pampered, lovely, and loved woman, a woman with full confidence in her sexuality, who after bathing here had moved to the next room and slipped on a silk slip and a peacock feather robe....

He remembered his childishly clumsy, excited hands once reaching for a pretty bottle...remembered how the bottle fell to the tiled floor.

A powerful, intoxicating perfume had hit his senses, overwhelming him. He remembered the intensity of that experience, how he had laughed and cried, his body leaping with the thrill of it. He had squatted down to soak his hands in the slick perfume on the tiles, and press them to his face. He had to be pulled away by an attendant because of the broken glass.

They had all been laughing and happy—it was not

his mother's way to shout over a broken bottle. Everyone had been delighted to see his infant ecstasy, the pure sensual joy of the child.

"Ah, what a happy woman your wife will be!" his mother had crooned, but it was many years before he had understood the reference.

Fourteen hundred years ago the Prophet, peace upon his name, had said, *It has been given to me to love perfumes, and women, and the coolness of prayer.* And in the Tribe of Aram it was still said that a boychild who loved perfumes would grow up to be a good husband and a good man, for like the Prophet he would love women and seek his guidance always from Truth....

He had understood the potency of the tribal custom on that long-ago night when Lana had stepped into his arms. That night his senses had been overwhelmed. He had been as wildly intoxicated by her as when the essence of a potent flower had drowned his childish self in an experience richer than any that had gone before....

In another age, another life.

All that was gone now. Only a dozen bottles of scent still littered the low table that had once been crammed to bursting. And one, on the floor, broken in two neat pieces, like his life: the shell remained, but the substance had gone.

He stared at her with a kind of angry intensity, and with a meaningless comment, not knowing how she had offended, Lana nervously replaced the bottle on the glass table.

They moved on. Some doors he passed by without opening, and she guessed that these were his father's and his brother's rooms and that he couldn't bear to see them empty. Not yet.

Soon they opened a door onto daylight. They had come to that part of the house that had been hit directly and was almost demolished, and now she stepped out into the weather, between walls without a roof. It was the section of the house highest up the slope of the valley wall.

Lana stood in the fall of thick wet snowflakes and stared around her at the ruin, a cluster of stone-built rooms without roofs, a pile of tragic rubble, already deep under snow. Window and door frames gaped empty, snow drifted high in the embrasures as if to emphasize the bleakness.

Then, under the pounding of the waterfall, she heard it. A distant sound...

"There is no need to explore here," Arash said.

She clutched his arm. "Arash, what was that?"

*Aaaaaa...*

"You heard something?" he asked, cocking his head.

A faint, faint cry, gone as soon as she heard it.

"Like someone crying," she whispered.

"What direction?"

She pointed east, towards the waterfall. Arash stepped across the snow-mounded piles of rubble and through a gaping doorway in the thick stone wall that had stood for centuries, and defiantly still stood. She followed him and discovered herself in the broad walled courtyard on the opposite side of the house.

In the centre of the open space was a square building surmounted by the dome she had glimpsed yesterday. Its windows were covered with wooden shutters, its walls piled high with drifted snow.

*Aaaa.*

Against the sound of the waterfall and the deadening effect of thick snow, it was difficult to get any bearing, but the sound was louder now than before.

"It is possible someone has taken shelter here, not knowing what part of the house is habitable," Arash said calmly. "Let's check the *majlis.*"

The *majlis* was a tribe's place of assembly, set aside by the sheikh for meetings and consultations with his people. In modern democratic countries the name had sometimes passed on to the elected assembly of the central government, but it was still used in its original meaning for these small local meeting houses.

She followed the path he beat through the deep snow of the courtyard towards the domed structure, which seemed largely intact. Her heart was beating uncomfortably. Was it a baby she had heard? If someone had spent the night out here without heat...it would be a miracle to find them alive.

The massive double doors of carved wood opened with surprising ease under Arash's hand, and he drew them wide and stepped through.

*Maaa. Maaa.*

Lana stepped inside after him. The darkness was relieved by the shafts of light coming through the cracks in the shutters. Nothing relieved the animal odour that hit their nostrils, nor the sudden chorus of bleating that arose in their ears.

"*Ya Allah,*" Arash muttered, more to himself than to her. "Is my father's majlis made a stable?"

"What is it? Sheep?" Lana inquired, blinking at the nervous shuffling shapes that crowded together in the darkest corner.

"Wait," he said. He wheeled around and went out

past her, and a moment later she heard the bang of shutters and muted daylight entered the room. He opened two sets of shutters and returned.

A small flock of sheep crowded into one corner of the room on the beautiful black-and-white-tiled floor, where straw had been laid to give them a bed. A few chickens and a rooster wandered around pecking the straw at random. A mule by a pail of meal stood patiently chewing, watching them over his shoulder.

"Oh, thank God they survived!" she exclaimed.

"Look," said Arash.

Farthest into the corner, facing the newcomers four-square, a ewe stood protectively over two tiny, perfect newborn lambs who suckled and pulled with crazy intensity, their tails waggling ferociously.

"Aww," chanted Lana, and then laughed with delight. "Oh, how brave of her, to lamb in the middle of a blizzard!"

"It is early for the valley. Lambing usually doesn't start for another two weeks."

"Are they warm enough?" she asked. The combined animal body heat had provided its own warming system, but the two lambs were so tiny.

"Lambs survive worse than this," Arash said. "But they will have a better chance if they are kept warm for the next few days."

She followed the direction of his nod. In the opposite corner there was a high iron stove; behind it was stacked coal and wood.

"I was hoping we could look after them in the kitchen!"

Arash flicked her an amused glance. "Try telling their mother that."

He crossed to the stove and, lifting off the plates on

top, looked down inside, then opened the door at the front and crouched down to begin manipulating the lever that shook down the ashes. She saw a glow of red.

"Well, we know that Sulayman or someone was here only yesterday," he said. He carefully picked up a few tiny bits of wood and began to feed them to the embers.

Lana crossed the room to help him, searching for dried leaves and twigs among the logs and passing them to Arash. After a few minutes the fire began to crackle and spit.

Plenty of fodder had been spread for the animals by someone who had clearly not expected to return for several days. But they freshened the fodder and the straw bedding, and took the oak buckets standing by the door and emerged again into the snowy day.

They worked together mostly in silence, and every time he seemed to anticipate her moves, or she anticipated his need, feeling stabbed her heart.

*We could have worked together to rebuild all this,* she told herself, as she watched Arash striding through the snow. *He would have accepted Dad's money if he loved me, and we could have…*

If only. There was no use crying over it.

Then, suddenly, a voice was murmuring, *Suppose I told him I loved him, asked him to marry me? Would he marry me for the sake of rebuilding his heritage? Would I marry a man who only wanted my money?*

But he didn't have to marry her. She had offered him help freely, no strings, and he had rejected it.

*Out of pride,* whispered the voice. *But if you were married, that would give him an excuse for accepting.*

*Buy a man with my father's money?* her other self demanded angrily. *No thanks.*

*You'll never get him any other way.*

She shook her head, shutting the voices out.

Arash crossed to where a narrow stream tumbled over a terraced wall in a tiny waterfall, and filled the buckets under it. Lana stood watching, then followed him back inside the building.

Standing in the doorway behind him while he topped up the water in the troughs, she saw that as he straightened his gaze was drawn as if irresistibly to the centre of the wall directly opposite the big entrance doors.

There was a large round shadow in the exact centre of the wall. She could not see his expression, but she saw how his back stiffened and he deliberately turned away from the sight.

"What was there, Arash?" she asked impulsively, before she could stop herself.

Arash turned to her blankly, as if surfacing from a dream. "Pardon?"

She indicated the wall. "What used to hang there?"

"The Shield of Aram," he said. "It hung in that spot for two hundred and fifty years."

His voice was without expression, but somehow she knew this had been the most precious treasure, was the worst loss of all.

"It was sold?" she asked quietly.

"Sold? No, it is impossible for the al Khosravi to sell Aram's Shield. It bestows sovereignty and right guidance upon us. Once, long ago, it was stolen, but the thief returned it. Now it has disappeared again. Who knows where it has gone?"

# Eight

**B**y unspoken agreement, when they returned to the kitchen, Lana began to make preparations for lunch while Arash filled the paraffin heaters and brought one into the kitchen and lighted it. The other he kept in the next room, where after a few minutes she heard the sounds of shifting furniture.

They had found supplies in various pantries and storerooms. There was enough food to keep them going; the amounts were small but there was more variety than she had feared they would find: olive oil, onions, apples and potatoes, dried lentils, chickpeas, apricots and milk, wheat flour and rice, and some bottles of home-preserved tomatoes. There were herbs and garlic hanging from the ceiling in one room, along with several joints of meat.

Gazing up at these, Arash had murmured, ''The protection of the *majlis* comes at a price.''

"And if you'll get me down one of those, please," she had responded dryly, "I'll try to find some way to cook it for your dinner."

But for now she was concentrated on making their midday meal, and the sound of Arash's activities next door became a companionable accompaniment to her own work. It was pleasant to feel that they were working together, on different tasks, towards their common good.

Back in London, when she had been falling for Arash and hoping he was falling for her, when she believed he was Kavi's bodyguard and had no inkling of his wealthy and aristcratic background, she had sometimes dreamed of a life like this, far away from the world she knew.

She had imagined them together maybe on a small farm, raising children and animals in a happy mix.

Lana had never wanted a marriage like that of her parents, where a close family life was sacrificed to the creation of wealth. Her father had been away most of the time, her mother taking sole responsibility for the home and family, at the end of ten years finding herself rolling in money but with little in common with her husband.

No, she hadn't wanted that with Arash. She had hoped for a life of sharing—the hard work and the joy, the pain and the pleasure....

But she wasn't forgetting that it was only because of her father's long hours of hard work that she was here now. If her father had been an ordinary man with ordinary goals, she might never have decided to go abroad to university, never have met Arash, would probably hardly have heard of Parvan or the Barakat Emirates.

And even if she had, she would have had no money to spend on the country's rebirth.

She had set some beans to soak earlier, and now she peeled, chopped and lightly fried onions and some canned tomatoes. She tossed them into the soup pot, added water and herbs and spices and set the result on the brazier to cook—a thick country soup—and removed the pail of water she had set to heat there.

Then, slipping her small bag of toiletries into her waistband, she picked up the pail of warm water and a lamp, slipped under the rug in the doorway and into the room beyond.

There she stopped in amazement at what she saw. "A stove!" she cried. "A real, honest-to-God *cookstove!*"

Revealed because Arash had removed a lot of the massed furniture and boxes, it stood in one corner—a marvel in black iron and chrome, dated and in need of a good polish, but otherwise looking serviceable.

"Imported from England for my grandmother. She thought it would make life easier for the cooks," Arash said.

"Does it work?"

"The pipe used to go out there, where the damage is," Arash told her, pointing to the missing section of roof and wall. "It will not be usable until I find some substitute for the missing lengths of pipe."

Lana looked around. There was also a large clay oven of the kind that was typical in the countryside. So this was the original kitchen. "Is that one in working order?"

"No problems there," Arash said. "What time will you want it hot?"

"Probably about three, is that okay?"

She indicated the pail of warm water. "If you don't mind, I'll go up to your mother's bathroom to wash. I guess the drains will be working, even though the water isn't."

He nodded. "I will carry the heater up for you." He suited the action to the word, bending to pick up the paraffin heater and leading the way along the corridor and up the stairs.

He was so caring, so protective, and she wished with all her heart that it was herself that he loved. Or that he loved no one, and she could hope, with time, to make him love her....

Did he know whether the woman he loved was still single? She wished she dared to ask. Suppose his love had grown tired of waiting and wondering and had taken second best? Maybe Arash was in a hurry to return home to prevent exactly that.

Maybe he was already too late. Was that the fear that haunted him, that was shadowing his eyes more and more darkly since they had come here?

Would Arash consider marrying her, Lana, if his true love were lost to him?

She was brought up short, seeing where her thoughts had inevitably led her. *It wouldn't work,* she lectured herself. To marry someone you loved more than he loved you was one thing. When he loved someone else, how could such a marriage possibly bring anything but heartache? A man who didn't even start out loving his wife would treat her badly, make her life hell.

*Not Arash,* her heart whispered. He was so careful of anyone for whom he was responsible—she had noticed that about him long ago. She was sure he was a man who would always be caring and protective of his wife, even if he didn't actually love her.

*Except for that moment last night,* she reminded herself ruthlessly. He hadn't been kind then. But then, what had that been, except an admission that he could still find her sexually attractive, even when there was nothing else between them?

If she married him, it would be important that he at least find her sexually attractive....

Absently she watched his tall, too-lean body moving with unconscious masculine grace ahead of her. Something in the very shape of him seemed to affect her mental function, her heart.

*Stop thinking like this!*

Ahead of her, Arash opened the door to his mother's bathroom and went in to set the heater down in the middle of the floor. Lana, following, set down her pail and slid the little lamp onto the nearest flat surface.

"You brought a light?" he asked.

She reached into her pocket and held up the flint, and Arash took it from her hand and lit the lamp for her. As he restored the glass chimney a comforting glow warmed the room. For a moment they stood looking at each other.

"Don't forget to make use of my mother's clothes."

"Are you sure she won't mind?"

"She will mind only if she learns that you did not use whatever you needed."

"Thank you."

He moved to the door, turned and looked at her.

"Will you stir the soup?" Lana asked, feeling the sweetness of ordinary things. "I won't be very long."

"The soup," he said slowly, as if he were thinking of something else. He moved his head and his gaze shifted. "Yes, I will stir the soup."

The bathroom and the dressing room were both well-stocked with mirrors, so when Arash said his mother was beautiful that was the truth. Well, she would have known that anyway, just looking at Arash.

Lana was one of those rare creatures—a woman unconscious of her own beauty. Perhaps because she had been raised without an adoring father to reinforce her sense of her own value, but also because since well before puberty she had been what other women considered fat. And although she herself had never worried about her weight, nor felt it to be a problem—she liked food far too much for that—the constant pity of her weight-obsessed fellow students couldn't help making a mark.

Of course men told her she was beautiful—even more beautiful because she didn't know it—but she had learned early to distrust that. Deep-set chocolate eyes with dark eyebrows, a straight, small nose, wide full lips and broad cheekbones carried all the ingredients of beauty, but she did not see them that way. Lana knew she was attractive, but if Arash had high standards of beauty…

She stood straight in the chill air, briefly examining her own naked body in the mirrors. She had lost a lot of weight since coming to Parvan, and she had cut her thick, once waving hair short, so that it curled around her head. Life was a lot easier this way, but she wasn't really used to seeing herself like this yet. Ever since puberty she had worn her hair long, had been well-rounded.

Now she was as slim as a boy. The rounded flesh had gone from her upper arms, her thighs, her abdomen, her bottom, and her body still felt strange to her. Her once-heavy breasts were smaller now.

She wondered if Arash would find this body attractive. Would he find pleasure, as he had once before, in stroking her neck, her thighs, her breasts? The thought of his touch, of touching him in love, abruptly made Lana go weak.

*I do not believe you have forgotten.*

She had forgotten. She had forced herself to forget. But now she remembered, and if he touched her again the way he had last night…Lana closed her eyes. She would be so helpless. If he stroked her, if he kissed her…

"Okay, this is what they call cabin fever," Lana muttered sternly, opening her eyes again. "Down to business."

She lifted a pretty smoked-glass bottle and tipped a few drops of turquoise oil into her bathwater.

"You found something to wear," Arash said, as they sat down to their lunch. Soup, and some stove-top biscuits, and apples for dessert.

She was wearing a flowing kaftan in a woven mix of deep indigo and purple wool. It was thick and warm as well as being feminine. And she knew the dark purply blue was good with her skin, enhanced the gold highlights in her hair.

What she didn't notice was that it also emphasized the shadows around her eyes, giving her skin a look of delicate porcelain, so that the past months of hard work seemed to have demanded too much of her.

Making her look as if she needed protection.

"You have been working too hard," Arash said, ladling soup into a bowl for her. He also had changed his clothes, from jeans into traditional Parvan trousers and cotton knitted knee-high moccasins, a long shirt, a dark vest. He was a mountain man now, no one could have mistaken him for anything else.

Lana stared at him. "All I've done is make lunch and a few preparations for dinner!" she exclaimed. "You're the one who's been throwing furniture around!"

"I do not mean here and now. I mean, you are less healthy than when you came to Parvan. I am glad Alinor makes you take this rest."

Accepting the bowl from his hands, she blinked at him in surprise. It was the nearest thing to praise Arash had ever offered her.

"I thought you resented my interference," she observed mildly.

He picked up his own empty bowl and paused to gaze at her. "Resented your interference, how?" he asked in astonishment. "In Parvan?"

Lana picked up her spoon and began to stir the steaming soup. She nodded wordlessly, not quite looking at him.

"That would be insane, if it were true. Because of you what would have taken years has been accomplished in months! How could any Parvani resent such interference?"

"You think I'm a poor little rich girl, playing at being Lady Bountiful, though," she murmured, staring at her soup with the fixity of a child hoping to find the letters of her name.

Arash finished filling his own bowl and set it down on the table with a clunk. "No," he said. "No, Lana, I do not think this of you."

The soup was nicely flavoured, the beans just a little undercooked. But they crunched satisfyingly this way. Taking another spoonful, she glanced up at his face.

There was a strange, indescribable mix of emotions on his face.

"Then why will you never accept help from me?" she asked reasonably, lifting an inquiring hand. "The way I see it, you'd rather let this place subside in a heap than take money from my father—or even any of the charity funds—to restore it. And that would be a pity, because it was beautiful and it could be again."

She held the full sleeve of the robe with one hand as she reached for one of the stove-top biscuits she had made, and carefully concentrated on breaking it in two. Its moist white centre steamed. Then she was forced to look at him again.

His dark eyes searched her face for a deeply unnerving moment when she could not read his expression at all, and just as it seemed something had to happen to break the tension, something inside him withdrew, as if by an effort of will. His gaze fell to his own bowl and he sipped some soup.

"It is not possible."

His tone was one she knew well. Remote, coming from behind a closed door. She knew from experience that the door was locked.

But she pushed against it anyway. "Why is it not possible?"

"But it does not mean that I remain blind to what you do for the country."

"But why can't you accept..."

"I cannot discuss this with you, Lana."

"I don't see why not. There's only the two of us here. Who is there to be offended?"

She thought she had made him angry, by the way he applied himself to his soup. He did not reply. Arash seemed always able to retreat into a world where he was alone.

They ate their soup in silence, while Lana wrestled with her feelings. She wanted to tell him, to say, *Look, I love you, I've just realized I'm crazy in love with you and have been right from the beginning, are you sure you don't love me?*

But she had done that once already.

Her words hadn't been quite so blatant, but she had been clear enough. Dumb with misery because he had left her without a word, she had written to him, in Parvan, as Kaljuki troops massed along the border and the world did nothing....

By then she had learned from Alinor who he was: not Arash Khosravi, a bodyguard, but Arash al Khosravi, Cup Companion to the Crown Prince and younger son of a titled sheikh.

Then she had understood, or thought she did: that was the explanation for everything that had happened. Why he had first seemed attracted, and then not, and then, when she threw herself at him, why he had been unable to resist. That was why he had said he could offer her nothing.

Because he could marry only with his father's approval, and his father would not approve of his interest in a foreign nobody....

In the letter she wrote that she was sorry not to have said goodbye, said she would miss him, said she hoped that peace was still possible, that she looked forward to meeting him again...and then she had written sadly that she wished he had been an ordinary man, without a title, because then, perhaps, they could have been more to each other....

As close as she could get to a declaration without

actually begging. In her dreams, Arash would write back, would confess the truth of his position, tell her why their love was impossible. In her dreams she then told him the truth of who *she* was, and asked him if this fact would change his father's mind.... She had had high hopes, because however aristocratic the family, she did not believe that the sheikh would object to such a marriage for his younger son. Arash was not his heir, after all.

So she had hoped. Arash replied with only the briefest of notes, thanking her for her concern. He had signed his real name, but there had been no explanation. There was nothing at all to give her hope. Not even the most tangential reference to the fact that he had made unbelievably wild and passionate love to her the night before leaving, that he had cried aloud, had wept and been shaken as he took his pleasure from her....

Nothing.

By then the Kaljuk army had invaded, the airports were closed to all but military traffic. Lana did not write again. She accepted what she should have understood from the biginning: he was never interested in her. He had made love to her because she had agreed to totally uncommitted sex and he was a man with normally functioning hormones.

There was nothing at all to regret except her own blind, self-centred stupidity.

And she was not going to go through the humiliation again of offering herself to the man who didn't want her.

When they had finished, Arash cleared their bowls from the table while Lana spooned coffee and sugar into a little pot and set it on the brazier, then set out a pretty hand-painted bowl with a few winter apples. They were wrinkled but still very edible, and with every sign of enjoyment Arash caught one up in one hand and bit into it with strong white teeth. The perfume of the fruit was suddenly deliciously sharp on the air.

"Are these from your own orchards?" she asked, taking one herself.

"I hope so," he said. "If they are not it will mean our trees are not producing."

Lana bit into the apple, feeling the juice spurt up into her mouth. The flavour was strong, richer than anything she could have bought at home, and under the skin the flesh was still firm and very white.

In spite of everything, she felt suddenly at peace with him. She thought, *I couldn't remain angry with him for long, no matter what he had done.*

"Is Aram an ancestor of yours?" she asked.

He was silent a moment, and over his face flicked a look that tore at her heart.

"Aram," he said, tasting the name. He nodded thoughtfully. "A long-distant ancestor, about whom we have many legends. He was the chief of this valley, a renowned warrior, a man who had attained deep mystical power."

"Is the shield really so old?"

"The shield, no. The stone—the central ruby of the shield, that was Aram's."

Lana smiled, biting into her apple again, and settling down on her cushions. "So it was originally Aram's Ruby?"

"That is what we call it. Aram's Ruby is carved with symbols that are said to draw power and seal it in the stone. The ruby was mined in this valley—in ancient times there were ruby mines here, and it was the finest and largest ruby to come out of those mines.

"Aram himself carved it, for only he had the knowledge that was required. Whether he wore it, or used it as a seal, is not known. So the stone was passed down from ancient times through this family. More than five hundred years ago, my direct ancestor had the ruby set into the centre of a ceremonial shield of gold, silver and copper, inscribed in such a way as to renew the power captured in the stone.

"The people of this valley believe—have believed for hundreds of years—that their good luck, happiness and prosperity comes from this shield, for as long as it is in the possession of their sheikh, he will be rightly guided. If a leader is rightly guided, no evil can befall the people."

He paused, thinking, seeming not to notice that he had let silence fall. She saw that he was contemplating an uncertain future.

After a moment, he roused himself. "The shield can bring such fortune only on its rightful owners, the al Khosravi sheikhs. It cannot be sold, and anyone who stole it would bring evil on his own head."

"Oh!" Lana had completely forgotten the apple in her hand. "You mean, there's a curse on it?"

He smiled and shook his head. "Not a curse. If an ignorant man sticks his finger into an electric socket, it is not a curse that kills him, but his own ignorance of what power is there, and how it must be used."

A little shiver of uncertainty threaded her fascination in the story, for his voice was the voice of a man explaining not arcane secrets, but simple fact.

"But, Arash...do you believe this?"

He gazed thoughtfully at her. "Lana, there is a hydroelectric dam at the head of this valley, bombed by the Kaljuks, which your father's money is at this moment helping to restore. Why?"

She was startled by the sudden change of subject. "Well, because electric power is so…it's so important to people's standard of living. What do you mean, exactly?"

"Do you believe in the electric power of this dam?"

"Believe? No—I mean, yes, but I don't have to *believe* in it, it's just there."

Arash smiled, then went on with his story.

"The shield, Aram's Shield, was displayed to the tribesmen at every meeting of the *majlis,* and when the present *majlis* was built—the building that now houses chickens and lambs and a mule—the shield was given a permanent home there.

"That was two hundred and fifty years ago. And over time, the *majlis* came to be called *Dar-i Khoshbakti,* the Gate of Good Fortune, because it was through its means that good fortune entered the valley."

When he paused, Lana remembered her apple and took another bite. She wanted to ask *Who stole it?* But the storytellers of Parvan did not need prompting. Storytelling was an art that all, from the simplest to the most sophisticated of Parvan's citizens, practised and understood.

"So the shield hung undisturbed through many years, and at every meeting of a *majlis* the men of the valley who had gathered to talk to their sheikh could see the proof that the sheikh's guidance could be trusted, and he could be given their loyalty.

"But word of the ancient stone and its strange properties spread. Men came from abroad, scholars and academics and seekers and charlatans and many others, asking to see Aram's Shield. At first, all such requests were refused. It was not until my great-grandfather's time that the first Westerner saw the shield.

"And one day in 1917 a servant tremblingly approached my great-grandfather with the dreadful news. Aram's Ruby had disappeared. The shield hung where it had always hung, but the stone had been prised from its place and the shield had no longer a centre."

Arash paused.

"What did he do?" Lana gasped, for, although Arash's voice was calm, she could almost feel the anger of the sheikh resonating down through the years.

"The day before, three men had visited the *Dar-i Khoshbakti* and viewed the shield. A Frenchman and two Englishmen. It was impossible to say whether they had worked together, or if one had done the deed alone. My great-grandfather's servants had not troubled to notice who had been left alone with the shield, or in what order the men entered and left the *majlis*— to them it was unimaginable that such a theft could occur."

On the brazier, the coffee suddenly boiled up in the little open pot, breaking the spell, and Lana snatched it from the heat. She had set two tiny cups, and she filled them with the thick, frothing liquid.

Arash stirred extra sugar into his while she asked, "What did he do?"

He smiled a smile that made her glad she was not the thief. She thought, *The old sheikh was probably terrifying. What a fool the man was to cross him.* "My great-grandfather of course did nothing. He shrugged his shoulders and wondered aloud that foreigners were such fools as to toy with their fate in such a way.''

Lana opened her eyes at him. ''Is that really what he did? Didn't he even try to find out who had stolen it?''

Arash shook his head.

''He summoned all the men of the valley at once to the *majlis* to show them the despoiled shield. He reminded them that the stone would bring evil luck on the thief, whoever he might be. He assured them that the Ruby would soon be back in his possession, not through force, but through its voluntary return by the thief, who would not be able to bear the weight of evil luck that would now befall him.

''And that is exactly what happened.''

Lana's mouth opened. ''Really?''

''Within three weeks the stone was returned to my father by a guide who had been paid a huge sum to deliver it, with a letter from one of the men begging forgiveness.''

''Is that all it said?'' she wailed.

''It said that nothing but evil had befallen him since stealing the jewel and he hoped to forestall more by sending it back to its rightful owner.''

She gaped at him, amazed. ''Arash, that's really strange!'' she said. ''Is it true?''

He smiled at her with a tenderness in his eyes that melted her heart with wishing. ''It is true. The letter was kept—it may even still be here. Certainly I saw it as a child. It was written in very stilted, broken Parvani that made me laugh.''

''Do you know what really happened?''

''No,'' he said. ''All that is known is that the ruby was returned by a very frightened man.''

Lana suddenly remembered the tragic sequel. "Do you think that will happen this time?" she asked.

Then she wished she hadn't spoken, for all the light went out of Arash's eyes as he was reminded of his loss. He shook his head.

"I know nothing of how it disappeared. Perhaps it was moved from the *majlis* and destroyed in the bombing. Perhaps it was stolen and the thief died without leaving a trace of where he hid it.

"I do not even know when it disappeared. I had not spoken to my father for many months before he died, nor my brother," he said. "We fought on different fronts. And there have been many strangers in the valley, during the war and after."

She didn't know what to say. "Is it…it must be extremely valuable," she murmured at last.

"It is one of the world's largest known rubies," Arash said flatly. "The engraving is unique. It is of inestimable value, both to collectors and to jewel merchants."

"I'm sorry," she murmured—because that made recovery of the jewel so much more unlikely. She had learned something of the antiques trade through her father's museum, and she knew enough to understand that if the shield had fallen into the hands of a private collector it might never see the light of day again. But at least in such a case it might be preserved intact.

The situation was a thousand times worse if an unscrupulous trader were to prise the ruby from the centre of the shield and recut it. It would still be valuable cut into two or more smaller stones, but the historical value of such a unique piece would be destroyed.

In that scenario, the shield would probably survive. It would still be valuable as a collector's item without the stone, but would be worth little if melted down. No one would trouble to destroy the masterpiece.

"But Arash, don't you think if a stranger—if anyone had gone out of the valley with the shield someone would have noticed and remembered? Have you asked people if they saw anything?"

"No one knows yet of our loss. Only Kavi, Alinor, and now you. Even Sulayman believes that my father removed the shield for safekeeping. When they learn the truth…" He shook his head and looked at her.

She saw desolation in his eyes. "How will I tell my father's people that, in addition to their other griefs, the source of their good fortune and right guidance has been lost forever?"

# Nine

"**A**rash," she whispered helplessly, putting a hand on his arm in an automatic desire to offer comfort. She looked into his face. "Will it mean so much to them?"

He gripped her hand and lifted it away, as though he couldn't take having her touch him. But then, having captured it, he didn't let go. Instead he turned it palm up, within the clasp of his own hand, and gazed at it as if the answer to his problem might lie there.

"Even now they say that the Tribe of Aram escaped the worst of the Kaljuk bombing because of the protection of the shield."

"Do you have to tell them the truth?"

His thumb stroked absently across her palm in a gesture of intimacy that shook her. It was as if they had a lifetime's history of turning to each other for comfort. As if, for this moment, he had forgotten the actual, ordinary circumstances of their relationship in favour of some deeper truth of what was between them.

Her heart leapt with the first hope she had felt since those distant days when everything had been possible.

"The meetings of the *majlis* must be reinstated as soon as I return to the valley. They will learn at the first meeting. There is no way to tell them. There is no way not to tell them."

She offered hesitatingly, "I suppose you wouldn't lie to the people about when it disappeared?"

He lifted his gaze to meet hers with the searching look that was so much his hallmark. She had seen him look at others like that, but not usually herself, not since she had come to Parvan. It had been as if he had no interest in the inner Lana Holding, not even as much as he invested in strangers at fund-raising parties.

But now his gaze pierced her, and she lost her breath because of the way her heart leapt with the desire to reveal herself to him.

"What do you mean?"

"If they attribute their relative good fortune in the war to the shield and you tell them it was already gone before intensive bombing began, doesn't it follow that their luck is not attached exclusively to Aram's Shield?"

The rich colour of his thoughtful eyes was something she would have been happy to drown in. She thought absently, *One day I'll have a home with a stained glass window that is just the colour of Arash's eyes....*

"Start my life as their leader with a lie for their own good," he pondered aloud. "Would it be the first evidence that the al Khosravi are no longer rightly guided?"

He shook his head, and smiled at her.

"They are men and women, not children. This would be to treat them as less than my own equals. I am the leader of my father's people because they have chosen it, because it is best for men to unite under a leader, not because they must accept me. Such a lie would violate the contract that my ancestors forged with the people."

Suddenly she saw how deeply honourable he was, with an honesty that went right through the bone.

"I'm sorry," she murmured. "You're right."

"There is no reason to apologize for offering me advice, Lana," Arash said with that same thoughtful frown. "Sometimes advice that is not taken is the method by which we find the right road."

"If you want my opinion," she said before she could stop herself, "the Tribe of Aram is safe in your hands with or without Aram's Shield, and give them a few weeks or months and they'll realize that."

He smiled at her, but the worried frown was still there, behind his eyes.

A thought was taking shape in the back of her mind.

"Arash," she murmured tentatively.

His dark gaze met hers inquiringly.

"You know my father is endowing a museum. What if—what if he put it out on the grapevine that he was willing to buy Aram's Shield, no questions asked? He could offer a massive sum, you know, and that might tempt the thief out of hiding."

He stared at her. "And what then, Lana?"

"Well, don't you see—if he was contacted by whoever has it, and tipped you off, you could have it seized and impounded as stolen property."

He was silent, considering. "And your father would

risk this? Such a person might be very vengeful, Lana, if he discovered your father was behind it.''

He was right. And her own connection to Parvan was so well known the thief would guess immediately that it was a deliberate trick. She dropped her eyes.

''Or he could just buy it,'' she said tonelessly, knowing what was coming.

He looked at her. ''The museum would fall down around his ears if your father tried to keep the shield there.''

''I didn't mean to keep.''

''You suggest he should buy it and give it to me?''

''Why not?'' She couldn't look at him, knowing in advance what his answer would be.

''Lana, Aram's Shield is worth perhaps many millions of dollars to a collector. Why should your fath—''

''On the open market.''

''What?'' He blinked at the interruption.

''On the open market, with bidding, I agree the sky's the limit with something like the shield. But what your thief has to face is that he can never sell it on the open market. It's stolen property, and no way can he ever hope to disguise that fact, from now till doomsday.

''So he has to take the money and run, Arash, don't you see? Whoever has stolen it, unless they stole it to order for a private customer, he has to take whatever he can get. He can't be hoping for more than a million or so.'' She paused, thinking.

''Maybe not even that. My father told me—''

She broke off because he was laughing. ''Only a million?'' he asked, with ruthless irony, as the closeness she had felt was washed away. ''Is that all? Well, then I will sell a few of the sheep that my father has left to me, and pay your father back!''

"A million dollars is pocket change to my father, Arash,'' she pointed out, with a rueful inward smile for what her father's reaction would be to hearing that.

She saw suddenly that she had angered him. ''I know it!'' he said. "He can buy and sell an impoverished sheikh, why not? What shall I give him in return, then, Lana?'' He stared at her, as if seeking his answer from her face, and she was caught and held by his gaze.

"What have I to offer except myself?'' He lifted his hand to her head, and she felt his fingers close ruthlessly in her hair. "Shall I marry his daughter so that his grandson will inherit an ancient title? What else is there to tempt him to do this thing for me?''

"Stop, Arash,'' she muttered uncomfortably.

"And you, Lana, you who can hardly stand to be polite to me—will you consent to being part of such an exchange? Your son would be a sheikh. Is that worth the sacrifice of your happiness?''

Her own fury blew up, consuming her with burning heat.

"How dare you!'' she bit out. "Where do you get off suggesting that my father would demand any return for what up to now has been pure generosity? How can you say such a thing about him? Or me?

"If I wanted to marry someone for his bloody *title,* Arash, I sure as hell don't have to choose you! You have an *obsession* about being bought and sold! What's your problem? All you have to do if someone makes an offer, you know, is say no!''

She stared at him. "Or maybe that's what you're afraid of, Arash! Maybe you're afraid of yourself!

Maybe you're afraid you *are* for sale, and you couldn't say no! What's the matter, is the shield too great a temptation? You might be seriously tempted to marry a woman you can't stand if it was to get your shield back?''

"I am sorry, Lana," he began, but she overrode him, jumping to her feet.

"Is that why you turned down my offers of help, is that why you'd rather be in constant pain every second of the day than go and have surgery paid for by me? Because it might be a disguised attempt to buy you?

"Well, set your heart at rest! I won't be putting in any bids in your direction. If I want to buy a man, there are lots of ancient titles in the world, Arash! Why should I stop at the sheikh of a tribe in a country no one's ever heard of? I could have an English duke's son for the amount of money my father can afford to throw around. I could probably have a European prince. You get to wear a tiara with a title like that, you know!"

He struggled to his feet. "I have apologized already, Lana. You must not insult my name."

"No, no, naturally I must not!" she agreed with bitter mockery. Of course her anger was given impetus by the thoughts she had been entertaining over the past day, and of course she was in no state to admit that to herself. She waved her hands in the air.

"It's open season on *Holding,* it's all right to suggest that my father's generosity is just a cover for the purchase of human beings, but *al Khosravi,* now, there's a name that…"

He grabbed her wrist in a hold that made her gasp. "Stop this!" he commanded. She could see that he was keeping his own temper in check only with difficulty.

"Let go of me!" she cried, twisting her wrist, but he held her firm. "Let go!" Her other hand came up to push against his chest, and suddenly, unbelievably, they were fighting.

"Stop it, Lana, stop it!" he cried, catching her other wrist, and then for a moment they were frozen, her hands in the air, caught in his grip, their bodies close, staring into each other's eyes.

*"Ya Allah!"* Arash cried helplessly, his jaw clenching. And then slowly, inch by inch, as if drawn by some powerful, slow-working magnet, he drew her arms around his neck, let go of her wrists to slide his arms around her, and wrapped her body tight against his. For one long second they gazed into each other's soul.

"I warned you," he said. "But you would have it so."

And then his mouth pressed hers in a ruthless, demanding kiss.

Her body was suddenly at melting point, and she moaned and clung to him, igniting him so that they burned together.

He held her head and tormented her with his kiss, a deep, hungry kiss that sucked her lips and nipped her tongue, that burned and melted her mouth, until she was whimpering with need. She cried his name under the pressure of his lips, fuelling his need, making him hungrier for the taste of her desire.

His mouth was a drug to her. The more he gave her, the more she needed. When his hands clenched helplessly in her hair and, drawing her head back, he tore away from one kiss to press another against her throat, she moaned aloud both pleasure and loss.

Then, one hand cupping her head, the other against

her lower back, he pressed her body against his, bending her back till she lost all sense of balance, making her feel his hard arousal and the assault of his tongue at once, and the world went black.

He pushed her onto the cushions and followed her down, his hands and his eyes burning her. He reached over her for more cushions, tucking them in around her, under her head, under her hips, so that she could be in no doubt of his ultimate intent.

He held her with such firmness, such strength, such possessive determination—and feeling the surge of passion in his blood that both thrilled and frightened her, she wondered dimly, *Is this what it means, to be safe in the lions' den?*

He was both danger and safety to her, and her blood trumpeted the knowledge in her temples, her heart, her whole being.

He did not smile as he looked at her. "Lana," he said, then bent to touch his lips to her eyelids, her temple, and trail kisses down the curve of her cheek to her ear, her neck, her throat, where the neckline of the kaftan left bare the pulse of her heart.

The kaftan buttoned down the front. He undid the buttons, one by one, his hand firm with purpose, his eyes fierce with need. Underneath, her soft breasts were covered only by the thinnest silk, and he pressed his lips against her flesh through the frail covering, so that heat rushed through her.

She lost track of time. What happened was measured by her heart only, beating, melting, sighing. Once only had she experienced this tenderness, only once before had her heart opened so trustingly to the being of another.

The air was cool on her skin when he drew off the

robe, but it only added to the passionate heat, the shivering desire that coursed through her.

Then she was above him, her body still encased in the silk garment she had taken from his mother's closet, her breasts on his chest, and she smiled into his eyes while his hand stroked her shoulder and arm, her face and hair.

"Do you give yourself to me like this, without conditions?" he asked, and she only smiled and helplessly shook her head.

"What conditions do you want me to make?"

"None," he said roughly. He gazed up into her face, seeking her response.

She only looked at him.

With a whispered oath his hands came up to encircle her head, and he drew her irresistibly down till, as if after a long age of need, their lips met in a kiss.

How much she had ached for his touch, through all the time of waiting and fearing to hear that he was dead, and afterwards, knowing that he disliked her, not knowing her own feelings…a flood of sweet yearning burst through her like an exploding sun, melting, burning, sweeping away everything in its path, as his lips, his mouth, his tongue pressed and devoured hers now with a hunger that bruised her.

"Oh, Arash," she breathed, when his hands and mouth released her at last. "Oh, Arash, your mouth!"

The violet eyes darkened as he gazed at her. He kissed her again, wildly, as if the taste of her lips made him drunk.

She undressed him, with passionate patience unbuttoning his shirt and pressing first her palm, then her lips against the heat of his chest, waiting with hungry eyes and melting being as he pulled off the moccasins, the heavy cotton trousers called *shalwar*...

Then she opened her lips on a soundless gasp, closed her eyes and opened them again, taking in the sight of his virile power...and the brutal scar that marked his leg from knee to groin.

He watched her from eyes that had gone black. Her gaze met his.

"How beautiful you are, Arash," she murmured and, his eyes leaping with the impact of her words, his hands slid sensuously up her thighs, drawing the silk high to expose her body to his need. Then he pulled her naked hips over his, parting her thighs until she was kneeling astride him, fitted himself to her, and drew her down onto his wild, desperate flesh.

# Ten

She lay in his arms and wanted to weep for pure joy. He had pulled a quilt over their heated bodies, and now he held her tighter than she had ever been held, his hands firm with possession. Her heart was wide open.

She lay against him in the clasp of his naked arms, his hands on her at hip and shoulder. She rubbed the flat of her palm lazily against his chest.

She counted his heartbeats, and listened to the everpresent rush of the waterfall, and thought they were the same. Everything was a manifestation of love.

And she asked, "Arash, do you love me?"

He stiffened. His hand convulsively squeezed her arm in warning. "Lana, do not ask this question."

Her heart, so open, began to shrivel with the hurt.

"Why not?"

"I have nothing to offer you. You know it." He

paused, but she could not say a word. "You yourself want nothing from me."

"You're sure of that."

"This," he admitted, stroking her arm from shoulder to elbow. "Of course, pleasure you wanted and you accepted. Let this be enough for both of us. Do not ask about my heart."

She lifted herself to look down into his face. It was tight with anguish.

She said, "I have a right to know one thing."

"Do you?" he asked, his voice resigned.

"When we were making love just now, Arash—were you thinking of me, or of her?"

He closed his eyes briefly and turned his face away. When he opened his eyes again he was not looking at her.

"Her?"

"The woman you love. The one who's waiting till you put your life in order. Were you making love to me, or to her?"

His chest rose and fell in a deep sigh. His mouth twisted. "You, Lana. I made love to you." His eyes moved to find hers again, and she saw the torment in them and pressed her lips together against a gasp.

"I'm sorry!" she whispered, not knowing why she said it.

"I am sorry, too. A man has no right to be so weak and still to call himself a man."

Tears burned her eyes, and to hide them from him she abruptly sat up.

"Are you—attracted to me against your will?"

"You know that it is so," he said flatly. "Why will you speak of it?"

He wouldn't be the first man who was sexually at-

tracted to someone because he thought her easy, while
reserving his love for someone pure. *The virgin-whore
fantasy,* she saw with sudden clarity, *and I am the
whore.*

A snort of bitter laughter escaped her. Cast as the
whore by the man who had been her only lover, who
had made love to her all of twice in her life!

"I speak of it because we should get it straight,
shouldn't we? I don't want you blaming me, Arash! If
you make love to me, that's your choice, not because
I seduced you, okay? I could just as easily—"

"I do not blame you. The fault is my own."

She shivered and reached for the purple robe, which,
she saw now, almost matched his eyes. No doubt that
was why she had chosen it. But it made no difference,
and she pulled the robe over herself. She found
strength in being covered.

She rubbed her fingers through her scalp, briskly ruf-
fling her hair, and turned and found his eyes upon her.
Eyes that, in spite of his best intentions, no doubt, were
still packed with desire.

It was like being kicked just under the ribs. Lana
took a deep breath.

"So what do you want to do now?" she asked.

"Do?"

"We've agreed that we have the hots for each other,
Arash," she pointed out brutally. "We're holed up
here together and now we've taken the lid off something you wish we hadn't.

"What are we going to do about that? Are we going
to spend our energy fighting it, are you going to be
loyal to your dream girl—or are we going to take the
next couple of days as a moment out of time?"

His eyes squeezed shut in a grimace of torment that

shocked her. "You drive me mad!" he said hoarsely. His hands closed painfully on her flesh.

"What vision is this that you conjure up for me? That we should love each other while we are here, freely, without thinking of the future, and when we leave, we leave it behind?"

She opened her mouth and closed it again. It would be a huge mistake. She knew that if she let him love her now he would bind her heart to his so that she would never be free of him again. After one night of his lovemaking, she had been left unable to let another man touch her.

She had tried, she had wished desperately to wipe his memory from her skin, out of her heart, with another man's touch. In the years between then and now other men had kissed her in passion. Each time she had hoped that this was the cure. Each time she had erupted with awful, uncontrollable rejection, pushing them away as if... No amount of apology could make up for what she had done, though she had tried. *I'm sorry, I thought I was over him....* After a while she had stopped trying.

If he made love to her again, if she gave in to the passion in her heart and in his eyes—she would be marked forever. When would she be able to settle into an ordinary life?

For him it would be a few days out of time. For her, it would be all of her life compacted into a few short hours. Hours of tormented, incomplete bliss. Her body sated, her heart still seeking. Or worse still, pretending. Hoping to change him, to see him fall in love with her.

But she swallowed and looked at him and knew she could not turn her back on her only happiness, even if it was destined to be only a crumb.

And she said, "Why not?"

Then, when the die was cast, she gasped with fear. But before she could take back the dangerous, foolish words, he jackknifed up, his hands encircled her head, and he drew her down and down, to drown in his ruthless, ravenous kiss.

His body grew hard against her thigh, as hard and hungry as if it had never tasted her flesh.

He was the lover she had always dreamed of. He was everything she ever wanted. He was passionate and tender, wild and firm, strong, loving, beautiful.

For two days and nights they made love, with such intensity and devotion she sometimes imagined that the world could only end on the third day. As if something inside them knew that the earth's life span was unbearably short, and they had to live all of life's passion in those two days, as if their frail human bodies carried the whole burden of expressing the joy of creation in the teeth of extinction.

Desire was a constant. He would catch her wrist as she lifted an apple, and the apple would fall from her suddenly helpless grasp, rolling away somewhere as her tongue tasted the sweetness of him instead of the fruit. It struck them anytime, everywhere. Their eyes could not meet without sparking the need.

She had not known so much pleasure was possible from the human body. And she made such discoveries over and over in the tiny moment of time that was allotted to her for joy....

He became to her the physical embodiment of her pleasure. Everything he did, all that he was, had the power to move her. He was a magnet, and she was a highly charged piece of metal. If he left the room while she sat in it she had to restrain herself from following him.

The lightest touch, a glance from crushed-violet eyes, even the movement of his hand in lamplight melted her. Made her yearn and ache for his kiss, his body, the wild explosion of delight that their bodies together created....

It was delicious, it was sweet, it was painful in its intensity. It was cruel in its lies, the voice in her head that whispered that he must love her, that such meeting and melting could not be possible unless he did....

It was like being drunk on the wildest champagne she had ever tasted. It was like flight on her own wings, and knowing she was too close to the sun. It was like dancing for him alone, wild, abandoned, freer than she had ever hoped to be...and knowing that the music would stop, soon, brutally.

"It's so hot!" she murmured on the second night, when they had awakened to need deep in the night and a wild burst of sensual excitement had made her sweat.

"The storm is over. Come," he commanded, standing up and drawing her up after him. She was drunk with sensuality; every cell seemed swollen with the constant shift between need and satisfaction. She followed him mutely, shivering a little as her feet touched cold tiles....

He opened the door to the outside and led her out into a black, snow-covered world. She stopped on the threshhold, blinking. The snow had stopped, the moon was high and bright in a silken sky, the world silent, magical, holding its breath as it waited for them...even the waterfall's music was muted in the darkness.

They were both naked, and she looked at him in

sensation-drugged shock as he lay down on his back
in a bed of snow and pulled her down after.

"Arash!" she cried.

He pulled her thighs apart over him, and his hand
found her centre with practised ease and she instantly
melted into the hot spiral of pleasure that coursed
through her. He fitted her to his body, and drove into
her, pulling her hips ruthlessly down.

Her knees deep in cool powdery snow, she fell into
the hungry rhythm, in spite of having been sated a
thousand times, and began to pant as his body in her,
hard and demanding, pushed against the floodgates in
her...it was a dangerous touch, giving him a connection not only to the deepest wells of pleasure in her,
but also to her heart.

Then, as the pattern built towards explosion, he
picked up a handful of snow and thrust it against their
flesh where their two bodies met.

The icy shock against the high heat they had created
was a system overload. Cold and heat rushed and
clashed in their bodies, creating a pattern of sensation
that made her cry out and laugh and gasp and moan.

Trembling with inexpressible pleasure, Lana's head
fell back and she cried her amazement to the sky from
an open throat, like a songbird who has just discovered
that morning has come again.

"Arash!" she cried, as his heat burned up into her,
and he pulled her down into his embrace and kissed
the word on her lips.

# Eleven

Under a wide, clear sky, two snowshoe-clad figures moved across the white valley towards the caravan route and the high pass. The sun that crept up over the mountain peaks was already warm, and all along the valley animals, their bells tinkling in the pure air, stepped gingerly out of their winter pens and sniffed at the deep white blanket that covered the valley.

Progress on snowshoes was difficult on the slope, and Lana had never used them before. But Arash went slowly, and she followed behind, trying to copy his step, his use of balance.

They had left money and a note on the table. It was customary in the mountains to leave some acknowlegement of the involuntary generosity of your hosts in such a situation, and payment if you were able. Arash of course was not a guest in his own home, but the money would allow Suhail and Sulayman to replenish their supplies.

They had renewed the animals' feed and water, and left the door of the *majlis* open.

A host of little tasks that reminded them that the real world would soon return. Only once, as they reached the crest of the ridge, did Lana allow herself to look back at the valley. The peace of it filled her heart, and she breathed deeply. She had spent a few days and nights of delirious pleasure in his valley, his home, his bed, his arms…and that would have to last her.

Under the thick fall of snow there were few visible reminders of the war, and she looked at the valley and imagined that this was almost how it had always looked in winter.

"Does it look the same?" she asked.

He bent to her lips, not having caught her words. "Pardon?"

"Is this how it used to look before the war? In winter, I mean."

He straightened and looked at the scene, considering. "It is not so different, I suppose."

She pointed to where a thousand blackened skeletons reached up through the snow, much more obvious now against the snow than they had been on the evening they had arrived. "What was there?"

"An apricot orchard," he said. "A bomb hit it in a dry summer."

"Whose is it?"

If things had been different, if there had been no war to take him away from her, might he have brought her here one day, to look at the valley not so different from what she now saw? If he had stayed in London, might the powerful physical bond have grown into something stronger, more durable?

"My family's."

"Yours, now?"

He glanced at her. "Mine, while I live. Mine to care for and pass on."

She said, "Arash, I'd…" She swallowed nervously, frightened of rejection. "I'd like to… would you let me replant it? Just that? We could bring in the saplings as soon as the snow melts…I hate it when trees…"

His lips tightened behind his curling beard. "Ah, did you enjoy it so much? What a compliment to me, Lana! Think what I can tell my sons in some future moment—this apricot orchard I earned in the bed of a rich American woman! How they will—"

"Shut up!" she cried, her voice ringing. "Shut up! What right do you have to say that?"

His face closed with anger at himself. "None. I have no right to say such a thing to you. Forgive me."

"Why did you talk to me like that?" she demanded, her voice breaking as she fought the quick tears. "Why did you spoil it?"

"In order to spoil it for myself. I am a man divided against himself," he said, his jaw clenched. "You know it. It is the road to madness."

He turned away up the path. "Come," he said.

The towers and domes of an *Arabian Nights* palace hovered shimmering above the capital of Central Barakat.

Lana unconsciously braked, her mouth opening on a slow gasp. "Is that it?" she breathed.

They had crossed the border into the Barakat Emirates and the Koh-i Noor mountains the first day. In the afternoon the road had begun to descend, and they entered the last long tunnel that the engineers had blasted through a mountain, emerging much lower down, in the foothills of the Koh-i Noor.

That night they had stayed in a village, where they were given an impromptu feast by the local chieftain, attended by all his neighbours for miles around.

This morning they had been escorted on their way along the sparsely travelled desert highway by a swash-buckling guard of honour in four jeeps. After an hour the guards had fired a farewell volley into the air and then, with grins, cheers and salutes, had peeled off in a wide sweep to return the way they had come.

"I suppose they've been doing that for centuries, only on horses," Lana marvelled.

"You suppose right. It's a very old custom, escorting your guests through hostile territory. Not quite as necessary as it used to be."

"Maybe he's a sheikh of the old school," she suggested, and he smiled.

"We are all sheikhs of the old school. There's no new school yet."

And even a simple sentence like that could melt her, she discovered—because she knew that the old code of behaviour, along with hospitality, generosity, and noble warfare, included giving sexual pleasure to your wife.

She flicked him a glance and was rewarded with the hard clasp of his strong, finely sculpted hand on her wrist as she held the wheel.

"Lana, it is finished now," he said. "We left it behind in the valley."

Last night in the village, of course, she had slept in

the unmarried women's quarters, in a tiny room with a high window through which she could see the moon as she lay awake aching for him.

"I know," she said.

Now the palace shimmered in the heat like a mirage, seeming to float in the air above the ground, as if her own mind had conjured it out of a fairy tale.

Arash nodded. "Omar's palace. It was the winter palace in the days of the old king. The court only spent certain months there—the rest of the time they were at the seaside or in the mountains."

"I can relate to that." Lana grinned. "It's hot enough already, isn't it?"

"Glad we've finally arrived?"

Not exactly. "I'm certainly looking forward to a shower."

The truck windows were open to the burning desert heat. Now and then, without warning, dust devils blasted sand into her face. She wore sunglasses to protect her eyes, and a large silk scarf around her head, because, however it ranked as a religious duty, covering your hair was a practical necessity in the desert.

Arash nodded and wiped a hand over his forehead. His face was streaked with sweat and dirt, and she supposed hers was the same. His hair and beard were dusted with sand.

She had a sudden vision of him as a middle-aged man, still strong and virile, his face lined with maturity, his hair greying, and her heart trembled with the desire to be with him then....

"A shower, yes," he said.

Suddenly there was a cloud of dust in the distance,

and they heard the sound of firing. Along the highway towards them, and off road, too, a phalanx of a dozen jeeps was bearing down on them.

Lana's heart sank. "Oh, God!" she cried. "Who are they?"

Arash said simultaneously, "Ah, we've been sighted! Omar must have sentries posted."

She had still to get used to the traditions of welcome. Hospitality, like generosity, was a high art in Parvan and Barakat alike.

She laughed. "For a moment there, I was regretting the sheikh's departed escort. I thought maybe we were being taken hostage!"

"What, so close to the palace? I think Omar would have something to say about that!"

In a swirl of dust, the jeeps surrounded them, guns firing on all sides. A few mintues later, they were escorted into Prince Omar's palace.

Omar's wife, Princess Jana, led her to a magnificent suite of rooms that was to be hers while she stayed in the fairy-tale palace. Two women servants were already unpacking Lana's bags.

"This is Salimah, who speaks English," Jana said. "She will take good care of you. Salimah, this is Lana Holding. And Fatima will draw you a bath."

The introductions performed, she led Lana out onto a broad terrace, cool, shaded, that faced on an internal courtyard where a beautiful fountain played at each end of a long still pool surrounded with bright flowers and rich greenery. Colonnades of delicately wrought arches surrounded the pool on four sides to provide shade. The sun entered through delicate latticework and fell in entrancing patterns.

"This is enchanting," Lana said.

There were drinks already waiting, on a low table between two comfortable chairs. Princess Jana waved aside a third servant as the two women sank into their seats.

Lana, still in dusty boots and jeans, was feeling very grubby beside Jana's stylishly cool white shirt and pants and gold sandals, but she certainly needed a drink before anything else. She chose the mixed fruit juice, and while they chatted Jana poured and handed her a tall glass of peach-coloured liquid.

It was at the state wedding of all three princes of the Barakat Emirates that Jana and Lana and Alinor had discovered they already knew each other. Although they had attended different colleges of the University of London, they had belonged to the same swim club. It had been a casual acquaintance—they had never even known each others' last names.

It was strange how much of a bond it seemed, now, so far from home.

"Alinor and I were terrified when that blizzard blew up," Jana was telling her. "We were on pins and needles. Thank God you made it to the valley! But Omar said right from the start that you were safe with Arash. He said it was just my own guilt making me worry so much."

"Why should you feel guilty?" Lana asked.

Jana floundered a little. "Oh, well, just because...you know how it is! I invited you, after all!"

"Yes, but—" Lana began, but her brain refused to concentrate on mental puzzles now, and she let it go. "Oh, isn't this wonderful! So beautiful—look at the way the sunlight falls through that lattice, it's just magical.'' She stretched luxuriously in the sun-dappled shade and drank the sweet mixture of peach and lime and other fruits she couldn't distinguish.

It was delicious. Lana sighed with satisfaction, listening to the fountain play. ''I suppose Arash's place was something like this, before the bomb,'' she remarked.

Jana sipped her own drink. Hurry seemed a million miles away.

''Is it very bad, the damage?''

Lana described what she had seen, the remnants of pools and orchards and arches, the beautiful tile work all broken, and then fell silent.

''I suppose now that you've seen it, you'll find some funding for him?''

Everything was too close to the surface for Lana to pass it off. She looked at Jana, no longer trying to disguise her hurt, from herself or anyone else.

''I've been offering money to Arash for ages. He won't take a cent from me.''

Jana's mouth was open in a small O of surprise.

''Really?'' She was mystified. ''But how ludicrous! And all this time we thought—but *why?*''

Lana shrugged. ''You tell me,'' she said, and the tears were suddenly very close to the surface.

''He won't even—not even the apricot orchard! He practically bit my head off—I mean, hell, Jana, what's a few damned *trees!* And I *know* his knee could be helped, it's a piece of shrapnel or something, but will he let me pay for the trip or the surgery? Will he, hell!''

She began to sniff, and set down her glass to hide her face in her hands.

''Oh, I'm going to cry! All this time...nothing! He

even helps raise the funds, for God's sake! I told him once if he only would accept the money that his targets donate after he's talked to them… but he just says, *Yes, use it on the valley.*"

"The valley but not his family estate?" Jana queried thoughtfully.

She nodded vigorously. "That damned dam the Kaljuks were so careful to—God, they were monsters! If you could see the careful way they targetted irrigation systems that have been there for centuries!

"All of that kind of stuff in the Valley of Aram— I'm allowed to fund that. They accepted their quota of the spring seed, and of course the teams went in and did mine clearance…. And we got a small textile factory going in one of the villages—traditional Aram textiles are really popular on the West Coast and in France, for some weird reason."

A sob rose in her throat as the pain that she had never allowed herself to feel came surging up.

"But that's all he lets me do. When it comes to…"

"Lana, he must be in love with you." The quiet voice cut through the misery in her brain like a whip.

*"What?"* Lana gasped, her breath trembling on whispered sobs.

"What other explanation is there?"

"Why is *that* an explanation? If he loved me he'd be able to take help from me!"

"If he lived in California, maybe. Arash is from the mountains. He's a Durrani *and* an al Khosravi, you know. Both fierce mountain tribes."

Lana gazed at her friend, torn between crazy hope and disbelief.

"Omar's a Durrani, too, so I know," Jana went on.

"The very fact that Arash loved you would make it impossible for him to accept your help. Up in the Koh-i Shir range a man's a man, and he looks after his woman."

*A man does not marry until he has something to offer a woman.*

"But he loves someone else. He told me so."

Jana stared. "Did he? When?"

A servant helpfully appeared with some neatly folded tissues on a tray, and with a grateful smile, Lana took a couple, and blew her nose.

"Boy, no staff problems here, I see!" she joked, as she wiped her nose. "He told me a couple of days ago. When we were up there. I think she's a girl from the valley. He said he wasn't going to marry her because it would take him years to rebuild and it would be a waste of her youth and beauty—as if she'd care about that if she loves him!"

Jana shook her head sadly. "Well, then I don't know what to say. Funny how we thought—" She broke off, and at Lana's inquiring murmur, merely shook her head. "You don't suppose he's lying to protect himself?"

"From what?"

Jana looked at her. "From you. If you had no money and needed him, instead of him needing your money— you might have a better chance, Lana."

"There was a time in England that I thought— maybe his father wouldn't want him to marry a foreigner. I wondered if maybe that held him back."

Jana smiled. "All I can say is, it never seemed to cross Omar's mind.

"Now, you must be dying for your bath, and here's

Fatima to say it's ready. *Shokran jazilan, Fatima*," she added to the servant, who nodded and disappeared again. "Fatima doesn't speak English. Most of the servants don't, but you won't need it with her, she's very capable."

Jana got to her feet.

"Omar and I are both scheduled to attend a banquet tonight in Barakat al Barakat, and then we're in talks all day tomorrow. So I'm afraid you and Arash will be on your own here for the next couple of days."

Lana blinked up at her. "What?"

"I'm so sorry, but there wasn't anything we could do about it. Of course, I'd planned on your being here a few days ago, and we would have invited you to go with us, but I'm not going to ask you to sit through a boring banquet tonight when you've only just arrived.

"I've left instructions for your meals to be served here on the terrace. I hope you'll make yourselves at home. There's a swimming pool, horses, cars, whatever you need—Arash knows the palace well."

Jana bent over her and kissed her cheeks. "I am sorry, I'd love to be able to sit and talk all night, but it'll have to wait. The helicopter has to leave in half an hour if we're going to be on time, and I've got to get into formal dress. But you'll be fine. Just ask Arash if you want anything."

Lana stood silently appreciative as Fatima rubbed her all over with perfumed soap, like a child. The touch of her firm hands relaxed the muscles that were stiff from long hours in the truck and sore from Arash's passionate lovemaking.

Afterwards she moved down the steps into the bath

and felt her body's grateful melting into the warm clear water.

She was trying not to think. Trying not to use Jana's words as the centrepiece of the puzzle that was Arash's behaviour. Trying not to hope…

He loved a woman but had never told her so. She remembered how his eyes had seared her as he told her that…was it possible?

It made sense of everything, and especially the wild passion of the past few days. If he loved her but could not marry her because he had "nothing to offer"— then the days of their lovemaking meant…

Lana closed her eyes and tried to banish the bright hope that flooded her to the roots of her being.

Thirty minutes later, totally refreshed, she stepped into the bedroom.

"Oh, how lovely!"

Salimah blushed with pleasure at the praise. "My mistress instructed me to offer you the use of her wardrobe, Khanum Lana. Seeing that you brought so little with you, I have chosen some for your approval tonight."

Several fabulous outfits were laid out, and Lana admired each in turn, though she knew from the first glance which she would wear. Salimah smiled in delight as she chose it.

"It is very beautiful, because it just reveals the skin," she confided, lifting the diaphanous black trousers that were crusted with gold embroidery around the ankle and handing them carefully to Lana. "Of course one wears no underwear—that would spoil the effect," she confided with a smile.

So Lana slipped on the flowing black harem pants and tied them at her waist and, putting her arms into the intricately gold-embroidered black jacket, watched in the mirror as Salimah buttoned it. Salimah was right—the gauzy fabric seemed opaque until her skin came in contact with it, and then it was revealed as diaphanous.

She used only the lightest of makeup, except around her eyes, which Salimah expertly kohled for her, and then dusted her cheeks and eyes with a gold powder that was all but invisible.

Then the maidservant placed a circlet of delicate gold leaf coins around her forehead, and draped the outfit's sparkling cobweb scarf around her hair.

Simple gold thong sandals and a few bangles on her arms completed the outfit. Lana stared at the vision of herself in the mirror. She would be staking everything on this night. What if he thought her a fool?

Well, why shouldn't he? She was a fool. A fool for love.

# Twelve

The table was laid by the fountain at one end of the terrace. She moved around to it under the beautiful stone colonnades, through the soft twilight, feeling as though she walked the path that a thousand women had walked before her, and with the same goal in mind.

The perfume of night flowers came softly on the desert wind, and a single star glinted down on her.

*Venus. Goddess of Love. Oh, shine on me tonight.*

He was there already, standing by the fountain, watching as her shape slipped from column to column, coming nearer to him.

He had said that it was over when they left the valley, but tonight he knew that it was not over yet. He had not been able to resist her in a snow-filled valley, a bombed ruin—how could he resist her now, when the heat of the desert night surrounded them, and she was dressed like the paintings of his ancestors' concubines, when the perfume of a thousand blossoms overwhelmed them, and her own sweet scent called up his blood?

She stopped at a distance, nervous, as though sensing his desire even that far. How had he been such a fool as to let his resolve weaken? To believe that there was such a thing as a moment out of time? He would pay the price of his blindness all the rest of his life, the memory of her clouding all that he did.

"Lana," he murmured. Her name was true for him as for all his countrymen. She had melted the heart of anguish, had softened the misery that life had created for him...but at what price? The pain of loving her he would never forget.

The gauzy, glittering scarf half-hid her smiling, trembling mouth from him, so that he saw instead the trepidation that filled her eyes.

He frowned.

"Why do you fear me?" he asked hoarsely. "How have I hurt you?"

Had his passion taken him too far? Sometimes he could not remember afterwards, so drowned was he in the taste of her....

She shook her head. "I don't fear you, Arash," she whispered.

She was lying, he could feel it. He knew her. He understood her with a directness that did not need words, now. If she feared him...

He would have more control in future. He would not allow himself to be so lost in her....

*A moment out of time,* he reminded himself. *There is no future. Tonight, yes, because anything else is impossible. But it will be the last.*

A servant noiselessly appeared to light and place

candles in clouded globes around the terrace, and they moved to sit at the table.

Tiny jewels all over her gauzy stole flickered in the candlelight with every movement, surrounding her head with a thousand fireflies. The fine gold medallions that rested on her forehead tinkled like fairy bells, creating a symphony in his ears. He had dreamed of her like this, in a glow of light and music, smiling at him.

"You are very beautiful in the costume of the East," he said softly, watching how the candlelight burnished the pale skin behind the silky black that covered and revealed her arm, her shoulder, her breast, as she moved. She was like a sculpted dancing girl in the bottom of a silver winecup, revealed and then hidden by the movement of the wine…like wine, she was intoxicating to the senses.

"Thank you."

He was a prince from the *Arabian Nights* himself, in loose cream-coloured Parvan trousers and a flowing, wide-sleeved shirt jacket that was open over his powerful bare chest. He was barefoot, his strong feet caressing the ground with full, deep connection. Just with that connection had he made love to her, and she felt the recognition of it in her deepest self….

Her eyelids drooped in seductive yearning as she looked at him, and his flesh stirred with the thought of her desire. She would not look at him like this if he had not pleased her. His hand clenched involuntarily around the crystal goblet, and he focussed his eyes and forced it to relax.

"Jana says the servants don't speak English."

"One or two, perhaps, but not those who serve us tonight. What is it you wish for?"

She smiled and shook her head.

"It's a beautiful night," she said softly.

More stars were appearing as darkness fell. Nearby an insect buzzed loudly as it sucked the sweetness from a night flower.

That was what she was in the glimmering black—a night flower. He thought how he had sucked the perfume from her, and a drunken madness flooded him, telling him to lift her in his arms now and carry her to his bed. If it was to be their last night, he must give her something to remember forever.

A beautiful night. *Beautiful,* he thought, *but cruel, for it has shown me my own weakness, how unequal I am to what fate has brought on me.* He thought of all that was in his heart, all that he could never say to her, even on a night like this....

"It is a beautiful night," he agreed tonelessly.

She looked at him from her dark eyes and smiled at him.

"I've never been in a place quite like this. Jana says you know the palace well."

"I visited often as a child, with my mother. During the war, I came here to—" He paused. "I came again."

"When you were wounded?" she suggested.

He inclined his head.

The servant placed food in front of them. Something luxuriously succulent, only to be expected from Omar's kitchens. The contrast to the practical, plain food they had eaten in the past hardworking months, and especially the past few days, was almost too shocking for their palates. They ate for a few minutes in silent, sensual enjoyment.

"It's been a long time since I tasted anything as delicious as this," Lana murmured. *Except for you.*

"Omar always has excellent chefs." He marvelled at his own ability to speak of nothing when the truth pressed up in his throat, urging him to confess, this once, all that he felt.

"Was it in Barakat that you had the surgery on your leg?" she asked.

He nodded. "Omar's company of Companions was with us that day. It was Omar's quick response that... He flew me himself in a helicopter. If I had had to take my chance with the field doctors..."

He did not finish. She gazed blindly at him, wondering how close she had come to hearing the news she had dreaded to hear. She licked her lips.

"I'm glad he was there," she whispered.

The waiter removed their plates and rolled a silent trolley near the table. It was a kind of portable grill, and he began to prepare some exotic flaming dish. They watched in silence as his skilled hands danced within the flames to produce the magic.

"Your hands are like that," she murmured, half-unconsciously.

He stared at her, the flames marking his face with leaping light and shadow. His jaw clenched. He could not speak.

"Dancing in flame," she explained softly. "When you touch me, it's fire."

Their eyes met and held. Blood leapt in his body. He closed his eyes and silently breathed.

After a moment the delicious odour of cooking arose over the table, and two plates of delicately sliced sizzling meat, redolent of sensual spices, were placed in front of them.

Lana inhaled the wonderful smells. It was as if the meal had been designed with seduction in mind, an assault on the senses—sight, smell, touch, taste.

"Do they eat like this all the time?" she asked. Even with all his money, her father didn't pay this much attention to food on a regular basis.

When they had finished serving, the waiters bowed and withdrew against the wall at a distance, where they stood like sentries.

"It is a cultural bias. Recollect how few sensual delights there are in the desert," Arash said. He looked at her. "We make the most of those we have."

She dropped her eyes to her plate. Oh, he did that, all right.

"In the desert, maybe," she managed to say in a normal voice. "Right here in this palace I've seen plenty, though. I don't know when I've seen so many flowers in one place."

"If you come to the Valley of Aram later in the spring, you will see flowers in great profusion," he began, and then broke off.

"But I won't be coming to the Valley of Aram later in the spring, will I?"

His jaw clenched. He made no reply.

"Tell me about the flowers in the valley," she begged. "Because I will never see them."

He swallowed.

"Please," she whispered.

He told her then, lovingly, because he described flowers to a flower. He told her a story from his valley, of the nightingale's love of the rose. How it yearned and pleaded from a distance, how it never won the rose.

He told her of his love thus secretly, knowing that her heart understood even if her ears did not.

Flowers, the shape of arches, the desert winds. Softly they discussed such things. But every word was a cloak for some other meaning. Every movement of his hand, her mouth, as they ate the tempting food, was a message of another kind. Every nod of her head made faint, sweet music.

Every sense was engaged on one theme: love.

Above them the stars became infinite in number, and the moon rose.

At last some rich honeyed cream, of unbelievable sweet delicacy, was served. The sweetness was painful to him, like his love, for it spoke of another world. A world where love and perfection were possible.

Lana slipped the spoon between her lips as he watched. He thought how he had taught her to taste his body between those lips, how willingly she had responded to his tutelage....

"So, it's over, our moment out of time?" she breathed then, as if reading his thoughts.

"Yes," he replied.

Then, because he could not resist: "Tonight—if you, too, wish it, we will have tonight. But it must be the last time."

She nodded, licking her lips. Just so had she licked her lips after...

"Is it because I don't please you, Arash?"

His hand gripped the stem of the gold-traced crystal goblet as his heart kicked a wild protest.

"It is not because you don't please me," he said levelly. "You know it."

"I pleased you?"

"I say that you know it! Why do you persist in this?"

"Because I would like to hear you say it. I think I have the right to hear it, don't I, if I've earned it?"

"What else have I been saying, here in the night? Did not you understand? You understood!" His jaw clenched, but she only gazed at him, silently pitiless.

"You pleased me," he said, and could have laughed—or wept—at how pale the statement was compared to the shimmering truth.

"My body is a source of pleasure to you?"

He stared at her with burning, crushed-violet eyes. "Your body is my torment and my delight," he said.

He closed his eyes against the flood that threatened him. So much feeling. How long had he kept it locked in? Would there ever be another woman who would respond to him as she did?

A wave of passion swept her at his words, and she swallowed and clung desperately to her purpose. She took another bite of the delicious dessert, and the creamy sensation on her tongue was as rich as the taste.

"I wonder," she said dreamily, "if you were a sheikh of old, whether you would have added me to your harem."

He moved jerkily, pushing his upper body back out of the candlelight. His eyes black, the deep purple lost in the shadows, he gazed at her.

"What is it you want, Lana?"

"Do you think you would have?"

"No," he said.

She gasped, and his eyes burned into her.

"The sheikhs of old did not add women such as you to their harems, Lana," he said bitterly. "Even they were not so lucky. Do not tempt me with such fool-ishness.''

Her mouth opened on a silent, slow, indrawn breath. ''Why not a woman such as me? How am I different?''

He did not answer.

Her cries in the night as his body moved in her, as his tongue caressed her, his hands gripping her of their own accord, saying that she was his. Would there ever be another woman like her?

''How am I different, Arash? Why am I good enough for three days in the mountains but not as a permanent resident of the harem?''

''Stop it. You are a rich woman, as rich as a queen! How should I have hoped to bring you to my harem?''

''Rich?'' She looked at him. ''Are you talking about money?''

He made no reply.

She took a deep, calming breath.

''What has my father's money got to do with anything?''

''I have nothing to offer you but sexual pleasure. Take that, one last time, and then let us forget.''

''After tonight, never again?''

His jaw clenched, his eyes closed, she saw his fingers unwrap one by one from the bowl of his goblet, as though taking all his concentration, as the servant silently appeared to refill it with clear liquid that splashed and sparkled in the candlelight.

''Aren't you forgetting something?'' she said.

He opened his eyes to watch her.

''I think it's a tradition amongst your ancestors, isn't it, when a woman has pleased you, to grant her some boon?''

His eyes flashed purple fire.

"If there is anything I have that you could wish for, I give it to you."

"You grant me whatever I ask without waiting to hear what it is?"

His head went up, and she saw the shadow of a long line of proud sheikhs behind his shoulder, men whose pride had expressed itself in generosity. She had heard stories of such leaders, and now she saw how deeply he shared their blood.

"Ask your boon," commanded Sheikh Arash Durrani ibn Zahir al Khosravi.

A chasm as wide as her whole life opened at her feet. On this moment's courage rested all her future. She thought of her father, the risk he had taken, borrowing ten thousand dollars and staking his future on his own talents. *My blood is the blood of risk takers,* she told herself, and picked up the dice of life.

She took a deep, trembling breath, and tossed.

"I ask you to marry me."

He sat unmoving, a statue, as though to contain his reaction to her words he had turned instantly to stone.

She waited to hear him say whether she had won or lost the toss.

"Why do you say this to me?" he demanded, when he could speak.

"Do you grant it?"

"I can neither grant you such a thing, nor refuse the gift I promised. Lana, choose something else."

"Why can't you grant it?"

"Why?" he repeated furiously. Then, as if goaded, he began to recite,

*"tora doost daram
wa chizi nadaram*

*joz sipar-i Aram,*
*ke tora nadadam.''*

"What does that mean?"

*"I love you, and there is nothing in my possession,*
*save for the Shield of Aram, that I do not give to you,''*
he translated. "It is what my ancestors have traditionally said to their wives on the wedding day. At such a
moment, in the Valley of Aram, a woman asks for her
dowry. What could you ask of me, Lana, what could
I give you, that you do not already have?"

She looked at him gravely. "The apricot orchard."

She saw the impact of her words only in the sparkling liquid in the crystal goblet that his hand en-
wrapped where it sat on the table. It trembled in the
candlelight.

"The apricot orchard is burnt," he whispered.
"What can you want it for?"

"To replant it."

"That is no dowry for a woman like you," he said
harshly.

"My father has money, Arash, it's true. So naturally
it isn't material possessions I seek for a dowry," Lana
said.

"You have a sense of purpose, a history, you have
something to build and nurture and pass on to future
generations. The apricot orchard is a symbol of all
these things, and it is also a symbol of the opportunity
to do things that matter in the world.

"That is what I ask as my dowry."

She lifted her head proudly and looked at him, a
woman negotiating her own marriage contract.

"On such terms, Arash Durrani ibn Zahir al Khosravi, will you marry me?"

# Thirteen

"**A**nd for this you wish to marry me? For a sense of history and the chance to do good?" He shook his head as if to clear it. "It is as you once said to me—you may find this anywhere. Marry a duke's son and save his heritage from death duties and the tax man."

"It is not for that that I want to marry you," she said, shaking her head. "I want to marry you because I love you. In keeping with your tradition, however, you have asked me to name my price. I—"

He leaned forward into the light so that the violet flames leapt to burn her. "You love me?" he burst out harshly, as if he could not bear to hear it. "Recollect that until three days ago you hated me!"

"I love you," she repeated, her heart swamped by the release of saying what she had kept hidden so long. "I have never hated you, though it is true you have hurt me. I've loved you almost from the first time we met, and everything I know of you tells me that I couldn't find a better man if I hunted for the next hundred years.''

''What has occurred between us is no basis for thinking you love me. It is sexual madness, Lana—''

''Is it? I wouldn't know.''

His eyes narrowed and he pierced her with a look that searched her soul. ''What?''

Tears burned her eyes as she smilingly blinked at him. ''I have nothing to compare it to.''

Arash got to his feet so abruptly his chair fell over. A servant moved on little cat feet, but was waved away.

''You drive a man mad.''

She gazed up at him, trembling with every emotion she knew, and some she'd never felt before. He stood over her and grasped her wrist.

''You have finished?''

It was a command. She dropped the tiny silver spoon, nodding mutely.

''Come!''

Her heart was leaping in her breast like a wild salmon struggling upriver to spawn. As Arash, waving away yet another servant, pulled back her chair, she stood.

In the furious, concentrated silence of forced control, still holding her wrist, he led her slowly along the colonnaded terrace and down the far side of the sweet pool that lay quietly reflecting the moonlight and stars. Flowers rustled as they passed, stirred by insects or the wind, and, with nature's generous abandon, released their perfumes on the night air.

Halfway along, directly opposite her own suite of

rooms, he opened a door and drew her inside. A beautifully furnished sitting room, like her own, that had been softly lighted by the hands of invisible servants...he led her through to the bedroom, closed the door and turned to her.

"Now," he said grimly. "Tell me the truth."

"There's only ever been you, Arash," she said. "So I'm a bit out of my de—"

"You were a virgin?" His voice was almost an animal cry.

She blinked slowly, gazing at him. "You didn't guess?"

He stared at her, seeing it all again, that moment when he had entered her and her throat had opened on a cry of pleasure, surprise...pain? But he himself had been so lost.

"How should I have guessed it? You offered yourself to me freely, you said nothing that a virgin might say in such a moment...."

"No," she agreed. "As I recall I said, *Make love to me, Arash.* Is that what I said? Is that what you remember?"

He closed his eyes.

"It is what you said." They were silent. He opened his eyes.

"Why do you tell me this now?"

"Well, because—" She took a deep breath, looking into the distance. "Because if tonight is our last night I guess it'll be a long time before I—"

She broke off.

"Do you tell me no other man has touched you since that night?" he demanded hoarsely.

"Touch is a funny word. They could touch me, they

could even kiss me. But there's always that moment, isn't there, when something changes? When it's not a kiss or a touch, when it's the first step to making love…''

She blinked, and he saw the spangle of tears on her lashes.

''I never got past that moment with anyone. No matter how firmly I told myself that this would be it, that I was getting you out of my system—I never made it.''

His eyes were narrowed with incredulity—and something else—as he stared at her. ''From then until now, how many years—no one? Why?''

''Because I loved you. And I suppose because—because you were fighting a war. Someone would kiss me, and I'd think, *I can't do this when Arash might be hungry and thirsty, or wounded, or having to kill someone….*''

She squeezed her eyes shut. ''I couldn't do it, not when you were on a battlefield somewhere…but the real truth was—not when it wasn't you.''

With a wordless cry, he wrapped her in his arms, and his mouth found hers, hungry, desperate. She swayed as passion swept her being, mind, body, self.

He tore his lips from hers, bent and lifted her up high in his arms, and carried her towards the bed. In the softly lighted room, his eyes devoured her. He laid her on the bed and sat beside her.

Her scarf glittered on the floor behind them, where it had fallen, a symbol of the unhappiness that had shrouded her. That, too, was floating away.

Gently he lifted the golden circlet from her brow, set it down.

''Lana,'' he breathed. ''I must learn to be less of a fool.''

He stretched his long body beside hers, lying above her on one elbow, and tenderly stroked her cheek, her ear.

The look in his eyes gave her courage.

"Arash, who is the woman you said you loved?"

"You know who she is."

Her stomach swooped. She closed her eyes, wondering if anyone had ever fainted from happiness, then opened them again to drown in the purple depths.

"It is you, Lana. It is you whom I love and have been afraid to love."

"Oh, Arash," she breathed, and his mouth sought relief in hers.

A little later, she asked, "Why were you afraid? You must have guessed how I felt."

"In London, perhaps. I at least dreamed that I could make you love me if I tried. And I imagined that I would try…."

He smiled down at her. "You knew. I looked at you, and I knew that you knew that one day soon…"

"Yes," she whispered. "But you never did."

"Jamshid and I realized that Kavian was also seriously attracted to Alinor—we had to check her background. It was our duty. You were her close friend, you lived with her. We checked yours, too."

"Oh!"

"It was necessary. Either or both of you might have been in Kaljuk pay—anything was possible. I hated it, but my duty was plain.

"I remember the moment that I discovered who you were. Who your father was. I looked at the report, I read the name. And I—I saw it all in that moment, Lana. I saw that war would come, that it would take everything from us. I would have nothing to offer you, or any woman.

"And I told myself that you could never be mine."

She was silent, taking it in. "Did you love me then? The night that I—that we made love?"

"I loved you, then and always. I told myself I loved you too much to try to bind you to me when I had no future. I had promised myself, *if the king's negotiations go well, if it is not as I feared, I will return and find her...* but I could not resist you when you came of your own accord into my arms."

Feeling coursed through her at his words, melting her.

"Why didn't you leave me a note, some word?" she cried involuntarily, remembering that anguish.

He took a breath and his lips tightened behind the black beard.

"I thought—forgive me, Lana. I did not know you loved me. I thought you only knew that I loved you, and you gave yourself to me out of charity, the way a woman will when a man goes to war.

"I stood looking down at you as you slept, wanting to wake you, to say to you, come with me, and let us face whatever comes together. But in that moment, your father's wealth rose up before me, and I thought—*How fortunate, to fall in love with a wealthy woman on the eve of war!* And I turned away and left you there."

She sobbed once. "I wanted to come with you. I wanted to help you fight. I'd have done anything...I wrote you, I tried to tell you."

She saw him close his eyes. "I was a coward, disguising myself as a strong man. When I came home, my sister said it. She said that a man afraid of a woman's money was no better than a man who feared the sword, but I did not accept it...."

"And when the war ended, you never thought of looking me up?"

He shook his head. "Lana, when the war ended, I was here, in this room, wondering whether I would live or die. My father was dead, my brother dead, the estate in ruins. I did not then know that the Shield of Aram had gone, but my wound—I feared that the injury had made me infertile.

"I believed that everything had been taken from me, Lana, including the future. Why should I think of you then? I could not even promise you a child. I thought the al Khosravi line would die with me."

"I wish I had known," she whispered.

"I recovered and went back to Parvan and the work of recovery. And then, there you were, exactly as you had been, beautiful, vital, and now bursting with pity for my country and with a generosity that could scarcely be believed. You gave everything, and took nothing."

She bit her lip. "And you would accept nothing from me."

"A man does not become a dog at the table of the woman whom he loves," he said fiercely, and she looked nervously into his proud face and made the wise decision not to press that mystery further.

"You couldn't look at me without gritting your teeth. I thought you despised me."

"Despise you?" His hand tightened fiercely on her arm, so that she gasped in protest. "I did not despise you. I despised myself, for still loving a woman when I had nothing to offer her."

She wrapped her arms around his neck, drawing him

close. "You offer me everything," she whispered, and it was true. He gave her love, he gave her past, present and future, and she had none of those without him.

As if he had been holding himself in check, she was suddenly startled by the ferocity of passion that blazed in him. His hands tightened on her, his mouth came closer.

"I love you," he said. "Will you marry me, my love, my life?"

"If you give me the apricot orchard," she replied, a smile teasing the corners of her lips.

But he was beyond teasing now. His mouth covered hers with a hunger that made the world go black. His hand, tight on her arm, lifted her against him, his other hand held her head, the fingers threading through her curls.

He rolled over on his back, drawing her with him, wrapping her tightly in his arms as his kiss hungered, tasted, drank. His hand in her hair drew her head away as his lips trailed from the sensitive corner of her mouth and along her tender cheek to her ear, then down the line of her jaw and underneath, to where her quick heartbeat pulsed.

His lips found her throat, then trailed little hungry mouthings up the line of her neck to her chin, and so to her mouth again.

Then his hands released her, and moved to the buttons of the silky jacket. One by one, as she raised herself above him, he undid the buttons, his mouth following the opening with its wet heat, down the center of her chest until the two sides of the jacket parted.

Her bare stomach was against the heat of his; her hips, nestled in his, felt the pulse of his need. Her full, round breasts swung free above him, and she whimpered her pleasure as his strong lips pressed the nipple and his tongue brushed it, over and over.

Then his hand moved up again to cup her head and draw her face down to his. His eyes searched hers, the deep wounded purple almost breaking her heart with love.

"Lana."

She was silent, gazing at him, still hardly able to accept the change that a few days had made in her heart, life, future.

"How handsome our sons will be," she murmured, her eyes stroking the broad white forehead, caressing the thick curl of black hair, the straight, serious eyebrows, the strong, narrow nose, firm lips, the curling beard.

"I hope they'll inherit your eyes. And the girls, too. Such a haunting colour. I used to dream of that colour.... That would be all I'd remember when I woke, just the colour. But I always knew it was a dream of you."

He kissed her hard. "Then we were together in our dreams, for I dreamt of you night after night on the battlefield."

She was entranced. "Truly?"

"It was as if at night, God sent me visions of you, to help me get through the days of war."

"Was it terrible, Arash?" she whispered.

"Terrible? Yes. If I had not had you there...there is a spring in the valley, in a protected place above the house, a spring of the freshest water, Lana. In the summer one bathes there, under the waterfall. Nowhere in the world is water so fresh, so pure, with such a taste.

"My dreams of you were like that water, as if my soul stood naked in a pure stream, and was refreshed."

She lifted her head and closed her eyes, breathing deep to calm her beating heart. "What did you dream?"

"Sometimes you waited for me, on a height, wearing white, and I struggled through forest or storm to reach you, and found peace. If I went to sleep thirsty your breasts flowed with milk or water into a cup, and I drank it and my thirst was quenched. If I was hungry you gave birth to peaches and offered them to me."

"Oh!"

"Yes, they were strong dreams, dreams of power. When I went to sleep tired, too tired even to sleep well, then you would come to me in a glow of sensual beauty, as you were that night, and you would say, *make love to me, Arash, make love to me,* and then strength would flood me, and I would love you, and the tiredness would be gone from my body in the morning."

He stroked her breast, cupped its weight in his palm, grazed the pad of his thumb over the tip.

"When I was wounded, you were there, too. Here," he corrected himself. "You were in this room. I opened my eyes and saw you, sitting by me. You said something to me, speaking very clearly, but afterwards I could not remember what it was...I knew only that it was required of me to fight and live.

"But mostly I dreamed of touching you," he said softly, suiting the action to the word, "of stroking your hair, your back, your thighs and breasts...and of you crying with pleasure. I dreamed of your face as it was that night, your mouth wide and your eyes squeezed tight, and my name on your tongue.

"Then I understood why women are generous with

men going to war. Because dreams and memories of that night—many times I had nothing else.''

She was too moved to speak, and for several minutes they looked silently, hungrily, into each other's face.

''I'm glad you had that,'' she murmured at last. ''But it definitely wasn't my conscious reason for what I did. I don't think I'd ever have guessed, even in my wildest moments of hoping that...''

''No? But perhaps you did not know everything that moved you. Perhaps you were nominated by God to give me what would keep me alive.''

She frowned as a jealous thought scratched her. ''But you would have remembered some other women if I hadn't listened to the call.''

In the warm shadows his eyes glowed deep, wet-velvet purple. ''Lana,'' he said. ''Have you not understood?''

She blinked. ''Understood?''

He drew down her head and kissed her. ''Lana,'' he murmured against her lips. ''There have been no other women for me. You are my first, my only love.''

Her breath rushed in in a long, audible gasp, and his arms encircled her naked back under the shirt as he pulled her down against him, her breasts flattening against the warm bare skin of his chest.

And then they were kissing with a renewal of that desperate urgency, a wild, hungry need of soul and body, that was half-tender, half-fierce. He pulled the black shirt down her arms and she eagerly dragged herself from its folds before moving her hands to the waist of his trousers to untie the drawstring....

Then at last they were naked, each open to the eyes and mouth and touch of the other, to the toying and kissing, the yearning and need.

And now there was nothing between them and love

He lay on his side, facing her, one hand cupping her delicate head with fierce tenderness, his fingers in her curls, the purple of his eyes melting her like wax. Her own hand was against his face, and she felt her love pouring through her palm and into him.

"Make love to me, Arash," she whispered, in the old incantation. "Make love to me."

He lifted her thigh with one impatient hand, and drew it over his hip, opening her to him, and then he fitted his flesh to her, and cupped her hips, and thrust home.

The stroke melted them both with sudden, impossible heat, with wild delight, with a burning of love that fired up and consumed them. They thrust hungrily against each other, each searching for the truth of who they were, knowing that it could be found in the Other.

Drunk, wild, they cried aloud into each other's being their joy, their increasing need. He clasped her, held her, but he could not get deep enough into her self. He rolled onto his back, drawing her over him, and she obediently knelt above him, giving him the deepest access. Now his body went his full length in her, and she cried wildly as each driving thrust pounded against the door that had never been opened in her, in him.

Under his guiding, passionate hands she rose and fell on the pounding waves of a storm at sea, sensing the wild depths they rode, magic with unseen riches, unsounded, deep, dark, overwhelming.

They rose and fell as the storm built, lashing them, and high waves lifted dangerous over them and smashed down, so that they gasped and choked on pleasure, and cried in amazement.

Then, after endless time on the cruel swell, a wave

climbed steep and stark above them, and they sensed its presence and gasped for the air they would need. It thundered down against their frail human forms, potent, perilous, too strong against their humanness. Then they were washed under, rolling, twisting, calling, sobbing, as Love tore a path through them into what we call the world.

Then they understood both pleasure and pain—the joy of Union, the pain of knowing they could not sustain it for more than these few moments of blinding sensation that were love, and joy, and life, and Truth.

# Fourteen

The heat of the desert soaked into their bodies, unravelling the strain of the past months and years. They rode Omar's horses into the desert, they swam in the swimming pool, they browsed in the souks of his city, where artisans engraved silver trays and cooks fried felafel, where charcoal sellers and apple growers offered their produce.

And always they escaped from the world back into the magic of his bedroom, where they loved, and toyed, and wept, and talked.

"Tell me how it was for you," she said once, and he told her how her body had thrilled him and troubled him, a young man going to a war from which he might never return, tasting a delight he might never know again, might never know but for her generosity....

"You were—twenty-two or three, weren't you?"

"I had just turned twenty-one."

"That's pretty old for a guy to be a virgin."

"In the West, it seems so. Not in the Valley of Aram. There it is still accepted that both a man and a woman will be virgin when they marry. We marry young—most girls are married by the age of twenty, men by twenty-two."

"Did your father and mother have someone picked out for you?"

"No, because it was understood from an early age that I would go to the palace and be named Cup Companion to Prince Kavian. And before that I must attend university."

"And you never met anyone at university?"

He smiled. "There was a girl, yes. But of course she expected to be virgin when she married. In Parvan this attitude is still common."

"And you never pushed her, never tried?"

"Not when I was not sure of wanting to marry her. If we had become engaged and the wedding could not take place immediately—then, perhaps. In Parvan a man does not lightly take from a woman what he can never restore to her."

"And then you came to England."

"Then I came, and I saw you, and I understood why I had not been sure of making Tahira my wife. With you doubt fell away, there was a certainty that nothing could hide from me."

"But—"

"But war threatened, and how could I in honour try to bind you to me when I could not see the future beyond it?"

"Well, I was bound to you anyway, so you might as well have."

When she spoke such things to him, he had no answer but a hungry kiss, and to draw her deep into drowning pleasure.

"Have you had a relaxing couple of days?" Jana asked.

They were on Prince Omar's private terrace, over-looking the swimming pool, the desert, the stars. A waiter was offering them flute glasses.

"Yes," was all Lana could say. She lifted a glass from the tray with a smile of thanks. "And how was your conference?"

"In some ways, fruitful." They chatted lightly, and without seeming to do so, Jana drew her friend aside so that Lana found herself settled in a comfortable chair, out of earshot of the men.

"Everything has worked out, I see," Jana said with a smile.

Lana blinked. "Pardon me?"

"Between you and Arash. I see that things are fi-nally settled. Are you—is it a formal engagement?" she went on, while Lana blinked at her, mouth open.

"Yes, but—"

Jana heaved a satisfied sigh. *"Alhamdolillah!* Oh Alinor's going to be *very* pleased. She was so sure' Have you told her yet?"

"Jana, what—what on earth are you talking about?" Lana asked faintly.

"You didn't guess?"

"No! Guess what?"

"Well, you see, Alinor told me that she was sure you and Arash were…the way she put it was, you were both deliberately ignoring the obvious. So we plotted a little for a way to get you together, and that's when

I started to press you to come for a visit. And Alinor somehow arranged that Arash should be your escort.''

"It was all *plotted?*''

"Not the storm." Princess Jana laughed. "That was fate taking a hand, I guess.''

"Alinor never said a word to me.''

"She didn't want to put you on your guard. Whatever was keeping you two apart—well, she didn't think talk would fix it. Are you making the announcement right away? Can we call her tonight and tell her she was right?''

At the other end of the terrace, Omar lighted a black cigarette and blew out the smoke as he nodded his satisfaction at what his cousin had just told him.

"Congratulations. It's good to see you so happy, Arash. I suppose the two of you will go home as soon as possible, and start to put your estates in order.''

"Yes," said Arash.

"Your people have been too long without security. They need you there, they need to see you, too, rebuilding. To know that it is finally and definitely over.''

"Yes," said Arash. "I wasn't raised to it, the way Kamil was. I have too much to learn. But I guess they understand and will suffer through it with me.''

"Your presence is the most important part of the equation. If you'll take advice from me…''

"I'll be very grateful for advice from you.''

"Then I suggest you don't wait any longer to get the Shield of Aram back into the valley, where they can see it. I know the house is pretty badly damaged, but they need to know it's there. I understand the *majlis* is still standing?''

Arash's lips compressed. "Omar, that's the worst part—"

"It's still in its protective packaging. I never saw any reason to unwrap it, but if you'd like to do so to be sure it's in good condition before taking it back, it'll be easy enough. The other pieces your father…Arash, what—?"

The flute glass had smashed into a hundred tiny fragments on the beautiful tiles. Arash pressed a hand on the stone balustrade, needing its reality.

"Sorry, Omar, did I drop my—*what did you say?*"

A servant was already brushing up the shards. Omar grasped his cousin's arm above the elbow.

"What is it, Arash?"

"*You* have the Shield of Aram?"

"Of course I have the Shield of Aram. And the other treasures your father sent to me for safekeeping. Did you imagine I had sold them?"

"Omar—*Allah!* Can this be true? I thought it lost—stolen!"

There was a long pregnant pause as each cousin assimilated what the other had said.

Omar spoke first. "Your father did not tell you? Not after Kamil was killed? Kamil certainly knew."

"I hardly spoke to him, all through the war. When did he send it?"

"About a year before the end of the war, at a time when the bombing had intensified. He had sent things here that were to be sold—we thought my agents would get the best price. At that time he sent all that remained, including the shield. We did it with night helicopter flights.

"Some of these treasures your father had earmarked to be held as long as possible, to be the last sold. They were the most precious, for reasons both of tradition and monetary value. He said that if they outlasted the war, either they could be sold to fund the rebuilding, or be restored to their place, depending. Many of those did survive, and are here in my treasury. Did you know nothing of this?''

''Nothing. I knew he had sent them out for sale, of course. The shield I believed lost. I thought everything gone.''

''I am glad to be bearer of such welcome news. Shall we go to the gallery now, so that you can see what is still in your possession?''

Arash blinked, his brain still reeling. ''Shall—'' Arash shook his head, trying to clear it, without success. He gestured towards the servant who appeared to summon them to the table.

''If your chef won't object to a delay—''

''To hell with my chef,'' said Omar.

''Oh my, is that *it?* Oh, how magnificent!'' Lana cried softly, as, under Arash's hands, the last of the protective covering was lifted away and the Shield of Aram was revealed.

They stood together in the cleaned, restored *majlis,* which sparkled with polish and new paint. Behind them the door was open on a rich late-spring day.

Outside, on the slopes, the sun burnished leaves and flowers, the wings of foraging bees and butterflies, the pelts of skittish horses, the sparkle of stones and springs, and the mighty rush of the waterfall.

Everywhere workmen sawed and plastered, men laid bricks, artists worked, artisans crafted and fitted and polished. Ploughmen worked the fields, and gardeners toiled among the trees and flowers. Further along the valley a thousand saplings waited to be placed in the dark, nourishing soil where the last of the blackened skeletons of their predecessors were being lifted out.

Inside the *majlis,* with a powerful heave, the sheikh of the tribe of Aram lifted the great shield of his people and restored it to its home on the wall of the place where for centuries his ancestors had advised and been advised by the people of his valley.

It glowed with deep power in the rays of the sun, blinding with its flashes of gold and silver, the ruby at its centre pulsing with deep, mysterious light that held the eye in a hypnotic grip.

He stepped back with only a faint trace of a limp now, and put his arm around his wife-to-be, and together they gazed at the symbol of good fortune and right guidance for them, and the valley and its inhabitants.

"It feels so right, Arash," Lana murmured, because she could find no better words. She turned to him. "I understand now."

He nodded. "Tomorrow," he said, "you take me for your husband here."

"Yes," she said firmly.

"You are not afraid?"

"I'm nervous, but not afraid." Unconsciously she touched her stomach, where the tiny seed of their union already nestled. "Anyway, it's a bit late for second thoughts!"

Sheikh Arash Durrani ibn Zahir al Khosravi turned and wrapped his love in the circle of his arms.

"Yes," he agreed, gazing down at her. "We will no longer look back. Now is the time for looking forward, my temptation and my delight. Now we face the future, and we face it together. You and I, and the child, and our people.''

\* \* \* \* \*

*Turn the page to read an exclusive extract from Susan Mallery's fabulous new story*
The Unexpected Millionaire.

*Available only from*
*Mills & Boon® Desire™ in December 2007*

# The Unexpected Millionaire

### by

### Susan Mallery

About eight seconds too late, Willow Anastasia Nelson realized there was a massive flaw in her plan.

She'd driven over to Todd Aston the Third's embarrassingly huge estate to give the slimy, no-good weasel a piece of her mind. But she'd never actually met the man, so she didn't know what, exactly, he looked like.

She had an idea, of course, sort of. Tallish, handsomeish, rich. But wasn't his hair dark and weren't his eyes brown? Why hadn't she thought to look him up on the Internet? He was probably on the front page of "JerksMonthly.com."

And if Todd Aston defined the whole tall, dark and yucky scenario, then who was the blond hunk and a half standing in front of her?

"Oh, hi," she said, smiling at the man who'd opened the front door and hoping she didn't look as out of place as she felt. "I was hoping to have a word with Todd. This is his house, right? My sister mentioned he lived here and…"

Willow groaned. That hadn't come out right. She sounded like a groupie.

"My sister knows him," she added helpfully.

Blond guy didn't step aside to let her in, although he did fold his arms over his chest in a move that got her attention. The man was *big*—really muscled, but not in a too-buff, action hero kind of way. This guy looked powerful, like a jaguar. She would bet he could snap her forearm without breaking a sweat.

His eyes were green and kind of catlike, she thought absently, continuing the whole "powerful cat" analogy. He had a good face—handsome, but also trustworthy. Not that she knew anything about him. He could be… She shook her head. She had to focus on her mission.

"Look," she said as forcefully as she could, determined to sound in charge and unintimidated by the burly guy's presence. "I need to talk to Todd. I'd like to do more, of course. He totally messed things up for my sister. Everything turned out in the end, but what if it hadn't? I get so mad when I think about it, I just want to pop his pointy little head. And that's the least of it."

The man in the doorway raised one eyebrow, then pushed aside the front of his suit jacket. Willow felt all the blood rush out of her head—no doubt fleeing to somewhere much safer than her body.

The man had a gun.

She could see it just inside his coat, tucked under his arm in some kind of holster. It was almost like in the movies, except for the cold knot of terror in her stomach.

"What is your business with Mr. Aston?" the man asked in a low voice that sent chills tripping down her spine.

So he wasn't Todd. She'd sort of guessed that, but now she knew for sure. "I, ah, he…"

The smartest move would be to leave. She wanted to yell at Todd, not get shot. But some stubborn streak made her plant her feet more firmly on the oversize and pillared porch.

"I think you're overreacting," she muttered, forcing herself to look away from the gun, back to the man threatening her with it. Well, not *threatening*, but intimidating. Something he was doing really, really well.

"I get paid to overreact."

"Has weasel-man already left for the office?" she asked sweetly. "I'll catch him there."

"You won't be catching him anywhere. Who are you and what do you want with Mr. Aston?" As he spoke, he reached out to grab her arm.

Willow had tried out every year of high school for the cheerleading squad. But in a world of amazons, she'd been too short. No matter how well she knew the routine, putting her in the lineup made them look off balance. Still, she'd been good at tumbling and turning and ducking.

The skills came back to her now as she faked a spin to the left, instead went to the right, then ducked under the big guy's arm. Suddenly she was inside the house.

Elation filled her. If Todd was here, she would find him. Then she would yell at him and her world would be set to rights.

She sprinted down the wide entryway, Mr. Big Gun and Cranky right behind her, then ran through huge rooms with soaring ceilings. This place was more like a museum than a house, she thought as she raced through what looked like a study and came out in a long hallway. She heard the man with the gun running behind her. She was fairly confident he wouldn't actually shoot her, but just in case, she wove back and forth and kept close to walls.

"Todd," she yelled as she ran. "Are you home? You need to get your lying, slimy butt down here. You don't have the right to mess with people's lives. It's wrong. You should know better."

Perhaps not words to put fear into his heart, but they would have to do.

She heard footsteps closing in and righteous anger gave her a burst of speed. Unfortunately that burst led her into a room with no other exits.

Panic energized her. She spun quickly, looking for a door, a big window, anything. Then she stared at the floor to ceiling drapes and headed in that direction.

Victory! A French door that led onto a patio as big as her elementary school had been. She burst outside and glanced around.

The grounds were stunning. The patio led to stairs that flowed into a terraced garden that reminded her of the grounds around Versailles. Beyond them was a forest of trees.

Didn't Todd know he was in the middle of Los Angeles?

"Stop," Burly Guy demanded as he ran out of the house after her. "Stop, or I'll make you stop!"

Ha! He hadn't been able to stop her yet, had he? But had he already called the police? Willow didn't wait to ask. She bolted for the trees.

Unfortunately the open ground gave her pursuer the advantage, mostly because his legs were a lot longer than hers. That combined with her erratic commitment to physical fitness and any sort of regular exercise program meant he gained on her far too quickly.

She dug down for more righteous indignation to give

her speed, or slow him down or something, but there wasn't anything left. Her breath came in pants, the sound of her rapid heartbeat filled her ears, and she felt the chilling fingers of defeat reaching for her.

"I will not be taken alive," she gasped as she surged forward, straining to reach the trees. Once there, she might have a chance. As for not being taken alive, okay, yeah, she had a slight dramatic streak.

She felt him reach for her and darted to the left, where a tree root jutted out of some grasses. She tripped over it, lost her balance and started to go down.

As she did, several things happened at once. There was an awful sensation of pain from her left ankle, she saw something gray and white and furry in a hollowed-out base of the tree, and what felt like a tank plowed into her from the rear.

She hit the ground, all the air rushed out of her lungs, and there were actual spinning lights where the rest of the world should have been.

She resurfaced to someone rolling her onto her back and telling her to take a breath.

Breath? She couldn't breathe. She really was not going to get out of here alive. Oh, God—she'd been kidding. She didn't want to die here. Now. Like this.

"Take a breath," the man repeated. "You're fine."

How did he know that? How could he be sure?

Willow opened her mouth and sucked in air. It filled her lungs. She did it again and again until the lights faded and she could focus on everything around her.

Gun Guy sat next to her. He'd removed his jacket. The good news was she could see he was all muscle and it was pretty impressive. The bad news was his gun was totally exposed and she couldn't pretend it wasn't there.

"Who *are* you?" he asked. "Some crazy ex-girlfriend? I usually know them, but every now and then…"

Willow raised herself up on one elbow. "Ex-girlfriend? No way. I wouldn't date Todd if the continuation of the entire planet depended on it. Well, okay, if it would save some endangered species, maybe. We all have to do our part. It's important for us to realize that for the planet to continue to be a renewable resource, there are some basic rules we need to follow."

He held up his hands in the shape of a T. "Time-out. Who are you?" he asked again.

"Oh. Sorry. Willow. My sister is Julie Nelson. She's engaged to Ryan, Todd's cousin. But rat fink Todd did everything he could to keep them apart and I can't let that go. I know I should just accept it and move on, but it was wrong. He thinks because he's so rich, he's king of the world or something. Idiot. Who are you?"

"Kane Dennison. I'm in charge of security."

"Here at the house?"

His expression hardened, as if she'd just insulted him. "For the entire company."

"Oh, sure. That explains the gun." She pushed herself into a sitting position and brushed at the grass stains on her sweater. "I wasn't going to hurt him, you know. I mean come on, look at me. Do I look dangerous? Seriously?"

He tilted his head as if considering the question. "You're short and scrawny, so I guess not."

The short she could handle—it was a reality she couldn't change. But scrawny?

"Excuse me? I'm petite."

"Is that what they call it?"

"I have curves," she said, really annoyed and just a little hurt. Maybe she didn't have big curves or a lot of them, but they were there. "It's the sweater. It's bulky, so you can't see what's underneath, but I'm very sexy."

She wasn't—not really. She tried, of course. But it was a losing cause. Still, to have this man just dismiss her like that was more than annoying.

"I'm sure you're stunning," Kane muttered, suddenly looking as if he wished he were anywhere but here. "I'm sorry you're mad at Todd, but you can't show up at the man's house and threaten him. It's wrong and it's illegal."

"Really?" She'd broken the law? "Are you going to have me arrested?"

"Not if you leave quietly and never come back."

"But I *have* to talk to him. It's just one of those things. He needs a good talking to."

One corner of Kane's mouth turned up. "You think you can scare him?"

"Maybe." Although in truth she'd kind of lost her passion for the job. "I could come back later."

"I'm sure Todd would be delighted to hear that. You have a car?"

"What?" she asked. "Of course I have a car."

"Then let's get you to it and we'll pretend this never happened."

# Mediterranean Men

*Let them sweep you off your feet!*

## *Gorgeous Greeks*

**The Greek Bridegroom** by Helen Bianchin
**The Greek Tycoon's Mistress** by Julia James
*Available 20th July 2007*

## *Seductive Spaniards*

**At the Spaniard's Pleasure** by Jacqueline Baird
**The Spaniard's Woman** by Diana Hamilton
*Available 17th August 2007*

## *Irresistible Italians*

**The Italian's Wife** by Lynne Graham
**The Italian's Passionate Proposal** by Sarah Morgan
*Available 21st September 2007*